THE
ALO
RELEASE

GEOFFREY ROBERT

First published in 2015 by Geoffrey Robert,
an imprint of Red Piano Limited.

Reprinted in 2016.
This edition published in 2025.
(Minor textual edits and new cover illustration included in this edition.)

ISBN 978-1-0670781-5-7 (Paperback)
ISBN 978-0-473-32897-9 (Ebook)

www.geoffreyrobert.com

About the author

Geoffrey Robert is a New Zealand author and former journalist, parliamentary press secretary, communications advisor, and news director. His diverse roles and experiences have shaped his understanding of the power of story — and the consequences when truth is manipulated or ignored.

He is the author of *The Alo Release*, *Finding Fabi*, *The Ghost Shipment*, and *All It Will Take*. His novels blend realism and allegory, often exploring themes of injustice, courage, and the resilience of ordinary people caught in extraordinary situations.

A lifelong traveller, Geoffrey has witnessed the widening disparities in wealth and opportunity that underpin many of the world's conflicts. From the dazzle of Times Square to the alleyways of India, the orderly streets of London to the chaotic bus stations of Kenya, and from the swagger of Sydney to the dirt-floor poverty of Timor-Leste, these global encounters continue to inform his writing.

His love of the outdoors and passion for keeping things natural have taken him to elephant watering holes in southern Africa, ancient mountain trails in the Sinai, remote villages in Myanmar, and the primeval rainforests of his homeland.

Geoffrey lives with his wife in Rangiora, New Zealand. He is the father of two daughters and the proud grandfather of two granddaughters.

Also by Geoffrey Robert

Finding Fabi
The Ghost Shipment
All It Will Take

Alo is a Latin word with several meanings, including sustain, nourish, support, maintain, keep, cherish.

Prologue

WITHIN SIXTY minutes it was well on the way to becoming the most watched *YouTube* video in a single day.

Before the last ember was doused and the crime scene turned over to the Los Angeles Police Department's anti-terrorism unit, edited highlights were leading news bulletins from New York to Beijing to London.

The footage had initially been uploaded to the *Grassroots Intelligence* blog from a stolen iPhone. It showed the audacious attack from the moment the Mazda Bongo pulled up outside the steel mesh fence to the simultaneous bursts of orange, yellow and white flames that reduced the controversial biotech lab in Pasadena to a heap of melted steel and ash.

And fragments of bone.

In between were jerking images of the security guards being overwhelmed, the alarm and sprinkler systems disabled. Skylights ratcheted open to increase the oxygen content inside the building. Green plastic buckets of accelerant strategically placed throughout by the six perps disguised tip to toe in gorilla suits.

The fire was so intense it was difficult to tell if any of the bone fragments were human.

Confirmation took three days.

Professor Roman Tolminsky, creator of the revolutionary Alo seed coating, was dead.

By then investigators determined the accelerant was a mixture of ammonium perchlorate, aluminum, eutectic salts and diesel fuel. The same cocktail used in arson trials at a fire technology lab in Longview, Washington. A recipe freely downloadable from the net.

The gorilla suits were purchased from Guise 'N Gals party rentals in Santa Monica by someone dressed as a carrot. He or she paid cash. The Mazda had vanished.

Over the following months, despite assurances of justice from the Governor of California to the President of the United States, no arrests had been made.

As the first anniversary of the attack approached, the world's attention was focused elsewhere.

1. Out of time

THE REMOTE LOCK on the office door clicked and in that instant Henry Beck understood. It was as if the commander of a firing squad had given the order to take aim.

A screech and burst of light forced his eyes and every muscle in his face to clam till he realized it was the security alarm. Yelling was useless.

He snatched at the desk phone. Dead.

He swiveled to face the monitor of his PC but could tell without touching a key it was frozen. The stylized Vestco logo and the words *Nourish, Sustain, Cherish* that normally floated across the screen were lifeless.

The alarm shrieked on off on off on.

He erupted from the chair, sending it crashing into the wall unit as he stretched for his suit jacket. Fumbled in the pocket for his mobile. The LCD screen stared back. Paralyzed.

He lurched to the window, raising palms towards his reflection as his hands touched the cold glass. The floodlit boxes of downtown Los Angeles sprawled beneath him like a giant Lego model. Thirty-six floors below, clusters of dots – drones on the early shift – flowed from the building and crossed the intersection of Fifth and Grand to form into orderly groups in Pershing Square. As per the drill manual.

They don't know. No one knows.

He grabbed a ceramic vase and hurled it at the window. It shattered against the reinforced glass like a slow-motion silent film as the alarm pierced on off on off in sync with the strobe. Laughing at him. Taunting.

Think Henry. Think.

He had come across the digital video clip by chance while deleting personal files of Professor Tolminsky. The *late* Professor Tolminsky. *They're nobody's business but the professor's, so let's preserve his dignity.* That's what the corporation's vice president, Chas Petersen, said. Henry was nearing the end of the deletion when the filename *megiddo.mov* attracted his curiosity. He'd spent three weeks as a volunteer on Kibbutz Megiddo during a college break in Israel. But the video had nothing to do with a kibbutz. It was unbelievable. He phoned Petersen to report the discovery, and the vice president said he was on his way down. Henry copied the file to a place he never thought he'd have to use, seconds before the screen froze and the lock on the door was activated from the central security suite.

Between bursts of alarm, a bell announced an elevator was stopping in the hall outside.

Desperate now, Henry scanned the office, drifting in and out of reality in the oscillating light. His eyes seized on his personal laptop recharging on the workstation. Reaching it in two steps, he hit the toggle and was staring at his wife. That lop-sided smile. Those dimples. Fingers splayed over her bulging pregnancy.

He wiped the moisture from his eyes and shook his head to refocus.

One keystroke and he was online.

Click.

Whoever was in the hall was unlocking the door from the keypad outside.

Henry opened *Mail* and typed m i l l b. The default address at millbrookfoundation.org appeared.

The doorknob began to turn.

Henry Beck was out of time.

His fingers *taptaptaptaptapped* over the keyboard, before toggling the cursor towards *Send.*

JAY DUGGAN strolled from the elevator into the lobby of the Millbrook Foundation for the last time in his life. The chatter of mockingbirds barely registered as he ambled towards the voices in the chief executive's office. The others must have arrived on time.

Should he feel guilty?

Certainly not for being a few minutes late. Or for failing to make a difference. His years of trying to save the world were over. Time to look after number one. If there was a tinge of guilt it was for taking advantage of Millbrook in the same way he criticized America on and on for exploiting the rest of the world. For self-interest.

Mostly though Jay Duggan felt relief. Twenty-two months, seven days and four hours since Peru, it was all about to end and he could finally fulfill his promise to Aroha.

He reached into his T-shirt and lifted her greenstone pendant to his lips.

* * * *

THE .380-CALIBER slug from the Lorcin semiautomatic slammed into the side of Henry Beck's head just above his left ear, rearranging the tissues of his brain and killing him instantly. The gunshot was drowned by the alarm.

Brad Kaufman closed the door, walked calmly past the workstation and placed the gun on the desk. It was acquired in the days following the riots in Ferguson, Missouri after the shooting of Darren Wilson. Sterilized and untraceable.

The Vestco security chief put his briefcase beside the gun and punched in a five-digit code to unlock it. From one of the compartments in the lid, he chose a plastic bag, lifted the gun carefully by the end of the grip, dropped it into the bag and zipped the seal. He put the bag into the briefcase, which he closed and locked.

He looked across at the body of the young IT specialist. What was left of his head was flopped beside the laptop. Blood pooled over the workstation and dripped from the wall onto the polished wooden floor, reminding him of his daughter's first attempt with watercolors.

Kaufman eased the laptop away from the head. The right side of the screen was smeared, but he could see an email was sent at 05.56.

He opened the message and stared at a string of letters and numbers. They meant nothing, but the name of the recipient's workplace, the Millbrook Foundation, sent his pulse surging.

He took the cellphone from his pocket and punched a series of numbers to silence the alarm, then removed his earplugs before hitting the letter *P*. A photo of vice president Petersen appeared on the screen as the phone dialed.

'Yes?'

'It is done. But we have an issue. Our boy sent a message to some clown at Millbrook. From his personal laptop. Hadn't counted on that.'

Kaufman heard a sharp intake of breath.

'What message?'

'Just a series of numbers and letters.' Kaufman read off the screen: '500mlETV 1gICE'

'Attachments? Did Beck send a file with the email?'

'Just the message.'

'Mean anything to you?'

'Looks like a list of ingredients.'

'Or some sort of password. Holy hell. We don't need this. Nine days to go. You can't take any chances with this Kaufman. Everything we've planned for. Right here. Right now. It's like you've just been told those 9/11 terrorists are in jets heading for the World Trade Center. Except we're talking millions and millions of lives this time. You've got to get to this guy at Millbrook. And that message, whatever it means, has to be eliminated.'

'Consider it done.'

Kaufman looked at the message on the laptop. He chose *New Message* and typed:

Sorry about that gibberish.
Spilt my coffee on the keyboard.
What I meant to say was - can you come over?
Got something interesting to show you.
Henry B.

He picked up the briefcase, walked to the air-conditioning panel beside the door, turned the dial down to fifty degrees and stepped into the empty hall. He locked the door, removed his gloves and slipped them into the pocket of his jacket.

The Millbrook office was just a short walk across Pershing Square.

2. One way or another

WHITE CLOUDS billowed across the screen on the wall of the Millbrook chief executive's office as the television weather update showed the day's high would reach just forty-eight in Los Angeles.

Jay chose an apple from the bowl on the coffee table, eased back into the sofa and pictured New Zealand summer sand between his toes.

No prizes for guessing the lead item on the news.

It was like nothing else mattered.

With just nine days to the much-awaited release of Alo — the seed coating set to revolutionize agriculture and bring humanity back from the brink of the global food crisis — we take a look at preparations for the historic day. Our coverage begins in India. We warn scenes in this report could be disturbing for some viewers.

The branding of the TV studio morphed into a colorless field near the small market town of Mandawa in Rajasthan. A bare-chested farmer in a faded red turban crouched on the ground, letting fragments of powdery soil run through his fingers.

Ishwar Singh has lost count of the times he's prepared this piece of land for planting. Last night he and his wife ploughed the field in the nude to appease the rain gods, a ritual based on an ancient Hindu legend. Farmers like Ishwar rely heavily on the southwest monsoon, which is critical for the all-important kharif rice crop. Last year it failed. So did the post-monsoon rains that normally fall from October to December. And the winter rains expected over the last two months. The drought has left Ishwar and millions of others throughout the subcontinent in a precarious state.

Jay tossed the apple from one hand to the other as a chaotic mob of rickshaws and bicycles and pedestrians were shown jamming an Indian street beneath a sign saying *'Grindlays - the bank that cares'.*

Wells have dried up in many areas, forcing migration on an unprecedented scale into cities like Jaipur, already bursting at the seams.

The high-definition plasma showed every cavity in the mouth of a mother howling over the crushed body of her child.

The death toll from this week's tragedy near Fatehpur, where thousands of people mobbed a train carrying drinking water from the state capital, has risen to four hundred twenty.

'Oh my heck. What's that got to do with Alo?'

Jay grinned at the woman sitting beside him. Cat Tayler had to be the only biologist on the planet who could string words like those together.

The Indian farmer dropped to his knees in prayer, eyes sunk into a face ridged prematurely by years too close to the breadline.

Today Ishwar is giving thanks to Brahma for a modern miracle created in a biochemistry lab in Pasadena, California. The Indian Ministry of Agriculture estimates more than one fifth of the nation's farmers will have access to seeds treated with the revolutionary drought and pest-resistant coating in time for this year's kharif planting.

A woman in a lime green sari ushered four children to join the farmer in the field. The kids beamed at Jay.

Ishwar and his family will be one of the first to receive the coated seeds after the global release in nine days.

Jay snuck a look at Cat, who was tapping her chin with four fingers while her head moved from side to side like one of those timing gadgets for a piano.

The rumble of heavy machinery jolted the room as the image panned from a close-up of a high-tech plough to an aerial shot of a vast area being cultivated. Trees bordering the field flung long shadows over soil so fertile you could drop an apple core in the morning and pick the fruit before sundown. The earth was etched in symmetric lines with eye-of-the-needle loops at each end. Sunlight glinted off tall grain silos spaced like silver tubes of lip balm in the orderly countryside.

In the Golden Triangle wheat belt north of Great Falls, Montana, farmers are preparing land for what they expect will be the first crop entirely free of wheat stem sawfly.

A farmer held a writhing black and yellow insect between his thumb and forefinger.

'I've wasted thousands over the years on pesticides to try and control these little varmints. None have worked. The extra money I've paid to order seeds with this Alo coating is less than half what I usually spend on pesticide. Top of that I'm told my yields will rise two-fifths. Sure as hell ain't gonna argue with those numbers.'

The farmer crushed the insect and flicked it into the air. The reporter came into shot on the edge of the field, posing with a loaf of bread.

'Those numbers are also good news for consumers of food made from wheat and other grains to be grown from Alo seeds. Today this loaf of bread sells for one dollar twenty. Next year the price is expected to drop below eighty cents.'

Bring out the violins, Jay thought, as the red earrings and lipstick matching the reporter's necklace were replaced with the ghoulish face of an African child blinded by conjunctivitis, too weak to brush away flies clinging to weeping sores. She was cradled in the arms of her mother who was frowning at Jay like it was all his fault.

There was a time when haunted eyes and bulging stomachs meant more to Jay Duggan. Yes, people were starving. Dying. He'd been to the camps. Seen and heard, smelt things they'd never show on TV. Foot-long worms writhing from the mouths of stick figures. Hyenas gnawing at the limbs of living skeletons. Nurses sobbing under mosquito nets night after night. Jay was sick of the way the fly-infested faces were exploited. Tomorrow the cameras would be pointed at a new photo opportunity. It was all a game to them, and he'd had a gutful.

It is here in east Africa where the most dramatic gains are expected. This woman and her daughter arrived last night at the relief camp in the Bakol region of southern Somalia, where the drought is so severe even camels are dying in large numbers.

A UN World Food Program lorry spewed up a caking of dust as it passed the skeletal remains of a carcass.

No rain has fallen here for more than a year. Even worse, the Drought Monitoring Center in Mogadishu is forecasting well below average rain for the gu season, the period between now and June when three-quarters of Somalia's grain is traditionally produced.

The caption identified an official from the WFP.

'We're optimistic the new coated sorghum and maize seeds will not only thrive in this harsh environment, but result in crops with as much as twice the nutritional content of the best harvests on record.'

'Oh. My. Heck.' Cat's arms punched the air as if leading a chant. 'When are these journalists ever going to acknowledge that for every starving African or Indian there's an overweight American or European?'

Back at the Somalian relief camp, the emaciated rug rat was propped in the arms of a reporter in a khaki safari suit and orange neck scarf. Her eyes fixed accusingly on Jay.

The revolutionary seed coating will almost certainly come too late for this child. The hope is that this will be the last year we'll see images like this.

* * * *

'FAT CHANCE lady. You'd be out of job.'

Cat Tayler aimed the remote at the TV as the bulletin jumped to a story about foreign leaders being hosted at Vestco headquarters later in the day. She stood to stretch, then turned to face her colleagues, hoping for support. Jay Duggan was juggling fruit, looking anything but the legendary eco-warrior. At the other end of the sofa, computer whiz Matthew Liddell twirled with his beard like he was waiting for a translation into HTML. Paul Deaver, chief executive of the Millbrook Foundation, brooded with his elbow on his desk and head in the palm of his hand. His voice was upbeat, bordering on patronizing.

'... know this is unfortunate.'

'Unfortunate? You make it sound like some first-grade science experiment and Mary-Lou put too much baking soda in the volcano.'

'I'm sorry Cat. We've given it our best shot. Just have to accept this thing's gonna happen and move on.'

If the words were supposed to make Cat feel better, he was wasting his breath. The campaign to stop the release of Alo had occupied every waking moment – and uncountable nightmares – for the best part of twelve months.

She turned her back on them and marched to the window. White blossom on the orange trees in floodlit Pershing Square was a surreal contrast to the stylized purple campanile and the glass and brick backdrop of corporate America. A world away from Somalia.

Cat was sickened by images of starvation in relief camps. It was so unnecessary. As a biologist she knew science had a pivotal role in feeding the world. But this Frankenfood seed coating was substandard science driven by the dollar, not by any concern for the wellbeing of African children or Ishwar whatever his name was.

The food crisis – so-called – was all about the insane drive for biofuel pushing the price of rice and maize and wheat through the stratosphere. Droughts came and went. Part of the natural cycle. Manageable by good farmers and better distribution systems. The world could grow more than enough to feed the world without resorting to genetic modification.

As director of science for Millbrook, an environmental organization set up specifically to counter the menace of genetic modification, Cat argued for the foundation to throw everything at the biggest player in the biotech game. Vestco. Creator, producer and ultimate beneficiary of Alo. Deaver agreed in the end, with one proviso, which he was now reminding them of.

'... known all along we've been working to a deadline,' he said, fidgeting with the band on his watch. 'A very specific deadline. I doubt there's a single person on the planet doesn't know the seeds will be released February eighteen. We agreed – all of us – in this room – if we couldn't stop Vestco by the end of January – eight days ago – we'd cut our losses. Move on to the next battle.'

Cat kept her mouth shut. Even she could see arguing was pointless. The initial deadline for the campaign was Christmas. After a long argument in which Deaver made it clear that continued opposition to something enjoying such overwhelming public support was undermining the foundation's credibility and bleeding support from funders, he'd relented and given them till the end of January. He redoubled his efforts, conjuring sponsorship from a hat and going into private debt to keep the campaign alive.

Then came her blackouts. The first ten days ago during a presentation to undergrads at Berkeley. Cat waved that away as fatigue. When she fainted again, crossing the street after a single margarita at Toppers, she got the message. Fortunately, Deaver was with her. And knew a physician just round the corner. The diagnosis was cardiac syncope, and Cat was ordered to take a complete break from work for two weeks. She protested, but was persuaded by the person who meant more to her than anything. Her father.

Deaver rubbed the back of his neck and avoided her eyes. 'Like it or not, the evidence may well be pointing to Alo becoming the greatest thing since sliced bread, hula hoops, Alexander Graham Bell and the Wright Brothers all rolled into one. And you guys have a plane to catch.'

Deaver's response to Cat's diagnosis was to shout her a vacation in New Zealand. 'A perfect opportunity to reflect and recharge,' he'd said. Jay had already indicated in his unassuming way he was 'retiring' from eco-activism and returning home to settle down. Cat and Matthew took the New Zealander up on his offer to show them around his country for a week or so before they returned to the States.

Cat glared at her watch. Check-in at LAX was less than two hours. The prospect of a vacation would normally excite her, particularly to a place so exotic. But her thoughts couldn't leave the campaign. Her campaign. Cat Tayler. Capital F for failure. What if a flaw in the seed coating was discovered while she was away? How would Deaver, whose background was in fundraising rather than science, cope?

'Leave me your private email addresses,' Deaver said, as if reading her thoughts. 'I'm sure I won't need to contact you, but if I do I'll use those. Forget about work. Have a great time. And thanks again for everything Jay. All the best with your forest. I meant it when I said there's a job back here if you change your mind.'

JAY HAD no intention of changing his mind. Bugger that for a joke. Deaver and the like, pen pushers in the flash offices of the environmental movement, thought of him as some kind of hero. Jay knew he'd failed to make a dent. Been farting against thunder.

'Just got to grab my laptop,' said Matthew as Jay reluctantly shadowed him into his office.

The room could have been out of one of those adverts in glossy magazines. Desk so spic and span it was unnatural. PCs and drives and add-ons that meant zip to Jay. Shelves of manuals. Boxes of software. Not a single living thing. Bare walls except for two posters – one showing the popping veins of Gollum from *Lord of the Rings*, another the blue face of the heroine from *Avatar*.

'Better check this,' said Matthew, referring to a flashing *Mail* icon.

'Give it a rest mate. You're on holiday.'

Matthew hesitated, then nodded. He shut down the computer and reached for a laptop.

'Sod it. Left the bleedin recharger at home. Do us a favor and take this suitcase for me. Tell Cat I'll see you guys at check-in.'

Jay shook his head in disbelief as the geek skived off towards one of the elevators.

The in-out board already showed Jay as gone, along with Matthew Liddell (Director IT) and Cat. Not Dr Catherine Tayler, with bullshit letters after the name like Dr Paul K Deaver MBA, BCom, Dip FIUS. Whatever they meant. Part of Jay was looking forward to spending a few days alone with Cat hiking in the mountains of New Zealand's Southern Alps.

'You're not leaving without saying goodbye I hope.'

Rosie Welsh. She who must be obeyed. Jay smiled for the umpteenth time at the sign above the receptionist: *Natura enim non imperatur, nisi parendo.* He'd looked up a translation of the foundation's motto once. It was from some English philosopher bloke and meant 'Nature cannot be ordered about, except by obeying her'. On the nail in terms of Rosie, who wobbled around to squeeze his arm and reach up to peck his chin.

'Gonna miss you round here kid.'

'You know where to find me Rosie. I'm expecting a visit.'

Of all the people at Millbrook who promised to come and see Jay in New Zealand, Rosie was the most likely to turn up. Hopefully with her two sons, who Jay had taken bouldering a few times at Joshua Tree National Park. The door to Cat's office opened and she flowed past in a wave of pinstripes, peach scent and a face that did not belong to someone on holiday.

'Where's Matthew?'

'Had to go home for something. Says he'll catch us at the airport.'

'He's cutting it fine.'

KAUFMAN SWALLOWED the steps two at a time and paused to scope his reflection in the glass doors. Non-descript black suit. White shirt. Gold silk tie. Black leather shoes and matching briefcase. The wig of reputable gray was undetectable and the lenses of the conservative glasses so clear you'd swear there was no magnification.

In the elevator to the fourth floor, the model LA businessman flipped through a stack of business cards and selected one from Impart Market Research. Before the doors completely opened he'd taken in the terrain of wood paneling, beige carpet, token plants in terracotta pots and prints of California redwoods. Irritating birdsong jabbered over an intercom as he approached the reception desk. He identified a secondary hall to the right with a single wooden door that was presumably a back entrance to the Millbrook offices. Double glass doors led to a stairwell.

A peroxide whale coated in greasepaint eyeballed him from beneath a picture of some bird flying over words in a foreign language. A glance at the staff notice board revealed the recipient of the email – Matthew Liddell – wasn't in yet and gave Kaufman the name of the receptionist.

'Morning Rosie,' he said, flourishing the business card. 'James Renshaw, Impart Research. Here to see Matt Liddell.'

The whale looked surprised.

'Matthew. He prefers to be called Matthew. I'm afraid you've missed him. He's just left.'

'Mind if I wait?'

'If you've got a week or so. Matthew's gone home to pick up a charger. He's off on vacation.'

Kaufman absorbed the news and recovered to pile on the charm.

'Lucky guy. I imagine computer experts like Matthew spend vacations at IT conventions unzipping their RAMs, mounting their hard drives.'

The whale blushed, tilting forward to parade her hideous chest.

'He's off to New Zealand,' she whispered as if it was a state secret. 'Though you're not completely wrong. He's going to see where they did that special effect stuff on the *Hobbit* and *Avatar* movies.'

This was heading downhill fast, but like a true pro Kaufman changed gear.

'Some people have all the luck. Guess I'll have to catch up when he's back.'

'Like to make an appointment, Mr...?'

'Renshaw. Call me James. When's he back?'

Rosie peeked right then left and lowered her voice even further. 'Not supposed to say really, James. Security and all that. They're gone till the fourteenth.'

'They?'

'Matthew's gone with two of his colleagues.'

Kaufman leaned towards her, hand beside his mouth. 'Won't tell a soul Rosie. Too bad. Deadline for our survey's the twelfth. Another time maybe.'

'Shall I leave him a message you called?'

Kaufman pinched his chin as if contemplating the question, his eyes drifting over her shoulder and resting on the name on one of the doors.

'Nah, let's leave it. I'll bump into him one way or another. You have a nice day Rosie.'

* * * *

THE GEEZER behind the redesign of Pershing Square got the balance between concrete and shrubbery spot on, Matthew thought, as he tightened his scarf. Traffic was already bunching along Hill, and the sidewalk was padding out with toilers.

Ten past six. Cat would be panicking, but there was heaps of time. He aimed for his favorite coffee cart in the northwestern quadrant, wandering in a wide arc to avoid a sponger hibernating under a silver tarpaulin. All they had to do was get rid of these deadbeats who dragged the place into a hairy no-go zone every night. Why couldn't they get off their backsides and find a job instead of forever holding out their hands?

The world was full of winners and losers. Matthew was a winner. Lad from the blotted side of the tracks in London using his wits to rack up the big dosh. Doing what he liked doing. How sweet was that? If you had to cheat or stretch the truth a little to rise above the gutter – as his father did – that was fine. Long as you didn't get caught.

He ordered a cappuccino and took a breather on a bench, positioning the laptop case on the ground and threading one leg through the strap. Just in case. Not that these bums would know what to do with it. Probably hock it off for less than five percent its actual value.

Matthew cradled the cup in his hands till the warmth spread to the tips of his fingers. Half a dozen Asian tourists were bundled near the orange grove in the center of the square, pretending to smile at one of their tribe filming on an iPhone. Matthew's eyes were wowed to an approaching jogger in red shorts and all-the-way-up legs. He raised his cup as she drew near and got a one-fingered salute for his trouble.

Bitch.

He had a quick look round to make sure no-one noticed, then drained the coffee, slung the laptop over his shoulder and trudged off through the group of tourists.

3. Wig and glasses

'YOU DON'T reckon living in the same block as the office is taking the job a bit too seriously?'

Cat ignored the jibe as she unlocked the door and moved aside to let Jay into her apartment. Two suitcases and a shoulder bag packed two days before were lined beside the sofa.

'Make yourself at home, I won't be long.'

Jay headed for the sofa and Cat tackled the list.

1. Confirm flight time/meal

She called Air New Zealand and was told the flight was leaving on schedule. Check-in was still the same time. And yes, her low-fat meal was still booked. 'Nothing has changed since you checked yesterday, Dr Tayler.'

2. Order cab

No need. She'd called from the office.

3. Change into travel clothes

A white V-neck tank, brown pin-tucked skirt and denim cargo jacket were arranged on the bed. She changed, slipped on a pair of sneakers, hung her suit on a clothes rack in the closet and folded and put her work blouse into the wicker laundry basket. The face staring from the mirror shouted *F*. Failure. Female. Foolish. Four eyes. And frowning. She ran a brush through her hair and refreshed the lipstick.

4. Check tickets/documents/cash

From the small safe in the closet, she took out a bum bag and parked on the edge of the bed. She leafed through the documents, rechecking the date and check-in time on the air ticket, the insurance policy covering everything from dental to emergency evacuation, confirmation of the reservation at the Hyatt Regency in Auckland, the expiry date on the passport. Three years to go. The passport photo was even more vanilla without the glasses.

She counted the unfamiliar banknotes. Thirty one-hundred-dollar bills depicting Ernest Rutherford, the New Zealand-born physicist who discovered the atomic nucleus.

5. Phone Pop

She fleshed out what he had planned for the next few days. Cat assured him she was feeling fine, there'd been no more dizzy spells, the money would still go into his account Monday.

'And I've ordered black pepper jumbo shrimp at Cha Cha Cha for the fifteenth.' Cat and her father shared a birthday and were yet to miss a joint dinner.

'Any idea if Mom will be in town?'

'Haven't heard from your mother in months.'

Nor had Cat.

'I'll calculate the time difference Pop, and phone most days from New Zealand to see you're OK.'

'It's you I'm stewing about Catherine. Take it easy out there. You deserve it after what you've been through. Live a little.'

'Love ya Pop.'

'You too sweetie.'

6. Isabelle

The ball of fur sleeping in the basket beside the tallboy growled as she was picked up, along with the assembled bag of accessories and instructions.

Jay was engrossed in a magazine. Cat hovered in the doorway to observe the first man other than her father to sit on that sofa for how long? Since before Millbrook.

She knew so little about the New Zealander, yet the storm-ruffled hair, take-me-as-I-come stubble and open uncomplicated face were curiously relaxing. Like a second glass of wine.

He looked up. Had he noticed her staring?

'Taking Isabelle across the hall to Mrs Appleby's. She'll be just home from work. Night shift nurse at Good Sam. Back in five, tops.'

* * * *

KAUFMAN TOOK the elevator to the floor above Millbrook and stepped into the futuristic lobby of a jewelry company.

Dwarfed by a huge print of an opal and gold pendant, two women were in tight discussion at the reception counter, which flowed in waves of perspex and wood mirroring the facade of the building. They never saw him jink to the right and through glass doors into the stairwell.

The whale was blabbing on the phone as he entered the Millbrook side hall and knelt at the locked door. A swift inspection of the keyway revealed a five-pin tumbler. Visualizing the internal parts of the lock, he used a small diamond pick to raise the pins to their breaking point and a tension wrench to rotate the cylinder and operate the cam. Within forty-five seconds he was inside a storeroom lined with shelves, filing cabinets, billboards and other junky propaganda. If his calculations were correct, the door on the left was the rear entrance to Liddell's office. The lock yielded in thirty seconds.

Kaufman paused to take in the monitors and keyboards and cables, then cocked his head to gauge sound carrying through internal walls, treading lightly to test the give in the floor. He edged silently to the desktop PC and used a gloved finger to hold the key suppressing the startup volume. He took a USB stick from his pocket and inserted it into a port. The program started automatically and took forty seconds to identify the password and open the desktop. He removed the USB, clicked the *Mail* icon, then opened the message inviting Liddell to come over. Moving the cursor to reply, he typed:

Be right over. Matthew

Cackling from the whale siphoned through the wall as Kaufman scoured the inbox till he found a message from Air New Zealand with the flight number and departure time from LAX. There was also a message from remotecontrolmail.com confirming they would be monitoring letters sent to the geek's apartment. Kaufman noted the address and flight details on the back of the business card. He went online and followed a series of links to the real estate company managing the Vestco building until he found a single-tenant floor plan. He recognized the layout of the thirty-sixth floor, showing the location of Henry Beck's office.

Leaving the web page open on the screen, he unlocked his briefcase and took out a plastic bag. Using fingertips, he picked up a blue Millbrook pen, dropped it inside and returned it to the briefcase.

Next he took a rectangular cigar tin and placed it carefully on the desk. He opened the lid, lifted the second cigar from the right and pushed a button invisible to the naked eye. The base of the tin clicked open to reveal the false bottom. Concealed inside was a small laser torch, containers of cyanoacrylate, glycerin, wood glue and theatrical glue, a tiny custom designed digital camera and laser printer, transparency paper and foil.

Within five minutes Kaufman detected and lifted a clear print from a coffee cup and transposed it onto the grip of the Lorcin. He wrapped the gun in a page of the *LA Times* from the trash basket, shoved it in his pocket and retreated unnoticed out the back door, down the stairs and onto Hill.

* * * *

THE LETTER lying open on the coffee table was too intriguing for Jay to ignore. The gold letterhead said International Federation for Biotechnology Information. Most of the world might be fooled by the official-sounding name, but it was nothing more than a front for the world's largest agri and biotech corporations. Big A and B.

Peel the outer layers of the onion and you reveal the federation's purpose in life – to manipulate public opinion and influence meetings of Codex Alimentarius, the body that sets international food standards.

The letter was an invitation for Cat to join a debate in Washington.

Two professors, one Jay recognized as a Nobel winner, were already confirmed for the opposing side. Despite her well-known stance against genetic modification, Cat was still well thought-of in the scientific community.

Poking out from under the invite was the corner of a second letter. Jay couldn't resist. With one eye on the door, he skimmed the words: extreme emotional stress ... cardiac syncope ... sudden decline of blood to the brain ... loss of consciousness ... life-threatening ... immediate break from work ... recommend vacation ... abroad ...

Jay inserted the letter back as if it was the only copy of some thousand-year-old parchment. He picked up the latest copy of *Discover* magazine and stowed away in the depths of the sofa.

He skimmed through an article on the emergence of *grassrootsintelligence.com* as one of the most powerful blogs in America. How breaking the story on the attack on Tolminsky's lab had catapulted the blog from obscurity to serious influence. Its continued exposés of big business had earnt it a following among liberals to rival the *Treehugger* blog. The article highlighted the example of *Grassroots'* exclusive on Del Pizza chain's announcement that it would only be serving food made with non-Alo ingredients in its 1200 restaurants across North America. How within hours the story had gone mega-viral on Facebook. The author speculated that because of its international reach, it was only a matter of time before *Grassroots* challenged the top dog in the blogosphere, *Huffington Post*.

About time, thought Jay. The new blog's popularity had resulted in an avalanche of leaks to the blog from corporate and government whistleblowers on both sides of the Atlantic. *Grassroots* posted them all, adding to its broad-based appeal.

Jay flicked to an article on the work of renowned geneticist Valmai Kane at a sophisticated biotron at Lincoln University in New Zealand. The biotron was a two-story affair with upstairs chambers simulating above-ground conditions and downstairs focusing on root systems. By controlling the air-conditioned chambers separately, Kane's team could see how very high temperatures affected leaf growth without cooking the roots. Made sense.

But didn't make Jay feel any less guilty about his home invasion.

He shifted his weight. The lump in his pocket was a cowhide climbing glove he'd used the day before at Rockreation. Two stories of sculpted wall in a stainless-steel building on La Grange Avenue. How pathetic his life had become. Working out in gyms beside steroid-popping jocks, spray-on tans. Dodging the creeps and junkies on night runs through MacArthur Park. No longer. He was going where he could taste the mountain air above the snowline, stay as fit as a buck rat through real exercise. Climbing, mountain biking, kayaking. Clearing exotics from the chunk of land he'd bought. Then planting.

From now on Jay Duggan was only concerned with replacing what Jay Duggan used. Two hundred and forty-three full-grown rimu trees, he reckoned, would replace the amount of paper the average bloke wasted or flushed down the toilet in a lifetime. He intended planting two *thousand* and forty. Just for starters.

He drifted towards the bookshelf lining an entire wall, running his finger along a shelf. You'd find more dust in your average library. In the middle were three framed photos. A man standing on the veranda of a white wooden house with a freckly girl laughing on his shoulders. Cat as a kid. Another was of three guys, jeans and long hair, taking it easy on a tattered sofa with weeds growing through the floorboards. Bloke in the middle holding a guitar on his crossed legs was a younger version of the man with the girl. Had to be Cat's father. Same impish smile. The third photo was a portrait of the guy in black and white, except for a gold arrowhead pendant round his neck sticking out in color. Native Indian design perhaps. Jay thought of the photo in his daypack. Every detail by heart. Side profile. Wet, dark hair pointing in jagged lines at the pendant round her neck that was now round his. He touched it through his T-shirt.

'We're going home, babe.'

Other than half a row on theater and stage makeup, Cat's shelves were sardined with books on science. David Baldacci and Lee Child didn't get a look in.

Jay knew people who stuffed shelves like this with books they'd never read. Feature walls they called them. Like hunters who mount animals, trophies, from countries they'd never set foot in. Bet Cat's read every word of these. She's even stacked them in order. Acheron to Yarrow. *Bloody frightening.*

He picked out a hard cover with a green jacket. *Seeds of Hope* by Roman Tolminsky. Creator of Alo. Many people expected Tolminsky's death would throw a spanner in the works of the coating.

The opposite happened, with Vestco fast-tracking commercial production and bringing forward the release date.

Haste that would seem indecent even to the most ardent genetic modification flag-waver if it weren't for the good old food crisis.

Jay stuck Tolminsky back on the shelf and took out the book beside it. *Hard Cell* by Professor K.M. Stedholme.

Inside the cover was a handwritten note:

Catherine.

I keep six honest serving-men, they taught me all I knew. Their names are What and Why and When and How and Where and Who. (Rudyard Kipling)

Many thanks for your affection and assistance.

Keith S.

The door opened and Cat came in clutching her to-do list. Today was the first time Jay had seen her kitted out in anything other than a business suit with pants to the ankles. The doctor had half decent legs. And her hair was untied. Another first.

'You know this bloke Stedholme?' he said, returning the book to the shelf.

'Keith was my mentor at Plant and Microbial at Berkeley. Moved back to England when he retired from teaching. Real character. Eccentric, but absolutely brilliant. We've kept in touch. Keith refuses to use email. Destroying the Queen's English, he says. Sends me screeds of handwritten advice for the campaign.'

She lowered her head and sighed, the edges of her downturned lips quivering, fingers tapping her chin.

'You all right?'

'Yeah. Just feel bad about leaving. You know, so close to release day.'

'No-one's done more to try to stop this thing than you, Cat,' he

24

said, glancing at the coffee table to check he'd left the letters as he found them. 'Anyone's guilty of jumping ship it's me.'

'Come off it Jay. You jump off ships literally, or so I'm told.'

'You believe everything you're told?'

She smiled with a hint of blush and looked at her watch, then the list.

'Seven. Turn everything off.'

She set the touch screen for the home entertainment system to *off*, then walked methodically around every room twice, disconnecting appliances, lamps, the computer, switching off lights. A horn blasted in the street below as she began her third check in the bedroom.

Jay hoped it was the cab.

* * * *

THE LANDSCAPE architect who redesigned Pershing Square wanted people using the five-acre space to get the idea they were in a great bowl surrounded by buildings, yet out of sight of the traffic.

The anonymity suited Kaufman as he casually dropped the screwed-up newspaper into a trash can, slipped the wig and glasses into his briefcase and blended into the early morning current of pedestrians on Olive. He entered the Vestco building via a side door.

Cold air and a breath of urine smacked him as he stepped into the office of the late Henry Beck. He pictured the crime scene as if he was back with the LAPD Homicide Special Unit. Georgie stretching the yellow tape to get photos from all angles. Bob dusting for prints. Doyle calculating the bullet trajectory. The Fox dissecting everything from a distance with hands glued in his pockets so he wouldn't touch anything.

Kaufman put on his gloves to inspect the corpse. The skin on the dead man's face was still tight and gray. Lips and fingernails not yet faded, though the eyes were starting to sink into the skull. No sign of the purple discoloration of livor mortis. The cold air in the room would slow the change in body temperature, which normally fell three degrees in the first hour after death. There was a faint smell of decaying flesh as digestive enzymes began eating Henry Beck from the inside out.

Satisfied his former colleagues would conclude the appropriate time of death, Kaufman unlocked his briefcase, opened the plastic bag containing the pen and tipped it onto the floor. He returned the air-conditioning dial to seventy degrees and took out his cell phone. Time to report this most unfortunate matter to the LAPD.

He punched in the numbers and was about to hit *talk* when he noticed the airport hub. An identical box sat beside Liddell's PC at Millbrook. The geek must have a laptop or tablet. The first email message would almost certainly be on that as well, and possibly on a phone. He had to get to Liddell before The Fox and his team started poking around.

Kaufman took out the business card and flipped it over.

Matthew L – 15B Metropolitan Apartments, South Flower St.

4. Deal with it

MATTHEW TENSED the muscles in his neck as he stretched back and let the hot water stream over his head. With the laptop recharging on the bar in the kitchen, there was time for a quick shower to freshen up before the cab arrived.

He turned and squinted as the water ran over his face and beard, then stepped back to let it massage his chest.

New Zealand had been on his must-visit list since watching the first movie of the *Rings* trilogy. The Kiwi special effects artists had taken things to a new level with *Avatar* and the *Hobbit* movies. Unlike most tourists heading Down Under, Matthew couldn't give a toss about real mountains or glaciers or leaping off a bridge with a bungee cord tied round your ankle. The sole focus of his trip was Weta Digital – the place where they made the 3-D computer model of Gollum and developed the ray-tracing software to manage the billions of polygons in *Avatar*. He was curious to get the inside goss on their use of sliders, and how they calculated the interactions between bones, flesh and hair. There were no public tours of the inner workings, but a friend of a friend knew a geezer who worked there as a systems administrator. The private tour would without doubt be the highlight of the trip.

Matthew knew sod all else about New Zealand, other than the All Blacks and the tongue-wagging war dance they performed before rugby games.

He hunched his shoulders to let the water flow down the middle of his back. Life was sweet. Enjoy it while you've got it my son. With all those young students coming out of universities, the shelf life of an IT professional was shortening by the day.

He rotated again and turned the hot up a notch. Five years, he reckoned. Then he'd be redundant. But with the dosh they were paying him at Millbrook, ridiculous dosh really, he'd earn enough to start his own firm and hire a bank of young nerds. Or would you call it a node of nerds?

When Deaver collared him in London with the offer of the job as Millbrook's IT director with a starting salary of $250,000, Matthew jokingly said he wouldn't consider it for less than $300K. 'Deal,' the CEO said without hesitation. He got to the States three weeks later to find the $300K was just basic salary. Benefits and bonuses added another fifty. Worth every cent, mind you. Kept the whole show on the road.

The best, though, was yet to come. Back in the UK Matthew couldn't give a toss about trees and endangered bleedin wetlands. Leave it out. Till he discovered working for a high-profile environmental organization went down a treat with the birds. So, he went along with the charade. Bloke's gotta do what a bloke's gotta do.

He increased the temperature another notch and closed his eyes as the water played with the back of his neck.

* * * *

LESS THAN one mile away, the custom-built blue Lincoln Navigator slowed to a stop in a queue of traffic.

The tinted windows were multilayered laminations of glass and polycarbonate, and the sides were made of ballistic quality steel. Kaufman tapped his foot impatiently on the grenade-proof floor and sneered at two gays walking past holding hands.

The queue wasn't moving. The driver was talking on his cell phone. Kaufman pushed the button to lower the divider screen.

'What's the holdup?'

'Sorry Mr Kaufman. The police are closing the street.'

'The hell for?'

'Motorcade due soon.'

'Dammit.' Kaufman slammed his fist into the leather seat. He'd forgotten about the banana republic brass visiting Vestco that morning.

'How soon we gonna be clear?'

'They're running late sir. Told it could be another 15 minutes.'

To their left was an orange City of Los Angeles service truck and behind was a Downtown bus. Three cars blocked movement to the front and concrete bollards closed off the sidewalk option. The Lincoln was wedged.

Kaufman took the business card from his pocket.

Flight NZ40. 10.25.

Not enough time to get to Liddell's apartment before the geek would have to leave to check in. Nor could he alert the police to Beck's murder. The Fox and his crew crawling over the Vestco building was the last thing the boss would want with these heads of monkey states in town. And it would be too risky to move on Liddell and his friends at the airport. He closed the divider screen and dialed Petersen.

'Yes?' The vice president sounded irritated.

'About our little issue...'

'Deal with it,' Petersen hissed, as if he didn't want whoever else was in the room to hear him. 'That's what you're being paid for.'

Kaufman took a deep breath and considered his options. There was only one. He phoned his secretary to make the arrangements, then took the small leather photo frame from his breast pocket and opened it. The trusting full-of-life face of his daughter, one arm round the chipmunk, grinned her cheeky grin. He swallowed. The shot was taken at Disneyland four days before she fell sick. A week of tests followed before the shocking diagnosis. Stage four neuroblastoma – the most aggressive and deadly form of the rare childhood cancer.

Month after month of induction chemo, stem cell collection, radiotherapy, immunotherapy. A rolling hell of vomiting, hair loss, burning temperatures, nose bleeds, gum bleeds, rashes. Then infection after infection that just hammered away at Eve's exhausted little body. The Schulerburg Klinik in Germany was now her only hope. And the million-dollar bonus Kaufman would receive the moment Alo was released the only way he could pay for the treatment.

5. Until now

'AFTER YOU.' Cat wasn't sure if she should be flattered or insulted, but the look on Jay's face was so sincere she let the display of chauvinism go and stepped past him into the plane.

A brown-skinned steward tilted his head in one of those phony customer service course smiles as he checked her boarding pass. Cat felt her face glow. For some reason she'd always visualized Maori people with tattooed faces and grass skirts.

'Welcome aboard Dr Tayler. 51K? In the rear cabin on your left.'

Perfect English.

'Can you tell me what time it is in Auckland at the moment please?' she asked, preparing to adjust her watch.

'New Zealand's twenty-one hours ahead Dr Tayler.'

'Which coast?'

'All of it.'

She began to thank him, but the head was already puppeting toward the next passenger. She shielded her arms so Jay and Matthew wouldn't see her make an L shape with her left hand as she shuffled down the aisle. She folded her jacket and put it in the overhead locker and had her seatbelt fastened before Matthew slid into the seat beside her, laptop bag perched on his knee.

'Do you sleep with that?'

'It's permanently attached,' chipped in Jay.

'OK OK. I get the bleedin message.' Matthew shoved the bag under his feet.

'You can't use them anyway,' said Cat. 'Not till we're in the air. They interfere with the electrics.'

She switched off her mobile and took the safety manual from the pocket. She noted the distance to the nearest emergency exit, felt under the seat for the tag to her life preserver, then looked up to work out which compartment the oxygen mask would fall from. She glanced across at Jay, who seemed a bit on edge. Surely he couldn't be afraid of flying.

A hostess zigzagged towards them, offering magazines and the *LA Times*. Her eyes lingered on Jay longer than necessary.

* * * *

AS THE BOEING 777-300 climbed through the clouds above Los Angeles and banked to the west, the man with the traditional Jewish yarmulke cap and flowing salt and pepper beard sitting in the back row of Business Premier class adjusted his half-frame spectacles as he scrolled through the passenger list downloaded onto his cell phone moments before takeoff.

He bristled at names like Fadallah, Musawi and Zadeh, but continued until he found what he was looking for. He noted the seat numbers.

The jet reached thirty-four thousand feet before leveling out and setting a course south-south-west over the Pacific Ocean. The seatbelt signs pinged off and this-is-your-captain-speaking advised the flight time would be a little less than the normal twelve and a half hours.

The man in business class asked for an in-flight phone and dialed the number for his home in the gated Westlake Village of Los Angeles.

'Kaufman residence. You're talking with Eve.'

'Good morning Eve. You're talking with your father.'

'Daddy! You'll never guess. I've just drawn this amazing meerkat. From that book, you know, Michelle gave me for my birthday. Can't wait to show you.'

'Afraid I've gotta go away for a day or two Princess.'

There was a pause.

'That's OK daddy.' It was the voice of an eight-year-old trying to mask her disappointment.

'Where you going?'

'Place called Auckland.'

'No! I hope you've got your gun Daddy.'

That rattled him.

'Because orcs are like the worst. Specially the pale one. Or when they cross them with trolls.'

'Orcs?'

'You know, chased Frodo in …'

'That was make-believe Eve. There's no orcs in Auckland. It's spelt different. They do have birds with no wings though, called kiwis.'

'You're joshing me now daddy. Like, all birds have wings. Even ostriches. And whoever heard of a bird named after a fruit?'

There was zip in her voice, which meant she was having a reasonable day.

She recited her counts like they were soft drinks. Elevated AST, ALT and GGT. Kaufman knew these related to her liver, but wasn't certain what each meant.

They spent several minutes talking about emus and pelicans and dodos. When Kaufman hung up he noticed the elderly woman across the aisle smiling in the conspiratorial way grandmothers enjoy the interplay between men and their children. The old bird's eye shadow matched the blue rinse in her hair. Kaufman smiled back politely.

He reached for his briefcase and opened it on his lap. Three manila folders, writing pad, digital voice recorder, pens, bathroom travel bag, cigar tin and a black plastic bag containing wigs, beards and accessories.

The first folder was marked simply ML. At the top of the first page were front and side profile photographs of Matthew Robert Liddell, born London. Age. Height. Weight. Hair color, currently worn with full beard. Eyes. Birthmark between index and middle fingers on left hand.

Blue rinse tottered off towards the bathroom. Kaufman checked his watch. 10.40 in LA. The monkey heads would have left the Vestco offices. He made three further calls. The first was to an LA number. A woman answered and was given instructions to place an anonymous call from a pay phone to the LAPD reporting she saw a man run out of the Vestco building about six-forty and drop something suspicious in a trash can in Pershing Square. He was about five nine, one sixty pounds, dark hair, beard.

The second call was to an unlisted number in Auckland.

The third was to his deputy at Vestco, who was told to wait ten minutes then call the police to report the murder of Henry Beck in his office.

'What the -?'

Kaufman cut him short. Blue rinse was returning to her seat.

'I'll explain later. I'll be out of town for a day or so. Call you back in a few hours to see how things are panning out.'

He returned to the dossier. The bottom half of the first page was a table of vitals based on the US Military Physical Profile Serial System, expanded to include information of particular interest to people in Kaufman's line of work. Ratings were given as percentages. Bold type indicated confirmed data, italics were estimates. Most of Liddell's life was in bold. The highest score, 92, was for academic intelligence; the lowest, 62, for current fitness. He rated in the 80s on practical intelligence, emotional stability, hearing and sight, but in the 60s for general physical capacity and upper and lower body strength. Your typical wimp.

By the end of the twelve-page dossier Kaufman knew Liddell was the son of a petty criminal with convictions in Salford County Court for false accounting and forgery of vehicle documents, resulting in short stints at Her Majesty's Prison, Manchester. Young Matthew came to the attention of Her Majesty's constabulary two years ago for allegedly hacking into the database of a reputable law firm in Kensington. The evidence was solid, but the charges dropped. Three weeks later Liddell moved to Los Angeles to work for Millbrook. There were details, all in bold type, of his salary, employment contract, social security number, medical and employment insurance. He had savings, checking and investment accounts at the Pershing Square branch of the City National Bank, with current cash assets totaling $156,000. He owed $3098.56 on his credit card as at 5pm yesterday.

He was listed as the sole tenant of 15C The Metropolitan Apartments, for which he paid $1880 rent per month. Four different women spent nights there in the last six months. He went to Casey's Irish Bar and Grill between Sixth and Wiltshire most Fridays from 6 to 7pm, always drinking happy hour martinis, was a regular patron at the Roof Bar at the Standard Hotel, and held a membership with Netflix online movie rentals. He voted Conservative in the last two British general elections, and although not entitled to vote in the United States, his political leanings were Republican. Liddell was baptized Anglican at St Aidan's Church in Lower Kersal, but was never a believer. He suffered from hay fever between the ages of six and thirteen, had surgery on his right elbow at the Nirschl Orthopedic Center in London when he was twenty-two, and was treated for food poisoning at Los Angeles Hospital fourteen months ago.

The dossier was a hardcopy summary. Web links highlighted in blue throughout the document indicated more detailed information was available. Kaufman accepted a glass of iced water from the hostess and picked up the other two folders.

The most striking feature of the photographs of Catherine (Cat) Tayler PhD was the red-rimmed spectacles. Several of her vitals were higher than Liddell, including physical strength, which Kaufman found amusing. She rated an impressive 97 on academic intelligence, but only 72 on practical intelligence. Hearing very good, eyesight appalling. He flipped through the rest of the dossier, the impressive academic record, history of environmental activism, noting with interest the woman had a very close relationship with her father, a guitarist with the eighties group, *The Buzzards*. He quit the band after injuring his hand and had since been supported on welfare and more recently by his daughter. Worth remembering.

The file on Jay Duggan was the lightest of the three, with a section covering the three-year period before he moved to California heavily italicized. That anyone could virtually disappear from the security radars of XecIntel, the executive intelligence firm funded by Vestco and a handful of other biotech corporations, was remarkable in itself. Kaufman got an even bigger surprise when he saw Duggan's vitals.

Academic intelligence was a hayseed 47. But physical capacity, upper and lower body strength, hearing, eyesight, emotional stability, core and current fitness and practical intelligence were all in the 90s. Core fitness was rated 96, just one point below the highest score Kaufman had seen. That belonged to a fellow snake-eater at Fort Bragg, nicknamed The Machine. But the rating that surprised Kaufman the most was Duggan's CUP – composure under pressure. It was always in italics for it estimated, among other things, the degree of torture a person could sustain before breaking. Kaufman prided himself on a CUP rating of 92, the only one he had seen above 90. Until now.

* * * *

JAY LIFTED his left leg, bending the knee and contracting the thigh muscles. Then with the other leg for the twentieth time.

He read an editorial in the *LA Times* ridiculing Del Pizza's decision not to use food with Alo ingredients. The chain's executives were labelled as off the wall, flaky, unscientific, harebrained and unstable, all in one paragraph. Similar articles, using similar language, had been appearing all week in the so-called mainstream media. The morons on *Fox News* had gone as far as calling Del's CEO unpatriotic.

There were only two half decent films on offer – documentaries on coral in the Red Sea and Mt Ramelau in Timor Leste. He'd seen the one on the reefs and had spent more time in the mountains of Timor Leste than he cared to remember.

Cat was asleep and Matthew was using the remote to Rory McIlroy his way round a golf course on the seatback screen. The route map showed the plane somewhere between the Marquesas and Galapagos Islands. Still eight hours from Auckland. Jay ordered another beer.

* * * *

THE ALARM on Kaufman's cell phone vibrated. He asked for an in-flight phone and called the office.

'Good news and bad,' said his deputy. 'LAPD have a suspect. One Matthew Liddell. Computer nerd from the Millbrook Foundation. You know, they're based over on Hill Street.'

'Excellent news. How'd they find him so quickly?'

'Our boy Henry Beck sent these emails to Millbrook this morning. When the cops searched Liddell's office they found a floor plan of our building on the nerd's computer.'

'You're having me on.'

'No shit. Guy's a real amateur. Some woman saw him drop a parcel in a trash can in the Square. Guess what was in it?'

'A Seagate drive?'

'Lorcin 380. Same caliber as the slug extracted from what was left of Beck's head. Forensics are running prints on it now, along with some other items they found in Beck's office.'

'You said there was bad news?'

'Seems Liddell's done a runner. He's on a plane to New Zealand with two accomplices from Millbrook. Interpol is onto it. Our man on the inside in Lyon says all three will be taken into custody soon as they land. Expects the notice to be upgraded from blue to red in the next hour. Anything you need me to do?'

Kaufman scratched the back of the wig. It was starting to irritate him.

'I want the layout of Auckland airport showing the location of the airport police. Emailed to my cell phone.'

'Ah... OK.' The deputy was clearly confused, but knew not to question such a request.

* * * *

APPLAUSE CRACKLED round the South Hall of the Los Angeles Conference Center like volleys of canon. From the wings, Petersen lifted his lapel to check the microphone was still in place as the chairman of Vestco Corporation raised his hands to calm the audience.

'Ladies and gentlemen, the current food shortage is without doubt the greatest crisis facing our planet. There is also no doubt the only viable solution to the crisis is to dramatically increase food production from the existing land set aside for agriculture. With the demand for biofuel, timber, forest conservation, not to mention land needed for the expansion of urban areas to house the world's growing population, opening up new land for growing food is simply not an option.'

The old man skipped the reference to carbon sequestration, but three out of four was acceptable. He was the one *delivering* the speech.

The crowd went mute, hanging on every syllable of Jozef Pyjas, as if the Vestco chairman was the messiah.

'Let me repeat. The only viable solution is to dramatically increase food production from *existing* agricultural land, much of which is already degraded or vulnerable to drought, floods and other extreme weather events hastened by global warming. Humankind, ladies and gentlemen, faces an extraordinary set of circumstances. Fortunately, we have in Alo an extraordinary solution.'

That went down as Petersen intended, and the chairman had to wait another thirty seconds before continuing.

'As you know, development of Alo and the science of genetic modification has had its critics.

A few boos. Half-hearted and planted for effect.

'Overcoming that opposition, ladies and gentlemen, has taken some incredibly bold and sometimes unpopular decisions. Not the least by the leaders of two countries in particular whose support for the release of Alo has been pivotal in getting us to where we are today. I'm talking of course about the great nations of China and India. I want to acknowledge the presence here this evening of Ambassadors Zhao and Paranjpe.'

The Vestco chairman waited for the applause to start fading before raising his hand for the final time.

'Starvation, ladies and gentlemen, is the worst of all tortures. That is one matter on which Vestco and the anti-genetic modification lobby – and *Grassroots Intelligence* – are in total agreement. The seeds that shall be sown in nine days will nourish and sustain humanity into the future.

38

Alo will make starvation history.'

On cue the nine thousand erupted as one. The clapping and cheering and foot stamping was deafening, and they sustained the standing ovation for as long as it took the chairman to shake hands with a dozen other pillars of society at the top table.

Petersen pressed the *record* button in his pocket and stepped forward to greet Pyjas as he came into the wings, flanked already by two of his bodyguards.

'Congratulations sir. Captivating speech.'

'Thank you Petersen.' The chairman was clearly on a high.

'I wonder if I could have a quick word sir. In private.'

The chairman motioned with his hand and the minders retreated from earshot.

'We may have an issue sir.'

Pyjas leaned close enough for Petersen to smell the dessert wine. 'Deal with it. Whatever it takes. I don't want to know. Just get us to the release. I'm counting on you.'

Petersen recognized the hulking frame of the Governor of California strutting towards them, so eased aside to let the two marionettes tangle in their mutual backslapping.

Chairman Pyjas was not the only one counting. Petersen was counting down to the biggest payout of his life. The sort of money never dreamed of during his career in politics. More than enough to fund a disappearance, a new identity, and in one dramatic sweep remove all the skeletons from the closet.

He took out the tiny digital recorder, hit *rewind* then *play* and put the machine to his ear: *Whatever it takes. I don't want to know. Just get us to the release.*

Priceless. The final pieces were coming together.

* * * *

KAUFMAN STROLLED in his socks down the aisle of economy class, through the gap between the lavatories and galley, and back up the other aisle, easing into seat 53G.

Most of the passengers in the darkened compartment were watching movies or bagging Zs. Those who weren't had no interest in an old Jewish man stretching his legs. In the fully reclined seat two rows ahead, Duggan appeared to be dozing, his eyes covered by a black mask. Beside his feet was a beer can.

Removing a blanket from its plastic seal, Kaufman slipped on a glove, rose and shuffled forward, pretending to drop the blanket as he reached row 51. He bent to retrieve it, deftly collecting the can at the same time. He caught a glimpse of what had to be a laptop bag at Liddell's feet. Out of reach.

Patience, Bradley. Patience.

Returning to business class, Kaufman put the can and cigar box into the travel bag and headed for the bathroom. Ten minutes later he peeled a layer of dried wood glue from a piece of foil, slid it inside a small plastic bag and put it back in the box inside the toilet bag. He rubbed his bald head before replacing the wig, beard and yarmulke and returning to his seat.

6. Never drank coffee

THE ARRIVAL video was playing on screens throughout the plane, but Jay didn't need to see the touristy shots of mountains and fiords and mud pools, or the warnings about threats to New Zealand's fragile biodiversity.

He was more interested in the movements of the hinged flaps at the trailing edge of the wing as the pilots adjusted the camber of the airfoil. He'd always been fascinated by how things worked. As a kid he'd driven his father nuts pulling apart and reassembling the family's four-stroke lawnmower. He was smarter than most of the kids in his school, but hated being confined in a classroom. When most of his mates went to university, Jay took a job as a diesel mechanic's apprentice. A degree was no use for the role he intended to play in life.

That role was determined at precisely 11.45 on the night of 10 July 1985. The moment a limpet mine ripped through the hull of the Greenpeace ship *Rainbow Warrior* in Auckland Harbor.

Jay could never forget the numbing silence when news came over the radio the next morning. His parents had been foot soldiers in the peace and environment movements since Adam was a cowboy. Protesting against the Vietnam War, French nuclear testing in the Pacific, American military bases, the rape of native forests. You name it. One wall of the kitchen was plastered floor to ceiling with a black and white of demonstrators marching against French testing in the

1970s. Mum and dad, front and center in matching headbands, were chanting under a banner saying *We don't pee in your Atlantic, so don't shit up our Pacific.*

In the days after the bombing of the Greenpeace ship, as details oozed out about the plot by the Direction Générale de la Sécurité Extérieure – France's foreign intelligence agency – disbelief turned to rage. It was the ultimate betrayal for a boy brought up on the heroic stories of his grandfather and great-grandfather, both killed fighting to defend France in the first and second world wars. As they say, the die was cast.

Jay lived two lives through his late teens. Working by day on bulldozers and trucks and tractors, fuel tankers, forklifts. Then spending every night reading. Planning his revenge. Against France. Against America, Britain. Any of the so-called powers forcing their high and mighty ideas on the little guys. Weekends were packed with climbing in the Southern Alps, taking on the wild rivers, hiking in the remote back blocks of New Zealand. The country he was roaring towards at 550 miles per hour. It couldn't come soon enough.

Noticing a change in engine power and pitch angle as the jet began its descent, Jay returned to his seat. The hostess who had been friendly to him during the flight avoided eye contact, making him check his fly wasn't undone. Imagining things.

Matthew had the laptop open on the tray table. Cat was congratulating him for lasting so long without a cyber fix.

'Blimey. Here's a blast from the past. Messages from an old friend who works for Vestco.'

Cat eyed him suspiciously. 'You never told me you had a friend working for the devil.'

'We were at university together in Manchester. Haven't seen him since.'

'What does *he* want?'

Matt stroked a key.

'ETV and ice.'

'What does this guy do, run their social club?'

Matthew ignored her. He read a second email out loud.

'Sorry about that gibberish. Spilt my coffee on the keyboard. What I meant to say was - can you come over? Got something interesting to show you. Regards, Henry B.'

The seatbelt signs flashed.

'Kia ora again ladies and gentlemen. First officer Romanos here. We're beginning our descent into Auckland. Please return to your seats, fasten your seat belts, put your tray tables up and ensure your seat backs are in the upright position. Please turn off all electronic devices until we've stopped outside the terminal building.'

'That's you Matthew,' said Cat, rechecking her seat belt.

He didn't move. Just gawked at the screen.

'Matthew, come on. You'll jam up the electrics. What's the matter with you?'

'He never drank coffee.'

'Who?'

'Henry Beck.'

'Well, he does now. Turn the thing off.'

'No he doesn't. It could kill him.'

7. From the embassy

LUMPY HILLS freckled with vineyards and etched with snaking rivers came into view as the jet sloped to line up for the final approach.

In the distance the syringe-shaped Skytower stood like a phallic guard over downtown Auckland.

The blue-green water of the Waitemata Harbor speckled with an armada of sails.

Cat rechecked her arrival card as the aircraft taxied towards the terminal. She didn't like the sound of up to five years imprisonment for a false declaration.

'You sure I don't need to declare the hiking boots?'

'Not new ones you've never worn. Only thing could cause you grief is all that New Zealand money wrapped round your waist. I was only joking when I said there's no ATMs.'

'But it says here you've only got to declare ten thousand or more.'

'Relax Cat. New Zealand loves tourists. Especially big spending Americans. They'll welcome you with open arms.'

* * * *

MATTHEW YAWNED and folded his arms as the baggage carousel began its sixth rotation with no sign of their suitcases.

'Mr Matthew Liddell?'

Four coppers turned up from nowhere.

'Yes.'

'Dr Tayler, Jay Duggan?'

'Is something wrong?' asked Cat.

'Come with us please.'

'What about our luggage?'

'Already taken care of.'

Drugs, thought Matthew. Just my bleedin luck to get done for a random search. He could feel the eyes of every punter on his back as they were led towards a door marked *No Entry* at the end of the customs hall.

'Thought you said New Zealand coppers didn't carry guns?'

Jay didn't answer. No one spoke as they were led along a corridor towards an elevator. The sound of the coppers' boots reminded Matthew of Darth Maul in that docking bay. He was wondering what a rubber glove would feel like up the arse, when the elevator reached the third floor.

The interview room had no windows and bare walls of cloud gray except for the white frame round a second door at the rear. Must be where they'll do the strip search. Three chairs were set up on one side of a table.

A Maori woman came in. She had balloon lips, trendy glasses perched on a squashed nose and some politically correct carving hanging round her neck. Looked like a fishhook.

'My name is Detective Inspector Hansen. Take a seat please.'

Her voice, like her haircut, could have been a man's. Three of the coppers left. The largest, a beefcake with biceps bigger than Matthew's thighs, remained beside the door. Fishhook sat opposite and opened a file.

'You know a Henry Beck?'

'Absolutely.'

What a coincidence, thought Matthew. The detective stared at him, assessing his reaction.

'When did you last see Mr Beck?'

'Haven't seen Henry since he went to work for the devil.'

'What's this all about?' butted in Cat, tapping her chin with four fingers.

'Mr Beck's been murdered.'

'Leave it out.'

'Oh my heck Matthew. Isn't that the guy who sent those emails.'

'Indeed it is Dr Tayler. Or was.'

Fishhook looked down at her file.

'The first was sent at 5.56am LA time. The second at 5.58. Mr Liddell's reply was sent at 6.40. Three hours before you boarded your plane.'

Matthew looked round the ceiling for the hidden camera. 'If this is Henry's idea of a wind up, I *will* kill him next time I see him.'

'Mr Beck sent you an email saying he had something to show you Mr Liddell. You replied that you'd be right over. The layout of Mr Beck's office was found on your computer.'

'That so?'

Part of the fishhook was made of bone, the rest of polished wood. Bound together with tight coils of string made to look antique.

'Mr Beck was shot in his office Mr Liddell. A male fitting your description was seen running from the building, dropping something in a rubbish tin. A gun. How do you explain that?'

'Jack it in lady. Someone's taking the Mickey.'

'Really? You won't mind if we take your fingerprints, then?'

'...some kind of mistake,' said Cat. 'I mean, we only got the emails a few minutes ago and he couldn't reply because of the electrics... Actually, fingerprints are a good idea Matthew. Show them this is all a mistake, and we can go and get our luggage.'

She was right. And fingerprints sounded better than a glove up the rear passage.

'Fire away copper.'

Fishhook stood, the legs of her chair rasping against the vinyl floor. 'Follow me please. All three of you.'

'What in heck do you want my fingerprints for?'

'This is a murder investigation Doctor. Mr Liddell is obviously a suspect. You both left the United States with him just hours after the murder. That makes you prime candidates for accessory to murder.'

Matthew reached for his laptop.

'You won't be needing that. And if you've got any other mobile devices, cell phones, tablets, leave them on the table. They'll be safe here.'

* * * *

KAUFMAN CHOSE the green *Nothing to Declare* lane and strolled through into the arrivals hall.

Expectant faces lined four deep on either side stared at him, but only for the split second it took each to realize he wasn't Cousin Sarah, brother Bill or Nora, Jim and the kids returning from Disneyland.

He walked past a florist and Vodafone booth, shifted a yellow *Cleaning in Progress* sign from the entry of the women's to the men's bathroom, then stepped into the vacant disabled cubicle and latched the door. The room was large enough for wheelchair basketball, with the sanitizing odor of airport bathrooms the world over. Close your eyes and you could be relieving yourself at LAX, Heathrow, Saint Exupéry.

A two-tone whistle came from the next cubicle. Kaufman replied and a Regency Duty-Free bag was slid under the dividing wall. The can next door flushed, and the courier left. The bag contained a Colt 45 with silencer, airport security tag, light pale blond wig and moustache. Kaufman slipped his gloves on and placed the sterilized weapon into the custom-made holster in the pocket of his trousers. He punched a key on his cell phone and studied the layout of the terminal. Satisfied, he removed his jacket, which he folded and placed into the briefcase along with the Jewish cap and beard. He hung the security tag round his neck, stepped out of the cubicle and attached the blond wig and moustache in front of the mirror.

He took the escalator to the departures hall, hurried through a food court and up another escalator to the Spinnaker Bar on the third floor. A circle of businessmen sharing a joke over a few beers ignored him as he moved towards an unmarked door, fingering the small pick and wrench in his pocket as he sized up the lock. Two children stood at the railing pointing at a replica biplane suspended between the second and third floors. Ten seconds later Kaufman had picked the wafer lock and was padding along a service hall.

* * * *

'RECOGNIZE THIS?

Detective Fishhook placed a photograph on the table in front of Matthew. The fingerprinting charade was over, and they were back in the interview room. Matthew picked up the photograph, a close-up of a Millbrook Foundation pen against blue carpet.

'Looks to me like a ballpoint pen. The little rotating ball at the end acts as a buffer between the ink and the -'

'I'm familiar with the technology Mr Liddell.'

'Call me Matthew. All my mates do. Including Henry Beck.'

'That pen, that *Millbrook* pen Mr Liddell, was found on the floor of your *mate*'s office. Any thoughts how it might have got there?'

The woman had a future on the stage. This was such a load of codswallop, Matthew was starting to enjoy himself.

'It's pretty obvious isn't it? I jumped out of the plane and my parachute got stuck on that pointy bit at the top of the Vestco Tower. So I Tom Cruised down the side of the building to the hundred and sixtieth or whatever floor Henry's on. Smashed through the window, topped him, then wrote a note explaining why I did it. Obviously I dropped the pen before legging it. Sloppy I know, but there you go. Found the note yet?'

Fishhook looked back blankly. Sense of humor was clearly not a requirement for promotion in the New Zealand Police. There was a rap on the door and an officer poked his head through.

'Results of the prints back Inspector.'

Bout bleedin time, thought Matthew.

'If you'll excuse me a minute.' She stood and whispered something to PC Beefcake on her way out. The constable unfolded his gorilla arms and flexed his hands, like a cowboy before a duel.

LESS THAN six feet away, Kaufman eased the spring-loaded tension wrench to bypass the false breaking points of the lock on the rear door.

Using a delicate seesaw action with his pick, he raked the pins until he felt them align. He slipped the small wrench and pick into his pocket, turned the handle and strode confidently into the room.

Within two footsteps he assessed the threat level, identifying the guard by the far door as priority one. The three greenies were doing goldfish impressions.

'I'm terribly sorry,' Kaufman said in a clipped English accent, advancing towards the guard.

'From the embassy. I was looking for the interview room.'

The guard hesitated, unsure whether to reach for the door or his gun.

He made the right choice, but a moment too late.

Kaufman casually flicked his right hand in the air then exploded forward, forcing the guard's gun hand down. He swung his left elbow into the man's chin, snapping his head back. The guard lashed out with his boot as he fell. Kaufman was winded but recovered quickly, pivoting to his right and pouncing on the guard as he tried to stand. The last sound Constable Mark Shaw heard was a snap as his cervical column gave way to the twisting force of the gloved diplomat.

8. Tsunami of panic

JAY'S FIRST instinct was to go to the aid of the cop. The subtle flick of the diplomat's hand before he lunged made him hesitate. Jay had seen that distraction technique before.

It was in the mountains between Afghanistan and Pakistan. Satellite images had been published suggesting staggering destruction of the famous forests around Kunar.

Every man and his dog knew it was being illegally logged. There was a lot of finger-pointing, plenty of jabbering. But Afghanistan was, you know, Afghanistan. The too-hard basket.

Jay volunteered to go in and get evidence of the destruction. Over six weeks he photographed the forest rapists. Meetings between Afghan warlords and Arab traders and Pakistani middlemen. Convoys of smoking trucks weighed down with timber anting along dirt roads towards the border.

On his way out through the Spin Ghar range of Nangarhar in the south, he came across a training camp.

Soldiers from an American Special Forces unit were being drilled by an Israeli instructor in what he later learnt was an advanced disarming technique called Krav Maga. The flick of the hand was intended to redirect a gunman's line of fire. It was used by elite professional soldiers, not diplomats.

And who wore gloves in the middle of summer?

As the cop and *diplomat* were grappling, Jay responded to a more basic instinct.

'Run.'

Matthew was out the back door in a flash. Cat was riveted to the chair, eyes bulging, fingers hammering away at her chin. Your classic rabbit in the headlights.

Jay gripped her arm and hauled her through the door. They sprinted down a service hall, the echoes of their feet clacking off the concrete walls. Shocked faces rotated like a row of clown heads at an A & P show as they rushed past a bar and onto an escalator.

Jay's mind was scrambling. The crazy allegations against Matthew. The weird email. The attack by the bloke claiming to be from an embassy. There was some serious shit going down here. He glanced back. No sign of pursuit. Yet. A blue-coated airport guide gave them the once over. Curious rather than suspicious.

'Look natural.'

'What in heck are we doing?' Cat spoke so fast the words banged into each other. 'We have to go to the police.'

'That *was* the police.'

Jay tightened his grip on her hand and shepherded her through a food court. Matthew was one step behind. Cat's movements were clogging as shock set in. Down another escalator and they were on the sidewalk. People grappling with luggage trolleys, duty free bags, talking on cell phones. A white Auckland Co-op taxi pulled into the curb and a passenger got out.

'We'll take that one thanks,' said Jay, pushing Cat into the back seat.

* * * *

KAUFMAN EASED the limp body of the police guard silently to the floor. The trio had cut and run, leaving the laptop and a small backpack on the table, along with their mobile phones.

There was no sign the scuffle was heard outside the interview room, but Kaufman was counting on seconds, not minutes. Killing the cop was unfortunate but necessary. It needed to be turned to advantage.

He slung the laptop bag over a shoulder and rifled through the backpack, pocketing a black address book and the phones. He took out the gun, pressed the tip of the silencer between the eyes of the dead cop and placed a single shot into his temple. Leaving through the back door, he retraced his steps to the bathroom, where he removed the wig and identity tag. He kept the moustache on, and added the half-frame spectacles.

The recently arrived traveler then waltzed through the door of the arrivals hall into the balmy early evening air. He crossed the road to a car park and selected a large Pacific Horizon RV. The lock yielded easily. He closed the curtains in the rear compartment, removed a baby changing kit from the table, opened his briefcase and transferred the print from the beer can to the grip of the Colt.

The roar of a departing Singapore Airlines jet was replaced by the wail of approaching sirens. He put the baby changing kit back on the table, opened the curtains and stepped out of the van. Two policemen appeared on the sidewalk near the main entrance, looking around uncertainly.

Kaufman walked between them and back into the terminal. You'd swear someone hit the mute button. Silent faces were drawn to a squad of police sprinting across the carpeted hall. More officers appeared at the top of an escalator and started running down. As eyes turned upwards, Kaufman eased the gun from the holster and placed it under a fern beside a tour group milling round a planter box.

An alarm started blaring. The word *bomb* was whispered in an American accent.

Kaufman was swept out the door in the tsunami of panic.

9. Where they least expect

THE CAB into the city was a fast-forward re-run of Cat's thirteenth birthday outing to the Rocky Point Haunted House in Salt Lake City.

Her heart was surely going to explode. Sweat needled her eyes. Closing them made it worse. Images darted from the terror of the airport and face of the psycho diplomat to her father grimacing at his mangled hand to we've gotta go to the police, the American embassy. She reached for her mobile, but realized she'd left it in the police interview room.

Baying sirens and red sparkles of light rippled on the edges of her vision from the opposite side of the freeway. Only when the cab slipped into the shadows of central city high-rises could Cat begin to focus, scour for anchors.

Old cars driving on the wrong side of the road. Signs, graffiti. All alien. Twilight was approaching but the sky was still way too blue to be natural. The innocent eyes of a young Muslim girl in a black headscarf – must be the driver's daughter – probed at her from a dashboard photograph. Seeing a burglar in someone else's home. A fugitive. The *F* word again.

The cab stopped at traffic lights near a stone building in two shades of brown with a clock tower. Jetties pointed fingers into the harbor. Two young Maori men in hoodies leaned against a wall. Cat stared into the heavily tattooed face of one. He poked out his tongue and laughed like a maniac. She reached over to check the door lock was down. Her hand was trembling.

Chatter on the cab radio. The accents and rapid speech were hard to follow. Something about disruption at the airport. Traffic jams. Roadblocks. Taxi rank moved. The cabbie switched to a commercial channel.

'... *apparently shot while interviewing three people detained on a flight from Los Angeles. Parts of the airport terminal have been cordoned off, causing massive disruptions to flights. Roadblocks set up on the main roads north and east of the airport have brought traffic to a standstill. Police warn that the three suspects – two men and a woman – are likely to be armed and extremely dangerous.*'

Cat locked eyes with the driver through his rear-view mirror. Eyebrows popped in recognition.

Jay reached over and ripped out the cord to the radio. The driver covered his head as if he was about to be hit. Cat screamed. Next thing she knew Jay was on the sidewalk yelling at her. She froze.

'Get the fuck out of the car.'

She fumbled with the lock, and Jay yanked open the door and dragged her out.

The tattooed face cheered.

* * * *

JAY LED them to the quietest corner of the Whitcoulls bookstore. The cooking section, under the *Ideas for Him* sign.

'Doesn't take a rocket scientist to work out something serious is going on here guys. We need to find out what.'

'Dammit Jay. We need to go to the police.'

'Not till we know it's safe.'

Cat turned to Matthew, but he stuck up his palms.

'I'm not goin back to that bleedin cop shop. Like I said, Henry Beck didn't drink coffee. I'm with superman here.'

Jay ignored the label. There was no time. 'Three of us together are sittin ducks. You two split up. Meet me over there.' He pointed to a public square across the road. 'Five minutes. And do something to change the way you look. Ditching those jackets'd be a good start.'

'This set me back twelve hundred bucks. It's an Andrew Marc.'

'You see any Andrew Marc shops round here mate? It's got Matthew bloody Liddell written all over it. Lose it.'

'Where are you going?' Cat's voice was a wafer, her fingers drilling her chin.

'Buying some time.'

He headed off through the store, which opened into the Britomart transport center. An electronic notice board showed trains leaving to the south and west in the next few minutes. He used his credit card to buy two tickets to Pukekohe and one to Henderson.

The saleswoman was a natural redhead with a leopard skin scarf and fingers stained by upwards of two packets a day.

'What you gonna do... clone yourself?'

'How'd you guess?'

'Whatever spins your wheels love.'

An escalator descended through a cage-like glass and wire structure to a landing. It was patrolled by a security guard built like a rugby prop forward, eyes sweeping diligently from side to side. A radio aerial stuck out of his pocket and keys hung from the belt. Jay walked straight for him, pointing to the lower floor.

'Is that the way to the trains?'

'Yes sir.'

The cavernous train hall was illuminated by a ginormous circular window in the ceiling. Water rippled in a pond above the glass dish and flowed down walls of stone on each side of the hall. Lights played on gardens of tree ferns, rocks and shimmering steel. Commuters were boarding trains at both platforms. Jay stepped onto a carriage, sat near the door and took off his jacket. Two teenagers shuffled up the aisle, shoulders back and using as little upper body movement as possible. Like it was uncool to walk. Eyeballs swiveled, checking out who was noticing them.

'Sup?' The wooden faces cracked into grins as the youngsters recognized a voice behind Jay. He used the distraction of the high fives and *sup sup sups* to slip out the door, leaving the jacket on the seat.

Back in the hall he turned into a corridor flanked by billboards. One advertised a Super rugby game between the Blues and Hurricanes at Eden Park.

Jay looked at his watch. The game would be starting soon. He hurried up three flights of stairs, piss-scented, and came out near the meeting place.

A Polynesian woman in a fluorescent vest was hustling a blue and yellow trolley heaped with brooms, brushes and buckets.

Sirens cried above the everyday din of downtown Auckland.

Matthew and Cat were huddled on a bench, hiding behind a map. The fancy jacket was gone, and Cat's was turned inside out. Her hair was tied back.

Nowhere near good enough. Jay sat at the bench facing the other direction.

'Here's the go. I want you to split up and each head up different sides of this road. Queen Street. Find shops selling something you can quickly use to disguise your faces. Caps. Sunglasses. Whatever. Both got New Zealand cash, right?'

'Yes.'

'OK. Try not to talk any more than you have to. Your accents'll probably set off the bloody fire alarms. And don't muck about. Most of these shops'll be closing soon. About three-quarters of a mile up there, Queen Street runs into Karangahape Road. K Road locals call it. See you both there in fifteen.'

* * * *

TWO BLOCKS away in the back seat of a corporate cab, Kaufman leafed through Duggan's address book.

It contained the names of dozens of people scattered throughout the globe, some already known to the security head of Vestco.

Others would be of great interest to Xecintel. Kaufman jotted down the names and addresses of the six people listed from New Zealand.

* * * *

CAT SINGLED out Jay by the way he was standing rather than his outfit. Must have broken into a construction site. He had on a yellow hard hat, earmuffs on top, orange vest over his T-shirt, frayed denim shorts, waist belt stuffed with tools. Steel capped boots.

She was pleased with herself. Using cash to keep small talk to a few grunts and nods, she'd bought a light pale blue tracksuit top with hood and matching track trousers. And committed the first criminal act of her life – slipping a box of auburn hair dye into her pocket.

Matthew was late. Across the road, a Westpac Bank security guard was giving directions to a couple on the sidewalk. On the opposite corner three people were waiting at a bus stop. An elderly couple and a businessman in a loud tie holding a bunch of flowers. Cat wondered if it was a wedding anniversary or an out-of-the-blue surprise.

She watched as Jay cut across the street to the bank, then up K Road. Moments later the businessman with the flowers headed off in the same direction. Cat sniggered. It was Matthew. She'd been so distracted by the flowers and ridiculous tie she hadn't noticed the beard. She waited until he was about fifty yards up the road, then followed him round a bend past the beginnings of a cemetery. Headstones discolored by decades of rain and wind and traffic fumes jutted out at odd angles. Across a busy street and down a flight of stone steps, she caught up with her fellow fugitives on opposite sides of an iron fence around the grave of William Hobson, first Governor of New Zealand.

'What about the British embassy?' Matthew was saying. 'I could get some sort of immunity till this is all sorted out.'

'Nearest embassy's hundreds of miles away in Wellington mate. Even if there was one here, not sure she'd be a good idea?'

'For heck's sake Jay. This isn't some *American Boy* adventure where everyone lives happily ever after. That guy from the embassy was real. That poor cop was killed.'

'Calm down Cat. If that bloke was from an embassy I'll eat my hat. And no way did he just show up to kill a cop. He was looking for something else.'

'What are you talking about?'

'The laptop, my mobile,' said Matthew. 'This is about that message from Henry.'

Cat was incredulous.

'He's got them now. So, what in heck are we doing here?'

'If he's got the laptop, he knows we looked at the message.'

'So?'

'Think about it. Whatever that message meant was worth killing a cop for.'

'And Henry,' Matthew added. 'Poor blighter must have been onto something.'

'But we don't know what the message means. Do we?'

She frowned at Matthew.

'Got my suspicions. Need to go online to find out.'

'Problem is,' said Jay, 'they *think* we know.'

'Who in heck are *they*?'

'My money says this is tied up with the release of Alo.'

'And,' said Matthew, 'if they're prepared to bump off a cop and someone as harmless as Henry Beck, they're not going to lose any sleep over three greenies.'

Cat clutched the iron railing to steady herself.

'You heard the radio. Not only is Matt being framed for murder in LA. The police here reckon he – we – killed the cop. Which says to me they don't know squat about our friendly visitor from the embassy.'

'And they said he was shot. What was that about?'

Another wave of sirens whined past on the road above, heading downtown. The sun was flagging, casting sinister shadows off the headstones. Street kids were ganging in the cemetery lower down towards what sounded like a freeway. In the distance Cat thought she heard a helicopter. She sidled closer to Jay.

'Look guys, don't ask me what the hell's going on. What I do know is we've got to get off the streets.'

'Where in heck can we go?'

'Where they least expect.'

'That would be a cop shop,' said Matthew. 'How bout we all just get bladdered and arrested for drunk and disorderly.'

'Not as silly as it sounds, mate. Problem is they don't have computers in police cells.'

'So where? This place gives me the creeps.' Cat expected the blond diplomat to leap out from behind a headstone.

'They'll expect us to try to get out of Auckland,' said Jay. 'Can't think of a better place to hole up for the night than in the middle of a city of a million people.'

* * * *

THE TUCKERED face squinting at Matthew from the mirror was some loser doing time at one of Her Majesty's prisons.

Sort of place where the cons, gangs of them and every one gone queer, do unmentionable things to weeds like him and the wardens don't give a toss. Loud voices outside made him jump. Get a grip. Just some people yahooing their way home from the rugby game.

Jay chose a house in this area because it was close to the stadium. Instructions on a cork notice board for feeding a cat suggested the owners of the villa in Mt Eden – Trevor and Alison Gatland – were away two more nights.

Both were into real estate, according to business cards on a desk. Number one son was into music. Number two played hockey. Goalkeeper by the look of pads in the wardrobe.

Matthew ran his fingers through his hair and walked through to the kitchen. Jay was adjusting the curtains to make sure no light could be seen from outside. Cat looked up from a tin of apricots.

'What do you make of that strange gibberish in the email, Matthew?'

'Henry didn't do gibberish. And he never drank coffee. Had a rare genetic sensitivity to caffeine. He knew coffee could trigger heart palpitations. Same with chocolate.'

'I could probably survive without chocolate,' said Cat. 'Couldn't imagine life without coffee. So, what about the email?'

Matthew sat at the breakfast bar.

'We came up with a few schemes in our early days at university. One of Henry's was to set up a business leasing out virtual safe deposit boxes. Idea was to create places on the net where people could store stuff. Private files. Passwords. Porn. Clips of bonking sessions with the secretary, stuff like that.'

Cat raised her eyebrows, but didn't interrupt.

'Only way you could access this virtual box was through a multi-leveled series of coded strings. To reach each level – there were always three – you had to answer two questions. One was based on general knowledge. Usually something to do with a person's job or whatever they were into. The other was based on the personal knowledge of the person leasing the box. That made it difficult for anyone else, including robots, to crack. We used to spend hours coming up with sequences then seeing how long it took the other person to open the box.'

'And you think this stuff about TV and ice was the code to one of these boxes?'

'Pretty sure it's the password clue to a first level.'

'Well, there's a computer,' said Cat, impatiently. 'What are you waiting for?'

'If only it were that simple. When Henry designed the software, he programmed it to permit only single entry at each level. Get it wrong and it sends you off on some wild goose chase, and locks you out from further attempts. Partly it was for security. Henry also wanted clients to come back to him to pay for another box.'

Jay interrupted. 'So, if that English bloke at the airport, who's probably got your laptop, entered the password into this system, no-one else can follow him in?'

'Only if he could solve the riddle. Which is our problem as well. When Henry and I were setting these up, the password doubled as a clue to the entry location. We'd usually attach the entry point to a password-protected portal on someone else's website. Like a parasite. If someone entered the correct password for their site, they'd get entry and go about their business unaware the portal was infected. If they mis-typed their password once, they'd be diverted to some random site, and not be able to enter again from that computer.'

'That could have caused chaos,' said Cat.

'Suppose so. We never stayed round long enough to find out.'

Matthew grabbed a piece of paper, wrote the message out, and put it on the table in front of them.

500mlETV 1gICE (16)

'The number in brackets means we're looking for sixteen characters. You guys see if you can make any sense of that while I have a chinwag with Mr Google.'

It was a desk-hogging eMac from the days before flat screens and pedestals. The operating system was years out of date. But the keyboard was a keyboard was a keyboard and the connection speed reasonable. The tension in Matthew's shoulders eased the moment he started tapping.

A search on *ETV* gave over nine million results. No surprises there. A search within the results, using the word *ice* narrowed it to 150,000 – from a problem-solving education program called *Disney on Ice* to an interview on the Entertainment Channel with a rapper called *Ice Cube*.

Jay threw in the towel first. 'She's out of my league. Reckon I'll spend the night dreaming about half liters of telly and a gram of ice.'

'That's it.' Matthew sat back beaming. 'It's got nothing to do with ETV or ice or measurements. It's an anagram.'

Google took 0.14 seconds to find 350,000 anagram programs. The first half dozen drew blanks, but a site called A2Z came up with 95 words. The longest were elegit, emetic and gimlet. They spent an hour trying to find an anagram that made sense, but got no further. Jay disappeared into one of the bedrooms. Cat made coffee and they continued. Tired, but like dogs with a bone.

'It's those bleedin numbers screwing it up.'

'Wait a mo. Look at the numbers Matthew. Five zero zero and one. What say the five is meant to be an S? The two zeros could be Os. The one either L or I.'

Substituting the one for I gave 630 words. Using the letter L gave even more, including teleologic which got Cat excited. But it didn't use all the letters. And it just wasn't Henry. *Vest* stuck out like a sore thumb, which led logically to Vestco, but there were scores of potential entry points on the Vestco website.

Cat quit next, curling up to sleep on the couch. Matthew was fading.

His shoulders were giving him grief, but he was not ready to give up. Time to reboot the brain. Come at it from another angle.

A search on death penalty came up with a description of an execution by electric chair by a US Supreme Court Justice.

'...*the prisoner's eyeballs sometimes pop out and rest on his cheeks... the body turns bright red, the flesh swells and his skin stretches to the point of breaking. Sometimes the prisoner catches fire... witnesses hear a loud and sustained sound like bacon frying, and the sickly-sweet smell of burning flesh...*'

Talk about a bleedin nightmare. This can't be happening. A microwaved packet of two-minute noodles and a can of coke fueled Matthew for another hour until jetlag finished him off.

'Looks like you won this round Henry me old china. And a gram of ice,' he muttered as he shut down the computer.

And. Could the space between the phrases mean *and*?

He switched the computer back on and added the letters A N D to the search. More than four thousand words scrolled across the screen, right up to gonadectomies. Sounded uncomfortably like castration. Also sounded more like Henry. But it still didn't use all the letters.

Matthew assumed Vestco was part of the mix, but not showing up because it was a proper noun. He deleted the letters v e s t c o and searched again. Still no word that used all the letters. Maybe it was a string of individual words. He scrolled through several times until he settled on log and in. He removed those from the search and came up with three words. One was obvious. Media.

VESTCO MEDIA LOG IN.

10. A mountain called Eden

PETERSEN FOLDED his arms and looked over the backs of heads in the public gallery of the federal courthouse in Los Angeles.

It was hard to believe the man cuffed in the dock was ever a newspaper delivery boy, let alone part of an award-winning team of journalists feted for its penetrating coverage of the most destructive day of the riots back in the 1990s.

The face, once respected and feared by politicians and city officials, was now gaunt and barren. Shoulders that confidently carried the burden of truth and revelation were hunched in capitulation. Eyes that witnessed the mayhem of violence, the looting and fires and the horror of innocent white motorists dragged from cars and beaten senseless, were now riveted to the floor as the Judge continued his monologue.

'And what, one might ask, are the inferences to be drawn from your continued insistence on silence? That this source does not exist. That he or she was a figment of your imagination. Created with cynical calculation to reignite a career that has gone steadily downhill since the lofty heights of a Pulitzer Prize.'

The Judge peered down on the defendant with undisguised contempt.

'Not only have your inventions besmirched the name of one of our country's most respected corporations. They had the potential to cause, at this time of global food insecurity, unfounded panic amongst countless millions of people. People whose only hope for nourishment may reside in this revolutionary development. What's more, you have falsely brought into question the name, the reputation, indeed the legacy, of a man destined to go down in history alongside the Norman Borlaugs of this world.'

Nice touch. It was the Judge's idea to compare Tolminsky with the Nobel laureate known as the father of the first Green Revolution.

Petersen looked across at the bank of television cameras in the media area doubled in size for the special sitting. Cameras from *Huffington Post* and *Grassroots Intelligence* rolled comfortably beside those of the big networks. How times had changed.

Judge and defendant were little more than extras in this theater.

The Judge cleared his throat.

'You are hereby ordered and adjudged in civil contempt of the Order of this Court and sentenced to five years in prison.'

The courtroom was suitably stunned by the severity of the sentence. All except the Judge and Petersen, who discussed the outcome during a supposedly chance meeting between fairways at the Hillcrest Country Club the day before.

An outcome, Petersen was sure, that would send a message to any other journalists even thinking about probing more deeply into the unfortunate demise of the great Roman Tolminsky. Or the questionable way in which he was courted by Vestco chairman Jozef Pyjas.

As the defendant was led from the court, he looked up at the gallery. For an instant his and Petersen's eyes met. There was a glimmer of recognition. Like someone you feel you should know but can't place. That was the secret to Petersen's true power – and survival. Ultimate power in public life was determined well beyond the public gaze. Once you became public property, your scope for maneuvering was severely curtailed.

This particular journalist came too close to knowing about Petersen and the role he played. For that he had to go down. The Vestco vice president allowed himself a sly smile. The now disgraced and former journalist was nobody. Latest in a growing list of people whose lives had been sacrificed during Petersen's relentless climb to the top. Yet another person who, if they knew half the truth, would have reason to want him dead.

In eight days, they'd get their wish.

* * * *

VIEWS IN downtown Auckland don't come much better than the outlook from the Sebel, one of several hotels built during redevelopment of the Viaduct Basin inspired by New Zealand's brief hold on yachting's oldest and most famous trophy, the America's Cup.

Guests dining on the balconies of the Sebel's marina rooms have front row seats to soak up the ebb and flow of charter vessels and sleek match racers or observe tourists strolling along the bricked promenade above the turquoise waters of the Hauraki Gulf.

None of which interested Kaufman as he drained his orange juice and picked up the morning's edition of the *Sunday Star-Times*.

Up since five, he'd powered through his hour-long routine of exercises, and forwarded all the contact information and data from the greenies' phones to Xecintel, before calling Eve for an update. She had stiff joints, and was lying down because sitting up gave her a headache and made her dizzy. Probably a sign the tumor was progressing. Not that she was complaining. Hardly ever did.

After the call, Kaufman studied a map of Auckland while demolishing a room service breakfast of bacon, eggs, sausages, grilled tomato, roasted peach chutney and Turkish pide, whatever the hell that was. Tasted alright, even if the name sounded like some Arab pissed on it.

OFFICER DOWN was the lame banner across the front page of the newspaper, above a large photo of the slain constable's grieving widow consoling two kids. Pages one through four were full of the 'execution-style slaying' and hunt for three suspects, one of whom was also wanted for the murder of a Vestco information technology manager in Los Angeles.

A Roll of Honor on page three listed the thirty New Zealand cops killed in the line of duty since 1890. *Thirty*. Big deal.

Radio news at six ran a story on the contempt verdict in LA. Nothing new on the fugitives, which suggested they were still on the run. From the laptop, Kaufman knew the email with the bizarre string had been opened. Computer and decoding experts at Xecintel offices in St Louis and Lyon spent the last few hours trying to make sense of the message. Unsuccessfully. Taking chances was not an option. Liddell and his two friends would have to be silenced.

Kaufman realized he needed help. He turned his attention to an Xecintel report on the New Zealand police and military. The police were under-resourced, unarmed and apparently determined to keep it that way. Armed Offenders' Squads used part-time volunteers on call. Their basic tactic of cordoning, containing and appealing to armed offenders worked in the vast majority of cases, which they claimed were resolved without the use of force. Try that in the gang jungles of Compton or North Long Beach.

The section on the military was even more depressing. New Zealand's pacifist anti-nuclear stance resulted in a steady decline in defense funding and morale since the mid 1980s. When a Minister of Defense in a previous administration was asked in Parliament what New Zealand peacekeeping troops should do if they were shot at, he had advised them to run. Jesus F Christ.

A handful of soldiers from New Zealand's modest SAS unit served in Afghanistan, but were so green they allowed their faces to be photographed by the media in Kabul. The country belatedly joined the international coalition fighting Islamic State, sending soldiers to train Iraqi security forces north of Baghdad. Most of the military, though, had no experience in counter-terrorism – international or domestic.

Things were, however, looking up.

The current administration in Wellington craved closer ties with Uncle Sam. The prime minister had privately assured the Secretary of State New Zealand's chicken-hearted nuclear-free legislation would be ditched in return for greater trade access to the US and covert help with a campaign to realign public opinion.

Kaufman's cell phone pulsed.

It was his deputy at Vestco.

'Yup?'

'Evening Brad, or should I say good morning?'

'There's zip all good about it. Hope this call's about to change that.'

'It just might. Someone in Auckland has logged on to the media section of our website using the code sent by Henry Beck to Liddell.'

'Got a trace?'

'You bet. They entered from a mountain called Eden.'

'When?' Kaufman was reaching for a map.

'Four hours ago.'

'What?'

'When we entered the code it took us to a site advertising incontinence diapers. We assumed someone was pulling our leg. Then with the time zones, jet lag and all that, didn't think you'd want to be dis-'

'You think I've flown all the way to this sleepy little shithole for a vacation? I want to know the instant you get another trace.'

'Roger that.'

'Jesus F Christ. This Mount Eden. Tell me you can be more specific.'

Kaufman scrawled the address on the map and located Esplanade Road. Using his thumb and forefinger, he figured the place was less than two miles away.

* * * *

AS THE orange passed in front of Jay's chin, he sent the apple in the opposite direction, pausing until it reached its high point before tossing the pear. Too easy. He wondered whether to add a passion fruit.

Matthew had filled them in on his discovery of the net portal, which led to the first level clue.

Rabbert ON 1gIGF2R OFF (12)

Cat, her hair still wet with dye, recognized part of the sequence of letters immediately.

'IGF2R is insulin-like growth factor 2 receptor.'

'Which is what exactly?'

'Causes problems in lambs. Calves too, when the receptor's de-activated. Embryos grow too big. Hearts become enlarged. Damages kidneys.'

'Could that be what the OFF means at the end of the clue? De-activated.'

'Makes sense.'

'This problem, this bloating thing, does it have a simpler name?'

'Large Offspring Syndrome'.

'And we know what and-a-gram means.'

'Which gives us L O S,' Cat said, beaming. 'This is going to be a walk in the park.'

Matthew was shaking his head.

'Don't get too excited. There's always two parts to each clue. The second will relate to something in Henry's personal life.'

'Or your personal life Matt. He sent it to you.'

'It's Matthew.'

'Does Rabbert ON mean anything to you?'

'Absolutely nothing.'

'Brilliant.'

Cat started grilling him on his relationship with the murdered Vestco bloke. He admitted the thing that drew them together at university in England was hacking. Matthew got so addicted to it, and had such success with some racket involving insurance premiums, he'd quit the course three-quarters of the way through the degree and lived the high life.

'What happened to your friend?'

'Henry was too straight up. Finished the degree, top student and all that. Then he was headhunted by Vestco. Started out as a foot soldier, but quickly moved up the ladder. Kept in touch for a while. Till I came to Millbrook. All contact was broken off, for obvious reasons. Haven't seen or heard from him since. Read on Facebook he'd been made governor of Vestco's IT department. Bit of a dab hand our Henry.'

'Why, out of the blue, does he suddenly email you?'

'You tell me.'

'And why just the first password? Why not the whole file? Would have saved a lot of trouble.'

'Been wondering that myself. Might have been in a hurry. Probably had the box all set up. Would have only taken a couple of keystrokes to copy a file into it.'

'How many others know about this virtual box caper?'

'We didn't talk about it to anyone else at Manchester. Henry was paranoid some punter would nick the idea.'

'So, it's possible you're the only one who knows?'

'Highly likely.'

'There's your answer,' said Cat, pacing the room. 'It came to you because you're the only one it would make any sense to.'

'But I'm the bleedin enemy.'

'What sort of stuff did you say can be stored in these virtual boxes?'

'Any computer file. Text. Audio. Images. Digital video.'

Cat sat back at the table and turned to a clean page of the pad, pen poised.

'Right. Let's break this down. First, Matthew's friend is the head computer honcho at Vestco, so presumably has access to their most confidential data and files. Second, out of the blue he sends his old friend the entry password to a virtual safe deposit box. Perhaps he was bored and just wanted to have some fun. But then he gets murdered. Let's assume whatever he put in this box is important. Third, this all happens nine days out from Vestco's release of Alo. And who does he send the password to? Possibly the only person on the planet who knows about these virtual boxes. But also, a person he knows works for Millbrook. Whatever's in that box, he's happy for us to see it. Wants us to see it.'

'Then why bother with the virtual box? Why not just send Matthew the file?'

'Maybe he didn't want Vestco to know what he was sending. Think about it guys. He might have been covering his tracks.'

'So why the second bleedin email, inviting me over?'

'And what about that embassy thug? What do they want with us?'

'They want us out of the way.'

'No offence Jay, but this place is about as out of the way as you can get.'

'Obviously not,' he said, sending a second orange into the air. 'Either they reckon we know what's in that box, or that our resident computer geek here'll be able to work it out. And they're prepared to kill to stop that happening.'

'Will you stop juggling Jay? This is serious.'

He caught the fruit and returned them one by one to the bowl, noticing the clock on the wall.

'Let's see what's on the news.'

The promo sequence referred to a startling development in the hunt for the murderer of the Vestco computer expert. The countdown ended with the face of the anchorwoman.

The hunt for the killer of Henry Beck, the computer expert for Vestco Corporation, has taken a dramatic turn in the last hour. Video footage sent to the Grassroots Intelligence blog shows the suspect — British born computer hacker Matthew Liddell — fleeing from the Vestco building in downtown Los Angeles at the time of the murder.'

The picture was grainy but clearly showed Matt running through Pershing Square with a laptop bag over his shoulder. The lower floors of the Vestco Building were in the background.

'The footage was captured by a Taiwanese tourist filming his tour group in the square 6.10am Friday. LAPD forensic pathologists believe Beck was murdered between six and six-thirty that day.'

'I was running for my bus, for chrissake,' protested Matthew, as the anchorwoman's face returned.

'Liddell's fingerprints were found on the handgun he was seen by another witness to drop into a trash can in the square.'

Fingers held a sealed plastic evidence bag containing a gun with a silencer.

'Examination by the Los Angeles County sheriff ballistics lab confirms it as the murder weapon — a .380 caliber Lorcin semiautomatic.'

'Oh my heck Ma-' Cat cut herself off as portraits of the three of them filled the screen.

'Interpol reports the manhunt has become international. And the body count has doubled. Within hours of the slaying in Los Angeles, Liddell evaded authorities and flew to New Zealand with two other activists from the Millbrook Foundation. Jay Duggan and Dr Catherine Tayler. The three were arrested as they stepped off the plane in Auckland, but overpowered and killed a police officer and escaped.'

A body in a black bag was shown being wheeled towards an ambulance.

'The officer was shot in the head at point blank range with a pistol which was later recovered in a planter box inside the airport terminal. Auckland police describe the murder as an execution-style killing.'

The TV showed a close-up of Jay, cropped tight round his eyes and mouth.

'The fingerprints of Duggan, an international eco-terrorist known to authorities throughout North and Latin America, Europe and Africa, were found on the murder weapon.'

'Welcome to the club, me old China.'

'This is such bullshit.' Jay had been called many things in his life. Never a murderer. A steely focus coursed through his body. The hunted. The sensation was familiar, strangely comforting.

'Vestco executives are downplaying speculation the murders are a desperate last-minute attempt to sabotage the global release of Alo on 18 February.'

A grim-faced Jozef Pyjas, chairman of Vestco, was shown surrounded by microphones and cameras.

'Our thoughts and prayers are with the family of Henry Beck, who was as enthusiastic as any of us about the potential of Alo. I can assure you, this tragedy will have no impact whatsoever on the countdown to the release. Henry would have wanted it that way.'

The anchor returned.

'Well-placed sources have told Grassroots, however, that at least one highly ranked security executive from Vestco is on his way to Auckland to assist in the hunt for the fugitives.'

Across the bottom of the screen flowed the words *NZ Prime Minister telephones US President, offers full cooperation.*

In breaking news, Interpol has just released these computer-generated images of the terrorists, wearing clothes they are thought to have stolen or purchased since their escape from custody at Auckland Airport. Police officers from other New Zealand centers are being rushed to the city to join the manhunt.

Jay couldn't believe what he was seeing. They had the construction vest and hard hat. Matthew had the green tie, Cat the tracksuit. The hood was off, and her hair was auburn.

* * * *

'THEES VILL do goot, dankeshurn. Deer by za zeebra crosseng.'

Kaufman folded the map and put it into his jacket pocket. By his calculations, Dominion Road was half a mile from the target, so if the cab driver heard later three bodies were discovered at a house in Esplanade Road, the German fare with the brown hair and goatee wouldn't enter his mind.

As the cab pulled away, he removed the goatee, stuck a cap on his head and began the short walk up View Road towards Esplanade. The sun was well above the rooftops and blasting a lot more heat than LA in winter. The leafy neighborhood of tidy villas hinting at comfort rather than serious money was almost deserted except for two kids playing on skateboards. But then it was already Sunday in New Zealand. Time to do the Lord's work.

* * * *

JAY PEEKED round the side of the sheet blacking out the window. The view was dominated by the Skytower. He'd been up there once, marveling at the panorama it gave of the city and harbor.

Now he saw nothing but irony. An act of international terrorism in that same harbor set him on the route to activism, driven by a desire for revenge.

It took half a dozen meetings to work out most environmental groups did little more than talk about the need to save the planet. Before his eleventh birthday he made his first move. Tracing the source of a small oil spill in a river to a wool factory. Towels he stuffed into an outlet pipe blew the boiler and cost the company thousands.

By his late-teens his sabotage shifted to the foreign-owned logging and mining companies ravaging native forests on the West Coast. He never liked the idea of spiking trees because of the risk to innocent workers. The knowledge he gained of heavy machinery through his apprenticeship enabled him to double the damage while halving the risk of detection. Disruption he caused cost millions and forced at least three companies to pack up and leave.

Didn't worry Jay that they all claimed it was for sound commercial reasons.

Now here he was, full circle. Back in New Zealand to retire from activism and plant a forest. Take care of his own mess. Mind his own business. Being labeled a terrorist by the Vestcos of the world came with the territory. In the early days it was a badge of honor. But to be accused of murder cut deep. It also changed everything. The trick to surviving all those operations overseas was anonymity. Always playing the ball, not the man, to borrow a rugby saying. A rule he followed religiously, even more so since Peru. He tapped the pendant under his shirt.

The *diplomat* had crossed the line.

Jay thought of his two workmates, searching the villa for new disguises. Cat had been badgering Matthew about his part of the clue. Trying to break it down into some one-two-three list. Matthew, in stress overload, had exploded.

Cutting and running was not an option. Cat and the Matthew were critical to cracking the clues to this virtual box. Could he trust them? Cat's heart was in the right place. Jury was out on the geek. Clearly he was being framed for the LA murder. He was such a wimp.

'I mean, how can the police be so blind?' said Cat, walking in holding a cushion. 'We all saw what happened to that cop. He wasn't shot. The guy from the embassy didn't have a gun. How in the heck can there be fingerprints?'

'I'm sure they would have found a gun. And I'm sure my fingerprints were on it.'

Cat looked confused.

Matthew, minus the beard and most of the moustache, was deciding between an Auckland Blues or New Zealand Breakers cap.

'Superman's right Cat. Seen plenty of films where the bad geezers plant fingerprints.'

'Come off it. This is the real world. The police would be wise to that.'

'Nine times out of ten it's the bleedin coppers doing the planting.'

'Well thank goodness I got to Pop before he saw the news. He didn't know anything about it.'

Jay glowered at her.

'Tell me you didn't just use the landline here to ring your old man in the States?'

'Just as well I did. If he'd seen the news before I had a chance to explain, he'd have a heart attack.'

'Right. Grab what you've got.'

'What's the matter?'

'Bugger me days Cat. Every policeman and his dog, and God knows who else, are converging on Auckland from all points of the compass. Can't believe you wouldn't have worked out your father's phone would be tapped by now. They'll be able to trace the call. We've got to get out of here. Out of Auckland. Now.'

11. The clock's ticking

CAT LOOKED over the top of her novel at the musician in the green T-shirt and bleached Levis. He was leaning back in a plastic seat, an Auckland Blues cap hiding his eyes, iPod headphones in his ears, one elbow propped against a guitar case.

Two rows back the young businessman in white shirt, striped tie, dark wrap-around glasses and gelled hair parted to one side pored over files in a real estate folder perched on the knees of stuffy black trousers.

All the prattle among the passengers – tourists heading for the Coromandel Peninsula, alternative life-stylers heading home, crew of the ferry – was about the murders. How little old New Zealand had shot to international prominence for all the wrong reasons.

The distant rise and fall of sirens turned heads back to the city as a fleet of police cars sped over the bow-shaped harbor bridge towards the North Shore.

Cat detected the hint of a smile at the corners of Jay's mouth as he pretended to study the real estate files. Perhaps his idea for a diversion was working after all. While she and Matthew had killed time downtown, Jay took a cab to a bus terminal on the North Shore from where coaches left for the Bay of Islands and the many small towns dotted between Auckland and Cape Reinga at the northern tip of the island. Using Cat and Matthew's credit cards, he'd withdrawn cash from an ATM and caught a different cab back to Britomart. From there it was a short walk to the pier to catch the late morning sailing of the ferry.

She shifted in the uncomfortable seat, adjusting the hem of the dress to cover knees too pale for summer in New Zealand. Careful not to dislodge the cushion tied round her stomach. Matthew showed with the flowers and loud tie the value of distracting attention away from the face. The pregnancy bulge also helped fill out the floral dress two sizes too big. She felt self-conscious at first, until she noticed most men were looking away awkwardly and women smiling in sympathy. There was no time to do anything about hair color after seeing her mug shot on TV. It was pinned up in a bun under a straw hat. The black paint on the frames of her glasses was a worry until it dried, but she doubted even her father would recognize her in this outfit.

A large white yacht approached the ferry. Cat searched faces on the deck for the blond diplomat, but it glided by and was soon lost in the maze of boats on the harbor. The City of Sails, she recalled from the arrival video on the plane.

The novel was a further deterrent to conversation. *She knelt to pick up the leaf, a symbolic offering of peace.* Must have read that sentence ten times.

Laughter pulled her back to Jay. A young woman, couldn't be more than eighteen, was talking to him, tossing her hair back over her shoulders. He was doing his best to look at her face rather than the large breasts. Cat couldn't compete with those, even with upward pressure from the cushion.

Matthew hadn't moved. After the argument at the villa, Jay warned her to back off. He was under enough stress and needed space to think straight. Cat hoped he was using the space to think about Rabberting On rather than wasting precious time listening to Ed Sheeran or Bruno Mars.

Jay extracted himself from the flirter and returned to the real estate files. It was hard to picture the business shirt and tie abseiling down buildings to unfurl banners, steering kayaks into the path of ships carrying nuclear waste, or zodiacs under the bows of whaling ships. Looks were indeed deceptive. Cat wondered what he must be thinking.

There was no question of his commitment. Nothing to prove. Would he think the same of her? Did she deserve it? All her life, others had taken responsibility for the big decisions. Professor Stedholme at Berkeley. Paul Deaver at Millbrook. Pop. Even Mom in the early days. What in heck must they be going through right now?

The deck shuddered as the ferry struck the first whitecap in the open water beyond the symmetrical cone of Rangitoto Island. For the first time in Cat's life, the buck stopped with her.

TRAPPED BEHIND a desk on the ninth floor of the Auckland Central Police Station was the last place Detective Inspector Hansen wanted to be at eight o'clock that evening.

Should be on the streets, breathing the investigation. Not playing tour guide. The order to meet the civilian flying in from America came from the highest levels. Higher than the Police Commissioner, if the gossip was on the mark.

Hansen was under enough pressure without political interference. She'd been on the go since the call from the Commissioner confirming as head of the murder inquiry and hunt for the three terrorists. After trawling through personnel files to assemble the best team of detectives available at short notice, she set up an operations center occupying most of the ninth floor, then spent a frustrating day chasing apparent sightings from Urawa to Pahoa in the Bay of Islands. All led nowhere.

The issuing by Interpol of a Red Notice for the arrest of the Englishman Liddell set off an avalanche of calls from journalists representing every media outlet from Abu Dhabi to Zimbabwe, jamming the phone system for ninety minutes until alternative arrangements were made. Things were about to get a whole lot worse. Every available seat on planes to New Zealand had been grabbed by journalists, and two charter flights of reporters from London and Washington were due to touch down in Auckland early in the morning. Then there was the Commissioner calling every hour on the hour, desperate for news of a breakthrough.

There was one promising lead. A bus driver saw the computer images on TV and reported dropping off one of the fugitives near Mt

Eden Reserve. Footage from a security camera in a car park showed Liddell and Duggan creeping from a patch of bush near a nursery. That led to the discovery of the brown skirt Catherine Tayler was wearing when they landed. Sniffer dogs were at that moment trailing a scent into the villas of Mt Eden. Which was where Hansen should be, rather than stuck at her desk.

She picked up a two-page bio on the American. Bradley Kaufman. Security executive for Vestco. Son of a soldier, attended such and such military school that meant nothing to Hansen, served in the Marines for several years, then with US Special Forces. Boxing and long drive champion at Fort Bragg. What an appropriate name. Why do men always put this crap in their bios? She was the top shot putter and javelin thrower at the Trentham police academy but would cringe if it showed up in a bio. For the last several years Kaufman had been head of security for Vestco, with a special interest in counter eco-terrorism.

Interesting to a writer of obituaries, but of little use in her hunt for the murderer of Constable Mark Shaw, father of two. She'd give the civilian five polite minutes, then get back to the real work.

* * * *

'WELCOME TO Auckland Mr Kaufman. I trust your flight was comfortable.'

Kaufman shook the hand of the overstuffed Police Commissioner.

'Fine thank you sir.'

'First time to New Zealand?'

'Fraid so.'

'Sorry it couldn't be under more agreeable circumstances. Traveling light I see.'

'Counting on a short visit sir.'

The day was a write-off. The Mount Eden house had been empty, although there were signs he hadn't missed the targets by much. More troubling was what he found there. Numbered lists showed the punks spent time trying to decipher the email from Henry Beck. Scribbled phrases like password, SD box and 3 levels confirmed the worst.

Kaufman tooth-combed the surrounding streets before admitting he needed help. To find them at least. Best bet was the local police. He didn't want them to know he arrived on the same flight as the targets, so a meeting with the head of the manhunt was set up via contacts in the States for two hours after the arrival of that day's flight from Los Angeles. Electronic airline, immigration and hotel entries were altered to reflect the change. Records of the in-flight phone calls to Eve and his deputy at Vestco were erased. After several wheel-spinning hours in a hotel room waiting for news of another hit on the website, he went out to meet the flight, reverted to his natural appearance, and returned to the city in an airport cab to complete the charade.

The lift juddered to a stop at the ninth floor. They stepped into a large open space with workstations, chunky computers, mismatched filing cabinets, whiteboards, maps and rota charts. The room was divided by gray chest-high screens, bare concrete columns and crisscrossed by cables stuck to the carpet with black tape.

'This entire floor has been taken over by the inquiry team, handpicked by Detective Inspector Hansen,' said the Commissioner.

Kaufman nodded politely and lied about how impressed he was with a room full of desk jockeys and other rear echelon mothers stuck in a re-run of *Hill Street Blues*.

'Made any arrests?'

'Detective Inspector Hansen is waiting to brief you.'

Kaufman went over what he knew of Hansen from a dossier emailed from XecIntel. Aged 40. One of the youngest ever appointed detective inspector in the country. A fast tracker in New Zealand's Criminal Investigation Bureau, thanks to leadership roles in two recent high profile homicide inquiries. Joined the police after a double degree in law and international politics. Top of class at the Trentham police academy. Ten months on secondment to the Australian Federal Police anti-terrorism unit in Indonesia and three months with another unit in the Oruzgan province of Afghanistan. Not married. No kids. Anglican. Always voted National. Usually vacationed on the Gold Coast of Australia. Drove a Prado four-wheel drive. There was a link to a photo Kaufman didn't bother downloading.

A handwritten sign on a piece of card taped to a door said *Pahi*. The Commissioner knocked once as he entered.

'Ah Inspector, I'd like you to meet Mr Kaufman from Vestco in Los Angeles. Mr Kaufman, Detective Inspector Chris Hansen.'

A woman.

That was unexpected. He'd visualized a hard-nosed chain-smoker with loose tie and shrinking hairline. Surprise number two was the color. Christine Hansen had brown skin like someone out of Honolulu, with eyes a shade or two darker and a ridiculous fishhook round her neck. Kaufman extended his arm. The handshake was solid, just like the woman giving it. Big lips parted in a forced smile.

'Mr Kaufman comes highly recommended Inspector. I'm sure he'll prove most useful to your investigation. Especially his experience in counterterrorism. I want you to take him along with you.'

The smile went west.

'That's most unusual sir. Nothing personal Mr Kaufman, but this is a police homicide inquiry, not some civilian celebrity…'

She had balls questioning the brass like that.

'… and it's a bit premature to call it terrorism…'

'Humor me Inspector,' said the Commissioner. Meaning *pull your head in*. 'This is a most unusual investigation. We can use all the help we can get. I'm sure Mr Kaufman's more than capable of looking after himself. Keep me posted.'

He left, and Kaufman could see Hansen was pissed off.

'Sorry about this Inspector. I'd resent the intrusion of a civilian as well if I were in your shoes. Look,' he reassured, palms open, 'I've been ordered over here to help in any way I can. Another pair of eyes. Last thing I wanna do's get in your way.'

Her shoulders softened. Fractionally.

'Better sit down then'. She pointed to a chair in front of the desk, barely visible beneath a pig's breakfast of paper, overflowing trays, a half-eaten Subway six inch and four coffee mugs.

'Your sons?' he asked, nodding at a photo of Hansen with her arms around two boys.

'Nephews. Too busy for children.'

'Tell me about it. Hardly ever get to see mine.'

'How many?'

'Just one. My little princess Eve.' He took the photo out to show her.

'Looks like she's got spunk.'

'Needs it. Few days after that shot was taken she was diagnosed. Big C.'

'Treatable?'

'Not normally. It's neuroblastoma. That's a rare cancer of the nervous system. Eve's got stage four. Worst type. Usually deadly. We've tried everything. Surgery, radiation, chemo, you name it. Tumor keeps growing. Only hope now is luminous mapping treatment at a clinic in Germany.'

'Luminous mapping?'

'Sounds weird I know. But it's for real. Krauts have found this way to make tumor cells glow using fluorescent dye. Means the surgeon, a Dr Berlangen, can pinpoint exactly what he has to cut out and what to leave behind.'

'So why isn't everyone using it?'

He noticed she'd doodled the words luminous and Berlangen on her desk pad.

'Very experimental. And expensive. Only twelve people – all with a similar prognosis to Eve – have gone under the knife so far.'

'And?'

'Seven survived. All in remission.'

'Tough choice.'

'Not really Inspector. We'll take seven out of twelve any day over zero, which is her chance using conventional treatment.'

Hansen shook her head.

'Always seems worse when it's a kid. You've gone for the bald look in sympathy?'

He nodded.

Hansen started shuffling papers to indicate the small talk was over.

'So what are you doing here Mr Kaufman? Frankly I'd have thought eight days out from the release of this wonder seed that's supposedly gonna solve the world food crisis, Ebola, bird flu, swine flu, flatulence and just about every other plague known to mankind, the head of security for Vestco would have more important things to do than fly all the way to New Zealand to pursue an alleged murderer.'

Supposedly and *alleged* were over-emphasized, but he let it go.

'I have a very able deputy back in LA Inspector. Stopping these terrorists has become priority one. We have reason to believe they're planning to sabotage the release.'

'New Zealand seems a funny place to do it.'

'What do you know about these people Inspector?'

'Interpol's supplied us background on the Englishman. We know very little about the American woman, even less about Duggan. He had a clean slate, well, reasonably clean, when he lived here. Certainly nothing to suggest a violent streak. I've got a team building up profiles.'

'I may be able to help there, Inspector. As you'll appreciate our corporation and others working at the cutting edge of biotech come in for special interest from groups claiming to have all the answers to preserving the earth. We keep tabs on the more extreme ones. Earth Liberation Army, Gene Shepherds, Millbrook. I can tell you that since leaving New Zealand your clean slate, non-violent tree-hugging Mr Duggan has become one of the most notorious eco-terrorists in operation. Linked to sabotage and terrorism in Europe and Asia. Was caught breaking into one of our soybean facilities in Guatemala but escaped before the police arrived.'

'Was he a suspect in the murder of Tolminsky, the firebombing of the Vestco lab?'

'No. He was in the UK at the time. Almost certainly involved in the hit on a field trial of genetically modified potatoes in Leeds. You may have read about it. Scientist in charge likened the destruction to burning university books seventy-five years ago.'

He paused to gauge Hansen's reaction. This seemed mostly new information.

'The Englishman Liddell is also not what he seems. He wasn't hired by Millbrook to set up databases for mailouts. They knew his reputation as one of the top ten most notorious hackers in the world.

He was, and as far as we know still is, known in the hacking underworld as Turtledove. That name is well known to the corporate and government intelligence communities both sides of the Atlantic. They've had to spend tens of millions repairing or replacing systems after incursions by Mr Liddell. In the last twenty-four hours he tried at least once to penetrate a highly sensitive section of the Vestco website. From right here in Auckland.'

Kaufman was sure little of this intelligence was in the background material accompanying the Interpol Red Notice.

But if Hansen was impressed, she wasn't showing it.

'The American doctor?'

'Catherine Tayler is a highly intelligent woman with extreme views on biotechnology in general and Alo in particular.'

'There's no law against having extreme views Mr Kaufman. Least not in this country.'

It was Kaufman's turn to feign a smile.

'As there was no law against Muslim students signing up for flight schools in Florida before Nine Eleven. Or Chechen brothers wandering around with backpacks near the finish line of the Boston Marathon. I'm sure I don't need to remind you, Inspector, about the critical state of the world's food supplies and the importance of Alo. The clock's ticking. Just as it was in the days before Nine Eleven. These terrorists must be stopped.'

'That's a little over dramatic.'

'On the contrary Inspector. The death toll from Nine Eleven was in the thousands. Sabotaging the release of Alo as good as signs the death warrant of millions.'

Kaufman's cell phone pulsed.

It was his deputy.

'Mind if I take this? Could be important.'

Hansen waved her hand to indicate *go ahead, you're going to anyway*, then stood to signal the end of the meeting.

'It's my deputy in LA. Liddell's just hacked into a secure part of our website from a place called Hot Water Beach?'

'How do you know it's Liddell?'

'Bound to be. He penetrated our site earlier today from a house in Mount Eden.'

Her eyes widened.

'We've had sightings of the suspects near Mt Eden. I've got dog teams there now.'

'Sounds like they've moved on Inspector. How far's this beach?'

'On the Coromandel Peninsula. Miles away. Don't see how they could have... Shit! The ferries. We didn't check the bloody ferries.'

'What's at this beach?'

'Motels, handful of beach houses,' she said, walking to the door.

'Sergeant, get me a list of landowners at Hot Water Beach on the Coromandel. Any word from the dog teams?'

'They found a house in Esplanade Road. Looks like all three were there this morning.'

Hansen returned to her desk, eyeing Kaufman with a bit more interest.

The sergeant was back inside five minutes.

'Got your names, Pahi. Eight of them. But you'll only be interested in one. Christine O'Gorman. American. At Berkeley same time as Catherine Tayler. Moved to the Coromandel three years ago.'

'Cheers. Send Max in will you.'

The officer in charge of the Armed Offenders' Squad, Captain Max Stafford, was more like a real cop. Tall. Athletic. Trim. Square jaw.

'How soon can you have a chopper ready Max?'

'Depends which one we use. Where we going?'

'Hot Water Beach, Coromandel.'

'Westpac Rescue's BK117 would be the quickest option. Fifteen minutes, assuming it's available. How many extras?'

'Just me.'

She looked across at Kaufman.

'Actually no. There'll be two of us.'

12. Regular little Erin Brokovich

CAT CLAMMED her eyes to make the waves slosh on a beach far away. With palm trees and coconut oil and reggae. Didn't work. The flurries of sulphur and water fizzing from the sand beneath her couldn't be anywhere else.

After helping dig the shallow pool and a trench to allow cold seawater to regulate the temperature of their natural spa, Jay went for a jog to check out the surroundings.

Matthew was up at the house, no doubt swearing about the speed of the dial-up connection on her friend's ancient PC. He had a hunch the other part of the clue related to a mutual acquaintance of Matthew and Henry's back in Manchester.

At least there was a computer. The rest of the place was a monument to Buddhism, escapism and a myriad other isms. The home of a Melville girl who'd never fitted in at school because she was an extreme non-conformist. She sounded happy enough when Cat called. Oblivious to what was going on, but not entirely stupid. When Cat filled in some of the details, Christine agreed it would be best if she were away from the house for the night.

The pool was getting too hot, so Cat pawed at the trench to allow more seawater in, reshaped her sand pillow and lay back with her shoulders under the water.

'Room for two?'

She hadn't seen or heard Jay approach, wearing a pair of shorts he found at Christine's. He pulled them down, tossed them casually as you like on the sand and squeezed in opposite her. Speedos rather than boxers. The shorter yellowy-blond hair looked as if it had been bleached, and reminded her she was now a flaming redhead.

Used to seeing him in loose T-shirts, she was surprised at the size of his chest. And intrigued by the spiral pendant dangling from a piece of string around his neck.

'What's with the pendant?'

'Just a thing.'

'A Maori thing, right?'

'Yeah. Greenstone from down south. Pounamu they call it.'

'Anything significant about the design?'

'Nah. Just a hunk of rock.'

He twitched. Obviously didn't want to talk about it. She closed her eyes to give him space. When she opened them he averted his gaze from her bra, hastily changing the subject.

'Crikey it's hot.'

She grinned at his awkwardness.

He raised his knees, brushing a foot against the outside of her thigh, and eased his shoulders into the water.

'Beaut disguises you came up with.'

'Guess all those seasons in the wings at Melville Junior High weren't a total waste of time. You and Matthew stayed in character really well.'

'Reckon we'll need new ones for tomorrow.'

'I'll check out Christine's wardrobe in the morning. Bound to be full of surprises.'

'Where is Melville? Never heard of it.'

'Nor have ninety-nine-point-nine percent of Americans. No more than a dot on the map of Utah. Day I was born took the population to twelve thousand four hundred fifty three. Melville's only claim to fame – more like infamy – was for the Antego chemical plant.

'Wouldn't have picked you for an Antego town girl.'

'Long story.'

'I reckon our geek up there'll be a while.'

She brought her knees up and wrapped her arms around them.

'Utah was Mom's idea. Had this great scheme selling houses to the Mormons. Opened an exclusive Mormon realty company. Pretended to be one, for heck's sake. Anyway, she made plenty of money. Melville wasn't all bad. Pop and I used to spend weekends, vacations, camping and hiking at Fish Lake and Dixie. Bryce Canyon. Guess that's where my interest in the environment started. Time I got to high school I was hooked on science. We were on this field trip to the Percy. That's a stream flows through a valley below the town. Found these dead fish. The teacher – we called him Bulldog Stevens – told me not to touch them. Said we were there to look at plants not fish.

'Anyway, I went back at the weekend. Found more dead fish. Dozens of them. Cut a long story short I did some digging around on the sly. Nobody was too worried about a thirteen-year-old with pigtails and buckets and plastic bags. Discovered that cyanide was getting into the river from a leak in a storage tank up at the Antego plant.'

'Regular little Erin Brockovich,' said Jay, smiling.

'No *happily ever after* ending to my story I'm afraid. Mom went ballistic when I presented my findings over the supper table one night. Flatly refused to let me tell a soul in Melville. Turns out she'd ploughed most of her money into Antego shares.'

'What did you do?'

'There was this poster at school for the Siemens Science Competition. That's a national prize for high school students. Mom said don't tell anyone in Melville. Thought I was being real clever sending my little report off to the Siemens Foundation in New Jersey.'

'You won, right?'

'Not exactly. There were mistakes in some of my calculations, and one or two of my conclusions weren't exactly scientific. But one of the judges was married to a lawyer who knew a journalist on the *Salt Lake Tribune*. One thing led to another and suddenly I was on the front page.'

'Good on ya.'

'That's not the way they saw it in Melville. Factory had to close. Over a hundred folk lost their jobs. We were shunned. I mean completely shunned. Got really unpleasant. They boycotted Mom's business. She had to close down. Then one night she just arrived home and announced she'd had enough and was leaving. Leaving town. Leaving Pop. Leaving me. Next day she was gone.'

'That's a bit rough.'

'It gets worse. Pop and I were walking home from Food4Less a few nights later and these guys – gutless thugs in masks – jumped Pop. Smashed both his hands so bad he's never picked up a guitar since.'

'Bloody hell. They catch the bastards?'

'Yeah.'

Cat could tell her voice was about to mush up, but it felt right to continue.

'The two guys they charged with assault had lost their jobs at Antego. Forty-two years' service between them. We tried to get the trial moved out of the county, but the Judge wouldn't allow it.'

She wiped her eyes.

'Jury, the good citizens of Emery County, came up with not guilty. Pop and I left town. Couldn't get out fast enough. Lived in LA ever since.'

'Ya wouldn't read about it,' said Jay, shaking his head.

Accented voices butted in from further up the beach.

Tourists.

'Your parents still together?'

Jay was still shaking his head, as if he hadn't heard the question. It was getting dark. Cat could only just make out the shapes of the cottages behind the beach.

'The old man went belly up a few years ago,' he said. 'The old girl's still kicking.'

'How will she be coping with her son being hunted as a murderer?'

'She's a tough old bird. Been dealing with bullshit all her life. Her and the old man were protestors since way back. Used to take me in a backpack to rallies. When they camped in trees to protest against logging native forests, they packed me off to an aunt on the West Coast.'

'We're being accused of something a bit more serious than camping in a tree, Jay. Your mom will be beside herself with worry. I know Pop is.'

He beamed and sunk lower into the water. 'It's the cops I pity. My mother won't be waiting for them to come question her. She'll be driving them nuts with her own interrogation. Just hope she doesn't go on another hunger strike. Getting a bit long in the tooth for that caper.'

'I'm really scared Jay.'

'You know you haven't been accused of anything yet. You could go to the cops, the media. Walk away from all this. Let Matt and me -'

He stopped mid-sentence, head tilted like a rabbit testing the wind.

The faint but unmistakable sound of a helicopter swelled above the surf.

'Bugger. They're onto us. Grab your stuff and scarper to that end of the bay. There's a shed, corrugated iron. Hundred yards the other side of those rocks. Wait for me there.'

He exploded from the pool and sprinted towards the house.

Cat thought immediately of the blond diplomat. She scampered out of the pool, grabbed the pile of clothes and money belt, and ran. Halfway to the rocks she remembered her glasses. She stopped and turned. The helicopter, its spotlight probing downwards like a golden net, was only seconds from the beach. Too late for the glasses. And not enough time to make the rocks. The bush was her only chance. Sprinting to her right, she scrambled up the bank and dived into the shadows, certain she was about to be hit by the spotlight

She lay dead-still for several seconds, then rolled slowly to see the helicopter bank over the water and hover above the beach below the house. Sand was being sucked up into the spotlight beam as the chopper landed. Fuzzy outlines of five figures jumped onto the ground and rushed towards the bank below the house.

Cat was paralyzed. Half the beach was lit up by a second searchlight rotating from the top of the chopper, sweeping to the edge of the bush only yards from her head. Tantalizing. The *thu-thu-thu-thu-thu* of the rotors was drawing her in like a giant vacuum cleaner, Jay's words echoing in her head.

You haven't been accused of anything yet. You could go to the cops. Walk away from this... It would be so easy. Just stand up. One, two, three paces into the light. Hands above your head like the movies. Happily ever after.

She took a deep breath.

Then turned and ran through the bush towards the end of the bay.

* * * *

KAUFMAN FOLLOWED Hansen and the Armed Offenders' Squad members up a slapdash path to an open gate with Buddha statuettes on each pole and a wooden wind chime clunking in the sea breeze.

The lawn in front of the house was bathed in soft green from a small light above the verandah. Other lights were showing behind curtains in rooms at each side of the house. Hansen signaled for the squad to split up, sending two men towards the room on the right, the other to go with her to the left.

'What about me?'

'Wait here Mr Kaufman. I'm assuming the offenders are armed. We've already lost one officer. Got no intention of losing another. Especially a civilian.'

Kaufman doubted the targets were armed, but buttoned his lips as the officers moved forward. He waited, hoping for gunfire – three rounds – but within minutes Hansen was on the verandah calling him.

'No-one here. Something you might be able to help us with, though.'

The reek of incense swatted him as he stepped into a hall resembling a junk store. Walls covered with African prints, borer-ridden musical instruments, Asian masks and carvings. He followed Hansen through a beaded string doorway into a small den cluttered with shelves of books and jars of preserved fruit and shells. Drying flowers hung upside down from hooks in a rough-cut beam.

In the middle of an oak desk was an ancient computer with a recognizable image on the screen. The Vestco logo. It was a page from the personnel section of the Vestco database, showing the curriculum vitae of Henry Beck.

Kaufman palmed his cell phone. No signal.

'Pahi! Out here,' called an officer from the back of the house.

Through another beaded string curtain was the kitchen. The wooden floor near the back door was smudged in gritty tread prints. Hansen was directing two of the officers to start searching behind the house.

'Seal off the whole area,' yelled Kaufman.

The officers hesitated, but after a nod from their captain filed out the door to follow her instructions.

Hansen turned to Kaufman with the sneer of a boarding school matron.

'I'd appreciate it if you'd leave the policing to us Mr Kaufman. And we don't need to be told to suck eggs. Of course, the area will be cordoned. When reinforcements arrive.'

She took a map from the front pocket of her vest and spread it on the kitchen table. Kaufman looked on as she pointed out landmarks to Captain Stafford.

'Two carloads of uniforms from Thames should be here in the next fifteen minutes. About the same time as the second chopper. We've got a busload coming up from Tauranga. And three more AO squads on their way from Auckland and Hamilton.'

The captain pointed to the area round Hot Water Beach.

'Looks like there's only a single access road to this place.'

'What do you recommend?'

'I'd contain them on this part of the peninsula. Put roadblocks here on the road to Hahei. And there on the main road at Whenuakite.'

'Agreed. But from what we know of Duggan's background, there's a good chance they'll go bush and head south towards Tapuaetahi. Covering this road's a priority. I also want a block at Tairua in the south. Another at this point east of Coroglen. And here at Kaimarama. Armed officers at every checkpoint. No vehicle allowed through till it's thoroughly searched, OK? Tell Jack to set up the command center there at Whitianga. And find me a local who knows this area like the back of their hand.'

Kaufman wasn't about to be sidelined.

'What about the chopper, Inspector?'

Hansen looked up as if she'd forgotten he was in the room. She turned back to the captain.

'What's the ETA on the second chopper?'

'Eight minutes.'

'Right. Mr Kaufman and I'll start looking to the south. When number two arrives, I want them to cover the areas to the north and west. After checking the beach.'

13. Back the truck up

THE TRAILER sailor was half a mile out to sea by the time the second helicopter arrived. Jay had spotted the boat on his jog along the beach.

Confident they were now beyond sight of the shore, he turned perpendicular to the wind and trimmed the sails.

'What beats me is how in heck they knew we were here?'

'I got into Vestco's mainframe,' said Matthew, clutching at the fairlead as the boat lurched. 'They must have traced the entry. Bleedin frightening what they can do with technology.'

'The frightening thing is how quickly they got here. We're in the middle of nowhere.'

Jay watched the searchlight sweep the beach near where they took the boat, hoping they wouldn't notice their prints in the sand. They were careful to use rocks when they could.

The chopper appeared to hover near the spot where they entered the water, then moved on to begin searching the bush to the north of the beach.

He kept the yacht heading south, thankful for the lack of moonlight. A veil of fine spray swept across them. Jay shivered. Still in his underpants.

Something was different about Cat. No glasses. He was about to ask, when she started grilling Matthew.

'So did you work out the answer?'

'No. Took me back though. Oxford Road. The Green Room was my pub. Ashburne. That's the university hall where I lived. Henry Beck was in Sheavyn House.'

'How in heck does that help us?'

Matthew held up a wad of papers.

'Got a printout of the names of all the geezers at Ashburne and Sheavyn while we were there.'

'How many?'

'Three hundred odd.'

'Great.'

Ducking under a canvas awning, Matthew used a flashlight Jay had grabbed from the house to search through the lists. Ten minutes of cursing, swearing and reminiscing ended in a load of drivel and no answer.

'Perhaps Jay's right about a Spanish connection,' said Cat. 'Let's assume L O S is the Spanish word for *the*. Go through the names again Matthew, looking for anything Spanish.'

He found two Garcias, a Cortes and an Alicante, none of whom meant anything to him.

'Must have missed something,' said Cat. 'Read them out again.'

'What? All of them?'

'You got something else you need to do right now?'

Jay gazed up at the sky as Matthew began. He'd almost forgotten how brilliant the nights could be in New Zealand, away from the smog and illumination of cities. There was something reassuring about the southern sky. The Matariki cluster. Capella on the skyline. Southern Cross to the southeast, above The Pointers.

'... Francis, Freeman, Fuller, Gant, Garcia, Gascoigne, George, Gifford, Golby, Graham, Granada, Greenwood - '

'Back the truck up mate. Did you say Granada?'

'Yeah, but that's as British as you get. Granada Television. That's Manchester, not Madrid. Coronation Street. Ken Barlow. Vera bleedin Duckworth.'

'There's also a Granada in Spain. I've walked up a couple of hills there.'

'Granada, Robert Vaughan,' Matthew read slowly. 'Bobby G. Software Engineering. Second Year. Bobby G was always going on about our generation being the young and the damned.'

'Gotta be it,' said Cat. 'Bert's also short for Robert. Rabberting on about the young and the damned. Fits perfectly. The Young and the Damned.'

Matthew was shaking his head.

'Too many letters. There's only twelve in the answer.'

'Could the whole shebang be in Spanish?'

'It's the sort of thing Henry'd do. Yeah.'

'I'm assuming neither of you are fluent. So all we've got to do is get a translation.'

'Could Google search it a millisecond.'

'You sure that's safe?' Cat's hands were riding her hips.

'They can't trace a bleedin Google search. Any idea how many searches there are per day? More than a hundred million.'

Jay interrupted. 'But once you've worked out the clue, you have to go into the Vestco site to get the next question, right?'

'Yep. That they *will* trace. Instantly.'

Jay adjusted the sail as they continued south. The creaking of the mast and swish of ocean against the hull filled the void in their conversation until Cat torpedoed the calm.

'OK. Listen to me. First, we find a place with a computer. Second, we do the deed and take off. Third, we'll need a getaway car waiting outside. Jay, that's your job.'

'Thanks.'

'Could do with high-speed broadband,' chipped in Matthew.

'And I could do with a pair of glasses,' said Cat.

By midnight the trailer sailor was gliding by the lighthouse on the eastern coast of Slipper Island.

* * * *

THOUSANDS OF miles away on the shore of Lake Turkana in Kenya, the chief of the local village rubbed the stubble on his chin and listened intently to the words of the wise one.

The witchdoctor lay in a shallow pit before him, the amulet of pebbles and necklace of colobus monkey bones rattling as the trance gained intensity. The wise one's voice fluctuated from high-pitched squeals to gurgles, but the answer to the chief's question was clear. The village should delay planting its maize crop until the new seeds fell from the sky.

Hundreds of miles to the west, a Canadian tourist at the Sunday market in the Ghanaian city of Daffiama sat at a bench in the shade and ordered a pot of pito. Behind pyramids of onions and tomatoes on a nearby table, three toothless old women were having an animated conversation. The tourist had no understanding of the local Dagaare language, but could tell what the women were discussing from the repeated use of one word. Alo.

On the other side of the Atlantic, at a sidewalk cafe in the Plaza Dorrego in Buenos Aires, a businessman scrolled to the tecnologia pages of the Spanish version of *Grassroots Intelligence* and began reading an article about an Argentinean-born geneticist working at the famous Vestco laboratory that replaced the firebombed facility in Pasadena. He felt so proud when he finished the article that, though his coffee was cold, he left a fifty-peso tip.

As the waiter was pocketing the money, the door of a van parked on a quiet suburban street in Los Angeles slid silently open. If anyone had been watching, light from a streetlamp illuminated the sign on the side of the vehicle: *LA County Department of Public Works Sewer Maintenance*. The occupant of the van closed the door, adjusted the zip on his coveralls, studied a note on his clipboard, crossed the street and walked up the side of a white wooden house with a carport covered in ivy. He slipped on a pair of gloves and connected a simple bugging device to the telephone line on the outside wall. He retraced his steps to the gate and crossed the street, ticking a box on the clipboard.

14. Heinz from Hamburg

MATTHEW HAD been stalling over the road from Whangamata Cyberzone for too long, willing the sole customer in the tea cozy hat to leave. Geezer must be composing a thesis.

If he were being straight up, Matthew had never felt lonelier and more vulnerable. Jay pissed him off every time he said *geek*, though if the New Zealander was on his shoulder right now he could call him *gutless nerd* for all Matthew cared. Just as well Jay was also being framed for murder. Otherwise, the guy might have legged it by now and left him to face the music. They were up to their eyeballs in some premier league stuff involving Vestco and this Alo. Matthew couldn't give a toss about the seeds. But he knew the only way to save his jacksy was to find what Henry Beck put in the virtual box.

He looked for the umpteenth time to his right up Port Road. Main street of this dozy town with the unpronounceable name. On the opposite corner, tables were being set up in front of this warped mural of an angel kitted out in blue knickers and sod all else as she roller-skated past some git with a guitar. *History is myth* written in a bubble beside her head. Matthew's stomach gurgled. He'd thrown up twice. On the boat trip through the night, and again on one of the kayaks they'd stolen from a beach house over the harbor to the north of the town.

Professor Tea Cozy was launching into another chapter. Now or never. Matthew risked the street, crossing his fingers that the sign bragging high speed broadband was more than a marketing gimmick. He hovered, checking his reflection in the window and muttering to himself in an accent he hadn't used since school: *Guten Tag Herr Liddell.* He felt naked, on view, with the freshly shaven chin, bowling ball head and *Küss mich! Ich bin Deutsch* shirt. Heinz from Hamburg.

The door had to have one of those bleedin bells. The *professor* looked around, but there was no sign of recognition from him or the manager reading a newspaper behind the counter.

'Internet ja?' Matthew figured if they couldn't speak German there would be no small talk. Seemed to work. He was given a blue plastic triangle with the number four and pointed to a terminal to the left of the professor. 'Danke.'

Matthew adjusted the seat upwards and went online. He was surprised by the speed of the connection. Google took 0.12 seconds to translate *The Young and The Damned. Los Olvidados* was a film made in 1950 *including some unforgettable sequences: the young girl Melche pouring milk over her bare legs to a very sensuous effect...* It was also twelve letters.

'Aces!' he said a little too loud for Heinz from Hamburg.

No one seemed to notice. The doorbell jangled and he spun round, fearing the blond assassin. The hair was blond, but the face tanned, good looking and Swedish from her accent. He smiled as the skirt sat at the computer to his right. She smiled back. Matthew tried to concentrate but found the dishy perfume distracting. He glanced at her screen and noticed she had opened a page called Grasröt Intelligens with the blog's familiar layout. How cruel. She was one of us, and here he was, the international celebrity hero saving the world. What a chat-up line. And he had to keep his trap shut. Bleedin Heinz.

He typed the URL for the Vestco media login into the address bar. His finger froze over the return key. One little tap and the wolves would be unleashed. This was daft. They had to get even more remote. He needed a mobile device. Something small and portable would make sense, but he'd never been a fan of smartphones or tablets. There was something reassuring about fingers thumping away on a keyboard.

Deleting the Vestco address, he searched Google's computer

category for a shop selling laptops. PCS Direct at Geysercity Plaza in Rotorua looked the best option. Jay wanted the mobile phone number for the Kiwi detective. Matthew had it in less than three minutes.

The shirt clung to his back. He sucked in a lungful, entered the URL, typed *losolvidados* in the box and hit return before letting the air squirt from his closed lips.

Nothing happened. The monitor seemed to have locked. The doorbell rang. Matthew looked daggers at the Vestco logo, hogging the screen like a bleedin two-story billboard.

'Er du nastan fardig?'

The male voice came from behind. Matthew exhaled as the lucky geezer took a seat on the other side of Miss Sweden.

A small square appeared in the center of the monitor. It started pulsing, then expanded to fill the screen. A stylized tick appeared, as if from fog. *Bit lame, Henry.* The tick faded away and was replaced by text. Matthew grabbed a piece of paper and started scrawling the next clue. He got halfway before the pen ran out.

'Shit.'

The professor looked up from his screen.

'Can I borrow your pen?' Matthew reached over before the guy answered. He finished writing the clue, considered downloading a serious history eraser, but there wasn't time. He deleted the files, the cookies, cleared the history and logged off. The chair fell as he stood. He picked it up, brassy as you like, and walked to the counter.

'How much mate?'

The man gave him an oddball look, like a double take, then ran his finger down a column in a notebook.

'Two bucks thanks.'

Matthew tossed a five-dollar note onto the counter.

'Keep the change. Cheers.'

It was only when he noticed the reflection in the door, he realized his mistake. Over his shoulder the manager was reaching for the phone.

* * * *

'WHAT CAN I see in front of me? Well now. There's a little swimming pool. Shape of a dog's bone.'

'It's summer over there right? How many in the pool?'

'No-one Princess. It's a bit early. I've got twenty after eight. What you got back there?'

'Twenty after eleven. That's like weird.'

Kaufman knew it was still Sunday in LA. He didn't want to confuse Eve with time zones. He pictured her lying back on her bed, clumps of hair on the pillow, tube in the nose.

'What's your mission today Princess?' She always set herself one task a day to accomplish. Something she'd never done before. Her way of keeping going, moving forward. Living.

'Thought I'd ring one of those radio talk shows. What else can you see Pop?'

Scum was what Kaufman could see across the road from the hotel in Whitianga. Two losers bagging Zs under a tree. Empty bottles lined up like notch counts on a rifle butt. Hooch no doubt pilfered on welfare.

'Over yonder's a beach. Real nice golden sand. Lots of sailboats.'

'What's the sea called?'

He had to think for a moment.

'Pacific. Yeah, must be. Same chunk of water we saw at Point Dume when I took you down to watch for the whales last week.'

There was a knock at the door.

'Gotta go Princess. I'll try to call you again tonight.'

'How long ya gonna be away daddy?'

'Just a day or two more. Business here's nearly finished.'

The stick insect of a hotel manager stood at the door holding a FedEx package. Going on about how it would reach thirty-five degrees and stay in the mid to high thirties most of the week. Like Kaufman knew what that meant in Fahrenheit. He extricated himself with a line about the guy giving up his day job and taking up weather presenting. You'd have to turn your widescreen on its side to fit the beanpole in.

The package contained an updated passport showing he arrived in New Zealand 11 February. There was also a boarding pass for the

Flight NZ42 on the same day. XecIntel would have doctored all the entries on the airline and immigration databases. His cell phone pulsed, and the excited voice of his deputy informed him the Vestco media login had been entered from an internet cafe in *Fongamarda*.

Kaufman studied his map of Coromandel. Nothing resembled *Fongamarda*.

'How do you spell that?'

'Starts with W H. The Maoris pronounce it like F.'

Smartass. Kaufman found Whangamata, a town on the coast well south of the cordoned area. The phone went again to show another incoming. Hansen. He took the call. She was yelling. Like in a storm.

'Morning Mr Kaufman. Good news. Liddell's been seen in Whangamata.'

He knew she was using the *Mister* to remind him he was a mere civilian. It was starting to get under his skin.

'Really Inspector? I'm confused. Isn't Whangamata outside the area you cordoned off?'

The background sound wasn't a storm. She was in a chopper.

'A little to the south.'

'At least you've caught one of them.'

'I said a *sighting*, Mr Kaufman. Haven't found him yet. Uniformed officers normally stationed in Whangamata were on the roadblock at Tairua. There are only desk-bounds left in town. Wasn't gonna send them near an armed suspect. I'm on my way there now with an AO squad. Landing in a few minutes.'

'The other chopper's coming for me, right?'

'My priority Mr Kaufman is to get armed officers and searchers into the target area. We're setting up blocks on the main road north and south of Whangamata. That'll take another thirty minutes cos most of our personnel were around Hot Water Beach. I'm sending a patrol car to get you.'

'I'm overwhelmed Inspector.'

'And we found a pair of glasses at Hot Water. Catherine Tayler's. Frames painted black with kid's paint. We've checked with her optometrist in Los Angeles and found she's very short sighted without them. Might slow them down. We're alerting every optometrist within a hundred miles to keep a lookout. Every optometrist in the country will have her prescription and mug shot by the end of the day.'

Waste of time, thought Kaufman. Tayler will be dead by the end of the day.

* * * *

THE DARK green Ford Mondeo was ideal. Roof rack with fittings for a kayak. Petrol tank near full. Parked in the cloaking shade of a pohutukawa tree. Jay saw the owner lock the car, then go into the rear entrance of a shop. Which meant she probably worked there and wouldn't miss the car for a few hours.

Breaking in was a breeze with a piece of plastic packaging tape he'd found in a bin at the back of a liquor store. A Bart Simpson windshield protector concealed him as he smashed the key mechanism and used a screwdriver from the trunk to manipulate the rotary switch. He turned it off and went back to the park to wait for Matthew. Cat was lying on her back under an even more impressive pohutukawa with a magazine resting on her tented knees. Light silhouetted her thigh through a muslin dress with a wide black belt. Aqua bangles on her wrists. Red hair tucked up in a tie. Makeup *borrowed* from the Whangamata Musical Society rooms altered the appearance of her face, accentuating the lines of her cheekbones, offset by drooping paua earrings.

Matthew was late.

Jay was about to go and see what the hold-up was when his bald head popped round the corner, jerking about like his nerves were shot to pieces. Cat was interrogating him before Jay changed into second gear.

'Were we right about the Spanish? Did you get the next clue? Did anyone see you?'

He handed her a slip of paper.

She read it out loud: 'The green Butcher takes a break round the toxic reservoir ($\underline{3}^c$ 12)'

'Why have you underlined letters in Butcher, toxic and the number 3?'

'The B, the t and the 3 were in italics.'

'What about the little c after the 3?'

'Seem to remember that meant circled.'

'As opposed to squared?'

'I guess.'

'OK. Let's break this down. First, Bt could be Bacillus thuringiensis. Especially since it's italicized.'

'What on earth is…'

'You're right about the earth. Bacillus thuringiensis is a soil-dwelling bacterium. I've no idea what the 3 signifies though. Any of it make sense to you Matthew?'

'I'm thinking.'

'Well think harder.'

'Give us a break. Only had the bleedin thing for two minutes.'

Whangamata mutated into a booming seaside town over summer holidays, its population bloated from four thousand to fifty thousand by surfers and other breeds of party animal, particularly round New Year. Schools had reopened a fortnight ago and the town had yawned, rolled over and gone back to sleep.

A school provided the only near-miss as they headed through town towards State Highway 25 and the south. As Jay pulled up at a stop sign pivoted on a metal arm by a child at a school pedestrian crossing, a girl started to wave. Till she realized it must be someone else in a similar car. Surely too young to know about registration plates.

They left the houses, passed the golf course and were soon in pillowing hills that hadn't licked rain for weeks. Jay wanted to get as far south as quickly as possible. Matthew was right about needing to get remote. First they had to get a laptop. Cat was studying a map book she'd found in the glove compartment, along with a box of tissues, a car manual, a dictaphone and two tampons.

Jay saw the flashing lights before he heard the sirens.

'Down,' he yelled, pulling the cap lower over his forehead and guiding the car towards the side of the road as two police cars came towards them. They streaked and faded in the rear vision towards Whangamata. The surge of adrenalin was something he wouldn't admit to the others. He thought of the English *diplomat* and the flick of the wrist used to distract the cop. The road was heading back towards the coast, approaching a small town identified by a yellow sign. It gave him an idea.

'What does this road do after Whiritoa?'

Cat looked back at the map.

'OK. First it goes south for a while. Then cuts inland to a town called Waihi. From there the main road splits. One way goes south, back towards the coast. The other heads west. Towards a gap in what looks like a forest.'

'You get the number of that detective, mate?'

'Is the Pope a Catholic?'

Jay turned onto Whiritoa Beach Road and drove the short distance to the dunes, parking beside public toilets.

'Pass me that dictaphone, Cat.'

'Where you going?'

'Gotta be quick. I'll explain in a minute.'

He weaved through a planted area of the dunes and onto the sand. The temperature was heading north by the minute, and he had to shade his eyes from the sun glinting off the water like stretched tinfoil. He held the dictaphone in the air and pushed *record*. Waves tumbled gently onto the shore. In the distance he picked up the annoying throb of a jet ski. A seagull was pulling at a hunk of seaweed. Jay threw a stone at the bird, which squawked obligingly. Back at the car he took a portable cooler out of the trunk and attached it to the roof rack with a stretchy cord. Something else for people to notice instead of the occupants.

Jay could tell from the arms folded tight and pinched foreheads that Cat and Matthew had been at each other's throats again. He headed inland, driving in thick silence for several miles until they were overtaken by a lime green VW Beetle.

'What was the name of that pub you and your mate used to drink in at Manchester?'

'The Green Room.'

'Don't suppose you remember seeing any blokes in blue and white striped aprons selling meat raffles?'

Matthew frowned.

'I've thought about the Green Room. Butcher taking a break means about as much as a teacher taking a tinkle.'

Jay reached his left arm back between the seats.

'Give us a look at the scrap of paper with the clue, mate.'

'Not while you're driving!'

'Calm down Cat. This is hardly the San Diego Freeway.'

There had been no more traffic since the green VW.

He held the piece of paper against the steering wheel with his two thumbs.

'This B in Butcher is the only letter in capitals. Mean anything?'

'B. thuringiensis would normally be written with a capital B.'

'So are bloke's names. Guess you've already thought of that?'

'No-one I can remember from the pub was called Butcher. Mind you, most of them only went by their first names.'

'Run 'em past us will ya, just in case.'

'Can't remember them all. There was Josh. Brooks was his last name. Henry Beck of course. Tennant Venton or Fenton or something. Wolfgang. Walter. Sam. Finbar. Lindsay. Don't know any of their last names. Plus Scruff and Four-X. No idea what their real names were.'

'No women?'

'Just the one. Four-X. Australian bird. Could drink us all under the table.'

'There must be something else you can tell us about Henry that might give us a clue?'

'Not that I can think of. He was into patterns.'

Jay pulled over at a country store on the outskirts of Waihi to buy a newspaper and ice creams. Hokey pokey flavor.

The consensus among her peers is that Dr Tayler has lost the respect of the science community.'

Cat was reading out loud from the back seat.

'Dana MacDiarmid, a one-time close associate at Berkeley, described Tayler as

a gifted biologist. But the longer she remains on the run, the more obvious her guilt.'

'Thanks Dana.'

'Renowned geneticist Dr Joris de Vocht, chairman of the International Foundation for Biotechnology Information, was more damning...'

Jay recognized the name. He was the one who invited Cat to the debate.

'Tayler, he said, was a woman of questionable scientific knowledge and even more questionable morals.'

'Wouldn't say that to my face, you two-faced piece of garbage.'

It was the closest Jay had heard her come to swearing.

The gap on the map was the Karangahake Gorge between two large forest parks – the Coromandel and Kaimai-Mamaku.

Just before the gorge, Jay spotted a public phone booth outside the Waikino Tavern. He dialed the number and pushed the play button on the dictaphone.

'Hansen.' She sounded annoyed by the interruption.

'Having a nice day, Detective Inspector?'

'Who's this?'

'Jay.'

'Duggan?'

'You won't find what you're looking for there.'

'Where do you think I am?'

'Doesn't matter. You're looking for the wrong person.'

'Don't take it personally Duggan, but I've heard that line before.'

Sounded like she had her act together. Jay also knew she would try to keep him on the line long enough for a trace. He kept an eye on the timer on the dictaphone.

'The person you should be looking for is a blond Englishman who knows advanced Krav Maga. He broke the cop's neck at the airport. If I was a betting man, I'd say British SAS. Good luck Inspector.'

He hung up. Two seconds before the recording finished.

15. Swarm of rubber necks

'FEED IT through again.'

Kaufman pressed the cell phone to one ear and covered the other with his hand to cut down the sound of the siren. The conversation between Duggan and Hansen was replayed as the patrol car accelerated across a bridge into Whangamata.

'They get a trace?'

'Nah,' said his deputy. 'Few more seconds they would've had him.'

Kaufman was getting regular updates via Los Angeles from the tap on Hansen's cell phone. He also assumed from the chatter on the police radio that the trio reached Whangamata in a small yacht reported missing near Hot Water Beach.

The patrol car slowed as it turned into Port Road. The driver pulled up beside a barrier and cut the siren. An Air force Huey was hovering over the town.

Another was patrolling the waterfront to the northeast. A third chopper, emblazoned with One News, was grounded in a car park. A cameraman was arguing with a police sergeant about the technicalities of a no-fly zone.

Kaufman waded through a swarm of rubber necks craning for a piece of the most excitement they'd ever see in their feeble lives. Beyond the barrier was a cluster of blue uniforms, charcoal body armor and orange and white patrol cars.

Crime scene tape was being fixed to metal barriers surrounding the Whangamata Cyberzone. Inside, Hansen was talking to two backpackers. She broke off when she saw Kaufman enter.

'Bit warm for gloves isn't it?'

'Never too hot Inspector. Screwed up a crime scene once by putting these mitts all over Exhibit A. Bad guy got off. Never again.'

She seemed satisfied with the explanation.

'Got something, Pahi.' The plain clothes officer was working one of the terminals.

'He erased his history, but I've recovered it. Looks like Liddell all right. Got into the Vestco website again. Also the police personnel database. And this. Search on an Acer netbook. That's a compact laptop. Led him to this shop in Rotorua. PC Unlimited in the main street.'

Hansen went to the counter where two officers were jawing over a map. She shoved them aside.

'If they're heading for Rotorua, Duggan must have called me from somewhere on the coast about here.' She pointed to where the main road reached the coast north of Katikati.

Kaufman couldn't resist.

'Duggan called you?'

'A few minutes ago, yes. Liddell must have got my number while he was here.'

Hansen looked back at the map.

'They have to pass through or close to Tauranga. There'll be computer shops there as well, so let's put a watch on them. And roadblocks on these roads into the city from the north and west. I want them in places they can't be seen till it's too late to stop.'

'What about the choppers Pahi? Got two more on standby in Tauranga and one in Rotorua.'

She tapped the map with her finger.

'You know what? Let's leave the choppers out of it for now. Don't want to spook them. There's a dog's breakfast of roads between Tauranga and Rotorua. Take forever to find anyone in there. That computer shop in Rotorua's our best option. Let them come to us.'

She gave instructions for squads to be split between the two cities, and for one of the choppers to pick her up outside in two minutes. She turned to Kaufman.

'It's time to introduce our American turuhi to the cultural capital of New Zealand.'

As she walked outside, Kaufman pulled one of the detectives aside.

'What did she call me?'

'Turuhi.'

'What does it mean?'

'*Tourist* I think, or maybe *visitor*.'

'What about this Pahi? Why does everyone call her that?'

'That's easy. Means *boss*.'

16. A stroke of genius

JAY COULDN'T understand why people chose to live in Rotorua.

Fair enough if you're a tourist, with its Maoridom-on-a-plate and hot springs and geysers and mud pools belching like oversized billies of porridge.

Downside was you couldn't get away from the stench like rotten eggs. Locals reckoned they became immune. Like living next to a railroad line or near an airport. But breathing in this sulphur-laden gunk 24/7 had to be doing violence to the lungs.

Across the road Matthew had stopped to look in the window of the Wild South Adventure Clothing Company. He took off his cap to scratch the bald head showing the first touch of sunburn.

Matthew was sure his accent gave him away in Whangamata, hence the new disguise. The polo shirt, trousers and boat shoes came from Save the Children and Red Cross second-hand clothing bins in Paeroa, the sunglasses from the trailer sailor.

The plan was for Matthew to go into the store and pick out the laptop he wanted, hopefully keeping his mouth shut.

Then Jay would truck up and buy it, using cash from Cat's money belt. His hair was parted and slicked back with gel. The frayed collar of the shirt was hopefully covered by the linen jacket. He was more concerned about the two-sizes-too-big shoes, not that anyone seemed to be taking any notice.

Matthew stopped at a pedestrian crossing two blocks from PC Unlimited. Foul steam floated from a drain beneath a banner advertising a Kids' Congress at the Rotorua Museum of Art and History. The sidewalks were hustling with shoppers and city workers at the beginning of lunch hour. Plenty of brown legs. Shoulder straps. Bored kids in buggies. Ice cream running through fingers. Cell phone heads. Plastic brand bags from Pak 'n Save, Camera House, Farmers.

Jay peered over the sunglasses, probing the road ahead. He wiped sweat from his brow, shielding his eyes from the sun with the palm of his hand. A glint on a rooftop registered for an instant before disappearing. Backing into the shadow of a shop entrance, he focused on the spot beside a brick chimney. Five seconds passed. Ten. He was about to move on when the light flashed again. To its right was a rectangular structure the size of a small car. Probably an air conditioning unit. Poking out from the far end was the black barrel of a rifle.

* * * *

'YOU'RE a genius, Petersen.'

The woman whispering in his ear was Shelley Sutherland, communications director for Vestco. The same woman who three months earlier scoffed when Petersen suggested hiring a global polling company to identify the five most respected people in the world, one from each continent, and invite them for dinner.

Here they were – an actor, golfer, television anchorman, football player and singer. All enjoying hors d'oeuvres of potato galette topped with smoked salmon and caviar and cream-laden asparagus bisque with the chairman of Vestco. The Hotel Bel-Air's captain, sommelier and waiters fussed over them like the living gods people thought they were.

Camera lenses zoomed and shutters clicked as the numerically most respected of all – a Bollywood megastar – proposed a toast to the imminent release of Alo, now precisely one week away.

If this intimate little get-together was considered a stroke of genius, Petersen wondered what phrase the guileless communications director would use to describe the rather larger and infinitely more telegenic gatherings primed for Beijing, Moscow, Mumbai and Boston in the next few days.

17. Surprise in an alcove

MATTHEW had his doubts. A rabble of kids in an art museum didn't sound a promising place to find a laptop, but Jay was sure he'd seen an Apple logo on the banner advertising the event.

Mind you, after the near miss on the way to the computer store – saved by a prearranged whistle from Jay – Matthew was up for anything.

Small fries in school uniforms were grazing on the lawn in front of the gabled Tudor style museum building as Matthew and Jay walked up the steps to the main entrance. A sign in the foyer told them the Kids' Congress was in the Bath House Pump Room. It was a large space with high ceilings, plaster moldings and timber beams. Up to thirty workstations were set up in the thick of Maori carvings and other clobber. There was at least one child looking after each workstation while their classmates had lunch. Some wore red T-shirts with Kids' Committee printed on their backs.

Matthew and Jay split up, pretending to show a tourist's interest in boring sepia photographs and hideous tongue-poking masks. Most of the computer hardware was old hat, but he got a surprise in an alcove off the main hall. A new MacBook Pro. A banner above the table said *Blast from the Past: Surrounded by so many cool artifacts, we'll each pick one object and either re-enact or create our own back stories from them, then tell our tales through video!*

A girl with pigtails and glasses was lost in a computer game. A nametag identified her as Bekki George and a label on the back of the laptop said Mrs Brown. Matthew found Jay and watched as he approached the girl.

'Excuse me, I'm looking for Bekki.'

'That's me.' The girl looked uncertain.

'Hi Bekki. I'm Mr Andrews from the museum office. Mrs Brown would like you to go and see her out by the pond. She asked me to look after the gear till you get back.'

The names worked. The girl saved her game and scrammed. Jay grabbed the laptop, and they waltzed out a rear exit.

18. Hamstrung since I arrived

THE POLICE Commissioner was trying to appear unruffled, but Kaufman could tell he was ready to spit tacks. The guy flew into Rotorua to take credit when the terrorists were caught, only to learn they'd slithered through the net. Again.

He turned away and put on an act of looking out the window.

'Where are they now, Inspector?'

'The car they stole from Whangamata was found near Government Gardens sir. Half an hour ago. Pretty sure they're here in Rotorua.'

'Pretty sure,' the Commissioner muttered to the window. 'I'm *absolutely* sure this is extremely embarrassing, Inspector. Not just to the force. The whole country. Tourism leaders have convinced the Prime Minister this bad publicity is costing their industry tens of millions of dollars. Every day these terrorists remain at large.'

He turned to face them.

'You must think us imbeciles, Mr Kaufman. Tell us, if you were in charge of this investigation, what would you do right now?'

'But Mr Kaufman is - '

'Perhaps better equipped to catch these fugitives than any of us Inspector.'

Enjoying Hansen's discomfort, Kaufman let the insult linger before answering.

'Duggan has outwitted some of the most advanced security

operatives in the world, Commissioner. And Liddell has penetrated top level and supposedly secure IT systems. They're obviously intent on sabotaging the release of Alo.'

'What would you have us do, Mr Kaufman?'

'With all due respect sir, I don't think you guys are taking this seriously enough. It's like you don't realize what's at stake. You don't stop terrorists like these with a few roadblocks and emails to optometrists. You need specialists. People highly trained and experienced in dealing with these madmen.'

Kaufman looked across at Hansen, seething in the corner. What he was about to do was a risk, but the clock was ticking.

'It would be helpful too if everyone was working from the same page.'

'What's that supposed to mean?'

'Frankly I've been hamstrung since I arrived. Sir.'

'That's bullshit. I've taken you with - '

'What about the phone call you got from Duggan, Inspector? When were you going to tell me about that?'

'Duggan called you? Christ Pahi, when were you going to tell *me* about that?'

The Commissioner's eyeballs were ready to explode from their sockets. Hansen tried to explain, but was cut short.

'I've heard enough. The Army has offered the services of the SAS. I'm going to accept.'

Kaufman saw his chance.

'I could have a squad of international specialists assembled and here within twenty-four hours sir.'

The Commissioner stroked his chin.

'Bringing in forces from overseas is outside my jurisdiction Mr Kaufman. But that's an interesting proposition. I'll raise it with the Prime Minister. In the meantime, I'm putting you in joint command of this operation.'

Hansen opened her gob, but nothing came out.

'The SAS are on standby and can be here within sixty minutes Mr Kaufman. What do we need to do?'

'Give them the green light, Commissioner. And seal this town. Immediately.'

* * * *

'YOU CANNOT be serious.'

Cat lifted a branch to try and see over Jay's shoulder. Grass browned off by weeks of moisture-sapping sun faded to the lake's edge, but Jay was looking towards the car park. The excited voices of children jiggled on the breeze. Cat cursed not being able to see clearly without her glasses, but she got the gist of the hair-brained scheme from the discussion between Jay and Matthew, who was looking for a stick of a particular shape. Now they had the laptop, they needed to get somewhere remote. Jay mentioned an old friend he trusted who ran a horse-trekking business in a national park to the southeast.

Other than working out the italicized 3 in the clue question meant there were probably three letters in the answer to part of the riddle, and 12 letters in total, they were no closer to a solution.

'Come on Jay, stealing a computer from a kid's one thing. Hijacking a school bus is completely different.'

'Not as serious as murder.'

'We haven't murdered anybody. This is insane.'

'Eye on the prize Cat. The big picture. We're running out of options here. You ready mate? Last one's getting on.'

'These'll have to do.' He handed Jay a stick that looked more like a withered banana than a gun.

'Tell me you're not gonna do this!'

Jay stuck the banana under his shirt. The bus engine started. He charged across the grass, Matthew a few paces behind. Cat followed in a crouching jog, as if making herself smaller would lessen the crime.

The last child was through the door. A large woman with a red folder identifying her as a teacher turned to see the two men rushing towards her. She jumped aboard, yelling something at the driver. Wheels skidded in the shingle as the bus started pulling away. Jay leapt onto the step, grabbing the handle with his free arm and jabbing his foot into the closing door. In a flash he was inside, and the bus shuddered to a halt in a muddle of dust. Then the screams. Cat followed Matthew through the door, dreading what she'd find.

The terrified eyes of twenty or more children, no more than first graders for heck's sake, pierced her. The ogre terrorist monster from all their worst nightmares. She felt two inches tall.

Jay was using the stick concealed under his shirt to herd the driver, teacher and another woman to the back seat.

'Hope you can drive this thing mate.'

'Give it a go.' Matthew didn't sound convincing.

'Right then. Cat, find something to tie these adults up.'

That sent the screaming through the roof.

'These poor children are terrified, Jay.'

The bus jerked as Matthew figured out the gears and edged towards the road.

'Which way?'

'Left. Then just stay on this road. Look for signs to Whakatane.'

'Fuck a what?'

'Whaka with a W H ya plonker.'

The screaming subsided. One boy started laughing. Unbelievable. Cat used belts and backpack straps to tie the hands of the three adults, apologizing as she did.

'How we goin?' Jay was holding a yellow plastic towrope he'd found in a toolbox behind the driver's seat. Using his free hand, he helped Cat thread it through the sets of hands, binding them together and using clamps to fasten each end to the base of the seat.

'Sweet as. Now all you grownups gotta do is keep those mouths shut, or I'll come back and gag ya as well.' He walked to the front, turned and whistled to get the children's attention.

'OK kids. This was a game.' He grinned as he lifted his shirt to reveal the stick.

The next few minutes passed for Cat like a traumatized blur of lake and forest interspersed with thoughts of bacillus thuringiensis, butchers' aprons, toxic lakes and reflected images of red hair, hideous earrings and makeup running in the heat.

By the time the bus approached the eastern end of Lake Rotoiti, Jay had most of the children laughing at his attempts to juggle their lunch boxes.

Sirens jolted Cat back to the present. She ducked down as three police cars overtook them at speed, followed by a police truck carrying what looked like wire farm gates. The bus rounded a corner. Up ahead the flashing lights had stopped at the side of a road beside an intersection. Half a dozen officers were putting on vests while two others were pointing towards the road, apparently discussing where to set up a roadblock.

'Let's all wave to the cops, kids,' said Jay as the bus slowed.

Cat squatted in the aisle and closed her eyes, bracing for the inevitable. Smooth gear changes. The ticking of the indicator as the bus turned right. Then the gentle vibration as they accelerated. Risking a peek through the back window, she saw a policeman walk into the middle of the road and hold up a white-gloved hand to stop the next vehicle.

'You'll never get away with this you know.'

The plus-size teacher had a beginner moustache and the self-important demeanor of a career vice principal.

'I beg your pardon. Get away with what exactly?'

'Kidnapping. Murder. Terrorism. These children'll be traumatized for life. And you call yourself a scientist.'

'Look, lady, I'm sorry, right! You think I'm doing this by choice? We just want to borrow the bus for a while. Then we let you all go and get on with your lives.'

'You're pathetic. Disgrace to science. Think of all those children who'll starve to death without Alo. We're talking mass murder lady. Geno - '

'Shut up.'

Cat had just noticed the little green ASA pin badge on the woman's collar.

It had never occurred to her that Vestco's propaganda reach would have gotten this far. As an Alo Science Ambassador, the teacher would have been invited to webinars and online chats, showered with brochures and classroom workbooks, almost certainly received grants for her school.

Cat rounded on her.

'Just shut the heck up. This Frankenfood has nothing to do with ending world poverty. It's all about money. And influence and pulling strings. They've exploited people's fears of the so-called world food crisis to over-ride just about every food safety rule imaginable. We've had no access to critical safety assessment data. We know nothing about the potential for introducing new toxins. We don't know enough about the molecular biological data characterizing the genetic - '

'Listen to yourself. You *don't* know. But we *do* know how many children die every minute from malnu - '

'Spare me the malnutrition lecture lady. A billion people don't go hungry because there's not enough food to go round. There's a billion people overweight.'

The teacher's mouth dropped. Cat thought of apologizing for what the woman obviously took as a personal insult. But there was nothing to apologize for, so she ploughed on.

'If the world's food output was added up and divided equally among everyone, each person would have 2700 calories a day. More than enough to get rid of hunger. If Vestco's so concerned about malnutrition and solving the food crisis, why does Alo have terminator genes that stop plants creating viable seeds?'

Cat had no intention of waiting for an answer.

'I'll tell you why. To force farmers to go back to Vestco year after year to buy more coated seeds. The word Alo has several meanings in Latin, lady. Vestco's always using the flowery translations like *nourish, sustain, cherish*. Alo also means *maintain* and *keep*, but the glossy publicity blurb doesn't mention that. Everyone's in cahoots with Vestco. Governments, big business, the media. It's a massive conspiracy.'

'What a load of nonsense. Those things just don't happen, for crying out loud.'

Cat's hostility evaporated.

'You know what? You're absolutely right. Thank you so much. I'm going to go and tell my friends we've made an awful mistake.'

She rushed up the aisle to Jay.

'Cry,' she whispered in his ear.

'You what?'

'It's the answer to my part of the clue. Cry as in Cry toxins. It's infuriatingly obvious in retrospect. Cry is short for crystal. The protein crystals synthesized when vegetative Bt cells undergo sporulation.'

'Clear as mud.'

She gave him a playful punch on the shoulder.

'Sporulation is the resting stage of a bacterium. As opposed to the active stage when it multiplies. Resting stage, get it? Taking a break.'

He raised his eyebrows in bewilderment.

'Long story short, Bt can act as a reservoir for Cry toxins. *Reservoir. Toxic. Taking a Break.* It all fits. And in three letters. C R Y.'

'Stone the crows.'

'And we have our stroppy teacher back there to thank for the answer.'

'You're wasted as a gypsy ya know.'

'You're wasted as a terrorist. You should run away and join the circus.'

'Stranger things have happened. How's the time?'

'Just after two-thirty.'

'This bus will be reported missing if it isn't back at school in the next half hour. We need to jump ship up here and head south.'

He leaned towards Matthew, who was approaching an intersection.

'Stay on this road, then look for a place off the side we can bail out.'

Half a mile past the corner a shingle track headed into the forest. Matthew drove in a short distance and parked out of view from the road. Jay checked the bindings on the adults and gagged them with rags from the toolbox, reassuring the children it was part of the game.

'Cat, check their pockets for cell phones. The kids too. And those bags up by the driver's seat.'

She found seven, as Jay cut some wires below the steering wheel. He took one of the phones and pretended to punch keys.

'Hi. Is that Kawerau Police? ... Just to let you know the Matata School Bus is sitting in bushes off a track about half a mile east of the

121

intersection with Highway 34. Everyone's safe. No dramas... Might pay to tell the parents they'll be a wee bit late back... They certainly are... Great bunch of kids... How long do ya reckon she'll take you to get here?... Really?... Can you make it a bit sooner? ... Appreciate it... Cheerio...'

He pushed a button to end the *call*.

'Cops'll be here as soon as they can, kids. Don't leave the bus. She's dangerous out there.'

Jay locked the door from the outside. Cat couldn't believe the kids were waving and smiling as she and Matthew followed him along a track further into the forest. As soon as they were out of sight of the bus, they dumped the cell phones and veered back towards the road.

19. Bigger pockets

PETERSEN CLOSED his left eye and squinted through the peephole with his right. The fishbowl lens comically distorted the man in the corridor outside, turning one side of his face into a caricature, but the beige silk kurta and white chudidaar pajamas gathered at the ankle were a giveaway.

He opened the door and ushered the Chief of Staff to the Prime Minister of India into the executive suite of the Biltmore. Petersen began briefing the man about arrangements for the following day, when the Prime Minister would be accompanying his country's first seed lots back to Delhi. The Chief of Staff showed little interest, his eyes settling on a white envelope on the coffee table between them. The latest installment of one hundred thousand in unmarked bills. The pretense over, the two men stood, and the Chief of Staff stuffed the envelope inside his kurta. They shook hands and Petersen escorted his guest to the door. He liked dealing with the Indians.

The little guy from the office of the General Secretary of the Central Committee of the Chinese Communist Party had been only marginally more cautious. He'd turned up in a business suit. Bigger pockets.

Petersen checked the calendar on his cell phone. Just the recipients from Indonesia, Russia and Moldova to go, with an annoying fifteen-minute gap between the last two. Regional conflicts could be so inconvenient.

20. Like startled twins

WHY DID they always use hackneyed phrases like *terrifying ordeal?* It was as if all anchors read from the same book of boost-the-ratings ladle-on-the-melodrama clichés.

Hansen was in the cafeteria of the Rotorua police station watching the lead item on the news. Images of the school bus in the forest overrun by camera flashlights and black body armor and M4 carbines were interspersed with children clutching Winnie the Pooh bags and sinister close-ups of fluffy pencil cases and a single shoe. Whatever they were supposed to signify.

The teacher with I've-been-crying-for-hours eyes came on to agree with the reporter how traumatizing the experience had been. It was like they were describing a different incident to the one Hansen and Kaufman were called to a couple of hours earlier. Most of the kids she spoke to seemed fine. One even described the hijacking as *cool fun.* Especially the juggler.

The camera zoomed from the heavily freckled face of a boy to show him being comforted by Kaufman, described in the voiceover as a decorated war hero and international expert on counterterrorism who'd been given special powers to assist with the manhunt.

'We now know what sort of terrorists we're dealing with,' Kaufman was telling the kid. *'They call themselves green. They've shown today they're nothing but yellow. Takes a special type of coward to go after kids like you.'*

Kaufman eyeballed the camera. *'Young Luke here and his buddies were incredibly brave today. Lucky they weren't killed. We're gonna leave no stone unturned until we've brought these terrorists to justice.'*

He turned back to the boy and held up his hand. *'Deal?'*

The tiny hand was coddled in the high-five of the American.

'That's what I call a man.' The compliment came from a female constable standing behind Hansen.

'Bit of a looker too,' added another.

'Oh p-lease,' said a male officer. 'He's from Hollywood. What do you expect? His concern for those kids will be as thin as those plywood facades on movie sets.'

'No. That's for real. Kaufman's daughter's dying of cancer.'

In the dead air that followed, Hansen couldn't believe she'd defended the man who humiliated her in front of the Commissioner just four hours ago.

The anchorwoman came back on.

'As the police prepare to bury the officer murdered at Auckland Airport on Saturday, the three terrorists remain at large, evading the biggest police operation this country has ever seen.'

Updated identikit pictures based on descriptions from the teacher and driver had been distributed to the media, but there'd been no sightings of the trio for several hours. Hansen knew about the theft of the laptop. There was a chance they'd gone to Whakatane, based on a comment in the bus.

There was little she could do on the ground until something showed up. She looked at the clock. The car would be waiting to take her to the airport for the flight to Auckland. As head of the investigation, her place was at the funeral. Family was family.

* * * *

ROSIE WELSH was near the bottom of her fourth gin so she couldn't be sure. That guy she'd just seen on the news, the war hero sitting beside the poor boy kidnapped on the bus down in New Zealand, looked familiar.

She drained the glass and reached for the bottle. One more wouldn't kill her.

No job to go to in the morning. Might never work again. Who would hire anyone who'd worked for Public Enemy Number One? More chance of getting a job if her resume said she'd done time in the state prison in Chino rather than as a receptionist for the Millbrook Foundation.

She took another swig and leant back in the chair, closing her eyes. Where had she seen that guy, dammit? Something about the mouth when he said... what was it? The kids had been lucky not to be killed.

Lucky.

That was it.

The mouth had been talking about Matthew being *lucky* to be going on vacation. It was that guy from a market research company looking for Matthew the day they left and everything turned to shite. But that guy had hair. And glasses. And said nothing about Vestco. Rosie would have remembered Vestco. Even after ten gins.

What to do? Couldn't ring the cops in this *state*. They'd never believe her. Paul Deaver, the former CEO of the former Millbrook Foundation. He'd know what to do. Fortunately, she had his private mobile, since the office number no longer existed. He answered after four rings.

'You're sure about this, Rosie?'

'S'lutely.'

'Who else have you told?'

'Not a soul. Saw him on the news not five minutes. What we gonna do Mr Deaver? Police. Gotta tell police. I'm in no really state right now.'

'Don't panic Rosie. I'll take care of it. Where are you?'

'At home.'

'Listen to me Rosie. Just stay where you are. I'll come round and we'll call the police together, alright?'

Relieved, she took another swig and staggered for her makeup.

* * * *

JAY WASN'T surprised to see no police on the tangle of shingle roads through the tedious pine forests south of Kawerau.

The forestry truck they pinched had four-wheel drive and a fair amount of grunt, which came in handy as he went off-road to avoid the odd intersection with side tracks leading to the beginnings of hiking trails into the back country.

Now they'd made it to the sealed highway at Murupara, he expected the shit to hit the fan. Only the main road from here on. Piece of cake for the cops to throw up a roadblock. But there was bugger all choice.

Cat stopped pummeling Matthew about his part of the clue only when he threatened to get out and take his chances alone. Had to be bluffing, but with stress levels deep in the red zone, Jay wasn't stopping to find out. The only sound for miles had been the throaty drone of the three-liter turbo-charged diesel engine.

Your main town in this neck of the woods, Ruatahuna, would make a great set for a time warp flick. Nothing different since Jay's last visit over a decade ago. The motel was probably still described in guidebooks as basic but comfortable, which was charitable. The roof of the Oputao Marae with its traditional carved tekoteko figurehead and sloping maihi panels at least had a fresh coat of red paint. The carpark outside the pub was still full, the main drag through town nodding off. Matthew picked up a handful of unsecured wireless networks, but wasn't game to stop to try the laptop.

Ruatahuna was in an open valley and from the air the white forestry truck must have stuck out like a sore thumb. In the seat beside him, Matthew's neck was craning in search of choppers. Nothing there but a flock of geese and the dogleg vapor trail of a jet chalking the endless blue. A few minutes south of the town the road re-entered the Urewera National Park. Jay relaxed his grip on the steering wheel as the greens of rimu, red beech, rata, tawa and kamahi meshed into a hood. He was among friends. And didn't the words *national park* give him some sort of protection as a Kiwi?

Through the rear vision mirror, Cat's eyes were full mooning.

'OK back there?'

'This place, this forest... it feels... enchanted. Like a fairytale.'

'Not as silly as it sounds, Cat. This bush is the home of the Tuhoe. That's an iwi, Maori tribe. *Children of the Mist* they called themselves. Some still do. Heaps of history in these mountains. Back in the early days when the British – the geek's ancestors – were stealing all the Maori land, there was this bloke called Te Kooti. Cunning bugger by all accounts. Led the Brits on a merry chase. Tuhoe gave him sanctuary up here.'

'I take it this was back in the days before roads.'

Jay nodded into the mirror. 'Then a few decades later there was another bloke, a Tuhoe prophet. Rua Kenana. Stood up to the British. Set up a community. You know, independent. On a sacred mountain over the back there. Homes. Meeting houses. Gardens. Couple of thousand people…'

'What happened to them?'

Jay sidestepped.

'Te Kooti eventually left. Think he was pardoned in the end.'

Which was true, if not the full story. Cat didn't need to know about the murders. The slaughtering of women and children, Maori and European, by both sides. The burning of houses and crops as the Brits tried to starve Te Kooti out.

'What about the other geezer, the one who thought he was a prophet?' Matthew's words dripped with derision.

Jay fought the urge to tell the smug little shit exactly what was on his mind.

That it was gutless wonders like him who forced the Maori off their land. Infected them with their poxy European diseases. Gutless wonders that brought police up here, to this sacred place, with their muskets to end Kenana's stand in a crazed shootout. Gutless wonders who killed his son and dragged the old man off to rot in jail.

'Well, with a bit of luck you're about to meet Rua's great great grandson.'

'That's all we bleedin need. What does he think he is? A - '

'So, your friend's a Maori from this Toohee tribe?' Cat butted in.

'Tuhoe.'

Matthew turned to Jay.

'Sounds dodgy to me. How do we know we can trust him?'

Cat tore into him.

'Don't be so racist. Are you saying anyone who's not white and middle class like you must be a criminal? Look at Vestco. Biggest, most ruthless, devious, murderous bunch of criminals on the planet. White. Middle class. Every last one of them. And predominantly male.'

Matthew raised his palms, mumbling something about *the bleedin mist when you need it.*

They drove on, stewing, until they passed Hopuruahine Landing and got their first view of Lake Waikaremoana. Cat wowed. Matthew stared straight ahead. You wouldn't know if he was impressed, sulking or away with the fairies. Jay let the windows do the talking as he followed the road around the eastern shore. Soon after the sign to Aniwanana, he turned off and parked the truck in a clearing behind beech trees.

'The hell are we doing here?'

'You wanted remote, didn't ya?'

'Yeah. But a bleedin net connection would come in handy.'

'Better find you one then.'

Jay wanted to walk the last mile or so through the bush, half expecting a welcoming party of flak jackets and handcuffs. He shepherded them through pillars of mature beech. The shadows released them from the heat, and the chiming of bellbirds and screech of kaka were a breath of fresh air after the diesel engine.

An unfamiliar three-part whistle stopped them. Jay turned and raised a finger to his lips. The forest drew breath. The whistle was repeated, this time from behind. They spun round, saw nothing.

Cat nuzzled behind Jay, her hand resting lightly on his shoulder, her face close to his ear.

'What sort of bird was that?'

'My money's on a greater spotted Kenana.'

Chuckling erupted behind an ancient rimu, followed by a face, heavily tattooed like an intricately painted mask. The grin was wide, but it didn't stop Cat and Matthew jumping like startled twins.

Jay moved forward to embrace his friend, touching noses in the traditional hongi of the Maori. The exchange of ha – the breath of life.

'Whatu, I'd like you to meet my colleagues, Cat Tay - '

'I know who they are, mate. These faces've been all over the TV. The Cat and the Matt. Pleased to meet ya, Doctor.' His hands were on her shoulders and their noses touching before she knew what was happening. 'And you young Matt.'

'It's Matthew.'

He put out his hand, which Whatu shook but still managed to hongi.

'I'm sorry for - '

'Don't talk crap Jay. You're always welcome here. When I heard yous were in Rotorua I thought ya might be heading this way. Beth will cook up a feed.'

'Not sure how much time we've got Whatu. What we really need is an internet connection so Matthew here can hook up his laptop.'

'No problem. My young fella's got all that computer crap in his van. What's this all about?'

'She's a long story. If it's all the same to you, let's get our geek sorted then I'll fill you in.'

'Sweet as.'

The horse trek base was in a clearing screened on three sides by slopes robed in thick bush. A meeting house at the far end dominated a dozen wooden houses. Stables. Barns. Outhouses. Horse paddocks. Sagging clotheslines. A scarecrow overwhelmed by the massive veggie garden. Tranquil was an understatement. Whatu walked up to the shell of an old caravan resting on tree stumps near two rusted fuel storage tanks. He rapped on the door.

'Maipi, get ya black arse out here. We got celebrities.'

Last time Jay saw Whatu's son, he was an awkward pimple-ridden adolescent. The young man who opened the door was twice the size, his chin covered in a similar tattoo to his father.

'Yo Jay. Sup bro?'

After hongi and introductions and jokes about Doctor Zeus, Jay pulled Whatu aside.

'Wouldn't ask you to do this mate unless it was really important.

Most of what Matthew needs to do on the computer's harmless. Surfing. Google searches. Whatever. Untraceable he reckons. But if he finds what he's after, he's gotta go into a website that will be traceable to here. I'll make sure he doesn't do that till we're just about to leave. And I'll make it look like we broke in. To cover your arse.'

'S'all sweet. What's this all - '

'Great spread you've got here.' Cat had joined them.

Whatu's grin distorted his tattoo into something resembling the tusks of a wild boar.

'Why thank you Doctor. We think she's pretty choice. Show yous round if ya like, while your friend's in cyberspace. Ya ride?'

'Matter of fact I do. Or can. Not for a while. I mean I used to ride all the time. When I was a kid.'

'Sounds like you'll have no trouble keeping up with Jay here. Couldn't ride a horse ta save himself. Let me get yous some gear.'

'Don't suppose you've got any glasses?'

'Coming out our ears. Beth – that's the missus - got more glasses than I've got saddles.'

He trudged off towards the houses. Jay turned to Matthew.

'How long d'ya reckon you'll need?'

Matthew looked at the wire drooping between the top of the caravan and a nearby tree. He shrugged his shoulders.

'Least an hour.'

'Right. We'll be back in forty-five. I'll smash a window or something to make it look like a burglary. Then you can enter the Vestco site, get the clue, and we'll clear out before the sky falls down on this place.'

* * * *

MATTHEW'S ESTIMATE of an hour was based on the rust, the weeds, the reek of horseshit, the out-to-lunch faces, and the assumption he'd be using old goat dialup.

He realized his mistake as soon as the door opened, and he was cuffed by a draft of cool air from a homemade air-conditioning system. Water from a large plastic bin was siphoning into a car radiator attached to the back of a fan. The caravan was hooked up to broadband through a cunning arrangement that included an empty pet food can and homemade satellite dish attached to the top of the flagpole. Program manuals and a retro CD spindle competed for space on plastic shelves with packets of instant pasta and rice. The microwave looked pre-war, the refrigerator was full of cans of a soft drink called *L&P*, the single bed got a lot of use, and through the back window was an impressive pile of old monitors and processors, keyboards, drives and fans. The desktop PC was a bit yesterday and there was no wireless, so Matthew connected the laptop and went online. The kid sat on the bed and watched as he unfolded the scrap of paper with the clue.

The green B̲utcher takes a break round the t̲oxic reservoir
(3^c 12)

If Cat was right about CRY, he could probably ignore *takes a break, the toxic reservoir* and the number 3. He crossed them out. That left *The green Butcher*, *round* and circled. Hadn't occurred till now that *round* and a circle around the 3 could be related.

First things first, me old China. Was there a Butcher who did the deed in the Green Room? Sounded like a game of bleedin Cluedo.

He Google searched his way through the names of drinking mates he could remember from Manchester. Nothing obvious there. A search of graduate lists gave him surnames for some of the others. Wolfgang Metzger, Sam Sherwood and Walter Lee. Finbar can't have lasted the distance. Wolfgang graduated with a BA in Environmental Management. That sounded pretty green, so he focused on him first.

He entered *Wolfgang Metzger Butcher* into the search box and nailed it. Metzger was a German word meaning butcher.

Under the clue question he wrote:
Wolfgang Metzger
Round
3
Wolfgang O 3
Wolf 3
Wolf circle

Matthew closed his eyes and pictured Wolf at the pub. The four of them in those bright red seats beside the window. Wolf, Henry, Matthew and Four X. It was a drinking game Four-X heard about from some toff went to Cambridge. You had to drink six shots, six pints and eat a raw onion – all in one hour. Four-X won hands down. In under thirty minutes.

Funniest thing was that everyone bawled their eyes out when they ate the onion.

Everyone except Wolf.

How did he explain it? Some bizarre medical condition – Riley Syndrome or something. Meant he was born without the reflex to produce tears. Wolf couldn't cry.

'You bleedin champion, Matthew Liddell.' He picked up the pencil.

WOLF NOT CRY

NEVER CRY WOLF

Twelve letters, with CRY in the center.

He knew before he searched that he'd cracked it. *Never Cry Wolf* was, according to Yahoo! Movies, an inspiring adventure story about man versus nature.

'Got it,' he announced to the kid. 'Now we just have to wait. Mind if I have one of those cans?'

'No worries,' said the kid, handing Matthew an L&P and taking one for himself. It was ice cold and tasted like...

'They say you're a half decent hacker.'

'You could say that.' Matthew eased back in the chair. 'Do a bit yourself do you?'

The kid smiled. 'Bloody oath. What handle d'you go by?'

'Turtledove.'

'Never heard that one.'

'Been out of the game for a while.'

'Ever meet the SwordPhish?'

'Several times,' Matthew lied. He almost met the legendary hacker once. It was at a London 2700 meeting the day after Turtledove appeared on the international cybercrime *wanted* list. He'd been going to hacker meetings for over a year, but it was the first time he'd been invited to the secretive inner sanctum where the big boys played. The SwordPhish had been there, but left before Matthew arrived.

'Rumor is he's based down south somewhere,' said the kid.

Matthew heard various rumors over the years about the great one living in Chile or South Africa or Australia.

'Can't tell you that mate. Sworn to secrecy and all that.'

'S'all sweet. What we waiting for?'

'Till the others come back. As soon as I enter the code, they'll know exactly where we are.'

'Who's they?'

Matthew didn't want to say he had no idea, so he reeled off a list of acronyms. 'CIA, FBI, MI5, NATO, ISIS.'

The kid nodded, impressed.

'So why don't you use a DA?'

Matthew had considered a distributed attack, which would involve logging into Vestco from multiple sites, confusing the hell out of anyone trying to trace the entry point.

'Take too long to set up.'

'I got one put together for a DDoS. We could modify that.'

The kid was full of surprises. And when he explained the attack mechanism he'd created for a distributed denial of service attack, using a client program to issue commands to zombie agents via compromised systems, Matthew was blown away.

'How many agents does each handler control?'

'A thousand per.'

'And your program's connected to how many handlers?'

'Twenty-two so far.'

'Unreal.' It would take ages to trace the source, and Matthew could surprise Cat and Jay by cracking the final level before they got back.

He modified the timing on the kid's trigger mechanism, loaded the password *nevercrywolf* and launched the program. Precisely sixty seconds later screens on twenty-two thousand computers and devices in God knows how many parts of the world froze simultaneously. Matthew laughed at the thought of someone called Heinz getting the white tick in Hamburg. He wrote the question to the final clue on a piece of paper and was about to start a Google search when he had an idea.

He removed the rogue active server page he'd set up on the Millbrook server and transferred it to sit as a bogus front page on his personal website. Anyone accessing the rogue page would unwittingly be opening a backdoor to their PC, giving Matthew a free look at all their files. He'd used the technique to monitor who was monitoring him at Millbrook.

'Bait on the hook,' he explained to the kid.

Turtledove was back in the game.

* * * *

IT TOOK the two men posing as detectives less than four minutes to enter the modest but tidy one bedroom apartment in the Los Angeles district of Mid Wilshire, end the life of the former Millbrook receptionist Rosie Welsh with a single stab to the heart using a carving knife from her kitchen, crack a joke about a whale becoming beached, and empty a few drawers to give the impression of an attempted burglary.

To help the police reach such a conclusion, a knife similar to the real murder weapon – bearing the fingerprints of a local misfit familiar to the LAPD – was left beside her.

* * * *

THE ROYAL New Zealand C130 plopped down at Rotorua's airport and lumbered along the runway like an overweight boxer whose trainer left the towels at home.

It didn't help Kaufman's mood to realize the Hercules was clocking up air points before he was born.

Hansen had hauled ass on a commercial flight half an hour earlier, off to Auckland to pay her respects and powder her nose. The terrorists had disappeared again. Checkpoints were in place here and there, though Kaufman got the impression there was a lot of guesswork involved. So vast and godforsaken was the central North

Island volcanic plateau, nothing was expected to happen in the hour or so left before darkness.

The years-old Hercules taxied behind an even older museum piece that arrived earlier with two Iroquois choppers, which were being prepared for action. Kaufman covered his ears as he walked over to greet the commander of the SAS. Captain Falconer saluted Kaufman and called him *sir*. A good sign.

The commander began issuing orders to set up a temporary base at the airport. As Kaufman watched them unload crates and boxes and gear from the rear end of the Hercules, he toyed with the idea of firing a round into the air to see how many would follow their former defense minister's advice and run. The soldiers appeared well disciplined and clearly respected their commander. They wore the same sand berets as the British SAS, but their kit was crap. Kaufman doubted any had seen live action, let alone killed anyone. Never mind. He only needed them to help find three misfits.

His cell phone pulsed. His deputy in LA sounded excited.

'The media login has been entered simultaneously from all over the world. More than forty countries.'

'And?'

'We ran a check against the list of names you sent from Duggan's address book. Narrowed it down to a tiny place called Aniwaniwa.

'Why in hell don't they just close the site down?'

'Got banks of nerds working on it. Gonna take a bit longer. All the release day comms stuff's linked into it.'

'How they going with cracking this code?'

'Still nowhere.'

'Keep me briefed.'

The deputy ended the call, but Kaufman kept the phone to his ear as he walked towards the SAS commander.

'Can you spell that for me Inspector Hansen? ... A N I W A N I W A... Yes mam... OK... You want us to check it out? ...Yes Inspector, I've met Captain Falconer. Very impressive unit. He's right here beside me if you wanna talk to him? ... A-ha... Will do Inspector.'

He pretended to hang up, and fronted the commander.

'There's been a sighting of the terrorists. Place called Aniwaniwa.'

'I know it. By Lake Waikaremoana. South-east corner.'

'Detective Inspector Hansen wants us to check it out.'

Captain Falconer hesitated, presumably uncertain about the chain of command, then started barking orders to deploy.

* * * *

THE FOREST was even more captivating now Cat could see properly.

The pair of glasses from Whatu's wife were close enough to Cat's prescription for her to admire the detail of lichen and mosses in every shade of green cloaking the trunks and branches of podocarps rising silently into the canopy more than a hundred feet above. Epiphytes like the nests of giant storks. And the ferns. Never had she seen such variety.

The stocky roan mare required no steering as it followed the mounts of Jay and Whatu up the trail above the camp, stepping with practiced ease over tree roots spanning their path. The two men had been chatting the whole way, their speech gaining in speed and laced with so much Kiwi slang Cat stopped trying to follow the conversation. Two words were repeated several times. *Aroha* and *utu*. Now and then they'd break into uncut laughter, which she found relaxing. Reminded her of a horse trek in the Tashar Mountain range with her parents in the carefree days before their world came tumbling down. The trail widened and Whatu waited for Cat to come alongside.

'Alright back there?'

'Blown away by the beauty of this place. Don't suppose you know what that plant is?' She pointed at a cluster of scarlet flowers, their uppermost petals curved skyward.

'Let's see now. You'd probably call it Clianthus puniceus. I'm pickin Jay here'd settle for the common name, kakabeak. We call it kiehai ngutu kaka. Don't see them so much anymore. In the wild that is.'

'I feel privileged,' she said, riding on beside him.

He smiled, showing gaps between his teeth.

'Hear that bird?'

'Which one?' The chatter of birdsong had been constant since they'd left the base.

'That chiming call. Korimako. A male. Bellbird they call it. Anthornis melanura.'

'Male?'

Whatu explained the subtle variations in the sounds of the cock and hen. How the song differed depending on the time of year, even time of the day. When a series of crystal-clear chimes sounded from a nearby tree a few minutes later, Cat was eager to show she'd been listening.

'Bellbird, right?'

Whatu stopped his horse and leaned forward in the saddle to look in the direction of the sound.

'Fraid not. She's a tui. Prosthemadera novaeseelandiae. White fellas used to call them parson birds. Here, use these.' He handed her a small pair of binoculars. 'You'll see why.'

The sight, when she had adjusted the focus to see with the glasses, made her gulp. The dark green-black metallic plumage was dazzling, but even more striking were the two tufts of pure white feather balls suspended from its neck. Just like a parson's collar.

'Cunning little buggers, tui,' Whatu continued. 'Mimic anything. They used to eat them in the old days. Or catch em, put em in cages an teach em to call greetings to people arriving at the pa.'

'A pa was a fortified village,' explained Jay.

They rode on, crossing an open ridge that dropped off steeply to one side before returning to the shielding shadows of the bush and descending into a gully.

Whatu kept up his fascinating commentary, impressing her with his knowledge of plants, from their reproductive attributes to medicinal uses.

The Latin flowed from the tattooed mouth with the same fluent authority as Maori names for trees like kamahi, kahikatea and totara.

'What university did you go to?'

The snigger was almost childlike.

'Stuff I know I heard from my father. He learnt it from *his* father.

Hokia ki nga maunga, kia purea koe e nga hau a Tawhirimatea.'

'Meaning?'

To Cat's surprise the answer came from Jay: 'Go to the mountains. That you may be cleansed by the winds of Tawhirimatea. The God of Storms.'

'Close enough,' said Whatu. 'Basically, means return to your roots to achieve self-knowledge before taking on the world. I tried to do it the other way round. Didn't work. So, I came back.'

Cat allowed her mare to fall back into line as she pondered the glimpse of spirituality from behind the rugged facade of Jay Duggan. They continued on in silence, as if words would break the spell. The dappled early evening light reflecting off the leaves like so many candles. The gentle shuffling of the horses' hooves gradually gave way to the sound of a waterfall. They dismounted at a clearing beside a stream flowing over rocks jutting from a steep bank. Jay and Whatu tethered their horses to branches and began climbing, using vines to pull themselves up. By the time Cat reached the top, the men were swimming in a clear pool above the waterfall. She felt sticky and unclean, so stripped down to her underwear and dived in.

The water was freezing so she didn't last long before getting out and stretching on a rock to dry in what was left of the sun. She closed her eyes, the rhythmic sound of the waterfall drowning out the thudding approach of rotor blades until she sensed a large shadow cross her face.

* * * *

'SIXTY SECONDS to target', the pilot announced through the headsets.

Kaufman nodded to himself at the familiar kick of adrenalin as he looked up from the topo map on his knees. Forest flashed beneath his feet in a tangled mass of hideouts and bolt holes in need of napalm. The chopper tilted and slowed as they approached a gap in the bush line, then banked to circle the clearing.

A slaphappy pile of buildings surrounded a circle of grass with a flagpole at the center. Spooked horses reared and sprinted round their corrals. The inhabitants of the shithole stood their ground, looking up and pointing or waving at the chopper like Santa was arriving with candy. Others came running out of buildings to join the show.

Kaufman pointed at a red, black and white rag limping from a flagpole, which had what looked like a hubcap stuck on the top.

'What's the flag?'

'Signifies something called tino rangatiratanga,' said Captain Falconer. 'Maori independence. Long story. Put her down over there by those stables, Phil.'

He gave final instructions as the chopper descended. Kaufman was to stay by the bird. At least they left him an M16.

'... and remember this is a Maori marae, gentlemen. You know the drill. Treat it with respect.'

As the soldiers fanned out in pairs towards the two main buildings, Kaufman stepped onto the landing strut. His eyes were drawn to the top of the flagpole. Not a hubcap. A homemade satellite dish.

He jumped onto the grass, yanking the charging handle of the rifle back as he stamped towards the pole. He blasted the satellite dish, the flag and the top third of the pole, stopping only when the magazine was spent.

21. A single shot

MATTHEW THREW up over the keyboard, the desk, his shirt. The screen of the laptop, which had been displaying a PDF on extradition arrangements between New Zealand and the States, pixilated then locked.

The kid recovered first, wriggling through the back window. Matthew's feet were bogged to the floor, his hands fused to the keyboard with regurgitated pasta. Through the open window he caught snatches of voices shouting over the uproar of the helicopter.

'... shootin at?

...dish on top of the flagpole...

...fuck you do that for?...

...ya bloody mind...

...sabotage Alo...'

The voices became clearer as the rotors were shut down. The New Zealand accents were surprised, angry. The American was calm, in control, and apparently talking into a phone.

'Tell me they're closing the site down... How long will that take? Ten minutes I can live with...'

Matthew knew losing the website could end any hope of accessing Henry's box.

The voices outside were arguing about the meaning of the bleedin flagpole. Something about *horny hecky*. He tried to isolate the sounds, forcing them into the background as if they were layers in a Photoshop image.

There had to be a way to get connected. Surely someone like Maipi who spent all day online wouldn't put all his eggs in a basket based on a petfood can and homemade dish. He looked at the kid's computer. Down the side below the ports was a Vodafone USB stick. Must be a dongle. Sellotaped to the back were the letters *kangarotekatoa* followed by *1234*. Hard to imagine a weaker security system, but then the kid was unlikely to be overrun by visitors this far from civilization.

Matthew stuck the dongle into one of the ports of the Macbook, entered the password and PIN, and navigated to the backdoor to the Vestco website. The only one Henry Beck never found. It had taken Matthew four months to open the initial door. All thanks to a dishonest employee who bypassed the firewall by plugging a modem into his or her computer and the other end into a telephone socket to download music tracks via another service provider. Henry had detected and eradicated the backdoor program and had the employee sacked, all within twenty-four hours. But not before Matthew set up dozens of other entry points. Over the next few weeks he marveled at the way Henry methodically searched and destroyed door after door until only one remained.

'Hey you.'

Matthew gagged, but there was nothing left to throw up. His chest was on fire. Shaking fingers hovered over the keyboard till he realized they'd found the kid. He forced himself to focus on the screen to find what he needed to download to recreate the critical part of the site.

'...go fuck yourself.'

The kid had balls. The voices were getting closer. Something smashed against the outside of the caravan.

'OK OK,' the kid was pleading. 'They're off on the horses. Heading that way, to the waterfall.'

'Lying little creep.'

The floor shook again as the kid was flung against the outside wall of the caravan

This time there was no response.

'He could be telling the truth sir,' said a New Zealand accent. 'I saw three horses in a clearing in that direction when we flew in.'

'Could have told me at the time.'

'Sorry sir. I wasn't sure who was in charge.'

'You know now. Let's go.'

'What about the boy?'

'He's not going anywhere in a hurry.'

The voices drifted off. The rotors of the helicopter rasped back into life. Matthew stared at the download bar, snailing slowly towards halfway.

* * * *

CAT STRUGGLED to stay in the saddle as the mare stampeded back along the trail. They'd rushed from the waterfall as soon as the helicopter passed. Gunfire a few minutes later from the direction of the base sent Jay and Whatu into another gear.

In the blink of an eye the forest mutated from a thing of beauty into a scene from a horror. Greens morphed to shadowy blacks and gray, illuminated here and there by sunbeams piercing the darkness like eerie searchlights. Tree trunks marched in a blur. Strangers in a mental asylum, their branches poking in accusation. The mare, uncertain now and needing to be coaxed to keep up, lurched and stumbled over jutting roots greasy with moss. Birdsong stood no chance against the pounding in Cat's chest.

How the hell did they know we were here? Matthew must have gone onto the Vestco website. Which means he might have the last clue. If he's still alive.

Up front, Whatu plunged through a stream and up a steep incline between two house-size boulders. As the mare cantered up to get better traction, Cat leaned forward, forcing her weight into the stirrups and clutching the mane to keep upright. The canopy thinned as they approached an open saddle. They broke from the bush and tore across.

The helicopter came from nowhere, the *chop-chop-chop* of its rotors shielded in the void beyond the bluff.

143

The mare shied, propping her front feet, twisting her body and taking three or four rapid steps sideways. Cat lost her balance, falling forward against the horse's neck, which she impulsively grabbed. She screamed as a figure swung onto the skid of the hovering chopper and drew a rifle towards his shoulder.

'Over here,' yelled Whatu, kicking his horse towards the edge.

Shots shattered the rock above his head as he disappeared over the lip. A sudden updraft tilted the chopper sideways as Jay charged after Whatu. The pilot corrected and the machine slow-motioned back to zero in on Cat. She tried to scream but her jaw locked.

Trekking horses are herd animals, programmed to take cues from those around them. Each has a place in the herd. Some are natural leaders. Some are more comfortable following. Upset the order and some will refuse to move. Others, like the mare, become flustered if separated from their mates. This personality trait saved her rider's life.

The horse jinked and bolted over the edge as bullets whizzed past Cat's ear. What appeared to be a sudden drop turned out to be an eroded shingle scree that fell away at a little over forty-five degrees for several yards before the bush line resumed. She clung to the mare's neck as it slid down on its front legs and backside, then catapulted into the bush in search of its mates. Cat found them hiding under an overhanging bank at the bottom of the gully. They could hear, but not see, the chopper prowling above the treetops.

'This is Captain Falconer of the Special Air Service. We've got you in the crosshairs. Stay where you are and put your hands above your heads.'

Cat obeyed the metallic voice immediately.

Jay looked up at the canopy, then across at Whatu.

'Reckon they're bluffin?'

'Have to be.'

'Lead the way.'

Whatu guided his horse round a fallen tree. Cat braced for the shot, but it didn't come. If anything, the chopper had moved further away. A few minutes later the trio were following an overgrown trail that seemed to run parallel to the one they'd been on.

Whatu's radio crackled into life.

'Kenana kainga to Kenana tahi.'

It was Beth back at the base. Whatu adjusted the volume and whispered into the mouthpiece. 'Sup?'

'Just had a visit from these army fellas. Headin your way in a chopper.'

'Fair dinkum? We'll keep our eyes open. Everything OK back there?'

'Maipi got roughed up a bit. Bastards blasted the shit outta his dish thing as well.'

Cat broke in: 'What about Matthew, is he OK?'

Whatu nodded at her. 'Where's the Pom?'

'Dunno. Guess he's still in there doin his computer shit.'

'We'll be there in a tick.'

The chopper was still somewhere above and behind, but out of sight. Jay insisted Cat ride in the middle. They rejoined the main trail just below the open ridge she remembered from the ride in. She held her breath and followed Whatu across, relieved to reach the safety of the bush on the other side.

A single shot rang out. She twisted in the saddle, just in time to see Jay hit the ground.

* * * *

THE LOOK on the face of the SAS commander was filthy. Kaufman returned the frown.

'You got a problem, Captain?'

'Our instructions were to capture these civilian suspects Mr Kaufman. Hand them over to the police to put on trial. Taking them out's supposed to be last resort, if any of our soldiers' lives are threatened. Tell me where shooting them in the back while they're riding away on horseback fits into those orders?'

'Clock's ticking Captain. And it's one hell of a big clock. Millions are gonna go belly-up without Alo. Ask them if they want time-out for some namby pamby trial.'

Kaufman looked at his cell phone. 20.45. Seven days to go. Multiple clocks were ticking. Alo. Eve. And Hansen. Until she came back, he was technically in charge. Better make the most of it.

The pilot's voice grated through the headset.

'What do you want to do, sir? I saw the horse fall.'

Captain Falconer looked at Kaufman for a response.

'Forget em for now. You heard the radio. Liddell's at the camp. Probably trying to crash the entire Alo system. Let's deal with him and wait for the others to arrive. Head north to make it look like we're going that way. Then loop back.'

HIDEOUS CURVED tusks jutted from the monster's jaws. Eyes death dark against the gleaming red of its head. Antennae needling forward as the back arched and the legs, raised in rows of spines and spurs, tensed for the strike.

Jay tried to back up, but his head was paralyzed.

A crack. Then a giant thumb and forefinger came into focus, tweezering the monster's armor-plated back and tossing it away. Again, the fingers. Valley lines on a palm, reaching for his throat. Fog on the sidelines.

'Y'right bro?'

Jay blinked.

The fog cleared, and he followed the hand to a tattooed face. Cat appeared over Whatu's shoulder.

'What in heck was that thing?'

'Just a weta. Devils of the night we call em. Not sure why, cos they're harmless. Been around since before dinosaurs.'

Jay held out his hand so Whatu could drag him to his feet.

Cat was tapping her chin, having a closer look at the insect that had been sitting on a branch just above where he lay after rolling from the fallen horse.

'Sure you're OK?'

Jay's head was one of those mortar bowls being dealt to with a pestle. His neck felt like it had been stuck in a vice and blood was oozing from a cut on his elbow.

'Good as gold.' He felt like a dickhead for falling off. The chopper had gone.

'We've got to get to Matthew before they do,' Cat said, climbing easily onto her mare and motioning for him to join her.

Jay staggered, but managed to climb up behind, wrapping his arms round her waist as she kicked the mare forward. Sunlight stabbed through a hole in the ceiling, forcing his eyes shut. When he opened them the edges of his vision were muddled. Where the hell was he?

Passing through a stand of rimu, regenerating younger trees, their weeping branches surrounding the rotting remains of a fallen giant. Flayed ponga tree ferns came sharply into view like a windmill of spears.

Another bolt of light and the haze was back.

He was on his mountain bike, pedaling like the clappers through bush on the South Island's West Coast. Towards the camp of McCully Industries, the timber and coal mining conglomerate logging ancient rimu. Exploiting an immoral loophole in the law. Jay was waiting for the last forest rapist to leave the camp for the weekend. Disabling the alarm. Smashing the window at the back of the office. Keys to every vehicle on a numbered board. Removing the oil filters. Cylinders of grinding powder. Dragging hoses. Opening valves to flood the site. Superglue into every lock.

About to squeeze the last drop into the filing cabinet in the manager's office. Stopping. Opening it. Reading the file. Details of a vast seam of coal on Mount Lees. Value estimated in the hundreds of millions. An attached timeline projected the application for a mining license at eight weeks.

It took Jay two days to come up with his plan and two weeks to carry it out. He was spotted in the area by geologists on his way back from moving the last batch. They couldn't prove anything, but he thought it best to leave the country till things quietened down.

He was celebrating his birthday at a hotel on the Kenyan island of Lamu when he heard the application for a mining permit was being challenged. A colony of endangered giant land snails – classified as nationally critical – had been discovered on the site. Funny, that.

Jay bummed around East Africa doing odd jobs. Mechanic for a British company taking people into the Serengeti. Tour guide leading groups up Mt Kilimanjaro via the Machame route.

The British company offered him a job in Papua New Guinea. Before long he was escorting eco-tourists up the Ajkwa River to stay with the Komoro tribe. He became incensed at the pollution of the river from a copper and gold mine high on the Jayawijaya Range. It was the sacred mountain of the Amungme people. What really got Jay's back up was a comment from the mine's chief executive that the environmental impact of lopping four hundred feet off the top of the mountain was like pissing in the Arafura Sea. Jay's friends from the Amungme tribe considered the mountain the head of their mother.

He planned an operation against the mine to coincide with a protest involving hundreds of tribespeople blockading the road to the site. It was the diversion. Jay went in and sabotaged the pipelines, making the river run clean for the first time in decades. On his way out he ran into a group from the radical Forest Liberation Front who had the same objective. They got talking. When they realized he'd achieved more by himself than they hoped to as a group with more resources and months of planning, they invited him to return with them to London. He was broke and would soon be a hunted man. Jail in Port Moresby didn't sound quite as appealing as London.

He met Aroha, a Kiwi lawyer for the Front, on his first day in the UK. Then came four years as a cell leader. Fighting the good fight from the forests of Afghanistan to the national parks of Irian Jaya. Each trip away from Aroha got harder. They just clicked. Both knew they'd found their soul mate. Everything was sweet. Till Peru.

Jay was to lead a small team of Lima-based activists against a natural gas project deep in the Amazon. Aroha had leave owing, so they decided to holiday together for two weeks before the mission. They wanted to avoid the crowds at Machu Picchu so took a multisport alternative tour, rafting the wild Apurimac, riding mountain horses and bikes along seldom used Inca roadways. The holiday ended. Someone pulled out of the mission at the last minute. There was a spare seat on the plane. Aroha begged. He caved in to those chocolate eyes.

They were in a raft heading towards their target in the remote Vilcabamba region. Drunk on love and the most amazing environment Jay had ever seen. Talking about going back to New Zealand. Planting a forest. Starting a family. Jay never heard the shot or saw her go over the side. It took him too long to find her, trapped underwater by an overhanging branch. Killed by his poor judgment and an unforgivable lapse in concentration.

From then on his heart was never in it. The Front started torching private homes in a campaign against urban development encroaching on forests. The firebombing of a forestry research lab was the last straw. Returning to New Zealand to plant a forest became more and more attractive, but he was broke again. So, when Millbrook headhunted him with an offer of ridiculous money, he accepted, calculating he'd give them two years and save enough to retire.

Jay imagined his forest – Aroha's memorial – would one day look like this... Except the trees would be black beech not red. Where the hell was he?

The whomping sound of a low-flying wood pigeon snapped him back to the present. He remembered. He'd been admiring Cat's bouncing butt when the shot spooked his horse. Couldn't afford another lapse like that. He eased the grip round Cat's waist as they pulled up near a ledge overlooking the horse trek base.

The camouflaged Iroquois squatted like a bloated dragonfly as the soldiers went from building to building. Sand berets. SAS.

Jay borrowed Whatu's binoculars and focused on the bald civilian who seemed to be in charge. The soldiers were concentrating their search on the houses. Jay swung the lenses across the compound to the caravan. It was partly obscured by the dented fuel tanks perched on wooden platforms.

'Wait here out of sight you two. Be ready to move quickly.'

Cat started to protest, but Jay held up his hand.

'Time's up Doctor Tayler. Just do as I say.'

22. Under our bloody noses

PETERSEN UNDERSTOOD the importance of images to television and social media.

Throw in the President of the United States, the countdown to the release and some manufactured tension over the security of the seed lots, and blanket coverage of the event was inevitable.

Cameramen and photographers dolled up in sterile suits and working under a pooling system had been allowed into the lab earlier to film the premium lots of seeds being inserted into sealed vials. Petersen's decision to allow a videographer from *Grassroots Intelligence* into the facility had won Vestco praise in an editorial piece in that morning's *LA Times*. *Transparent* and *gracious* they called it.

Now the President, standing on a raised platform beside the Chinese Premier, was smiling at the swarm of cameras as they jointly pushed a button to raise the barrier arm, sending the first consignment away from the secure environment of the laboratory that had been built to replace the one destroyed in the fire a year ago.

From there the seeds were being driven under heavily armed escort to Edwards Air Force Base to await their flight to Beijing. Chinese J-11 Shuangzuo and American F-16 fighter jets passed overhead in a powerful and totally unnecessary show of strength and the brotherhood of nations.

As the Chinese Premier was ushered from the platform, the tech crew began dismantling the Great Wall section of the giant montage to reveal a Taj Mahal backdrop for the Indian Prime Minister who was up next.

Petersen nodded as the President's Chief of Staff approached.

'Everything alright?'

'Sure sure.'

'Sorry for keeping the President out so late.'

'You kidding? I'm told this is the biggest audience in the history of Chinese television. Add that to the hundreds of millions in India in a few minutes. What politician would turn down a TV audience of one point six billion? Not to mention social media, the gazillions of Americans who'll see our man as the ultimate international statesman over their breakfast cereal. Should be worth two or three points.'

The aide steered Petersen away from the pack of journalists.

'About this little issue down in New Zealand. I'm sure I could get the President to lean on their Prime Minister to allow a Special Forces unit into the country. We could dress it up as a formal request from New Zealand, so the good folk down there don't get touchy about some foreign invasion. The New Zealanders won't object. Hell, they want this sideshow sorted as much as we do.'

'Appreciate the offer. But my man on the ground assures me he's got everything under control. A Special Forces unit would give more attention to the sideshow than it warrants.'

'Your call. Offer stands though. Say the word and I'll put things in motion. And thanks again for this. You sure I can't lure you to the White House? The President was impressed with what you achieved in those elections in New Jersey and Virginia.'

'Appreciate the offer Al. I'm happy where I am for the time being.'

They shook hands, and the aide strutted back towards the masquerade. If he only knew.

* * * *

'HE'S NOT here sir. We've searched every building.'

Kaufman looked across at the pack of flea-bitten dregs the SAS soldiers found hiding in the shacks and outhouses. They were lined up beside what was left of the flagpole. He walked towards them.

'Liddell's here somewhere Captain. One of these low-lifes knows exactly where he is.'

Most of the brown faces glared back in defiance. A couple looked ready to crap themselves, if they hadn't already. Kaufman stared at one after another until he saw what he was looking for. A raisined old witch, sinister black tattoos on her chin, glanced nervously to her right. He followed her line of sight. All he could see was a fuel tank, bush, a rusty hunk of scrap and more bush.

He stepped over the remains of the satellite dish and stood beside the flagpole.

Facing back towards the fuel tank, he scanned the surroundings, slowly rotating his head. Light reflected off a metallic object high in a tree to the right of the tank. A red cable snaked round branches and down the trunk towards the hunk of scrap, which he now saw had an axle at its base. Some sort of vehicle perhaps.

His cell phone pulsed. He took the call, keeping his eye on the spot beside the fuel tank. It was Petersen, telling him about the offer of Special Forces.

'You're right. That won't be necessary. Any word on the other men I mentioned?'

'Both have been located and should arrive within forty-eight hours. The Israeli took a while to track down. Pushed a very hard bargain. Better be worth it.'

'He is.'

'And we're announcing a one-million-dollar reward for information on the terrorists. That oughta smoke em out.'

Kaufman hadn't taken his eyes off the hunk of scrap.

'I don't think that'll be necessary either. If you'll excuse me, I've got something to take care of here. I'll call you in a few minutes with some good news.'

He cocked the M16 and advanced towards his quarry.

* * * *

CAT FOCUSED the binoculars on the bald man.

The phone call distracted him, but now he was moving towards the caravan again.

Matthew had to be warned. She opened her mouth to shout, but her voice was swamped by an explosion that jolted the caravan several feet into the air.

* * * *

MATTHEW WAS catapulted into the ceiling above the bed, along with the chair, the laptop and shelves of pasta.

A moment of weightlessness before he was lost in a stinging, suffocating, stinking void. Floating between up and down. Arms grabbing, lifting, dragging. Something sharp jabbing his stomach. A flickering light. Autumn. A child carrying a teddy bear. Then the chilling realization – the instant before passing out – that he was being taken deep into the woods to be shot.

* * * *

CAT REACHED for her blouse to wipe the tears and realized she was still in her bra and knickers.

The air reeked of smoke and burning fuel and the whinnying of terrified animals. Flames skipped from the roof of the stables. Figures rushed to rescue animals trapped inside. Others were waving their hands in the air or running round like headless chickens. The soldiers had regrouped after the explosion and were moving tentatively towards the overturned caravan. Sirens could be heard approaching from the road.

It didn't matter anymore.

'Mind if I have a look?'

The voice startled her. She'd forgotten about Whatu.

She threw the binoculars at his feet and stalked off.

'The hell d'ya think ya goin?'

'To give myself up.'

'Whatya wanna do that for?'

Emotion overwhelmed her. And anger. At Whatu. At Jay. Most of all at herself.

'It's all over. This whole mess. It's insane. Matthew's dead. Jay as well for all we know.'

'Bugger all chance of that with you yakking loud enough to wake the dead.'

It took a moment for Cat to register the voice, as Jay staggered onto the ledge with Matthew slumped over his shoulder.

'Dammit Jay. What in heck have you done to him?'

'Nice to see you again too,' he croaked, sounding hurt. 'Our geek's got a bump on the head's all. Be a bit drowsy for a while. Should be good as gold.'

'Drowsy? He's unconscious. We shouldn't be moving him.'

'Crikey Cat. You might fancy gettin shot at again. I'll pass. We've gotta hit the road. Hey pronto.'

'It's hopeless Jay. There's only one road and its blocked.'

Whatu stepped forward.

'There's a trail about half a mile through there. Joins up with the walking track along the Ngamoko Ridge. Comes out near Kaitawa at the southern end of the lake. It's your best bet. Specially now she's gettin dark. Take the horses.'

'Thanks mate. Owe you one.' Jay handed Matthew to him like a blackened sack of flour and jumped onto Whatu's horse. 'Toss the geek up here. Unless the good doctor wants to lug him with her.'

Whatu half lifted, half pushed the limp body of Matthew until it lay across the saddle in front of Jay. Matthew moaned, lifted his head, then flopped against the horse's back.'

'See? He's right as rain. Let's hoof it.'

'This is insane,' Cat protested, walking to the other horse.

Jay tossed a cigarette lighter to Whatu.

'Sorry bout your tank mate.'

'How'dya blow it?'

Jay chuckled.

'If I told ya, I'd have to kill ya. Let's just say it involved a tray under

154

the outlet pipe, a rag and a beer bottle.'

'Cunning bastard.'

'And sorry for dropping you in it Whatu.'

'I'll give yous ten minutes to reach that track. Then I'll go down and spin some cock 'n bull yarn about you knocking me out an pinchin the horses. Haere ra, my friend. Pleasure to meet ya, Cat.'

* * * *

THE SAS soldier climbed out through the door of the overturned caravan and Kaufman could tell from his face the news was not good.

'No-one in there, sir. But I found this.' He held up a laptop, its lid buckled and screen cracked.

'Search the bush around here. Little prick can't have gone far.'

They found signs of tracks, but the ground was so dry the marks could have been left by animals.

'Excuse me sir.'

Kaufman turned to see the pilot with a fistful of wires.

'Chopper's out of action sir. Someone's cut through a chunk of electrical wires right under our bloody noses.'

Duggan.

Kaufman ignored the shaking heads and what-do-we-do-now looks as he walked towards a pile of firewood. He snatched at an axe and took out his frustration on what was left of the fucking flagpole.

23. A thing called a backup

CAT PUT the curling tongs down and used her fingers to gently shake out her hair, now dyed black.

A bath in green tea and lime leaf salts followed by four hours sleep on a pillow-top mattress and wool overlay had soothed the aches and scratches, bringing a hint of color back to a face that was an anemic mess when they arrived at the farmhouse in the middle of the night.

She recalled little of the trip after leaving the horses at the end of the trail. Jay stole a pickup – a ute he called it – and drove without lights through a bewildering patchwork of forestry roads and farm tracks, with Cat on the open deck cradling Matthew's head. He was asleep now in the bed behind her. They still didn't know if he had the final clue.

Letters and receipts in a desk in the living room showed the house belonged to a Major Eric Thorne-George and his wife Diane, due home later that day from a vacation on Australia's Gold Coast. Photographs on the mantelpiece suggested the major had retired from the army.

Cat squirted some hairspray, using her free hand to scrunch the curls to keep them in place. She opened the heirloom closet and chose a floral dress to go with the horn-rimmed glasses from Whatu's wife.

* * * *

WHEN MATTHEW opened his eyes he knew he'd died and gone upstairs.

Her butt was a firm nine-point-five bordering on ten. Miss Great bleedin Britain. In his room. Getting her kit off. First the skirt, a wriggle of the butt, down to the knickers. Then the top. Button by button. Peel off the shoulder. Bra straps. Fingers through the hair. Adjust the glasses. What's goin on there, darlin? *Bit retro.*

As she turned to face him and Matthew realized who it was, he shut his eyes. And waited. *Out to it.* Cat said nothing. He waited some more, then eased one set of lids apart. She had her back to him again, but was putting clothes *on* rather than doing the full Monty. He waited till there was nothing more to see, then stretched his arms, gave an exaggerated yawn and lifted his head from the pillow.

'Matthew! About time. Jay, he's awake.'

The back of Matthew's head was screaming for a handful of aspirin. 'Where am I?'

'On a farm. Somewhere near Napier. Jay knows. How do you feel?'

'Like I've been duffed up something fierce.'

'I'm not surprised. That horse ride was rough enough in a saddle. The pickup was a nightmare the way Jay came. You drifted in and out of consciousness. Muttering something about Johann's backdoor. Kept you as still as I could. Some of the bumps. Just couldn't see them coming in the dark.'

Jay appeared at the door the same time as the smell of fried onions. 'Grub's up, if you can stomach it.'

Matthew was peckish. His ribs gave him grief as Cat helped him out of the bed. When he stood he was surprised his legs were steady. The dining room had Boy Scout symbol wallpaper, oatmeal carpet and a stucco plaster ceiling with a gaudy chandelier.

Matthew was using bread to mop up the remains of the fry-up of sausages, eggs, onion and grilled tomatoes when he noticed Cat staring at him, fingers drumming her chin, pen primed in her other hand over a notepad.

'What?'

'Did you get it? The clue?'

'Course I did. *Keep following the rush before the queen young man, and check the home of Johann's footsteps.* Thirteen letters.'

Cat got him to repeat it slowly as she wrote it down.

'OK. First, Johann must be Johann Miescher, the guy who discovered nucleic acids. The molecular substrate of the genetic code. You know, DNA. That would fit with the genetics theme from the other clues. Second, I've got a feeling Miescher was Swiss. Or was he Austrian? Should be easy to check. Find out where he lived. What about your part of the clue Matt? Any ideas?'

'It's Matthew. Not really. There was this geezer at university. Everyone called him the Queen.'

'Makes sense,' said Cat, scribbling on the pad.

'Yeah. But cracking the password might be the least of our worries,' said Matthew. 'Bastards shut down the Vestco website.'

'Meaning?'

'They've worked out what we're up to. Must know about the media log in. Couldn't stop us using it, so they've nuked the whole bleedin site.'

'Where does that leave us?'

'Up the spout as far as entering the last password goes.'

'So why are you smiling?'

'I downloaded what we need to recreate the important part of the site.'

'Hate to break it to ya mate,' said Jay, 'but that caravan and any computers inside it – including your laptop – are toast.'

'That's why, me old china, we have a thing called a backup. I copied the file to a CD while Rambo was looking for you in the helicopter.'

'And this disk is where?'

'Pocket of me jacket.'

'Jay, I threw the jacket in the trash can out by the back door.'

He went outside to retrieve it.

'Why use a CD, Matthew? Wouldn't it have been simpler, and a heck of a lot more convenient, to back it up to the cloud?'

'I had to use a public wifi network. Encryption on those things is notoriously weak. Data would have been too vulnerable during the upload. Piece of cake for Vestco to hack and destroy. Low tech was the safest bet.'

'Would never have thought of that.'

Jay returned balancing a smoke-blackened CD on the end of his index finger.

'So you're telling us the fate of Alo, not to mention any chance we have of getting to the bottom of this mess, rests on this flimsy hunk of aluminum and plastic?'

Matthew nodded.

'Reckon another one of ya backups might be in order mate.'

'But there's no computer in the house.'

* * * *

JAY PEERED through the binoculars. Tip Top ice cream. Hot pies. Sandwiches. Filled rolls. New release DVDs $2. A blue, red and white hotchpotch like any suburban corner store in the country.

Other than plumes of smoke rising from fires north of the city, the scene was typical Tuesday morning. A mother pushing a child in a buggy. Pensioners complaining about the heat.

You could smell the tar seal melting on the road. He adjusted the *Farmers Always Know the Ground Rules* cap, put on the glasses with the seventies flip-up tinted lenses and stepped out of the shadows. The walking-stick clacked as he shuffled across the street. Back bent. Legs bowed.

The shelves were packed with brands that transported Jay back to his childhood. He filled a plastic basket with Sanitarium weet-bix, Watties baked beans, Griffins snax, Purex loo paper and a copy of *Hawkes Bay Today* as he waited for the shopkeeper to serve another customer. He cleared his throat and approached the counter.

'Looks like another hot one today,' he said, adding scratch to his voice.

The shopkeeper, an Indian migrant in a red dastar, smiled as he took the items out of the basket and rung them up on the till.

'That will be fourteen twenty please.'

'And I don't suppose you sell blank computer disks?'

'CD or DVD?'

Matthew hadn't said anything about that. Jay took a stab.

'The first one.'

'Sony or Verbatim?'

'Better make it one of each.'

* * * *

THE STANDING room only turnout at the Holy Trinity Cathedral in Auckland was no surprise to Hansen.

Deaths in the line of duty were thankfully rare in New Zealand, and the size of the country's police force meant everyone knew everyone. She was sitting in the third row from the front, waiting for the service to start.

'What I don't understand,' whispered the detective beside her, 'is why they bothered shooting him after breaking his neck. If they were in a hurry to get away. Autopsy showed he was almost certainly dead when the bullet entered his head.'

'Duggan wouldn't have known that. Probably wanted to make sure.'

'And where did he get the piece? They'd just stepped off a plane from the most security conscious country in the world. Doesn't add up. Nothing in Jay Duggan's history suggests violence. Quite the opposite. And *he* wasn't the one being fingered for the murder in LA. So why kill a cop? Twice!'

'There's a lot we don't know about Duggan,' Hansen said, thinking back to her first conversation with Kaufman.

She looked across at the impressive stained-glass windows with their colorful Polynesian designs.

'Assume you've heard about this *Jaywalker.kiwi* blog claiming the sun shines out of Duggan's arse?'

'No. Is it something I need to worry about?'

'According to the *Herald* this morning it's been getting a lot of hits, comments.'

'Can we keep tabs on it, find out who's behind it?'

'Can't be that hard to find out. Leave it with me.'

Hansen's cell phone pulsed. Her second-in-command would only be calling if it was important. She leant down behind the pew in front, concealing the phone as best she could.

'Yeah?'

'Duggan's been seen in a shop in Napier. Got a call to the hotline from the shopkeeper.'

'Who've we got down there?'

'None of our guys. They're still tidying up after Waikaremoana. There's a CIB unit in Napier. SAS are on their way. Armed Offenders' Squads too. And your American friend was heading down that way last night.'

'Kaufman?'

'Don't think he was very impressed with the hospitality being offered in Waikaremoana.'

'Right. Arrange for a car to pick me up as soon as the funeral's over. Get me on the next flight to Napier.'

She tossed up whether to tell Kaufman. She'd been briefed on the fiasco at the horse trek base, ending with the crazed attack on the flagpole. Pretty ironic given the place of flagpole attacks in New Zealand history. Kaufman wasn't to know that.

Bells started to toll as the family of the slain officer began filing into the church. She dialed Kaufman and passed on the information.

'Appreciate the tip-off Inspector. Liddell's downloaded some incredibly sensitive material from the Vestco website. The corporation has arranged a small reward for information. Should get the phones ringing.'

Hansen wondered what he meant by *small*. She was about to tell him it might encourage false calls when a tap on the shoulder told her the funeral service was beginning.

24. Mrs Senior Net

GRANDPA JAY took a bus into the center of the city, slinking off at Tennyson Street near the Municipal Theater with its la-di-da Egyptian columns and door lintels.

Tourists might fancy these art deco buildings stuck up after the earthquake in the 1930s. To Jay they looked out of place, a tarted-up reminder of colonialism. He turned into Dalton Street beside the concrete jungle Public Trust Building, and found The Cybermouse Cafe.

He was directed to a terminal and took out the paper with instructions from Matthew. The blackened CD from Waikaremoana loaded on the second attempt, but he was unsure what to do next. A loud bead of sweat tiptoed from his forehead to his nose. He wiped it and rattled the cap.

'Shit.'

'Having trouble love?'

The woman beside him was late sixties, with thin white hair, red-blotched cheeks and a community smile.

Jay remembered he was dressed a similar age.

Scratchy voice.

'I'm trying to copy this fandangled thing for my grandson.'

Mrs Senior Net talked him through the process of saving the file to the desktop, ejecting the CD, inserting the blank.

'Then you save your copy onto there and click *burn*.'

'Thanks. That's got it.'

'You're welcome.'

He paid and left, heading for the post box in a pedestrian mall round the corner. He slipped the copied disk into the envelope he'd addressed and stamped back at the farmhouse and poked it through the slot. Laid-back as you like. A local guidebook said buses left from the corner of Dickens and Dalton. Grandpa doddered off. Walking stick pattering. Head down through the throngs of sandals and toe polish, ankle socks and trainers.

* * * *

THREE WEEKS out of police college and already Constable Graeme Wilson felt like-a-glove in the stab resistant vest many older colleagues griped about having to wear.

He straightened his cap and set off on his beat along Dalton Street. A photo of an old codger using a phone in an advertisement on the wall of the Telecom Shop reminded him of the radio bulletin describing the appearance of the terrorist spotted at a store in the suburbs.

So he got the shock of his short career when he turned the corner into Dickens and bumped into the suspect. Literally. The old man's walking stick was jarred to the sidewalk. Constable Wilson had the guy on his back in a flash, pinned to the ground with a knee on his chest. As he fumbled with his cuffs, Duggan raised his hands together in submission. Conscious of the gathering crowd, and murmurs of *shame* and *go easy on the old bloke*, the constable clipped the cuffs onto each hand, even though he knew they were supposed to be attached behind the back.

As he pulled Duggan to his feet, the cap was dislodged, revealing a mop of yellow-blond hair. The word *terrorist* was uttered. Suddenly everyone was cheering.

Constable Wilson radioed in to report the capture.

'*Need backup?*'

Duggan showed no sign of resisting. He knew he'd met his match. 'Negative. All under control. Bringing him in.'

'Good work constable. Take him to Onekawa. Lockup's more secure over there. I'll radio ahead. Got our hands full here at central dealing with these fires without some bloody celebrity circus.'

This was the sort of break you dreamed about in police college. Constable Wilson paused to wallow in the adulation, even bowing to his fans before marching the dangerous international terrorist to the patrol car. Another cheer went up as the terrorist was shoved a little harder than necessary into the back seat. Constable Wilson doffed his cap to the appreciative crowd, got in the driver's seat and switched on the siren. For icing.

* * * *

KAUFMAN COULD never work in a place like this. The whiffy burrow out back of the store was a soup sandwich of papers and magazines, cartons and jars up to here, and a spaghetti of cords and plugs.

The gook's breath reeked of fish as he repeated in broken English the description of Duggan to the detective who arrived the same time as Kaufman.

The radio on the cop's hip came to life, relaying the message that Duggan had been picked up in the central business district and was being driven to Onekawa Station.

'Which way will they go?' Kaufman tried not to sound too interested.

'It's a station in an industrial estate on Austin Street. Most direct route's along Taradale Road.'

Kaufman headed for the door.

'Everything's under control sir.'

'I'll believe that when I see Duggan's corpse.'

25. Our own branding

RENT-A-CROWD. Cat leered at the television and the beaming Californians cheering the arrival of the first truck at the gates of Edwards Air Force Base.

Mass-produced placards bleated *Nourish, Sustain, Cherish* and *Together we're making starvation history*. They didn't even bother concealing the Vestco logo. Green T-shirts and face paint to show how much they all really cared for the environment. More balloons and stars and stripes than a Republican convention. A good proportion of Asian and African Americans, she noticed.

The camera panned across this sea of contrived jubilation to the fawning reporter, struggling to be heard over the din.

'*...scenes unprecedented in peacetime. As you can see behind me, Californians have come out in their hundreds of thousands to farewell the first shipment of seeds, to play their part in history.*'

Aerial shots of the convoy, a smiling President, a lone protester in a white boiler suit trying to hide behind a hand-painted *Weed Not Seed* sign rolled across the screen, followed by close-ups of seed containers as the voiceover continued.

'*... designed secure containers made from recyclable plastic...*'

'How gullible can these reporters be?'

Images from a camera over a driver's shoulder showed the first truck turning into a hanger and pulling up beside a gaping ramp at the back of an aircraft. A yellow forklift glided towards the truck, already ringed by soldiers in camouflage uniforms, rifles facing outwards.

'... *into the C-130Js for flights to every continent. The first shipment, to India, is scheduled to touch down in New Delhi within twenty-four hours.*'

'And kiss goodbye to all that fancy security the moment they reach the Third World with their corruption and phony degrees.'

Matthew looked up from a map. 'That's not very politically correct, Doctor. I thought Vestco and your Uncle Sam were the bad geezers here.'

'At least they take security seriously.'

The news returned to the New Zealand studio. Beside the anchor's shoulder was a graphic showing three silhouette figures inside a ticking clock.

'Got our own branding now I see,' said Matthew.

'Shhh..'

'... *has announced a million-dollar reward for information leading to the capture of the three terrorists still at large in New Zealand.*'

'Bleedin cheek. I'm worth at least two - '

'Will you shuddup!'

'... *sighting was near the southeastern tip of Lake Waikaremoana late yesterday...*'

Armed police were shown turning away cars at one of the entrances to the national park.

'*The police have repeated the warning that the terrorists are extremely dangerous and should not be approached. Anyone with information is asked to call the manhunt hotline.*'

An 0800 number appeared on the screen.

The transition back to the studio caught the anchor off guard as she was reading a piece of paper.

'*In breaking news, we have an unconfirmed report one of the terrorists is in police custody in Napier. Perhaps New Zealand is about to get another millionaire. We'll bring you more details in our bulletin at midday.*'

'Jay!' Cat shrieked. 'No. No.'

Matthew was at her side, raising his arms to her shoulders.

She shoved him away.

'No! Not Jay.'

She brought her hands up to cover her face as the screams trailed to sobs.

'Probably a trick,' Matthew was saying. 'Bait to lure us in...'

'How can it be a trick? You heard it. Napier. They weren't supposed to know he's anywhere near Napier.'

'If they've got superman, they've got the disk. It's curtains.'

26. Déjà vu

JAY HAD been in this situation before. Handcuffed in the back of a police car. Brazil. Last year.

An in-and-out hit against a Vestco facility in the heart of the Amazon, where thousands of square miles of rainforest were being destroyed to plant genetically modified soybeans. Police and Vestco security guards were waiting in ambush in the silos. Must have been tipped off.

Jay was taken to the police station in the nearby city of Santarem. Thrown into a cell to wait for the local police chief, who was at some wedding. Three hours weighing up the chances of surviving twenty years in a Brazilian jail before discovering the door to the cell had been left unlocked. Others in his situation might have put it down to a lucky break. Jay didn't. Nor did he find out who tipped them off. The only person back in LA who was supposed to know about the hit was Deaver, the Millbrook CEO.

Déjà vu. Another police car. Heading for another cell. Handcuffed again. Heat almost as stifling. Siren sneering. Static on the police radio. Chatter about the spread of wildfires.

Jay could see three distant columns of smoke tacking into a darkening cloud hundreds of feet into the air. The young constable was looking too, see-sawing to get a better view. Jay's eyes moved from the back of the young cop's head to the cuffs chafing his wrists.

The car slowed a gear as it neared a roundabout. Jay eased forward till he had enough play on the seatbelt, and as the car rounded the traffic island he swung up and to his right, smashing the metal cuff into the side of the constable's head.

Hands knee-jerked off the steering wheel, sending the car into a skid. It hit the verge and flipped, rolling twice before landing on its roof against a paling fence. Siren still sounding off.

Fine fragments of dust choked the inside of the car. The constable was coughing about his leg. Jay managed to unclip the seatbelt that had probably saved his life, kick out the window and crawl out. He scrambled over the fence and tore down an alley between a furniture warehouse and engineering factory, dropping anchor in the shadows at the sound of squealing tires.

Through a gap in the fence, he saw a white Holden park beside the overturned patrol car. A man got out. Same bald guy he'd seen at Waikaremoana. Must be a plain-clothes detective. The man hustled to the driver's door. Wearing gloves, which was odd in this heat.

* * * *

KAUFMAN KNELT beside the driver's window. The young officer was conscious, but wedged.

There was no one else in the car, no sign of Duggan. Other vehicles were pulling over beyond the roundabout. A couple of guys were walking towards him, uncertain how close to come.

'Stay back. I'm a detective,' Kaufman yelled. 'This is a crime scene.'

The driver coughed.

'My leg. Think she's busted.'

'Have you called for backup?'

'Can't reach.'

His right arm was jammed between the smashed-in door and the airbag protruding from the buckled steering wheel. The impact had pushed the upper part of his body sideways and his left arm was stuck under his thigh.

'Keep still officer. I'll call in for you.'

He reached across for the radio handset.

'What's your name, son?'

'Graeme. Constable Graeme Wilson.'

'What's our location here?'

'Ah... Taradale Road. Near the roundabout.'

Kaufman pushed the transmission button. 'We've got an officer down at Taradale roundabout. Near the roundabout. Repeat, officer down. Constable Wilson. We need back up. And an ambulance. He's injured pretty bad. Think his neck might be broken.'

'What the...'

They were his last words as Kaufman clutched the officer's head with both arms and yanked the jaw up and over the shoulder, snapping the windpipe.

27. Tiny ray of compassion

CAT WAS slumped in a La-Z-Boy chair while Matthew paced the room bleating about ways to give himself up without getting his brains blown out.

'How bout we call the media before we ring the coppers? Can't shoot us in front of bleedin cameras.'

'Whatever.' Cat was past caring. She was gazing through the lace-curtain sheers, hungry for distraction in the antics of a black and white dog herding sheep onto a truck two fields across. The television was still on in the background. Some crap American reality show.

'Can you turn that thing off?'

'News is on soon.'

She looked back out the window. The dog was a machine.

The lead story was about the overwhelming gathering at the funeral of the slain cop in Auckland. The grieving wife, the Prime Minister reading the eulogy, rows and rows of blue uniforms watching on a big screen outside the church. Then the casket. The blue policeman's cap sitting on top, beside a doll from the six-year-old daughter too distraught to attend the service. Cat used her sleeve to wipe away the tear scolding her cheek.

Then came a story about the arrests of Whatu and his son. The young man's banged up face was barely recognizable as he was led into a police van. They didn't even show Whatu, who the reporter said had been shot in the arm trying to escape.

'That's it,' Matthew announced. 'I'm ringing the reporters.'

'Shhh...'

The silhouette and ticking clock graphic appeared beside the shoulder of the newsreader.

'News has just come in of a shocking new development. We're crossing live to Neville Kemp in Napier.'

The reporter was surrounded by a crowd restrained by a section of yellow tape.

Officers in white boiler suits and fluoro vests were crawling over the wreck of a patrol car in the background. Parts of the overturned vehicle were concealed behind a white canvas screen.

'... rolled several times before coming to rest against a fence. It seems the officer, who hasn't yet been identified, broke his neck on impact. The car was being used to transport Jay Duggan, the New Zealand-born terrorist wanted for the murder of Constable Mark Shaw. Duggan had been apprehended in Napier minutes earlier.'

The television screen divided in two as the reporter was interviewed by the anchor.

'Any word on the condition of Duggan?'

'Not as yet. Standard procedure is to transport prisoners in the rear of a patrol car with their hands cuffed behind their back. The police aren't commenting on what has happened to Duggan. A cordon was put up around the car soon after the crash.'

'Doesn't sound good for Duggan...'

'Well no. I have to say most of the police activity is focused around that back seat area. And they're all forensic rather than medical people. We may be talking two deceased here.'

Cat gagged as the muscles in her chest, neck and shoulders knotted and a tingling spread down her left arm.

'... video clip, amateur footage from a mobile phone sent to Grassroots Intelligence minutes after the crash, which I've got to warn you is pretty graphic...'

The quivering video showed the car on its roof, siren blaring, then panned to the back of a bald-headed man kneeling by the front window, cradling what appeared to be the driver's head in his arms.

'First on the scene was Bradley Kaufman, head of security for Vestco who is in New Zealand helping the authorities hunt down the three eco-terrorists. We're told

Mr Kaufman managed to keep the officer alive until an ambulance arrived, but he died soon after.'

Cat wheezed. The image of the cradled head glimmered like a tiny ray of compassion in the thick of the grief and terror and darkness. Another tear rolled down the side of her face. This time she let it reach her neck, barely registering the slamming of a vehicle door outside.

28. Hardly rocket science

MATTHEW NOSED over to the window. A *Furniture Direct* truck was in the driveway.

Coppers don't drive round in furniture lorries, he thought, as the front door slammed, and footsteps bulldozed along the hall. Had to be the psycho from the airport. He shielded himself behind Cat's chair and stuck his hands in the air.

'We're in here. Unarmed.'

The door opened.

Jay walked in. Blood scabbed round a cut above one eye. His shirt was shredded, and he was wearing handcuffs. Cat jumped out of the chair like she'd won the National Lottery. Matthew extended his arms even higher to make it look as if he was stretching.

'I was held up,' Jay said before either of them could ask the obvious.

'But the car,' said Cat. 'That poor cop. And you. I thought you were – '

'Fill you in later. Once I get these bracelets off.'

They followed him across a yard to a workshop. Inside were racks of gardening tools, pesticide spray backpacks, tins of paint, a lawnmower, golf clubs, dartboard. Lengths of timber were stacked in the rafters. A workbench took up most of the rear wall, under a board clogged with tools, and nails and screws in upturned jars. Power tools were arranged on a shelf under the workbench.

'That angle grinder, mate. Green handle. Should do the trick.'

Matthew plugged it in as Jay laid his hands on the bench and explained the best way to cut through the link between the two cuffs.

'Perhaps we should leave them on,' said Cat. 'Give the bad guys a sporting chance.'

Matthew tilted the blade into position.

'What happened to that cop in the car?'

'Had to make it crash. Only way I could escape.'

'For heck's sake Jay, you killed him.'

'What ya talking about?'

Cat's answer was drowned by the high-pitched whine of the grinder.

'The policeman's dead,' she said when the cuffs were off. 'On the news. His neck was broken.'

'Bullshit. His leg looked a bit crook. Nothing wrong with his neck. Or head. He was yakking away to me.'

'But that guy from Vestco, the Kaufman guy. He only just managed to keep him alive until - '

'Explains it,' said Jay, rubbing his wrists. 'Mr Kaufman and our friend who gate-crashed the interview at the airport are one and the same.'

'But he was blond. And Eng - '

'Seems you're not the only dab hand at disguise, Cat.'

'We're going to the police this time. Right?'

'They'll never believe us. And with the clout behind Vestco, he'll be able to cover his tracks easily. No-one's coming to bail us out. We're on our own.'

'Hear about Whatu and his son?'

'No.'

'Both arrested. Whatu shot in the arm. Boy beaten up bad.'

Jay turned and shot daggers.

'Why the hell didn't you wait till we got back to go online? You knew they'd get a fix on the location.'

'Wasn't my doing. Kid had this program, from a DDoS. We hit that site with over a hundred thousand computers from here to Timbuktu. Had to be a flaw in the program for the coppers to narrow it down so fast. Or the kid was stringing us along about the number of zombies.'

'For heck's sake Matthew. You put everything at risk. I mean they could have been killed. Not to mention ruining our best shot at finding out what's in the box.'

Matthew couldn't believe this. After everything he'd gone through, they were making out like *he* was the villain.

'You can stick your bleedin box.'

'That's rich coming from you. If you'd applied yourself - '

'Settle down you two.' Jay was holding up both hands. 'This is as much my fault as anyone's. Cops must have my address book. It'll have Whatu's details in it. We're not gettin anywhere pointing the bone at each other. Eye on the prize. How you guys goin with your clues?'

'We both need to get online,' said Cat.

'What's the story with the disk? asked Matthew. 'Was it corrupted?'

'Seemed OK.'

'So where is it now?'

Jay reached for his pocket.

'Bugger me days. Must have fallen out when the car rolled.'

'The cops will have it.'

'Won't do them much good. Got bunged up when I was tackled by the constable.'

Matthew couldn't believe it.

'So, we're right up the bleedin spout.'

'Not quite. I made your copy. Posted it to Ross on the West Coast of the South Island.'

'Oh my heck Jay. That's miles away.'

'It was the safest place I could think of. Wasn't expecting to lose the original.'

'And if they've got your address book, they'll know about Ross.'

'Name and address wouldn't be in there. Know it like the back of me hand.'

'But think of it. They'll have every known acquaintance sorted out by now.'

'Doubt it. Only been to Ross once in the last twelve, fifteen years.'

'So first we can email Ross. Second we get the CD sent back.'

'Email? Crikey. There isn't even a phone.'

'What is it with this bleedin country? It's like we're in a time warp.'

'What about a friend?' asked Cat. 'Neighbor?'

'Only one. Lives over the back fence. Can't be bothered with phones either.'

'How bout we send another letter, asking for the CD back.'

'Take too long. Three, four days. Least that long to get back. And where would we get it sent to? Less you're planning on twiddling your thumbs round here for a week?'

'Haven't got a week. Alo releases in six days.'

'She's hardly rocket science then. Gotta get down south.'

'And away from this place,' said Cat. 'Owners are back in a couple of hours.'

'Righto. I'm gonna need some other clothes.'

'All sorted back in the house. I'll get them.'

Matthew waited till she left.

'Cat nearly lost it back there, Jay. Pleaded with me to give ourselves up.'

'Forget it. She's stressed to the hilt.'

'Surprised there's any chin left, she's been thumping it so much. I'm gonna crack this code Jay. Teach those bastards.'

'Good on ya mate. Show's not over till the fat lady sings, eh? Do us a favor and drive that truck in here. Sticks out like a flare from the road. And the air.'

'We're walking to the South Island, then, are we?'

'Nah. Gotta better idea.'

29. Run out of places to hide

HANSEN ARRIVED to find the police station in pandemonium. One of their family had been killed.

The young constable might have been new to the force, but he was well known locally as the former head boy and captain of the first fifteen rugby team at Napier Boys' High.

The media road show was gushing into the small seaside city, adding to the pressure, and the heat wave stifling the east coast for the past few days had triggered scrub fires, one of which was out of control and threatening houses in Napier's western suburbs. Half the district's police roster was still making its way back from Waikaremoana. To top it off, the police hotline was besieged with calls of possible sightings of the fugitives from all over the country – and one in London – since the announcement of the million-dollar reward. Investigating them was sucking up vital police time.

'Press conference starting, Detective Inspector. They want you in there.'

'What press conference?'

Hansen was directed to a door marked innocently as *Cafeteria*, but entered to blazing lights, television cameras and microphones thrust in her face. The Commissioner's spin-doctor appeared at her shoulder to guide her through the mob. She was too relieved at being rescued to wonder what he was doing there.

At the front of the room, she took a deep breath and spun to face the music. A commotion at the main entrance drew the cameras away like a magnet as the Commissioner marched through the door with the Prime Minister.

'Sorry to hear about the death of Constable Wilson.' The accent could only belong to Kaufman, who appeared at her side. 'Tragedy for his family. No-one should have to bury their kid.'

'Truly shocking,' she said, thinking of Kaufman's daughter.

It was Hansen's first sight of the Prime Minister in the flesh. He was smaller, more fragile than she'd imagined. Dwarfed behind the scrum of microphones on the lectern. The voice though was strong and reassuring. Fatherly.

'Thank you all for coming at such short notice. As you know, today we lost another police officer. I'd like to begin by offering my condolences to the family of Constable Graeme Wilson. I'd also like to take this opportunity on behalf of the New Zealand people to thank Mr Brad Kaufman from Vestco for his efforts to save the life of the young man.'

Kaufman nodded as the cameras swung round and flashes popped.

The Prime Minister cleared his throat and adjusted his royal blue tie.

'Ladies and gentlemen. We are faced with an unprecedented international emergency. We are six days to the hour away from the release of Alo. I don't need to remind anyone here of the significance of that event. It has become clear in the last few days these three armed and incredibly dangerous terrorists will stop at nothing in their attempt to sabotage that event. Two police officers have been slain here in New Zealand. A Vestco employee has been murdered in Los Angeles. Innocent school children and their carers have been kidnapped, terrorized.

'Extraordinary circumstances call for extraordinary measures. I am therefore announcing as of this moment new anti-terrorism legislation that will extend the powers of our law enforcement agencies to treat any person aiding and abetting these fugitives as terrorists themselves.

'Further, I can tell you I have been in talks this morning with the leaders of our coalition parties in the New Zealand Parliament, and have their backing for legislation to introduce capital punishment for crimes covered by the new anti-terrorism laws. Parliament is being convened under urgency this afternoon to enact both pieces of legislation. Thank you.'

Hansen was astounded. So was everyone else in the room, judging by the silence. The death penalty had been abolished in New Zealand decades ago. No one executed for more than half a century. The Prime Minister was almost at the door before a reporter recovered enough to fire a question.

'Prime Minister, can you tell us whether these new anti-terrorism laws will apply to the Waikaremoana father and son arrested for helping the fugitives?'

'Absolutely. The laws will apply retrospectively from the moment the three terrorists arrived in New Zealand. They have run out of places to hide.'

30. Maori for middle-of-nowhere

A SAUNA would be bleedin heaven compared to this, Matthew thought as he leaned forward and peeled the shirt away from his back.

Saunas didn't stink of urine and their floors weren't covered in shit and oily hunks of wool. They were boxed in by sheep in the middle deck of a three-tiered truck. Matthew shuffled as close as he dared to the opening at the side of the pen. The heat was still suffocating.

Jay was stripped to the waist. Sweat sparkled off his chest and biceps like a right poser.

Unfortunately, Cat hadn't followed his lead. She sat against an internal cage in her flowery dress and those ridiculous glasses. Curly black hair did her no favors. She'd blathered on at him for miles about his clue till the heat and stench shut even her up.

They passed through places with unpronounceable names like Ongaonga, which had to be Maori for *middle-of-nowhere*.

The truck slowed through the gears as it descended into a drab valley dotted with red spots that made Matthew think of ladybirds. And cabbage. The place stunk of it.

On one side of the road four red mechanical harvesters were wading through acres of dead-looking brown stuff. Fields of ploughed grayscale stretched away on the other side, flagged every hundred or so yards by green banners announcing this was about to become an Alo farm.

Workers were loading the coiled remains of an old wire fence onto the back of a truck.

Here we go again, he thought.

Dr Tayler came in on cue.

'Check that out. I mean, it's a classic example of what's wrong with these seeds. This land would have been your traditional mixed farm, right Jay? Different crops rotated field to field so parasites couldn't get a foothold in the soil. Now they've pulled down the fences and I betya, betya, they're gonna plant one type of seed in this entire valley.'

'Cabbages?'

'Oilseed rape. Same family as cabbage. It's a brassica.'

'Isn't oilseed supposed to be yellow?'

'When it's flowering yes. They wait for it to die and dry out so they can harvest the tiny black seeds. They're crushed for biofuel.'

'I thought biofuels were, you know, the holy bleedin grail. Reduce dependence on oil and stuff.'

Cat threw back her head and stared at the ceiling, less than a foot above.

'Have you learnt nothing from your time at Millbrook? Biofuels are a bigger part of the problem than the answer. They could plant every square inch of the world's arable land in rapeseed, and it would only produce enough biofuel to replace a third of the oil we use. It's insane Matt.'

'Matthew!'

'And this mad dash to produce biofuel is swallowing up land that should be growing food. It's happening everywhere, for heck's sake. Farmers back in the States are subsidized to grow corn for ethanol. Europe's just as bad. That's what's driven the price of rice and maize and wheat through the roof. Far more people are starving because of biofuel than drought. You could feed an African family for twelve months on the amount of grain needed to fill the tank of one SUV.'

She pointed to the ploughed fields.

'Now these schmucks have ripped out what was probably a perfectly healthy crop and they're gonna plant oilseed rape coated in Alo. All for a few extra bucks.'

Matthew couldn't resist baiting her.

'Sounds like efficiency to me.'

'You of all people should know the perils of monoculture. The Irish potato famine - '

'Don't lump me in with the bleedin Irish –'

'... decimated the population because they relied on one species of potato that was wiped out by a phytophthora.'

'Fighto what?'

'Hundreds of thousands died. Millions of others were forced to leave your homeland.'

'Give it a rest.'

'Even if this Frankenfood was safe, Vestco has exploited people's fears of a food crisis to create a monopoly. A super global monopoly that's gonna make every farmer in the world reliant on Alo. By next week, Vestco and three other multinationals will control two-thirds of the global commercial seed market, and more than 80 per cent of plant breeding research. Under the guise of intellectual property rights, Vestco's lapdogs at the World Trade Organization have devoured the rights of farmers to save seeds to plant in future years. If Johnboy Pitchfork so much as tries, Vestco will sue the bejesus out of him for infringing patents.'

Matthew tried closing his eyes, but she didn't get the hint.

'We're not talking about some benevolent agency like the United Nations driven by the need to feed the world. Vestco is a privately owned multinational corporation with only one goal. Money. They can hike the price whenever they want.'

Her fingers were hammering at her chin, the veins in her neck twitching. Matthew looked to Jay for backup, but he was asleep. Or pretending to be. Cat was in full flight, chest heaving. Might have been a turn-on if they weren't up to here in sheep shit.

'If you believe Vestco's propaganda machine,' she droned on, 'the amount of land to be planted throughout the world with these Frankenfood seeds over the next two months is thousands of times the acreage of potatoes in Ireland at the time of the famine. For heck's sake Matthew, do the math.'

They continued in merciful silence for a few more miles until Matthew realized from a sign that they were getting close to the intersection with the main road.

He kicked Jay's foot to rouse him.

'Big junction coming up. This road meets State Highway 2 west of a town called Takapou or something like that.'

'Bound to be a roadblock at the intersection,' said Jay. 'Even if there's not, main road'll be watched closely. Time to bail out.'

They crawled through sheep towards the back of the truck and Jay reached out and loosened the catch on the door.

'Soon as we slow, we're out of here OK?'

He looked across at Matthew. 'The hell did'ya know about the intersection?'

'From a map at the farmhouse.'

'What can you tell me about the country to the south of the junction?'

'Thought you knew this bleedin country like the back of your hand.'

'Gimme a break. New Zealand's about the size of the UK. I know the South Island fairly well. Bugger all about these parts.'

'I was concentrating mostly to the west heading for the university at Palmerston North,' said Matthew, visualizing the map. 'Two lines I remember. One could have been a railroad passing through this Takapou from the east and heading south. The other had circles at regular intervals. Cut through Takapou as well, heading south-west on a diagonal.'

'Probably a line of power pylons,' said Jay. 'What about roads?'

'Fairly sure there was a spider's web of minor roads to the south. They go virtually all the way to the bottom of the island.'

'What a memory, Matthew,' said Cat. 'You've got to get out more.'

'Can't get out of here fast enough girl.'

The truck slowed near the top of a hill. There were no cars behind them, so they were able to slip unnoticed out the back door and into a ditch at the side of the road.

* * * *

KAUFMAN TRIED the door. It was locked but loose, and gave way to his shoulder.

The outbuilding smelt of grease and arc welding. On one side tools were neatly arranged on hooks. Old signs and vehicle registration plates covered the doors of a tall wooden cabinet. A bunch of empty picture frames hung from a wire attached to a rafter, and at the far end were barrels of grain and seed and a large drum filled almost to the brim with what looked like molasses. On the other wall at eye height was a gun cabinet. Padlocked.

He could hear a chopper approaching. He slipped on a pair of gloves and grabbed a long-handled bolt cutter. As the hum of the bird grew to a growl and the walls started vibrating, he broke the padlock and opened the cabinet. Two hunting rifles and a Smith and Wesson replica revolver. Kaufman chose the rifle with a scope and dropped it into the drum of molasses. A few bubbles and it disappeared into the sludge. The revolver went into his pocket, along with the gloves. He opened the door enough to see there was no one between the outbuilding and house. Hansen was talking to someone on the front verandah.

'Inspector. Come look at this.'

As soon as she saw the open gun cabinet, she called for the farmer. While they were waiting, she handed Kaufman a plastic bag containing a sheet of paper.

'They found this in the house. In between the doodling there's letters and phrases like MU and Center for SB. Pretty sure it means Massey University down the road in Palmerston North. It has a Center for Structural Biology. Forensics also found traces of hair dye in the bathroom, so I'm guessing at least one of them is jet black. A heap of clothing's been dumped in a forty-four-gallon drum out the back of the chook house. I've got the farmer's wife sorting through to see what's missing so we can narrow down their latest disguises.'

'Good work,' said Kaufman. 'Where'd you find the paper with the writing?'

'Table by the phone.'

The farmer came in, looking harassed.

'I assume that gun cabinet's usually locked, Major?'

'Bloody hell.'

'Can you tell us sir, what, if anything, is missing?'

'Course it was locked Inspector. Bastards. They've taken my new rifle. Browning X-Bolt it was. Only used the bloody thing once. Stone the crows. And my son's pistol. Called a Daisy Power Puff or some poncy name like that.'

'I need you to give all the details to the constable here, Major. And constable, I want this shed sealed off. Fingerprints, photos. You know the drill.'

Kaufman followed them towards the house, past officers in white jumpsuits searching through cartons. Barking announced the arrival of a police dog team, which had to wait for a path to be cleared through the throng of reporters and rubber-neckers beyond the front gate. Inside the house more officers were dusting doorframes and window ledges for prints. Yellow numbered tags dotted the floor, and flashes were going off as photographers captured every angle.

Kaufman found the table beside the phone. He quietly removed the top page of the pad, folded it and added it to his pocket collection.

31. Beamed from the deck

DELHI HADN'T seen a crowd like this since the funeral of Mahatma Gandhi.

People lined the streets in their hundreds of thousands to watch the procession from the Rashtrapati Bhavan to the iconic sandstone arch of India Gate. The President and Prime Minister beamed from the deck of the lead vehicle, soaking up the adulation, even though they realized the masses had turned out to see not politicians, but the glass encased seed vial displayed on a dais between them.

Soldiers flanked the vehicle four deep on all sides as it made its way slowly along Rajpath, followed by more than a mile of smiling dignitaries, elephants, camels, school children, musicians, dancers and representatives of every political party and ethnic group on the sub-continent.

32. A paddock car

NO ONE had mentioned the clue questions since the farmhouse, but visions of Johann Miescher and footsteps and double helices goaded Cat like a nagging mother whenever she closed her eyes.

The gasoline gauge had been showing empty for over an hour, so it was no surprise when it finally conked out.

A *paddock car*, Jay called it. Four wheels, no windshield, riddled with rust and bodywork more cratered than the moon. Through some miracle of mechanics – and a few well-aimed kicks – Jay had coaxed the vehicle along more than sixty miles of rutted tracks and riverbeds since stealing it soon after leaving the sheep truck.

They were on a hill overlooking cattle yards and a milking shed in front of a red brick farmhouse and vegetable garden that could feed half of Melville. Cat was starving and stiff and stunk to high heaven of sheep droppings and urine. The floral dress was a soiled write-off and the hair she'd spent so long curling flopped in annoying matted clots on her forehead. She looked at her watch. 9pm. Just after.

'Now what?'

'Wait here.'

Jay shouldered the door open. Cat was about to ask where he was going but checked herself.

He'd been acting differently since Waikaremoana.

A little aloof, as if he was annoyed at her. Probably the pressure.

She watched as he sidled down the slope towards the milking shed, doing his best to keep out of view of the house. A light was flickering in a front room. Television, she guessed. He disappeared from view just as a dog started barking.

Cat grabbed the binoculars and focused on the house. A black Labrador was chained to a kennel beside the back door. It opened and a woman in T-shirt and track pants appeared on the step.

'Shut the hell up,' she shouted, tossing a bone toward the kennel and going back inside. The barking stopped. A window at the back of the shed swung open and Jay dropped, out carrying a green can.

Matthew, who had been sleeping on the back seat, stirred as Jay thumped his fist into the side of the car to open the gasoline cap.

'Where are we?'

'Few miles southwest of Martinborough. Fifteen, twenty shy of where we need to be.'

Jay pulled a newspaper from under his shirt and two cans of Fanta soft drink from his pockets.

'These'll have to keep you going for a while. Bit warm for my liking.'

He hotwired the car back to life and drove off. The light was fading as Cat looked at the crumpled edition of that morning's *Wairarapa Times Age*. The front two pages were missing, but the countdown to the release still filled most of page three.

'Protest marches are planned in several parts of the world tomorrow,' she read out loud, 'including one in Wellington. Police expect protesters to be outnumbered by supporters of Alo.' She tilted the newspaper to get a better view in the light, spilling some of the orange soft drink onto the page.

There was another story about the Police 0800 manhunt hotline being swamped with calls, and a plug for a website and email arrangement for passing on information to the inquiry team headed by Detective Inspector Chris Hansen. At the bottom was a teaser for an article on page eight titled *Gene Jeanie: Master of Disguise*. Intrigued, Cat leafed through the pages.

'Oh my heck' she said, stifling a laugh. The photograph of her face had been taken at Berkeley during a workshop on genomic imprinting.

The tailored black jacket, ridiculous heels and designer jeans belonged to someone else. Journalistic license meets Photoshop. She read the article to herself, dread mounting with every paragraph. There were quotes from classmates back in Melville, references to how she'd maliciously forced the closure of the Antego factory, 'ripping the heart out of the town that never recovered'. Margot Donaldson, the high school drama queen turned B-grade Hollywood actress who began treading the boards on the stage at Melville Junior High, recalled Catherine Tayler as a gifted make-up artist and master of disguise.

And renowned Los Angeles clinician Dr Lorna Buchanan 'felt compelled to break patient confidentiality in the public interest'. She confirmed the terrorist had been 'exhibiting unstable tendencies for some time and was diagnosed with an antisocial type personality disorder bordering on psychopathic' before she fled the United States. Worst of all was a quote from one of the lowlifes who attacked her father, claiming Bob Tayler had assaulted him in a drunken rage.

'Sonofabitch,' Cat swore under her breath, letting the newspaper fall to the floor.

Don't take it seriously, she tried to convince herself. If the cruddy local rag was prepared to superimpose faces on bodies to justify a headline, there's no telling how far they'd stoop with the words. *Assuming* it was the local rag. She reached for the page. Photo courtesy of *Grassroots Intelligence*.

The blog must have been duped. And Pop had subscribed to *Grassroots* since the day it broke the news of the firebombing of Tolminsky's lab. What would he make of this? How was he holding up?

Cat closed her eyes and rested her head against the seat. The breeze through the open window was soothing. Pop'll manage, she thought with a smile. *Worrying is counterproductive*, he'd be saying.

She must have drifted off because the next thing she knew the car had stopped and Jay was shouldering his door open. The smell of salt and seaweed hit her before she heard the rolling of the waves.

From the top of a tussocky mound, they looked over the tiny fishing settlement of Ngawi, coddled between gray windswept hills and the

Pacific Ocean. Vintage bulldozers on the beach. Boats of various sizes and degrees of seaworthiness. Across the water to the south, the top of a mountain glowed in the twilight.

'That'll be Tapuae-o-Uenuku,' said Jay. 'Highest peak in the inland Kaikoura range.'

'You climbed it?'

'Tapu's just a baby. Less than ten thousand feet. I'll take you up one day. She's a glorified hike, specially this time of year.'

Cat liked the sound of that. In different circumstances.

'I'd settle for sea level anywhere in the South Island right now. How in heck are we going to get across?'

Jay looked through the binoculars, sweeping from the cluster of cottages to the stony beach, settling on something near the water's edge. Cat squinted in the quarter light. A person in white boots was dragging a dinghy over the stones.

'Wait here,' said Jay. 'This could be our ride.'

'He's gone barmy,' said Matthew. 'It's twenty bleedin miles. I'm not going across in that pint-sized thing.'

Cat ignored him as she watched Jay walk up to the man, say something, then help him pull the boat the last few yards. They stood talking, ankle deep in water, Jay pointing out to sea and the man shaking his head. Jay suddenly broke away and jogged back to the mound.

'He won't take us across. Too far out of his way, he reckons. He's heading back to Island Bay tonight though, and'll take us to Wellington. For a price.'

'There's a university in Wellington, right?'

'Yeah. Victoria University. Big one. Should be easier to get to the South Island from Wellington, too. And that's the last way they'll expect us to arrive in the capital.'

'Is that thing safe? asked Matthew as they reached the water's edge.

'Safe enough to get us to his cray boat. That's his between the pontoon and the runabout.'

The fisherman – just call me Skip – was a Maori in his late fifties. Short clipped hair, grey stubble and a lispy voice slithering through the gap once occupied by his front teeth. A black singlet struggled to cover an enormous stomach spilling over the front of his denim shorts.

Jay pushed the dinghy into the surf. Skip started rowing, his eyes fixed on Cat's chest. What is it about men and breasts? She tried to stare him down, but he just poked his tongue a little further through the gap in his teeth. Halfway to his fishing boat, he started cackling.

'Something wrong?' Cat asked.

'Those cops couldn't find a pint in a brewery. They think yous fellas were going to that wananga up at Palmy. Had the place crawling with cops all day.'

'He means the university at Palmerston North,' Jay translated.

Cat was relieved to find Skip's boat had life preservers and was large enough to have a cabin with galley, bunk and toilet. The deck was more than three times the size of the paddock car, though Jay warned space would become limited during the night as the cray pots were hauled onboard. She rechecked the straps on her life preserver as Matthew helped Jay winch up the anchor.

'How do we know he isn't gonna have the coppers waiting for us when we dock?' Matthew was asking.

'Wouldn't blame him, just quietly,' Jay replied. 'Million bucks'd buy half a brewery.'

'This geezer knows about the reward?'

'Course he does. I told him.'

'You what?'

'Look mate, here's the deal. We've gotta trust someone. Skip here's fishing outside the cray season without a quota. He'll think twice before calling the cops. I reckon he's straight up.'

Cat recalled the way Skip was ogling her breasts and had a horrible thought.

'You mentioned he'd take us for a price. What does he want?'

'Let's find out.'

The boat had left the bay. They waited for Skip to finish attaching an orange buoy to a rope, then popped the question. His eyes drifted back to Cat's chest.

'Whatya got?'

She jumped in quickly. 'I can give you one thousand American dollars.'

'They don't take that monopoly money at the pub.'

'We've got about five hundred New Zealand between us,' said Jay.

Skip scratched the stubble on his chin as he considered for a moment, before holding out his hand.

Jay gave him the cash.

'Course I'll need extra for danger money. With Rambo comin for yous fellas' arses.'

'What do you mean?'

'That Yankee fella. Kaufman is it? Fore ya know it he'll have a whole fuckin posse of Marines and Seals and surface to air, anti-ballistic, inta-continental heat-seeking an all that shit. Put a red dot on ya from outta space and bam, ya history.'

'That's all the New Zealand money we've got.'

Skip's eyes hadn't left Cat's chest.

'That jacket'd look good on the missus.'

Cat was so relieved, she sobbed.

'You got it,' said Jay. 'When we get to Island Bay.'

'Fair enough.'

After a swim to wash the flock of sheep from her pores, Cat was savoring her fifth raw mussel, washed down with a cold beer.

Jay and Matthew were helping Skip haul up the first cray pots. Red bodies and legs and feelers squirmed to escape the black mesh-covered frame.

'What do you use for bait?', she heard Jay ask.

'Possums mostly. Roadkill. Burn em up a bit on the barbecue first. Crays love em.'

Matthew accepted another can.

'Cat over there's worried you're gonna turn us in for the reward.'

'The hell for? Got all I need. Sleep in till ten most mornings. Get to play with the mokopuna. Few beers with me mates every second night. Come out on the boat and escape the missus every other night. The hell would I do with all that money?'

'Buy a bigger boat. Catch more. Sell more. Buy a fleet of boats.'

Cat knew where this was headed. She'd heard the Heinrich Böll story about the decline of the work ethic. Skip obviously hadn't, so she helped him out.

'How long would that take him, Matthew?'

'Five, ten years.'

'Then what?'

'Branch out to exporting. Open offices closer to his market. Turn the one million into twenty.'

'Then what?'

Jay delivered the punch line.

'Well Skip, you could stay in bed till ten in the morning, play with the grandkids, go to the pub every other night...'

It was the first time Cat let go and laughed in days.

She adjusted the spare life preserver she was using for a pillow, lay back on the deck, closed her eyes and was soon lulled to sleep by the rocking motion of the boat.

* * * *

PETERSEN POURED another single malt and walked across the Isfahan rug to the desk in his study.

There were three messages.

He wasn't expecting one from the private email address of his insider on the board of the *New York Times*, so he opened that first.

Just out of briefing with editor-in-chief. He's determined to go ahead with story we're co-publishing with Grassroots linking you to voting irregularities in California, New Jersey and Virginia. Has agreed with blog to hold until day AFTER Alo goes live. Accepted elections story unrelated to your role at Vestco, and not in national – or international – interest to jeopardize release. Hope you've got a good attorney. PS: We're running a story tomorrow with the latest international blog rankings. Grassroots has taken over from Huffington as the most influential on the planet.

Petersen drained the glass and opened the second email. Analysis of focus group research suggested a significant proportion of people still undecided about the safety of Alo would be swayed by an unequivocal endorsement from an internationally credible opponent of genetic modification.

The third message had an attached PDF showing the billboard cover of the special issue of the world's largest English language news magazine. Due in stores on every continent within hours.

The cover, with its familiar red border, featured a photograph of Jozef Pyjas, Person of the Year.

The smiling Vestco chairman was standing on a hill in Somalia, one hand holding a vial of seeds and the other draped around the shoulder of a beaming African child wearing a t-shirt with the words *Nafaqayn, Xajin, Tarto*.

Dinner and two bottles of Montrachet Grand Cru at the Batard in Lower Manhattan was all it had taken Petersen to persuade one of the magazine's editors that the Somali words for *nourish, sustain, cherish* would be more authentic than the English.

He knew without reading the story there would be no mention of the shadowy path he and his old college buddy Pyjas trod to reach the pinnacle of that hill. How Jozef had been a research manager at one of the world's largest seed corporations when an enthusiastic scientist called Tolminsky made his breakthrough seed-coating discovery. How Petersen persuaded his old buddy to ensure the discovery was never reported and Tolminsky was convinced it would never get the backing of the biotech giant. Wasn't difficult, with the industry focused back then on helping farmers in rich countries because of the prohibitive cost of winning regulatory approval. There would be no mention in the *TIME* article or anywhere else of how Pyjas left the other corporation within months to set up Vestco, with Tolminsky as chief scientist and Petersen using his considerable contacts in government and the darker side of the business world to ensure a smooth passage through the minefield of obstacles. Legal and otherwise. The former Pulitzer Prize-winning journalist who came closest to revealing the truth had unfortunately taken his own life shortly after his day in court.

Petersen looked back at the *TIME* cover. In the background over the child's shoulder were thousands of white tents, like maggots on a gray carcass. Pyjas had never been to Africa, let alone a relief camp.

That was not the point. Within forty-eight hours, thirty million people would have read the magazine and billions in streets, roads, squares and plazas would see the billboard and the clear message it conveyed. Almost every television station, radio station, newspaper, news website and blog on the planet would run stories about who *TIME* chose as their Person of the Year.

Timely indeed.

Before turning in for the night, Petersen placed a call to Cambridge, England; then to Mumbai, Moscow, Beijing and Boston. He was particularly looking forward to what he had planned for Boston.

33. For the Missus

THE BOOM of a ship's horn nudged Jay from a sleep so bottomless it took an age to get his bearings. The tang of fish cooking. Tickling pitch of the waves. Bitter taste of sea breeze. Gulls. Could be anywhere.

'But that is so inhumane.'

'S'a bloody fish, woman. The hell can ya be inhumane ta somethin not human?'

Cat was scowling in front of the skipper, who was holding a wriggling cray above a pot of boiling water. Two halves of one of its cousins were sizzling away on a small barbecue rack beside the pot. She turned to Jay, who propped himself up on an elbow.

'He's going to boil that poor creature alive.'

'Only way to cook em.' Jay tried to keep eye contact so she wouldn't see the crustacean's death dance in the pot. Cat was still wearing the orange life preserver over the floral dress. Probably slept in it, if she slept at all.

'There must be more humane ways to - '

'She's all over in a few seconds, Cat. Not a bad way to go I reckon.'

'I've never heard anything so barbaric.'

The chin was getting an early morning workout. Behind her, Skip had plucked the cray out of the pot, cut it in half and removed the brown bits from its head. He was brushing it with oil...

'Wait till you taste it.'

... sprinkling what Jay assumed was a mixture of salt and pepper...

'There is no way in heck I'm going to - '

The pieces of cray hissed as they landed on the barbecue. Cat spun round and gave Skip an eyeful. He just smiled and poked the first cray with his tongs.

'This fella's bout ready if ya wanna feed.'

'I'm a starter,' said Jay, getting to his feet. They were a third of the way between Baring and Sinclair Heads. The boat dipped and rose as it struck the wake of a container ship entering Wellington Harbor to their starboard. Jay took a couple of legs and went back to sit with Matthew in the stern.

'Here mate. Wrap ya laughing gear round this.'

Empty pots were stacked behind plastic containers filled with live crays in water.

'Looks like ya had a good night Skip.'

'Pretty choice. Keep the missus happy I reckon.' He reached over to switch on the boat's radio.

'What's the plan?' asked Matthew, tossing shell over the side and wiping his mouth with the sleeve of his shirt.

'Skip here knows a restaurant. Called Kai in the Bay. Cousin of his that runs it might be able to help us get across to the South Island. Tonight, with any luck. And Doctor Tayler needs to get to the university.'

'Quiet you guys,' said Cat, finger to lips as she tried to hear the radio. 'They're talking about us.'

Through the static came snatches of conversations between boaties and the radio base operator.

Searching Wairarapa... sheep truck ... stolen car... east of Carterton... Rimutaka Hill crawling with cops...

Skip was shaking his head, sniggering like a kid.

'Them coppers. Wouldn't know their arse from their elbow.'

Jay scanned the coastline ahead. They were rounding Rat's Island, a small natural breakwater that gave Island Bay its name.

'Where's Rimutaka Hill?' asked Cat.

'It's the road over from the Wairarapa into Wellington. If they're searching in Wairarapa it could buy us some time. Won't take them long though to work out where we're heading.'

'How big's Wellington?'

'Two hundred thousand in the city at the last census, half a million in the region.'

'For heck's sake Matthew. Your memory's frightening sometimes. It's not natural.'

A few minutes later they were alongside the jetty. Matthew walked off first, followed at a suitable distance by Cat, wearing a toweling hat and Mrs Skip's blue coveralls.

Jay offered his hand to Skip. 'Thanks mate.'

'No worries young fella.' Reaching into his pocket, the fisherman pulled out the wad of New Zealand banknotes and thrust them into Jay's hands.

'You fellas're gonna need this more than me. Think I'll keep the jacket though. For the missus.'

'Cheers.'

Jay met the others at a pre-arranged spot behind a children's playground.

'Trainspotter Matthew here tells me there's a thriving red-light district in Wellington. How do you fancy being dressed as a transvestite, Jay?'

'I'll pass on that one thanks. What time's that Alo rally?'

'Three o'clock.'

'Anyone got two dollars?'

Jay took the coin from Cat and walked across the road to a phone booth. The tattered back half of the local White Pages was hanging from a string.

East, Hayden. 542 Rajkot Terrace, Broadmeadows.

Had to be him. He put the coin in the slot and dialed the number.

* * * *

HANSEN WAS struggling to concentrate over the noise of the dog, which hadn't stopped yapping since the chopper carrying her and

199

Kaufman landed beside the farmhouse in Wairarapa.

'She barked at something about nine last night as well,' said the owner's wife. 'Thought it was just a rabbit, didn't we Bill? Then we heard on the wireless this morning those terrorists were in the area. Bill here checked the sheds, didn't you Bill? Noticed the petrol can gone. That's when we called your hot phone thing. Isn't that right Bill?'

Bill grunted. It was obvious who wore the pants in this household.

Hansen spread a map of the lower North Island over the kitchen table. If the trio reached here by nine last night, they probably weren't heading for Wellington. She pointed at one of three fingers jutting into the sea at the end of the island.

'What's down there?'

'Nothing to speak of. Seal colony. Few baches. You know, holiday homes. Bit of a fishing outfit, isn't there Bill? Lotta folks have baches they use at weekends. Isn't that right Bill?'

Kaufman butted in.

'Fishing? Maybe they're after a boat to get across to the South Island.'

It was a possibility. Duggan was from down that way. His elderly mother, who turned out to be the instigator of the amateurish *Jaywalker* blog threatening to take on a cult following, lived just across Cook Strait in Takaka.

'And isn't Alo releasing in the South Island.'

'Correct. At Lincoln University, near Christchurch.'

Hansen looked across at the couple.

'Can you show us where most of the fishing boats are located?'

The woman pointed to the tip of one of the fingers.

'Ngawi. Plenty a fishin boats down there at Ngawi. Isn't that right Bill?'

* * * *

'HOW'S YOUR daughter doing?'

Hansen's concern caught Kaufman off guard. They were flying south towards the coast over hills sucked colorless by drought.

'Hangin in there. Spoke to her last night. She'd just got home from eleven hours of transfusions. Hemoglobin slipped dangerously low. Had to pump her back up slowly so it wouldn't put too much strain on her lungs and heart.'

They spotted the car at the same time, in a hollow behind the hill near the edge of the fishing village. After circling and confirming it was empty, the pilot landed in a field about a quarter mile away.

'Better wear these,' Hansen said as she tossed Kaufman a pair of gloves.

The car, if you could call it that, had once been blue. Possibly. Rust covered most of the roof and half of one side. Three of the doors had been replaced at some point in its long and tortured life. Kaufman offered to check the surroundings while Hansen inspected the wreck. He waited till he was out of her sight, made sure he couldn't be seen by the chopper pilot, then dropped the revolver in some long grass before continuing on a few yards and sitting down.

When Hansen called out a few minutes later, he stood up.

'Over here.'

'Pretty sure they used the car,' she said as she walked towards him holding a newspaper. She was so busy looking at the paper, Kaufman thought she'd miss the gun. Until she stood on it.

'What have we here? Daisy Powerline. Just like the one stolen from the farm in Napier.'

'They've still got that hunting rifle,' he said. 'Wonder what they're planning to use that for?'

Hansen held up the newspaper.

'This could give us a clue. There's a fresh stain, looks like juice, on a story about the protest march in Wellington today.'

'They're hardly likely to hit one of their own protests, Inspector.'

'True. Though according to this story, the protesters will be outnumbered by Vestco's fan club. And there'll be a lot of police. We've already lost two officers.'

Kaufman wasn't going to argue.

'Why come here though?' she continued, walking along the track towards the beach. 'They could have got over the Rimutakas to

201

Wellington before we sealed it off. While we were mucking around in Palmerston North.'

A man in black singlet and white rubber boots – a fisherman of some sort – was walking towards them, presumably attracted by the sound of the chopper. Hansen introduced herself and asked him where the boats went from here.

'Everyone's got their favorite spots love. They don't let on, if you know what I mean.'

'Many cross to the South Island?'

'Not worth the trouble, love. More fish round here.'

'How about boats coming over here from the South?'

'Not very often. Chaps head round from Island Bay for the crays though. Usually come in the afternoon. Back over at night.'

Kaufman cut in: 'Where's Island Bay?'

'A suburb of Wellington.'

Blackjack.

34. Headphones on. Oblivious

THE *GO WELLINGTON* trolley bus stopped near the Metro supermarket on Willis Street and Cat watched the other passengers as Matthew got off.

No one gave a second look to the student with the gold Hurricanes rugby jumper, canvas knapsack and Leichner number eight shading along the side of the nose that took five years off his age.

Somebody's grandmother stuttered up the steps, took too long to pay the driver, waddled down the aisle and fell into a seat as the driver's patience ran out. The old duck smiled at Cat, who smiled back.

If it wasn't for cars on the wrong side of the road, central Wellington could have been Fresno, Long Beach or Sacramento. There was Coke. McDonalds. Starbucks. The tentacles of multinationalism. Vestco was muscling in on the game with *Nourish, Sustain, Cherish* banners above the street, Alo posters in store windows and an odious two-story digital billboard: Four days, 23 hours, 59 minutes, 42 seconds... 41... 40... 39... 38...

Melville: The Sequel.

Only difference was the name of the corporation. Antego employed Uncle Burt and brother Ernie, sponsored the little leaguers, donated to the school and church and the garden club. Antego this, Antego that. Even replaced the engine for the Melville Volunteer Fire Brigade.

Cat glanced around her fellow passengers.

The man beside her was reading a *Grassroots* sports story headed *Springboks pack threat to All Blacks*. If everyone else around them wasn't talking about Alo and the hunt for the terrorists, they were reading about it.

The morning's *Dominion Post* was cover to cover, from the front-page photo of the Vestco chairman with a beaming President outside the White House to hints on the best vantage points for the afternoon's rally in Wellington.

The bus stopped near a bookstore on Lambton Quay. The smiling grandmother got off with Cat, who held the woman's arm to help her onto the sidewalk.

'Thanks dear,' the woman said, before leaning closer and whispering behind her hand. 'Or should I say *Doctor*?' She winked and shuffled off.

Cat was so shocked she stood in the middle of the sidewalk a full thirty seconds till a parking warden asked if she was alright. She sprung over to the window of a pharmacy, pretending to look at the display of sunscreens. Reflecting back was a student with short black hair barely showing beneath a charcoal beret, last year's sunglasses and an easy-going smile through fullish lips of Carmine number two. All the clothes, even the commerce textbooks in the hessian shoulder bag, belonged to Skip's daughter who graduated from Victoria University in December. How in heck did the old duck recognize her?

Cat felt defenseless without Jay. She took a deep breath and slipped into the flow of office workers on lunch break. The abundance of white shirts and take-themselves-too-seriously faces suggested a fair proportion of government staffers. Head straight, avoid eye contact. Right into Cable Car Lane.

Matthew's head was buried in a book under a sign saying the next cable car was leaving in four minutes. Cat ignored him. Her eyes were drawn to the words *Grin Reaper* scrawled in crude graffiti across a *TIME* billboard leaning against the window of a bookstore. She went inside and took a magazine from the shelf, putting it on the counter with a twenty-dollar bill so she didn't have to speak.

Ignoring the smug cover of the Vestco chairman and photos inside of excited faces in Delhi, she rummaged through the text for ... what? Dissent? Balance? Even a semblance?

The closest it got was a shot of a cute girl in a white hooded windbreaker holding a sign saying *Mr Pyjas Don't Poison Our Children.* Jozef Pyjas smiled condescendingly at her from a panel in the next column. Beside a story about fire bombings at several Del Pizza restaurants and the CEO having a mental breakdown.

Cat always thought her scientific knowledge and passion would lead to some world-changing discovery. To be honest, it became an obsession. Landing the job of science director at Millbrook gave her, she thought, the perfect platform. How naive was that? Simply making an earth-shattering discovery was not enough. Nowhere near. She had to overcome greed, politics, manipulation. And public cynicism led by an unbelievably gullible media. Did *Grassroots* have the only journalists prepared to ask the tough questions?

The cable car arrived, and she took a seat three rows from Matthew, beside a girl with pimples and sensible glasses and Biol 101 written neatly on a ring binder on her knees. Could have been Cat the first day at Berkeley. Bursting with enthusiasm and idealism, ready to take on the world. Antego, Vestco. Melville, LA, Wellington. Antego this. Vestco that. Nothing had changed.

She folded her arms, steeling herself for round two. Cat Tayler didn't do *F*.

* * * *

KAUFMAN STUDIED the bank of screens. Cameras were positioned to cover the entire protest march to the steps of Parliament.

Images were fed to the liquid crystal monitors casting blue glows onto the faces of the officers in the darkened surveillance vehicle.

'Could be a ploy to distract us,' said Hansen. 'Wouldn't be the first time.'

Tayler's credit card had just been used at an ATM within spitting distance of the march, confirming Kaufman's hunch they'd be running out of cash.

'No. They're here,' he said. 'You can smell them. Duggan's always been one for the grand statement. This is his stage. They'll be getting desperate. And we know he's got a rifle. How long ago was the card used?'

'Ten minutes. Got a bloody nerve if it was them. ATM was around the corner from the police station. Less than fifty yards from the front entrance. We had officers there within two minutes, but there was no sign of any of them. We've cordoned off two blocks and we're searching every building, but this is the central business district. Thousands work in these offices.'

Fingerprints found on the steering wheel of the car at Palliser Bay had been confirmed as Duggan's. A cray fisherman had come forward to report his boat was hijacked by three people, who forced him to bring them to Wellington. He gave detailed descriptions of what they were wearing.

Kaufman concentrated on the monitors. Several banners promoted *Jaywalker*, the blog full of broken record crap about Vestco and genetic modification.

Two, four, six, eight, Alo will Con-Tam-In-Ate.

The childish chant, started by some jerk dressed as a corncob screaming into a megaphone, was taken up by the rest of the rabble as the head of the march reached Midland Park. Ten thousand people tops. Amateurs.

'Might have something, Inspector.'

Kaufman stepped beside Hansen to look over the shoulder of the operator, who was toggling to zoom in on an image taken from the first floor of a department store. Two men in beige cricket tops and toweling hats waving flags. The Stars and Stripes and the Vestco logo. A woman in blue overalls and a straw hat took something out of a shoulder bag and touched the corner of each flag. They burst into flames.

'Can we zoom in?'

'I have, Inspector. That's the best we can do from here.'

'Let's take em out,' said Kaufman.

'We're not even sure it's them.'

'Course it is. They match the fisherman's ID right down to Tayler's hat. Take em out. Use your snipers for Chrissake. Before Duggan makes the hit.'

'Can you see a rifle, Mr Kaufman?'

Her calm, patronizing tone was pissing him off.

'It'll be in Tayler's bag.'

'Doesn't look big enough for a rifle to me, Mr Kaufman.'

'Jesus F Christ. What is it with you people? Been pissing around for days with your backyard Keystone Cop routine. And what've these terrorists been doing? Laughing in your faces. Now they're doing it again. Burning the fucking flag right in front of you. And you're gonna do what? Dial 911 and ask for the fire department?'

'You're way out of line, Mr Kaufman.' *Mister* was spat like a snake.

'Out of line? I'm in joint control of this operation dee-tective. And I say take them out.'

Hansen turned to her offsider.

'Captain. Tell AO squads Echo and Golf to move in carefully from each side of the street and apprehend the three suspects. Use the backup uniforms in the HSBC building for crowd control. Mr Kaufman and I are just stepping outside for a chat. Take over for a minute please.'

She virtually pushed him through the door onto the sidewalk.

'I don't give a rat's arse what you say, *Mister* Kaufman. Far as I'm concerned you're a consultant. A civilian consultant. Read the orders. Joint control means joint decision-making. If we can't agree, I call the shots. If you can't live with that arrangement, *Mister*, get the hell out of my face. And never, ever, speak to me like that in front...'

The captain's head appeared in the doorway.

'You gonna want to see this Pahi.'

The bitch turned her back and stomped back into the van. He followed her, fuming. One of the officers was pointing at a monitor showing images from a chopper hovering over the march. Three other people, also dressed in beige cricket tops and blue overalls, were walking behind a large yellow banner. The image was sharp enough to show the trio were too old to be Duggan, Tayler and Liddell.

'Got another lot near the rear,' called the operator at the end of the line. Three more protesters, Maori this time but wearing the same clothes. Pushing supermarket trolleys carrying kids in school uniforms holding three placards. *Alo. Da. Bollocks.*

'They're having us on. Taking the piss.'

'Thank you Captain. Tell those AO units to move in only if they can make a positive ID.'

Kaufman was thankful for the darkened room. He was sure his face was glowing red.

'My apologies, Inspector. You seem to have everything under control here.'

He stepped out into the daylight and glanced at his watch. The plane was arriving in just over four hours. They couldn't come soon enough.

* * * *

MATTHEW FOUND what he was looking for on the ground floor of the library. A single computer terminal at the end of a row where he was unlikely to be disturbed.

He sat down and put on a pair of headphones to dissuade other students from talking to him, then eased the tips of his fingers onto the keyboard as if greeting an old friend. The fear and mayhem of the last few days faded with each keystroke.

Logging on to the student server was a piece of cake and he spent some time searching for answers to his part of the clue. *Keep following the rush before the queen young man.* There was the geezer everyone called the Queen at Manchester, but Matthew couldn't remember his real name. There was no reference to Queen in any of the Manchester University student lists.

A little distraction might help reboot the brain. He navigated to the rogue page he'd set up on the front of his website. Within minutes he had a list of hundreds of media organizations, police forces, intelligence agencies, hackers and punters who had viewed his site in the last forty hours.

More importantly, he had access to their computers. A search on

Kaufman came up with details about two passengers arriving on a flight later that day from Brisbane. He noted it on a piece of paper, along with the American's mobile phone number that was listed as part of his digital signature.

He scrolled the visitor list, stopping at a tag including the string *SwPh15h*. Curious. On the off chance it belonged to the famed SwordPhish, Matthew tracked one of its email addresses and fired off a brief message about the CD, Jay's friend Ross, and a hunch he had about television coverage of the Alo release.

Back to business. A search on *queen* netted 180 million results, but an image of the band Queen at the top of the first page jogged his memory. The Queen at Manchester was named after some rock star. The lead singer of Queen was Freddy Mercury. Matthew re-searched the student lists and, sure enough, there was an F. Mercury in computer systems engineering.

Mercury. *Keep following the rush before* the Mercury. He looked for answers using the planet, then tried the table of elements. Before mercury came gold. *Gold rush* sounded likely. But what followed, or came after a bleedin gold rush?

Time for another reboot. He tracked an entry from a computer at the Forensic Investigations Unit of the New Zealand Police and was surprised how easy it was to gain root access to the national website. This was too good an opportunity to pass up. He found his way to the administrator set up, which led him to the page displaying the latest identikit images of the three eco-terrorists. A few keystrokes and he'd superimposed the heads of Arnold Schwarzenegger, Bart Simpson and Mother Teresa onto the three bodies. For good measure he inserted a spreadeagle virus, triggered to kick in at midnight.

* * * *

CAT WAS getting nowhere in the science section. Johann Miescher was born in Basel and studied there as well as in Gottingen, Leipzig and Tubingen, returning to Basel to make his celebrated extraction of DNA from the sperm of salmon.

What in heck did *in his footsteps* mean? Miescher had a son called Guido, but that was too obvious. She found a reference to a thesis on Miescher's work written by Valmai Kane, now a professor at Lincoln University in New Zealand's South Island. The library did not hold a copy of the thesis, and it would be too risky to phone the woman.

Cat was handicapped by not wanting to ask for help. She'd already mistakenly greeted a janitor. Although her American accent didn't seem to register, she didn't want to take any more chances. Frustration levels were rising. She decided to try the history section.

'Are you, like, going down?'

A young woman student was holding the elevator door open. Cat got in.

'Bad hangover, eh?'

'I beg your pardon!'

'The shades,' said the student, pointing to Cat's sunglasses. 'It's not, like, bright in here.'

'Migraine.' Cat turned her head away, hoping the conversation would end there.

'What part of the States you from?'

'East. Virginia.' Cat was counting on the young woman's knowledge of the United States being as limited as most American's knowledge of New Zealand. Wrong again.

'No kidding? My brother did AFS in Virginia. That's like American Field Scholar. You know, like an exchange. Where'd you go to school?'

'Virginia Heights.' Cat was making it up.

'Which part's that? My brother's school was in the north I think.'

'South.'

'Whatya studying here?'

The black hole was getting deeper.

'Biotech.'

'Didn't know they offered that.'

'Post grad. I'm doing a doctorate.'

'Right. Who's your supervisor?'

The lift reached the ground floor.

'Hey, I'm running late. Nice talkin to you.' Cat walked off, numbed by the eyes surely burning into her back. She padded calmly calmly calmly towards the exit, concentrating on her breathing, craving fresh air.

Approaching from the other side of the glass door was Kaufman.

Cat turned aside at the last moment and snuck behind the issues desk. Through the open doors she heard a helicopter approaching. The American stood in the foyer, his eyes fixed like a cat stalking a bird at a point on the far wall. Cat followed his line of sight and saw Matthew looking at a computer screen. Headphones on. Oblivious.

* * * *

A SEARCH on *footprints* took Matthew to the YouTube video of a song by Leona Lewis. She was a bit of a looker, though the clip was spoilt by Spanish lyrics superimposed over the footage.

Something else was wrong. Footprints. It was *footnote*, not footprints ya bleedin tosser. Cat's barking up the wrong tree. He scrawled FootNOTE on the scrap of paper and logged out. He was about to take off the headphones when reflected movement on the screen made him wet himself.

He grabbed the note and bolted. The headphones still on his head yanked the monitor from its stand and sent it crashing to the floor. He made it to the end of the row and tore across the open space, hurdling a coffee table and scattering a group of students beside a vending machine.

The American tank blindsided him from the right, knocking the wind from his lungs as he smashed into the periodicals.

Forcing one eye open, Matthew saw the shocked face of Cat on the other side of the shelf, tapping furiously at her chin.

'Foot...' was all he got out before something slammed into the side of his head.

35. Sticks and stones

'WHAT about those, such as the one hundred eminent scientists questioned by Grassroots, who still insist Alo is too risky, there are too many unknowns with this sort of genetic modification?'

Hansen took a sip of coffee and looked up at the television on the wall of the cafeteria at Wellington Central. Jozef Pyjas tilted his head slightly and smiled at the interviewer.

'I can assure you Alo has been tested and re-tested more times than any agricultural product in history. And history, as you know, is full of examples of discoveries and inventions that would never have been made if scientists and their sponsors listened to the doomsayers. Vaccination. Penicillin. Refrigeration.'

He counted them off on his fingers.

'I could go on. Imagine where we'd be today if Edward Jenner listened to the critics back in the eighteenth century who said inoculating people with a cow pox virus was too risky, too many unknowns. Smallpox used to kill as many people as cancer or heart disease today. Now, thankfully, smallpox is history.'

'Fair point,' said a sergeant, before tucking into a filled roll as the Vestco chairman started waffling about the investment Vestco was making to train scientists in recipient countries.

'By the way, Pahi, congrats on collaring Liddell.'

'It was Kaufman who nabbed him. And we've got an alert cleaner to thank for the tip off.'

'Where's Liddell now?'

212

'At the hospital. Under guard. I'm hoping to question him in an hour or so, once he recovers from the trauma of his arrest.'

'He resisted?'

'Not sure how much of it was resistance or over-exuberance by Kaufman. Matthew Liddell doesn't strike me as an aggressive person.' The sergeant didn't need to know that if Hansen had arrived in the library seconds later she'd be questioning a corpse.

The Pyjas interview moved on to the manhunt.

I understand one of the terrorists is in police custody.'

'How the hell does the media know that? We haven't released it yet.'

'... a specialist international anti-terrorism unit is arriving in New Zealand in the next hour or so. We're confident the remaining two terrorists will be behind bars very soon.'

Hansen almost choked on her coffee.

'Anti-terrorism unit. What the hell's that about?'

The sergeant shrugged.

'Why has it taken so long to catch them, Mr Pyjas?'

'Well, you know, I'm sure those folk down in New Zealand are very good at catching house burglars and cattle rustlers. When it comes to international terrorism, they lack experience.'

'Surely this is a matter of international importance?'

'We believe so. I spoke to the New Zealand Prime Minister just before coming on air. He's agreed the specialist unit will be under the control of an American with vast experience in these matters.'

* * * *

IF THE owners and staff of the Alcove on Hillhurst Avenue had an inkling of what Petersen did for a living, they might have objected to him becoming such a regular customer. The cafe was one of his favorite places for off-the-radar meetings in LA, and the management's stated commitment to 'sourcing locally grown and organic produce whenever possible' made most conversations deliciously ironic.

His guest, dressed in a *Young and Reckless* t-shirt, jeans and purple denim trainers, had his own reasons for anonymity.

The International Federation for Biotechnology Information had served its purpose. Genetic modification critics in every country had been countered and discredited by an army of 'independent experts', often dressed in white MD coats and stethoscopes or weighed down with enough science degree acronyms to fill both sides of their business cards. The same experts had bombarded the world's media, penning op-eds and guest blogs, appearing on chat shows, keynoting conferences, moderating panels, peddling the results of questionable research. Thanks to the federation, Codex food standard meetings had become exercises in rubber stamping, and the World Trade Organization had ruled that labelling of genetically modified food violated trade treaties because it unfairly disadvantaged imports.

But even those achievements were small beer compared to the mother of all acronyms: TAFS. Opposition to the Trans-Atlantic Food Security pact had wilted under the doomsday glare of the food crisis. Buried in the fine print of the pact, fast-tracked to meet Alo's deadline, were the terms 'regulatory merging' and 'investor dispute protocols'.

In plain English that until now had never been fully explained to the masses, it meant the EU's tough stance on genetic modification had been altered to match America's far more sensible regulations, and governments could be sued for loss of profits caused by their policies.

Game, set – but not quite match.

The Community Coalition for Food Safety – another creation of Petersen – had become a Facebook phenomenon with 'likes' to rival rockstars. It had been so well set up, no-one suspected the group standing up for the rights of ma and pa consumers and family farmers was fake.

The mother page had spawned offspring from Abbeyville County in South Carolina to Zapata in Texas, with its hometown content carefully managed over time to ensure conversations remained, if not pro-genetic modification, at least neutral towards Alo. It had exceeded Petersen's expectations. Until this week.

Anti-genetic modification propagandists had propelled the fine print of the TAFS pact into the headlines, and manipulated the balance of argument on Facebook firmly against Vestco and Alo.

Which had prompted the meeting at the Alcove Café. The young man sitting across the table finished his hearth-baked toasted bagel and wiped his moustache with a serviette.

'It can be done. Are you familiar with the term Sybil Attack?'

'No.'

'It's a sock puppet technique named after a woman with multiple personalities.'

'I've heard of sock puppet software being used to sway online polls, but I thought Facebook had found a way to block multiple puppets.'

'Not entirely. I have a product that trawls Facebook pages for keywords, assesses their level of risk or offence to the client, and creates counter arguments, with links to authoritative sources.'

The young man paused, glancing around the café to check he wasn't being overheard.

He moved his chair fractionally closer and lowered his voice.

'But given your time constraints, I'd recommend another of my products. Sticks and Stones.'

'I'm listening.'

'Psychologists have found that one of the most effective ways to stop people thinking rationally is to swear at them and call them names. Sticks and Stones uses the same trawling software to identify risk words and phrases, but instead of countering them with rational arguments and science, it flings abuse.'

'And this works?'

'Not with everyone. But if applied correctly, most people get so wound up they disengage with the conversation. Instantly.'

Petersen stroked his chin.

He liked the idea of a Sybil Attack, but if science hadn't convinced these people by now it wasn't going to change their minds before the release.

'How long would it take to activate this Sticks and Stones?'

'With the kind of money you're talking about, six hours. Have to warn you though, the Community Coalition site will go toxic within 48 hours.'

'So be it.'

'YOU CAN see him now, Inspector. Doubt you'll get much though. He's pretty drowsy. Amnesia's common in cases like this.'

Matthew kept his eye closed – the one he could open.

Let them think I'm out to it. Hearings still bleedin twenty-twenty.

'What are his injuries, doctor? Looks like he's been in a car wreck.'

'Traumatic brain injury, though the angiogram showed limited signs of intracranial hemorrhage. Fractured clavicle. Facial contusions and lacerations, as you can see.'

'In English?'

'Concussion, but no bleeding in the brain. Broken collarbone. Few cuts and bruises.'

'Why is he not being kept in a secure room like I asked?'

'It's being prepared Inspector. They'll be moving him down shortly.'

Matthew snagged a whiff of perfume and sensed the Kiwi detective standing over him.

'Hello again Matt. Detective Inspector Hansen. We met briefly at the airport. How you feeling?'

He slowly opened his good eye, took in her face, then looked over her shoulder.

'I'm alone Matt. Just me and the doctor. Were you expecting someone else?'

With an effort, he raised his head from the pillow.

'Name's Matthew. Your Yank friend, Kaufman. He locked up yet?'

'Why would I want - '

'For murder. He killed both your coppers.'

'Don't be ridiculous. Mr Kaufman wasn't even in the country when Constable Shaw was killed.'

Matthew sunk back into the pillow, closed his eye and turned on the waterworks.

'I need to ask you some questions.'

'Fraid you'll have to wait Inspector,' said the doctor. We need to top up his pain relief.'

* * * *

CRIME SCENE tape cordoned off half the ground floor of the library, from the monitor Matthew had been using to the bookshelf where Cat said the screwed-up piece of paper landed.

Jay tried to look under the shelf from different angles, but needed to get closer for a decent view. Cat, who'd managed to slip out a side door before the building was overrun, told Jay there was something deliberate in the way the piece of paper left Matthew's hand as he was tackled. Did it have the answer to part of the clue? Who knows? Now the geek was busted, it was their only chance.

Part of the shelf where Matthew got clobbered lay on the ground where it fell. Jay could see it had periodicals on anthropology.

He found a terminal that hadn't been logged off, worked out how to do a catalogue search, and found a reference number for a journal called Transforming Anthropology.

He wrote the library code on the back of his hand, pulled the hoodie tighter round his face and walked as confidently as he could towards a sergeant standing behind the tape.

'Excuse me sir. I need to get this journal.'

'Sorry son. Can't come in here.'

'Look I realize you're just doing your job officer, and like, I don't want to be a pain. If I don't get this reference, like tonight, I'll miss the deadline for my assignment in the morning and fail my whole degree.'

'No can do.'

Jay stole a look under the shelf, saw nothing.

He raised his eyebrows, turned and headed for the door.'

'Hey you.'

He froze.

'Give us that number. I'll get it for you.'

Jay exhaled.

'Thanks. Sergeant is it? Appreciate it.'

'I had a daughter at uni. I know about assignments.'

The officer knelt and ran his finger along spines.

'You sure this mag's here?' he called out in a voice to rouse the dodos.

'Should be. Computer says it's not checked out.'

The next twenty seconds took twenty minutes.

'Here we go.'

The cop walked back, holding up a thin journal with a cover story headed Racialized Publics.

'Thanks sir. You've saved my arse. Take the rest of the night off.'

'I wish.'

Jay retreated to an empty desk beside the lifts and feigned interest in the legacies of race and class privilege in the United States. When he looked up, the focus of everyone's attention was back on the police and bright lights and white boiler suits. Beyond the tape, huddles of students were pretending to study but fooling nobody. A cleaner was wheeling a trolley towards the elevators. She pushed the down arrow. Must be a basement.

Minutes later Jay was rifling through a rubbish skip. Newspapers. Food wrappers. Half a bottle of Tropix Vodka Raspberry Rush. Three hypodermic needles. And a rimu tree's worth of paper. Almost all of it scrunched up into balls. Took twenty minutes to find it.

Kaufman 771 400 17

Norton/Abdiel QF27 from Brisbane tonight

Gold

FootNOTE

13 letters.

36. The whole works

KAUFMAN IGNORED the ogling and finger pointing as he roamed through the arrivals hall. Anonymity was blown out the water with his mug on TV every night, so there was little point covering up.

He knew he impressed the hell out of these peasants in the camouflage field jacket and pants he'd had sent out from the States. If they thought he meant business, they were on the money. Civilian my ass.

This little venture, through no fault of his, had gone downhill ever since the tree-huggers set foot in New Zealand. The comedy of bungles, political correctness, inexperience and sheer incompetence of Hansen and her lot made Fatty Arbuckle and Charlie Chaplin look like an elite force. Two of the three were still on the run and their continued liberty was beginning to threaten the smooth running of the release in five days. Ditto Eve's shot at treatment.

All that was about to change. After the stoush with Hansen and pulling a string or three, the New Zealand Police Commissioner granted his request to operate independently of Hansen when necessary. He looked up at the arrivals board. The Qantas flight from Brisbane had landed. Any minute now the personnel required to help him finish off the trio would walk through the door.

They came separately, their shorts and t-shirts, sunglasses, caps and sandals – even suntans – blending with groups of passengers returning from vacations on Queensland beaches. Who would have guessed these two men had wasted more people between them than you could fit in the airliner they'd just arrived on?

Norton Deakes alone had clocked up over two hundred fifty with the United States Army Marksmanship Unit, including a Taliban dune coon from 2190 yards during Operation Anaconda in Afghanistan. That was before the South African went private and stopped counting. Abdiel Nazim, the Iraqi Jew and former Mossad agent who specialized in elimination through mechanical or chemical means, had struck more often than the businessman walking in front of him had celebrated Christmas.

Kaufman loathed the term *mercenary*.

Deakes and Nazim were private soldiers who would carry out orders without question, without a manual, without a trace.

As per pre-determined instructions the three men made their separate ways to the cab rank, where they agreed to share a ride to a hotel.

Other than comments about the weather and the flight, the only information they conveyed was a coded confirmation that the package was being transported to a warehouse near the airport.

* * * *

JAY'S STOMACH was bellowing for a refuel, but he had one more task to complete before the feed.

The day had started well.

He wanted the cops to think they were at or near the protest rally, to give Cat and Matthew a free run at the university.

Making the ATM withdrawal and getting his old Greenpeace friend Hayden East to arrange trios of protesters to dress up worked a treat. All were hauled in for questioning then released.

Then Matthew got nabbed and things turned to custard.

Perimeter security at Wellington Airport was virtually non-existent, so Jay was there to see the white Transit van with diplomatic plates pull up on the tarmac beneath the Qantas jet.

The custom molded crate was the first item unloaded from the cargo hold.

It took two men to transfer it to the van, which was driven to an unmarked building on the western boundary of the airport.

Less than a quarter of a mile as the crow flies, Jay squatted on the roof of a Rebel Sport store, fingering the computer chip in his pocket. Time to up the ante.

He took out the cell phone he'd 'borrowed' at the university, enabled the GPS function, and punched in the numbers.

'Yes?'

'Evening Bradley. Hope your mates enjoyed their flight.'

'Who's this?'

'You disappoint me. Didn't pick you for a sandwich short of a picnic.'

'Duggan?'

'As you say in Hollywood, I'm asking the questions. Did Norton and Abdiel pass the Krav Maga course as well, or are their skills in a different field?'

'You're so out of your depth.'

'I'll take that as a *yes*. That was a curious item of luggage arrived on the plane from Brisbane, Bradley. Pity your handlers didn't treat it with the respect it deserved. Or didn't you tell them what was in it?'

'You're full of horseshit.'

'Call me old fashioned Bradley, but I thought that fancy Barrett rifle was supposed to be shipped out *with* the computer chip for the optical ranging. Got this sneaking suspicion you might struggle to find replacement parts for that type of weapon in little old New Zealand.'

'You're bluffing asshole.'

Jay heard a soft beep on the line. The trace was being activated.

'Let me give you some friendly advice, Bradley. If that's really your name. You made a mistake coming here. Prize cock-up. Picked on the wrong people. Wrong country. You've dug yourself into a hole. The more you dig the deeper and darker she's going to get. I'd cut my losses if I were…'

'I'm quaking in my…'

'You should be. I know what happened to those two cops. Saw you with my own eyes. Now I've got eyes watching Matthew. If anything happens…'

'Listen here you little…'

Jay cut him off.

A landscape supplies truck was trundling along the road towards him. He tossed the cell phone into a pile of bark mulch in the back and dropped the computer chip down the storm water outlet in the spouting of the building. Time for that feed.

* * * *

KAUFMAN TURNED the rental car into the visitors' park at Wellington Hospital. His heart was back to normal since discovering Duggan had managed to get inside the warehouse, open the crate and disable the Barrett.

Deakes said the rifle was as good as useless without the chip that determined the temperature, barometric pressure and tilt.

An alternative weapon would have to be sourced.

Kaufman did not like being made a fool of.

He called XecIntel to demand they find out more about Duggan's background, using whatever means necessary. Unfriendly visits would be made to all Duggan's address book entries.

Yes the New Zealander was good. But so was the man sitting in the white doctor's coat beside Kaufman. Now to deal with Liddell. And call Duggan's bluff. Kaufman punched the number for his annoying local sidekick.

'Hansen here. What do you want?'

'I've just had a phone call from our mutual friend, Mr Duggan.'

'No kidding? Any idea where?'

'We've triangulated it to somewhere between three cell phone towers near the airport. Pretty sure I know where he was calling from.'

'I'm listening.'

Kaufman described a line of buildings between Cochrane Street and the western runway.

'And you know this how?'

Jesus she could be irritating.

'Duggan was talking about something he could only see if he was nearby.'

'How long ago?'

'Just got off the phone,' he lied. 'Sixty seconds.'

'Mind if I ask what you were doing in an industrial zone near the airport this time of night?'

'Not at all Inspector. I was sightseeing in your beautiful city.'

'Save the prattle, Mr Kaufman. I'll check it out.'

Atta girl. He knew Duggan would be miles away by now, but that should tie her up for a while. He waited till Hansen and three uniformed officers emerged from the front entrance of the hospital and drove away in two patrol cars. He turned to his passenger, who was fitting a stethoscope around his neck.

'All set, *Doctor* Nazim?'

* * * *

SKIP COULDN'T have been clearer. Be there on time for the powhiri – the traditional Maori welcome. Or be snubbed all night.

Jay shifted the weight to his right leg and brushed the bush aside to get a better view of the restaurant and surrounds. Half a dozen people dressed for a feed stood awkwardly in one corner of the courtyard. Where was Cat? If she was there, her disguise was good.

High-pitched chanting by two women signaled the beginning of the ceremony, the karanga. A car pulled up and a middle-aged couple got out and headed towards the entrance, framed by carved wooden po. Jay jogged across the road and slunk through the gate. He merged with the other guests just as a warrior began the haka powhiri, the dance of welcome to symbolically draw visitors onto the sacred marae. Grass skirt. Bare chest. Tattoos. Snaking tongue. Popping eyes. The whole works.

* * * *

THE PILLOW came over Matthew's face before he had a chance to call out.

Gasping for air, he got nothing and panicked.

He tried to bring his hands up, but they were restrained. His head was pinned and being pushed like a great weight, sandwiched between two pillows.

Claustrophobia.

A strange, muffled darkness.

Pain stabbing his forehead, heart pounding, chest crushed.

The sensation of bile rising.

Then the sound of the machine monitoring his vitals going berserk.

'Shut that thing off!' hissed a voice.

The ringing died, replaced by an intense light as the pillow was plucked away. Matthew sucked in a mouthful of air just before a huge hand clamped over his mouth.

'Call out and you'll be dead before you hear the echo.'

The accent was American. The face unmistakable. For the second time that day Matthew wet himself. He was vaguely aware of a figure in a white coat kneeling behind the monitoring machine.

'Now we're going to have a wee chat, Matthew. If you want to live, I strongly advise you cooperate. Piss me off and you're dead meat. We understand each other?'

Matthew nodded and the hand came off his mouth. He gulped.

'Why are you so keen to break into the Vestco website?'

Matthew knew this was the hero slot. The moment to resist. Tell the arsehole to go fuck himself.

'There's a virtual safe deposit box. Henry Beck. He did it. Put something in it. It's Cat and Duggan want to open it. Not me. Couldn't give a toss. They're up to the last clue. But they can't do it without me, and they've got the wrong - '

'Where are Duggan and Tayler now?'

'I don't - '

The pillow came back so fast, so unexpected and with such force Matthew was sure his nose was breaking.

He tried to inhale but couldn't get his lips open. The pressure on his head intensified, his lungs were on fire and the tingling in his fingertips shot up his arms.

Searing light dazzled him as the pillow came off. Air charged into his lungs.

'You were saying?'

'The restaurant. We were supposed to meet there tonight. Something in the Bay. Pie in the Bay. Kai. Yeah. Kai in the Bay.'

Kaufman turned to the white coat.

'You set?'

'Ken.' The Hebrew word for *yes* was the last thing Matthew heard before he passed out.

37. We are one

THE OYSTERS were divine. Served raw on ice and topped with pesto made from fern shoots with the delightful name of *pikopiko* that tasted like bitter asparagus.

Cat picked up a hint of grapefruit in the sauvignon blanc. Not the gooseberry and nut flavors quoted by the waiter who recommended a Matahiwi vintage from 'over the hill'. The live traditional music was fabulous until Jay mentioned one of the flutes was probably made from albatross bone.

The most pleasant surprise for Cat, though, was the company. They were seated in a private alcove known as the Rangitira Table with Sir Jack, who Cat discovered was not Skip's *cousin* in the conventional sense of the word. Anywhere from sixty to eighty, he had a bald head, spherical face mottled with freckles, flattened nose and double chin. His blue silk tie had a white logo circling three crowns and a book. Around his neck hung an intricately carved Manaia, a mythical half human half bird creature with eyes inlaid in abalone shell, known locally as paua. When Sir Jack spoke, the words seemed to float from far away, with a measured calm that exuded wisdom.

Cat rearranged her cutlery and studied the menu card. The Rangitira Table was described as a meal experience about sharing ideas and challenging philosophies as you eat and drink. They'd certainly done that. Conversation ranged from genetic modification to the Maori concept of whakapapa, which Jay translated as genealogy. The story of Sir Jack's family history, traced back to the arrival of a canoe on the east coast centuries ago, was carved into the walking stick leaning against his chair. It was the inherited responsibility of every Maori to protect their land, Sir Jack was saying.

'We call it kaitiakitanga. It comes from the word *tiaki*, which means to guard. Keep watch over. To protect, not to control. Every part of the world – natural and divine – is linked by its mauri. Life force. Kaitiakitanga places an obligation on us to protect the mauri of all other species. Which is why genetic modification or engineering or whatever you want to call it is wrong. It mixes the mauri of different species.'

He reached for his walking stick and held it up. The inlaid shell eyes near the handle sparkled in the candlelight.

'Through my whakapapa, I am linked to the land. We are one. To mix the mauri, change the natural order, is to change my whakapapa.'

The words were spoken with such humble simplicity, they sat in silence for several minutes. Cat had only come across one other person like Sir Jack. An elderly native Indian she met on a study trip to Canada. She pictured his blistered lips as he spoke: *Sunlight leaves no mark on the grass. We too must pass silently.* There was as much wisdom in these two old men as in all the professors she'd had the privilege to meet. Like Whatu's knowledge of plants at Waikaremoana. It was one thing to possess knowledge. To align that knowledge with passion and feeling for the land brought a deeper wisdom.

Until a few days ago, Cat would have dismissed anyone without a university degree. Her view of education was being turned on its head.

She looked across at Jay, another man with an intriguing, almost spiritual side, though right now he was staring at the *beauty* spot just above her top lip. Waterproof brown mascara. Painted on like the rest of the disguise lifted from a year-old *Cosmopolitan* magazine. Strip eyelash extensions. Glossy lips filled out with liner and a dab of lip balm to accentuate the pout. Pearl earrings and matching fake necklace. Flowing wig. Black cocktail dress. No photograph or identikit image of Cat Tayler looked anything like this.

Jay held her gaze for a few seconds before patting his lips with a serviette and standing.

'If you'll excuse me. I need to have a word to our waiter. About a boat.'

* * * *

KAUFMAN DRUMMED his fingers on the steering wheel as he waited for a *Tangaroa Fisheries* truck with one headlight to pass in a trail of exhaust fumes.

He turned into The Parade and parked over the road from the Kai in the Bay. Through the back window of the restaurant Kaufman could see a guy in a white chef's hat working in the kitchen. Smoke rose from a pit in the corner of the car park. Only three cars. The fewer witnesses the better. He directed Deakes to the rear door and headed for the front. Safety off. Gun cocked. He pushed open the door and fired a single shot into the ceiling.

The joint was empty except for an old man sitting at a table in the corner. He reached for something beside the table and Kaufman sent another shot above his head, shattering the glass covering a framed parchment. The old guy didn't flinch. He grabbed a walking stick, calmly stood and started mumbling in an unintelligible language

'Sit the fuck down Grandpop and put your hands on the table where I can see them.'

The old buzzard ignored him, and started walking forwards, pointing his stick at the door. Must be deaf, thought Kaufman, firing another shot into the floor in front of him. He aimed at his chest. The man kept advancing. Deakes appeared at the door to the kitchen.

'Back's clear. No-one here except the kaffir cook and two ousies washing up.'

The old man stopped in front of Kaufman and was now pointing the stick at him.

'E mua ãta haere, e muri tata kino.'

'Anyone out the back speak English, Deakes?'

'Nee. Just mumbo jumbo like this krimpie.'

38. Freakish luck

ON DAYS LIKE this, Dave Lowe thanked the Lord he worked in television. The footage from Mumbai and Moscow and Beijing was pure gold, and the package he was putting together for the main bulletin had a Peabody for executive producer written all over it.

Food riots had broken out simultaneously in Tiananmen Square, Red Square and in Mumbai's hellhole of cardboard and humanity made famous by the movie *Slumdog Millionaire*.

Thanks to tip-offs, the network's cameramen were right there to capture helmeted thugs from the People's Liberation Army lashing out at grandmothers, Russian soldiers firing teargas to disperse a group of school children, and a shrieking woman holding the broken body of one of the stars of the Oscar-winning movie crushed in a stampede for sacks of rice.

Pure gold.

A red light flashed on the console.

Lowe took the call from his executive assistant.

'This better be important.'

'Trust me, it is. *Grassroots* has just posted from Boston Common. Massive demonstration over food stamps. Largest crowd since the Vietnam War. The mayor gets up on stage, tries to calm them down. This bum walks up. Shoots him. Point blank.'

'Pictures?'

'You betya. *Grassroots* had a camera right behind this guy. Freakish luck.'

The digital clock on the console showed eight minutes to deadline.

'Thank Christ for that joint-use agreement with the blog. Right, lead in with Boston. Strip in sixty. No. Make it eighty. Move the stiff kid from the slum into slot two. Get Marcia to redo the voiceover. Play up the double tragedy. Run Moscow and Beijing as three and four.'

'What do we lose?'

Lowe scrolled through the bulletin list.

'The anti-Alo rallies are ninety secs. How strong's that piece?'

'Very. Size of the crowds turned out in London, LA and Paris were a real surprise. Shows support for the release of this thing's not as strong as everyone thinks.'

'How good's the footage?'

'Well, no-one gets assassinated, Dave.'

'Drop it. Give the overflow to Boston.'

* * * *

DEL BOVILL was a creature of habit.

Every morning, she would quietly get out of bed so as not to wake Tony, get dressed and walk the loop from their home on Cedar Street, along 11th Ave, Erickson, 20th and Canyon, past Prince Charles School and the Creston Post Office all the way to the corner, then back beside the railroad line home.

After a shower, Del would prepare breakfast. This morning it was turkey and pineapple on organic wheat bread, with avocado and organic honey mustard. Tony was addicted to the honey mustard sold at the local Vital Health store.

After breakfast, Del would take her cup of wild licorice tea and her iPad onto the porch and check Facebook. Her granddaughter had introduced her to social media as a way of keeping in touch while she was volunteering for Projects Abroad in Laos.

Del was especially eager this morning, to see if there was any response to her comment about aloe vera.

There had been an interesting conversation on British Columbia's Community Coalition page about natural remedies for acid reflux. Tony had suffered for years, until they discovered that half a cup of aloe vera juice before a meal soothed the irritation.

Del logged on, and almost spilt her tea.

Seventeen comments.

'Something wrong, dear?'

She handed the iPad to Tony.

He thumbed through the comments, his head shaking in disbelief.

Del went inside to find the piece of paper her granddaughter left with instructions what to do if this sort of thing happened.

When she got back to the porch, Tony was smiling.

'I see where you went wrong. You missed the 'e' in Aloe.'

'Still, there's no excuse for that sort of language.'

Del went into her profile and tapped 'Likes'. The Community Coalition for Food Safety was top of the list. She jabbed the 'Unlike' button with a little more force than necessary.

39. A national bloody treasure

MEETINGS, meetings and more meetings. It was the part of the job Hansen despised. Lack of sleep compounded the misery.

'What exactly is the status of these mercenaries?'

'Let's not get melodramatic Inspector,' the Commissioner replied as they rode the elevator to the ninth floor of the executive wing of Parliament, known locally as the Beehive for obvious reasons.

'They are operating under the same autonomous arrangement as Kaufman, and answerable to him.'

Hansen started to protest.

'This has gone on long enough, Inspector. It's becoming a serious embarrassment. You, we, need all the help we can get.'

They were met by a secretary who guided them into the Prime Minister's private office.

Around a large wooden table matching the wall paneling and the shelves displaying gifts from heads of state sat the members of the inquisition. All men, but Hansen was used to that. She recognized the head of the Security Intelligence Service, National Assessment Bureau, Chief of the Army, American Ambassador, the Prime Minister's press secretary. Couple of unknown suits.

And Kaufman. What the hell was he doing here?

As they waited for the Prime Minister, there were murmurings about canceling leave, emptying out the national police college, re-swearing in retired officers, roping in territorials, the impact on tourism.

The word *catastrophic* was used twice. Grassroots got a mention, as did the Jaywalker blog. Hits had increased twenty-fold since a story on last night's television news, and almost all the comments on the site were now anti-Duggan, pro-Vestco. Kaufman looked smug.

The Commissioner was asked for an update on the manhunt. He deferred to Hansen. She cleared her throat.

'As you know, we have one of the suspects in custody. All our resources are being thrown into containing the other two in the Wellington area. The airport, railway stations, roads, bus terminals, port, wharfs are under intensive surveillance.'

A side door opened and a needled looking Prime Minister scudded in. Everyone started to stand, but he motioned for them to remain seated and for Hansen to continue.

'We believe they may be trying to head for the South Island, with a likely target being Lincoln University where the New Zealand release of Alo will take place. In addition to the tight net we've drawn round Wellington, we've got people watching airfields and ports on both sides of Cook Strait and the Navy patrolling the water in between.'

'So, in point of fact Inspector, these terrorists could be on Uranus for all you know?'

'I, we...'

'And this fiasco last night at the Maori restaurant?'

Hansen was dreading that question. Kaufman came to her rescue.

'Completely my fault, Mr Prime Minister. I acted on what I understood to be good information, realizing Inspector Hansen was busy following up another lead. Turned out to be a false alarm.'

'Just as well. Sir Jack's considered a national bloody treasure in this part of the world, Mr Kaufman. All hell'd break loose if anything happened to him.'

'I accept full responsibility sir. I was wrong. I was out of line. It won't happen again.'

'I sincerely hope not. Let's move on. Have you any good news, Commissioner?'

'The police website is back up and running, sir. It was knocked out for several hours by a virus we suspect was put there by Liddell before he was apprehended.'

The Prime Minister glowered down his nose at Hansen.

'I trust you can confirm Liddell is still in custody. That you've at least got one thing right.'

Bastard.

'Of course, sir,' a little sharper than necessary. 'The Englishman has been moved to a secure room in the hospital, with armed guards outside his room. Others at the entry to the ward. The hospital grounds are being patrolled 24/7. He isn't going anywhere.'

The meeting broke up and Hansen pulled Kaufman aside.

'Thanks for covering for me.'

'Forget it. I screwed up. And sorry about that old Maori guy. Couldn't understand a word he was saying.'

'Sir Jack speaks better English than you or I. He's got a PhD from Oxford.'

Kaufman's mouth dropped.

'You must have really done something to piss him off.'

'Must have been my accent. You said Liddell's been moved. Is he, you know, coherent?'

'He's in a bad way, but he'll live. The machine monitoring his vitals malfunctioned. Electrical fault they reckon. Fortunately, it had only just happened when they went to shift him, so they managed to resuscitate.'

* * * *

PETERSEN glanced out at the blue-gray waters of the Bo Hai Gulf as the Lear jet closed in on the coast of China southeast of Beijing.

'Mr Pyjas is streaming on channel four sir.'

'Thank you Penny.'

He pushed a button on the arm of his chair and a monitor folded out from the cabin wall. The Vestco chairman was announcing a large donation to ease the suffering of slum dwellers in Mumbai, making appropriate noises about the food riots and how Vestco was a responsible global citizen.

The death of the child star from Slumdog Millionaire, visiting relatives at the time of the riot and whose tragic demise had captivated the world's media, was an unexpected bonus. Everything was falling into place. Except the terrorists.

Petersen switched off the video and looked back outside. Through wispy cloud, the rooftops and streets of Tianjin city blended into a vision of a rusting battleship. Had he overestimated Kaufman? He'd seemed so ideal for the job. Raised in a rigid military family under an iron-fisted father. Lived, worked, breathed in military environments all his life. Told what to do, what to think, when to fart. Follow orders or be damned. Highly skilled yet easily manipulated. Known skeletons in the closet. We all had them. The knowing was important. Cheating on the psychometric testing to get into the Special Forces, at least three serious indiscretions while seconded to the LAPD. The guy ticked all the boxes, including the *ace*. The weak link.

Eve.

Petersen knew all there was to know about his security chief's daughter. And more. How Kaufman prematurely retired from foreign ops when Eve was born so he wouldn't miss the childhood years like his father had. The cancer was icing on the cake, the generous medical expenses clause the clincher. After arranging for Kaufman to be bombarded with information about cancer and treatments till he was overwhelmed, Petersen came in like a white knight, introducing him to an oncology consultant who would take care of everything. Coming from such a trusted specialist, Kaufman was bound to believe the information fed to him about the clinic in Germany. Then at a critical moment of vulnerability, daddy dear was offered a large bonus to be paid the day after Alo was released. Enough money, coincidentally, to cover the prohibitive cost of his daughter's treatment.

Money earmarked for surgery of an entirely different sort.

40. The trap set

KAUFMAN HAD forgotten how grody and uninspiring general hospital wards could be.

At the Center for Cancer and Blood Diseases at Los Angeles Children's Hospital – Eve's second home these last eight months – the elevators were guarded by giraffes and the floors cushioned with peacock mats. He could picture her now, jumping from one feather dot to the next. Hours spent creating a ladybird to stick on the mural in the Love Bug Garden. And her favorite place, the rehabilitation unit known as The Dome, with rafters and skylight and hot air balloons painted on the wall. The number of times Eve dreamt of floating away on one of those balloons...

The echo of footsteps on vinyl brought Kaufman back to the waiting room outside the ward at Wellington Hospital. Numb walls. Cold floors. Lingering disinfectant. Library voices.

Updated information from XecIntel prised open one of the shutters screening the murky past of Jay Duggan. The mere sight of a room set up for water boarding was enough to persuade a Scottish environmentalist listed in Duggan's address book to come clean about a venture in South Africa that closed a diamond mine for several weeks. There were others in Spain and Canada. But the one of most interest to Kaufman was in Australia. After a botched attempt to sabotage a Rio Tinto mine west of Darwin, Duggan managed to spring an injured companion from a hospital. Under the noses of police guards.

Perhaps it was a blessing Liddell survived the equipment *malfunction*, as Hansen put it. Duggan was bound to try to reach the English nerd. Deakes, armed with a replacement Stoner sniper rifle, was stationed in a nearby second floor apartment with a clear view through the barred window. Nazim was at the kitchen table of the apartment, monitoring live footage from inside the hospital after hacking into the closed-circuit video surveillance system.

From the waiting room, Kaufman could see the only entrance to the hall outside Liddell's room. With the trap set, he scratched the top of his headpiece, gently brushed the matching moustache with his thumb and forefinger, and adjusted the hearing aid in his left ear. Nazim was coming through clearly.

41. The money sentence

'FOR THE record then, Vestco is sticking by its pledge that, for example, a peasant farmer back in Bangladesh is going to triple the amount of rice he can grow despite the drought, despite the threat of yellow stem borer, despite the fact he has absolutely zero experience with these new seeds coated with your Alo?'

The Dhaka reporter for *Grassroots* held the phonebook-sized copy of the Vestco Pledge in one hand as he glanced skeptically round the room full of journalists.

'Sounds like science fiction to me?' he said, shaking his head.

'Fair question,' thought Petersen, watching the media briefing from several camera angles on monitors in a room beside the ballroom foyer of the Park Hyatt in Beijing. Years of experience taught him the trick with these briefings was to make the questions *appear* curly. Patsy ones were too obvious, even to journalists like this bunch flown in from developing countries. It also helped if the journalist believed he thought up the question himself. The science fiction line had been planted over dinner at the China Grill, the highest restaurant in Beijing with 360-degree views over the city and main course prices exceeding the monthly salary of the young man from Dhaka.

Vestco's communications director, Shelley Sutherland, was nearing the end of her well-rehearsed answer.

'... better than that. Farmers in Bangladesh currently average a yield of between one and one point two tons per hectare. The fourth part of our pledge was to triple yields. That was a minimum. After our latest round of laboratory tests, we are confident farmers throughout Asia, Africa and South America, despite drought, despite pests, despite never having seen Alo, will average five tons per hectare.'

Petersen saw from the scribbling pens and sideways nods the answer had the desired effect. It was the money sentence that would be read and heard and seen by hundreds of millions in the hours before the poll was taken. He leant towards the microphone and pushed the transmit button.

'That will do Shelley. Wrap it up.'

'Last question,' she said, pointing at a reporter from the *New Light of Myanmar* who enjoyed the Wagyu sirloin, medium rare, for dinner last night, but struggled with the chocolate lava cake.

'Damn it. I said wrap - '

Too late. A snappily dressed African woman in the second row had shot to her feet.

'Any comment on the fact two of the terrorists are still roaming at large in New Zealand, and the threat they pose to the release of Alo?'

Petersen cursed as red lights come on above several cameras and he realized they were only starting to record. If the communications director didn't answer, her refusal would become the story. The downside of staying out of the public eye was relying on others to take the spotlight. Shelley was good, but not perfect. She tried to gloss over the unexpected question, but fumbled. Petersen could see the headline coming.

Time to ramp up the pressure on Kaufman.

42. Root access

HANSEN OBSERVED him through the door before activating the *record* button on her phone and entering.

Twenty-four hours and the bruising was lighter, the swelling down, the right eye half open.

He was sitting up in bed talking to a nurse.

Almost perky.

Hansen opted for the soft approach.

'I'm sorry about the malfunction with the equipment, Matt. The technicians here assure me it won't happen again.'

'It's Matthew. You still don't get it do you? It's not the technicians here you've got to worry about. It's that crazy Yank. Tried to kill me like those coppers. He's the one should be locked up.'

The nurse left.

'Still on about that are we? Look, we've checked the airline logs. Mr Kaufman didn't arrive in the country until the day after Constable Shaw was murdered. He couldn't possibly - '

'Means nothing. Logs can be changed. Old mate of mine at university, Phil Dixon, did it once. Was going out with this stewardess who did the dirty on him. Phil worked out the airline's staff mail server sat outside the corporate firewall. You could use any IP address to telnet into the server. Phil'd been bonking this bird for months. Knew all sorts of personal details. Took him less than ten minutes to figure out her password. From there he got root - '

'Root?'

'Root access.'

'You've lost me. Can I have the short version in English?'

'He hacked into the mail server and got access to the passwords - '

'What's this got to do with airline logs?'

Liddell raised his good eyebrow.

'He wanted to piss her off, right? So, he re-routed her to all these out of the way places. Like Addis Ababa, Lima. Silly tosser went too far and got caught. If all he'd wanted to do was change one flight log no one would've noticed.'

'Surely it can't be that easy.'

'Piece of cake if you know what you're doing.'

The guy was full of bullshit.

'We'll check it out, OK? I need you to tell me where Jay and Catherine are.'

'You're dreaming lady.'

There wasn't a lot of conviction in Liddell's voice. His eye kept darting over her shoulder. Sensing he was terrified of something, she tried a different approach.

'I promise you I'll look into Mr Kaufman's movements. Between you and me, I also have some concerns about the way he operates. What would need to happen for you to tell me where Jay and Catherine are? And what the three of you are really up to?'

'You'd need to tell those guards out there Kaufman's the one they need to keep away from me.'

'Done. I'll give specific instructions that he is not allowed near this room. Anything else?'

'A guarantee I won't be extradited back to the States.'

'Isn't that where you live?'

'Those barbarians've still got the death penalty.'

Obviously he hadn't caught up with the news about New Zealand's re-introduction.

'That's not an issue here, Matthew. You've been arrested for your part, alleged part, in the murder of one, possibly two of our police officers. Those are matters for the New Zealand courts.'

He seemed to relax.

'Make you a deal, Matt.'

'It's Matthew.'

'Sorry. Cooperate and I'll guarantee no extradition. And protection from Bradley Kaufman. But we can't protect Catherine and Jay from him if we don't know where they are.'

'I want it in writing.'

'That can be arranged.'

'They're going to see a friend of Jay's. Lives in the South Island.'

'Why? What's this all about?'

He told her about a virtual safe deposit box that must contain incriminating information about Alo. How they'd reached the last of three entry levels. Something far-fetched about the footnotes of the geezer who discovered DNA.

'This friend of Jay's? Who is he? Where in the South Island?'

'Name's Ross. That's all I know.'

* * * *

CLEAR SKY and afternoon sun hadn't altered the rusted hulk appearance of Tianjin as the Lear headed east on the return journey to LA.

'Your call to the White House is on line one sir. The TV producer is holding on two.'

Petersen dealt quickly with the President's chief of staff, taking up his offer of a Special Forces chopper for New Zealand. The second call was more important.

'Sorry to keep you waiting Dave. What you got?'

'Is this line secure?'

'Naturally.'

'Good news is that exit results from countries west of the dateline... we're talking China, Russia, the eastern states of India ... indicate upwards of eighty percent approval. Bad news is my superior's talking about broadcasting the poll results a day earlier than scheduled.'

With figures like those, any time would be acceptable. But for maximum impact it would be better on the eve of the release, as planned. Petersen hadn't got to where he was by settling for *acceptable*.

'What are the chances of convincing your superior to stick with the original time?'

'Slim. We've been leaked some rare footage from inside a nuclear facility in Pyongyang. They're putting together a special segment. She wants to run it in your prime-time poll slot.'

Petersen didn't answer.

Just left the silence hanging.

'Some of our brass are getting nervous about this two-headed hosting arrangement for release day linking the network's mainframe to yours. Worried how it will look, like we're compromising editorial independence.'

'We've been through this many times, Dave. You know as well as I do it's the only way to get the simultaneous live feeds we want from all the release sites.'

'I know. I know.'

Another pause.

'There may be a way to discredit the North Korean source.'

'I'll make it worth your while, Dave.'

'Can you be more specific?'

'We'll double your payment.'

'Hope for both our sakes this line's as secure as you say. I'll see what I can do.'

Petersen hung up and looked at his watch. The call from the oncology consultant would be going through to New Zealand in a few minutes. He dialed Kaufman.

* * * *

KAUFMAN LEFT the waiting room to take the call from Petersen.

'Everything's confirmed for Frankfurt. First class tickets with Lufthansa for you and Eve from LAX Wednesday next week. That's two days after the release. A limo will meet you at the airport and take you directly to the Schulerburg Klinik in Bad Nauheim. You and Eve have a two-bedroom suite and Eve has three dedicated nurses – all American – who will be at her beck and call 24/7. How's she doing?'

'Hanging in there. I spoke to her earlier today. Pretty tired after the last round of transfusions.'

'Say hello to her for me when you talk to her again.'

'Thank you. I – we – appreciate everything you're doing for us.'

'Pleasure's all mine Brad. Any news from down there? I'm counting on you to make sure those greenies don't spoil our party.'

Kaufman's cell phone beeped to indicate a call waiting.

'I'll let you take that Brad. Might be important.'

It was Kaufman's deputy back in the States, with a recording of part of the interview between Hansen and Liddell.

'Feed it through.'

He smiled at Liddell's concerns about 'that crazy Yank', Hansen's sweetener about opposing extradition, and the wimp opening up about the virtual deposit box, the CD and Ross.

'Pass that stuff about DNA and footprints onto the team working on the clue. That has to narrow it down. We know anything about this Ross? I've seen that name somewhere.'

His phone beeped again. Kaufman recognized the number of Eve's specialist in Los Angeles.

'Dr Hamilton. Can you hold for just a moment sir?'

He switched back to his deputy.

'So, about this Ross guy?'

'Ross is not a person Brad. It's a place. Little town on the West Coast of the South Island of New Zealand. Ross was one of the words we found pressed into that sheet of paper you sent us from the farmhouse in Napier. Someone had written an address: 10 Tokoma Street, Ross, Westland.'

'Excellent work.'

'And Brad.'

'Yep?'

'We don't think the New Zealand cops know about the house. We picked up a call between Hansen and the Commissioner. She suspects the town, not the address.'

'Let's keep it to ourselves. Gotta go.'

He took the call from the specialist.

'Sorry bout that Doc. Everything alright?'

'I'm not going to lie to you Mr Kaufman. Eve's condition is deteriorating faster than we expected. I'm afraid we've done all we can here. Her only hope now is Dr Berlangen's treatment at Schulerburg. Unless he can pinpoint and remove the tumors, she's down to weeks, if not days.'

43. Home ground advantage

JAY STOPPED rowing and allowed the dinghy to come round so he could get his bearings.

The distant snow-covered tops of Aoraki and Tasman glimmered in the moonlight like hewn pillars supporting a ceiling speckled with stars.

'Kia tuohu kotou, Me he maunga teitei, Ko Aoraki anake,' he whispered, head lowered, then plunged the oars back into the water, spun the boat round and propelled them towards the shore. The lights of the *Tangaroa* hoki trawler that had taken them from Wellington, around Farewell Spit and down the western coastline of the South Island, drifted further out to sea.

'What was that about?'

Cat was sitting in the stern, gripping the sides as if they were riding grade six rapids.

'An old Maori saying. *If you must bow your head, then let it be to the lofty mountain Aoraki.*'

'Which one is it?'

'The highest. Mount Cook most people round here call it.'

'Have you climbed it?'

'Most of it. We stopped a few feet shy of the summit.'

'Why? I thought the whole purpose of climbing a mountain was to stand on the top. Hold a flag. Get your photo taken.'

'Not on Aoraki. She's special to Ngai Tahu. Sticking a flag in the top'd be like dancing on your grandmother's grave.'

Jay rowed on. The rhythmic sound of the oars breaking the water was gradually swallowed by the roar of surf crashing on the shore. He spun the boat round once more to pick his landing point. The mountains had disappeared behind cliffs of clay and boulders rising dozens of feet into the bush. He tried to guide the little boat through a channel but miscalculated the surge of the tide. They slammed against one of the rocks.

Cat panicked, tried to stand, lost her balance and toppled out. Jay jumped in after her. It was only waist deep. He lifted her in his arms and carried her onto the beach, putting her down under an overhang in the cliff. Other than a bump to the shoulder and looking miserable, she seemed fine.

Jay heard the helicopter before he saw the searchlight frisking the coastline about a mile to the north. He ran back into the water to retrieve the dinghy, pulling it up beside Cat and using his foot to disguise the dragline in the pebbles. He made it to the overhang seconds before the arched silhouette of the New Zealand Air Force Iroquois passed overhead, its single beam illuminating the beach. Could have been a scene from *War of the Worlds*.

'It's hopeless Jay. They know we're here, or where we're heading. They've got Matthew. There's only four days to go and I'm no closer to sorting out my clue. Even if Matthew's worked out his. I've lost my glasses again. Let's face it, we're sunk.'

He put his arm around her good shoulder. She was soaked and shivering and the chin was taking a battering. The chopper was gone. For now.

Salt and seaweed and the fishy scent of the ocean fused with the dank earthy coarseness of the bush. Jay breathed deeply, sucking in a draught of his old mates Tane Mahuta and Tangaroa. Guardian spirits of the forest and sea. In all the jaunts he'd been on overseas he seldom got to choose the theater. This time he could. Odds that had been stacked against them were tilting.

Half time. Change ends. Home ground advantage.

44. Red sun on a brown square

HANSEN SUSPECTED the town of Ross as soon as Liddell said the word at the hospital in Wellington. Her inkling was confirmed when they discovered Duggan spent several school holidays there as a kid.

Didn't matter they hadn't worked out which of the five hundred houses his friend lived at.

Hansen had no intention of letting the two fugitives reach any of the houses.

There would be no more deaths on her watch.

The little West Coast town was surrounded. Armed police and soldiers in houses and buildings and sheds at every intersection and on every road from the Harihari Highway in the northwest to Aylmer Street in the southeast. So well concealed, even the media pack hadn't cottoned on to the new frontline of the manhunt.

Kaufman and his mercenaries were somewhere on the Coast, lying low, which suited Hansen fine.

She rotated her aching shoulders and looked at the clock on the wall of the motel room. Half an hour to midnight. Satisfied there was nothing else she could do and that her second in command would alert her the moment anything happened, she decided to spoil herself with some much-needed shuteye.

* * * *

248

WITHOUT GLASSES, Cat could see no further than the blurred outline of passing bush and farmland.

The stench of stale beer, male sweat and the apple and cherry wood aroma of pipe tobacco smothered the cab of the truck as it lurched along the road in the dim moonlight. The driver had no name and no interest in theirs.

'Less ya know the better,' he'd said when he pulled over to pick them up just out of Okarito.

He also saw the helicopter and had his own reasons for not wanting to be collared by the cops. Under a canvas tarpaulin on the deck behind them was a load of clocks and bowls made from illegally milled rimu he hoped to sell at the Wildfoods Festival in Hokitika later that day. Jay started to give him a hard time about it until Cat, wedged between the two men with the gear stick between her legs, squeezed Jay's thigh to shut him up. He sulked for several minutes, fiddling with a flashlight he'd found in the door cavity.

Cat kept her own mouth shut to avoid blowing their identity, though it soon became clear No Name hadn't heard of the manhunt, Alo or deodorant.

Since Okarito they'd pulled off the road and hidden twice to avoid the helicopter's searchlights. No Name was convinced it was the police or 'Customs jokers' looking for drug dealers working the coast.

He wasn't taking chances.

At every opportunity he'd driven off the main highway, if you could call it that, onto side roads or dirt tracks.

Every judder was a painful reminder of the bruise on Cat's shoulder.

They were approaching the outskirts of Ross from the west when the truck swung into a shingle driveway and stopped behind an old corrugated-iron barn.

'What's the matter?'

'Cops,' the driver grunted, pointing through a line of poplar trees to the property next door. 'Over there, beside Digger Townsend's woolshed.'

* * * *

MATTHEW LOOKED at the digital clock on his bedside monitor. 2.45am. The bonking nurse would be coming in soon for her final check before going off duty.

She and her colleagues had kept him up to speed with goings on outside. He knew Cat and Jay were still on the run. Attitudes towards him had changed since his near-death experience, which everyone insisted was caused by an unfortunate equipment malfunction. Things relaxed even more with news the search for his partners in crime had shifted to the South Island. He was no longer strapped to the bed, although a hospital security guard remained in the reception area.

The bonking nurse was pleasant to the point of groveling. The malfunction happened on her shift, while she was hard at it in the storeroom with one of the security guards. So, she was happy to sit by the bed and answer the patient's innocent questions about her life and family. And her netball, which Matthew discovered was a passion. When he asked if he could stretch his legs she convinced the guards it would be therapeutic to walk up and down the corridor, under supervision of course. Which was when he spotted the computer two doors down on the right.

The nurse walked into the room and Matthew pretended to be asleep as she read his vitals and noted them on the chart clipped to the end of the bed. Through squinted eyes he watched her check herself in the mirror, pursing her mouth as she touched up her lipstick. Boot steps approached. The nurse padded out to meet them. Excited whispers. A door opened and closed.

Matthew took the tube out of his arm and eased out of bed. The corridor was empty and the other guard at the end had his back turned. He crept past the storeroom and through the door on the opposite side. The computer was switched on, awaiting a login. The seventh attempt confirmed the nurse's password as *wingattack*. Humans were always the weakest link. He scrolled through his emails, opening one from Deaver back at the Millbrook Foundation in LA. He'd been asked to pass on a message from the CIA. In exchange for Matthew giving himself up and leading the police to the other two, he'd be given immunity from prosecution for the killing of Henry Beck. The second part of the email stunned Matthew. Deaver told him to seek out a guy called Bradley Kaufman, 'an old friend of mine you can trust with your life'.

You conniving arsehole, Matthew thought. The Millbrook CEO was up to his armpits in this bleedin caper.

A stifled squeal of ecstasy from across the hall refocused him on the screen. *Keep following the gold rush young man.* A Google search came up with an album called *After the Gold Rush* by Neil Young. He knew he was close, but the answer could only be one word.

Shouts in the corridor. Stampeding boots. They must have discovered the empty bed. Matthew concentrated on the screen. Keep following... Keep following... What the hell follows *After the Gold Rush*?

Doors were flung open down the corridor. They were searching the ward.

He typed *after after the gold rush* into the search field and hit the return key as the door burst open.

'Freeze and put your hands above your head.'

He raised his arms but kept his eyes on the screen. The answer - the title of Neil Young's subsequent album – was written across a red sun on a brown square.

Harvest.

* * * *

KAUFMAN HAD never known anyone talk so much. The old girl followed them room to room as he and Nazim searched the rattletrap excuse for a house.

If she was to be believed, a letter arrived a few days ago from Duggan, who said he was in the country and would visit her as soon as he could. She'd thrown the letter out, along with 'one of those metal donut thingamajigs'.

Or so she said at first. Her memory was clearly going west and the story changed by the hour. Perhaps she hadn't thrown it out at all. Perhaps she'd hidden it somewhere. Better check.

'Better safe than sorry, dear.'

Kaufman told her he was a friend of Jay's from the States. She got excited when he said Jay was meeting him here. She'd prattled on about young Jay visiting in school holidays, helping out at her stall at the Wildfoods Festival. 'Bound to be coming for the Wildfoods dear.'

She yakked away like a pinball on steroids, telling them what was in every room, even suggesting places for them to look. Insisted they search the backyard, the outhouse, the laundry-come-woodshed with possum pelts hanging up to dry. 'Trapped em and skinned em myself dear'. There was a foul odor out back, a mixture of the pelts and sewage wafting across from the property over the back fence. Kaufman had been relieved to get back inside the house to the down-home smell of frying bacon and mushrooms and onions and baked pastry. The old girl was still asleep in her bedroom. Snored all night, after downing several 'medicinal brandies' before going to bed.

Kaufman peered through the flimsy lace curtain in the front room. Dawn was bracing. From the tap on Hansen's phone, he knew the chopper crew reported nothing during their searches through the night along the coast. Roadblocks also drew blanks.

Eve sounded stable when he spoke to her on the phone. They obviously hadn't told her about the deterioration. Good idea.

Across the road was a double-story wooden house with paint peeling off a *For Sale* sign on the picket fence. There was no movement behind the upstairs dormer window, as you'd expect in a house unoccupied for months, if not years.

Nothing to suggest one of the world's finest marksmen was in position, with orders to shoot on sight.

45. Don't fight the rock

IN 1865 a party of gold prospectors decided to camp for the night in a place known as the Totara Valley, a few miles south of the West Coast town of Hokitika.

One of the men wandered down to the river to fill a billy. When he didn't return, his mates went searching. They found him picking gold out of cracks in rocks in the riverbed.

News of the discovery spread quickly, and before long thousands of diggers arrived and the town of Ross was born. Within a year, rich gold-bearing layers were found deep underground.

According to a local newspaper, one could see as many holes as in a nutmeg grater.

All Cat could see without glasses were the fuzzy shapes of buildings stretching away like rows of children's soft toy blocks. They were crouching behind a pile of rocks on a hill overlooking the town, ears ringing with a dawn cacophony from the forest at their backs. Jay was peering through the binoculars.

'How does it look?'

'Peaceful. Pretty much as I remember it.'

'Then what in heck are we waiting for?'

'Well, on the roof of that shop, behind the jade factory, is a marksman. There's two more over there on that water tower. Another on the crane to the right of the fish and chip shop.'

'But you've got a plan. Right?'

'Course.'

She followed Jay back into the forest and over a saddle into a gully on the other side of the hill. Two-thirds of the way down, he stopped beside a massive log that must have fallen across the gully in one of the storms for which the West Coast was apparently renowned. Water was trickling in a stream nearby. They slithered under the log and Jay pulled back some foliage to reveal the entrance to a cave about two feet high by eighteen inches wide.

'You're kidding.'

'She's not as bad as she looks. First bit's a smidgen tight. This cave leads to a tunnel that takes you to the main shaft of the old Fraser claim. From there you can drop down to the tunnel to the Cassius junction and you're away laughing.'

'How do you know this?'

'Used to spend hours exploring down here as a kid.'

'Won't the police be guarding the tunnels?'

'Highly unlikely. Entrances were all sealed off years ago after a tourist came a cropper in the Ross United Shaft. Took them over a week to find the body.'

'How long ago are we talking about?'

'Forty, fifty years.'

'That was before you were born. You said you came here as a kid?'

'Not many people know about it, but these tunnels were used by protesters during the campaigns to stop logging down the road at Okarito. My old man helped fix up some of the tunnels bunged up in the seventy-seven earthquake.'

'I don't know Jay. Sounds dangerous.'

'You can wait here if you want Doctor,' he said, smiling and taking No Name's flashlight from his pocket. 'Gotta tell ya though, Aunty's possum pie's not to be missed.'

He wriggled through the opening, leaving her little choice. She regretted it instantly. The walls were frigid, slimy and too close, and within seconds her heart was pounding so loud she thought someone was hammering on the rock.

'Next stretch's a bit tight.' Jay's voice amplified off the walls. 'Keep one arm out in front all the time. And don't let your elbows get too far behind your shoulders. Last thing you want's to end up lying on your arms. She'll be slow going at first, but it beats getting stuck.'

'I can't do this Jay.'

'Don't fight the rock Cat. She'll always win. Just relax. Breath evenly. One foot at a time.'

The first twenty or so yards were a terrifying crawl through shallow water. Then the cave branched, and they left the stream and headed down an incline high enough for a bent-over shuffle. It was surprisingly cool. Lack of glasses was no handicap as Cat held the end of a piece of rope Jay had tied to his waist. She focused on his feet in the ring of light from the lamp. After a while they passed through a three-sided wooden frame into what Jay said was one of several horizontal tunnels running between the main vertical shafts sunk by gold mining companies back in the nineteenth century.

The Fraser Shaft was a vertical chasm, about six feet square and braced every few feet by thick beams of timber. A wooden ladder with several rungs missing descended the near side. A change in the air suggested a large void as Cat followed Jay down, thankful she could see only to the edge of the lamplight. Another horizontal tunnel took them to a shaft twice the size of the Fraser and ringed by a ledge wide enough to walk on. Tunnels led off in three directions.

'Welcome to Cassius Junction,' Jay announced, his voice echoing.

Cat jumped as a bat flew close to her shoulder.

'Have you any idea where we are?'

'About thirty feet below the corner of Gibson Street and Simpson.'

'How did they know we were coming here Jay? They must know about your aunty.'

'Doubt it. She's not a real aunty. Got a completely different name. Mum and dad never talked openly about her because her place was a safe house for protesters in the old days. Used these shafts myself after a wee job at the McCully's site. Aunty Joan was an activist from way back. Kept it quiet cos towns like this are full of rednecks.'

'Sounds familiar. So how *did* they know we were coming?'

'The geek I reckon. Wouldn't take much to get him blabbing.'

'Jay. That's not fair!'

'Come on. He's about as green as a bottle of tomato sauce.'

'So he's not the world's most committed environmentalist. But he's not stupid. Matthew knows solving this thing's his only route to freedom.'

'Hope you're right.'

'We haven't got much choice right now, have we. Who knows? Matthew might turn out to be our diamond in the rough.'

'More rough than diamond I reckon.'

'That's a bit rich coming from you.'

The sides of the shaft shook as a vehicle passed overhead, sending a shower of dust onto their heads.

'Here, you take the torch. Keep close and right behind me for this next section. Runs directly under Gibson so she's taken a bit of a clobbering over the years. And don't stand on any boards. Never know what's under them.'

The going was much slower as they picked their way over piles of collapsed rubble and broken beams, edging carefully through frames that looked too flimsy to support the weight of the rock above. Several secondary runs led off the main tunnel. Cat was surprised to see some had doors. Jay turned into one of the side runs, and by the time they'd climbed down yet another shaft to reach yet another tunnel, Cat was totally disoriented. She was about to complain when Jay stopped beside a wooden door with a brass handle. It was locked.

'Shine the light up here.'

He fumbled behind a wooden beam and produced a large key. The door groaned open, and Cat sensed a change in the air, indicating another shaft. A plank of wood the width of a diving board had been placed across the shaft, ending beside a ladder on the far side. She followed the beam of the flashlight as Jay looked up. The ladder led to a trapdoor in the ceiling, which appeared to be made of metal.

'Town grew so fast back in the gold rush days,' he said as he stepped onto the plank, 'by the time they worked out the best gold was deep underground, half the flat was covered in buildings. So, they started sinking shafts. Under houses. The church. School. One of the hotels. Even the bank, which is directly above us.'

'We're breaking into a bank? How's that going to help us?'

'Hasn't been a bank for over a hundred years. These days she's a house.'

* * * *

KAUFMAN WAS tucking into his third egg when his cell phone went off, the panel showing it was Deakes across the street.

'You've got company.'

Obviously not Duggan, or he'd have a bullet through his heart by now. There was a knock on the glass door and the old girl padded along the hall to answer it. Kaufman couldn't hear the early exchange of greetings. The voices became clearer as they approached the kitchen.

'Jay's friends are here. They're having breakfast in the kitchen. Have you eaten, dear?'

Hansen appeared at the doorway.

'What the hell are you doing here?'

'They're here to meet Jay, dear.'

The look on Hansen's face was priceless. Surprised. Dog-tired. Pissed off. Uncertain how to react in the presence of the old girl. All in one very confused expression.

Kaufman seized the initiative.

'You told us to arrange our own accommodation. The town's booked out for this Wildfoods festival and your entourage. Aunty Joan here was kind enough to let us spend the night.'

'Don't bullshit me Kaufman. How the hell did you know about Joan?'

'Her address was imprinted on the pad at the farm in Napier.'

'Why didn't you tell me?'

'You had the top sheet of paper. I assumed you knew. Course I could ask you the same question. When were you planning to tell me about Aunty Joan?'

'I've just found out from the Post Office check.'

'Poached or fried dear?'

'What?'

'Your eggs. Would you like them poached or - '

'Neither. Thank you. I've already eaten.'

* * * *

JAY REACHED the top of the ladder and cupped his palms against the trap door. He braced his legs between the rung and the wall and pushed upwards.

A bit more pressure and the door moved, releasing years of dust into his eyes. Cat coughed below him. Jay hauled himself through the opening.

The beam from the flashlight circled the old strong room, washing over shelves chokka with preserving jars, rows of books and *National Geographics* dating back to the Ark. Tins of all sizes. Diving masks and oxygen tanks. Shoe boxes by the dozen. Stacks of vinyl records tied with twine.

A length of dowelling sagging so low under the weight of clothes, the tuxedo and clown suit in the middle flowed onto the floor.

'How old did you say Aunty Joan was?'

'Early nineties, I reckon.'

'She's a scuba diver?'

'This isn't her house. This is Aunty Fay's, her neighbor over the back fence. She used to dive for paua. What you'd call *abalone.*'

'How many aunties have you got?'

'Just the two round here. Like I said, they're not real aunties. More like old family friends.'

'Like Skip's cousins?'

'Sort of.'

A graunching sound made Cat gasp. As the reinforced steel door to the vault creaked open, stabbing the room with light from the hall outside, Jay felt her arm slip round his waist. The grip tightened as the barrel of a gun appeared through the opening.

Like a slow-motion replay, inch by twenty-eight inch of the barrel was revealed.

A finger on the trigger. Steady as.

The polished wooden stock of a sixteen-gauge Winchester.

A hand.

Denim arm.

The slippers gave it away. Pink and fluffy. Then the face. Wrinkled like one of those Chinese Shar-Pei dogs. Glasses with lenses half an inch thick. And a smile as warm as a coal range in a snowstorm.

'Cat Tayler. I'd like you to meet Aunty Fay.'

'Bout time you showed up young man. I'll put the kettle on.'

The old woman lowered the barrel, nodded at Cat, then turned and pattered down the hall. The musty smell of age took Jay back to the days when Joan brought him over here for tea and nibbles. Always Anzac biscuits. Big as fists.

Ten minutes later they were wolfing down a feast of bacon, sausages, mushrooms, fried eggs, onions and homemade toast. Time took a breather. The coal range. Fabric-covered wireless. The framed tea towel with the Irish blessing on the wall. Even the crocheted cozy covering the teapot from which Fay was pouring a brew strong enough to put hairs on the chest of a Girl Guide.

'Who's doing the night cart rounds now you've retired Aunty.'

'Cheeky blighter. Retiring's for old people. I'll be doin the rounds till I'm six feet under. Folks are countin on me.'

'You've still got your driver's license?'

'Not exactly. No one's asked to see it yet. Touch wood. It's good to see you again Jay. Joan's been expecting ya.'

'I'll pop over and see her in a while.'

'Best to wait a bit I'm thinkin. What with the town crawling with coppers and what have you. And poor Joan having to get the pies sorted for the Wildfoods. She'll be in a right flap. Specially with those queer folk been poking around since yesterday. '

'What folk?'

'See for yourself. Clear as day from the window upstairs.'

Jay and Cat climbed up the narrow staircase to a tiny bedroom that hadn't been used this millennium. Through the lacy sheers Jay looked across the yard into the back of Joan's house. The silhouettes of two men sat at the kitchen table. Cat's hand landed gently on his shoulder and stayed there.

'Tell me Mr Duggan. How in heck do you propose getting to her?'

'With cunning and guile Doctor Tayler. Ounce of luck wouldn't go astray either, just quietly.'

46. Designed by some half-pint

TALK ABOUT overkill. Matthew was boxed up on a white fiberglass chair inside a steel cage in the back of a police van.

Facing him were two Armed Offenders' Squad officers, helmet to boot in black with only noses showing through the gaps between masks and scarves. Their rifles were aimed at his head and chest through a small rectangular opening in the mesh. Like he was going to snap the cuffs binding his wrists or the shackles leashing his ankles. Through the small rear window he could see a line of police cars, lights flashing like a presidential escort. The irritating whine of a siren at his back told him there was at least one other car at the head of the convoy. Plus the helicopter overhead.

He cold-shouldered the guards and looked through the tinted glass of the side window. A bus stop. Grass verge. Letterbox. The leaves on a tree. Would this be the last time he'd see such things?

The van swung into a street bordered on one side by a high netting fence. The gloom worsened as he saw the razor wire along the top, then the sign for the Royal New Zealand Army Base Trentham Camp. The convoy slowed at the entrance, just long enough for a glimpse of cameras and microphones before pulling up in a compound of tarmac and khaki.

Around the back of a three-story concrete tomb out of sight of the media Matthew was escorted, still in handcuffs and shackles, into a reception area designed by some half pint who dropped out of architect school.

'Welcome to Trentham, Mr Liddell.'

The geezer identified himself as Colonel Wood, commanding officer of the Corps of Royal New Zealand Military Police. A huffy fellow with Photoshop blue eyes and a head permanently tilted to one side that made you think rotate tool.

Five degrees counterclockwise should do the trick.

'Pleasure to be part of the team,' said Matthew.

'Captain Ogilvy here will escort you to your cell.'

'Excellent thank you, old chap. I'll just get settled in then. You know, freshen up a tad, then pop down for a quiet one before dinner. You can order for me if you like.'

Nothing to lose, thought Matthew as he was led away.

'Oh Mr Liddell...' Colonel Wood called out as they reached an elevator. 'In case you're wondering, this entire building has been stripped of all electronic equipment. My instructions are to ensure you do not come within a hundred yards of anything so much as resembling a computer.'

47. Can't see the clown

KAUFMAN would die rather than admit it to her face, but Hansen was right. This was Duggan's kind of place. Thousands of people. Open public space. And Aunty Joan.

The Wildfoods Festival was an excuse to turn the tin pot town of Hokitika into an orgy of outrageous clothing, loose behavior and, by the look of some of the food on offer, loose bowel motions.

The annual event had become so popular organizers capped the number of tickets at fifteen thousand. It was Hansen's idea to let Aunty Joan set up her stall and stake her out, hoping Duggan had the balls to show up.

Everywhere you looked were green balloons emblazoned with JayStalker, the new name for the blog that had been hijacked by pro-Vestco nerds and was now being used to incite people in the street to help hunt down the terrorists.

Standing on a small rise between the Kaniere School Spit Roast and Cricket Satay, Kaufman could see anyone approaching Aunty Joan's stall.

Plain-clothes police were everywhere, as well as dozens of uniforms and Armed Offenders' Squads standing by at the perimeter.

Aunty Joan was raking it in, her possum pies more popular than neighboring stalls selling fish eyeballs and wasp larvae ice cream. The hand-painted signs were enough to make your stomach squirm.

Plump White Huhu Grubs. Deep Fried Grasshoppers. Mealworm Jell-O. Gourmet, my ass.

Mountain oysters sounded manageable till someone told Kaufman what they were. Fried lamb's testicles. You'd have to have a cast iron gut to hold this stuff down. Or be drunk, which many people seemed to be. His attention was lured to a group of children's entertainers dressed as characters from the Wizard of Oz. The Tin Man was tossing candy from a metal bucket to an excited swarm of kids. He thought of Eve. Disneyland.

He looked back at Aunty Joan's stall. A guy, Duggan's build, in a striped football jersey and jeans was talking to the old girl with his back to Kaufman. He moved to get a look at his face. Too young. The Tin Man's bucket was empty, and the kids were zeroing in on a clown juggling eggs. Hoots of laughter as he let one plop on his cap. Kaufman felt a tug at his jacket.

'Hey Mister. Out of the way. I can't see the clown.'

He turned to see a girl, no more than five, plastered in freckles, her mouth buried in a pink mass of cotton candy.

* * * *

JAY KEPT juggling as the American stepped out of the way and bent to apologize to the girl.

He'd been close enough to Kaufman to see the red swelling round a sandfly bite on his forehead.

Raised voices yanked eyes towards the tent of the Legalize Cannabis Aotearoa Party, where a couple in matching hemp hats were offering take-the-piss masks of the terrorists using photographs from police identikit pictures.

A group of young rednecks were arguing with the dope heads. Pushes led to shoves. The stallholder wearing the Matthew Liddell mask was thrown into the Westport RSA band, his elbow smashing through the skin of a drum.

Then it was all on, as inebriated hoons rushed from all corners to join the brawl. Two uniformed policemen tried to intervene but were overwhelmed. One of the cops fell and was pounced on by the mob.

Jay glanced over at Kaufman, who was talking into a mobile phone. The American started running towards the downed cop, grabbing bodies and tossing them aside like pieces of straw.

This was Jay's chance.

He headed for Joan's stall, still juggling.

Aunty beamed when she realized who was standing in front of her.

'Sorry Joan. Only got a few seconds. Did you get the thing I posted to you?'

'Came the other day kiddo. I sent it to the person at this address in Governor's Bay, just like the man asked.' She handed him a scrap of paper.

'What man?'

'No idea. Said he was a mate of your friend Matthew. He knew about the CD. And about John Fitzgerald. I thought I could trust him.'

'What the? What did he look like?'

'Never saw him kiddo. He got me on the phone at the Save the Children shop. Sounded American.'

This sounded ominous.

'Have you told anyone?'

'Course not. I spun a line to that Yanky bloke. Said I'd biffed it out. Don't think he believed me. Mind you I gave him the Alzheimer's treatment, so anything's possible. That Maori police inspector's sharp as a tack though Jay. She's at least got people searching the rubbish dump.'

The shouting was fading.

'Better skedaddle kiddo. Look's like the police officers are getting things under control.'

48. So many parallels

THE CLAW-FOOTED bath was so long Cat could lie back and immerse her entire body. It was remarkably soothing, though more likely from the temperature of the water than the three cups of apple cider vinegar Aunty Fay insisted on adding. Or the phase of the moon the dear old thing swore was favorable for opening the pores.

Not that Fay had any monopoly on irrational thoughts.

Since the first night on the fishing trawler, Cat had been haunted by the vision of red, white and blue double helices morphing into a giant hourglass. Sand poured through the neck to gradually bury her. The first time she was in her Melville school uniform.

At other times, she was trapped in the bottom with Pop, with Keith Stedholme, Jay. Once she was buried up to her neck with sand piling on top of her doctoral hat.

Bonkers.

She looked up, half expecting to see falling sand.

A plastic chandelier hung from the high ceiling of what used to be the banker's front office. Where once there would have been scales to weigh gold there were now bathroom scales, rolled up towels, stacks of cinnamon and oatmeal soap and homemade oils.

Cat stepped reluctantly out of the bath, dried herself, and bent down to look in the mirror set at the height of her host.

Back home she would never have thought of short black hair.

Aunty Fay was waiting outside the door with a shoebox full of spectacles.

'Every pair I've owned since Adam was a cowboy.'

The lenses on the more recent styles were too strong, but she found a pair with translucent gold frames dotted with rhinestone studs that were remarkably close to her own prescription. So retro they were almost back in fashion.

'Got those in September of fifty-four. Wouldn't have been much older than you, dear. Had Phil Taylor in those. Course I took them off. And young Digger Townsend out the back of his old man's woolshed.'

'Really?' Cat tried not to sound shocked.

Aunty Fay took her on a tour of wardrobes and boxes and suitcases and trunks in search of clothes to match the glasses.

Cat kept away from the windows with their lacy curtains and glimpses of snow-capped mountains and a yard cluttered with chicken sheds, some sort of tanker truck and other bits of rusting machinery. She wondered how anyone could live in such disorganized chaos, but Fay knew where every single thing was. Thanks no doubt to her remarkable memory.

'Wyatt Rogers, 1943, back seat of his father's Model T,' she said as Cat tried on a velvet dress with panel stitching and Peter Pan collar. A nylon floral number reminded Fay of Blocker Simpson, 1957. Digger Townsend was back on the scene for a gaudy pink and purple geometric skirt on New Year's Eve 1973.

'He had a bit of trouble keeping it up that night. No Viagra in those days, more's the pity. Don't suppose Jay has that problem, eh dear?'

Cat blushed.

'So how long is it since you saw Jay?'

'Last time would have been when they came for Joan's birthday. Jay and ... Aroha.'

Fay's voice trailed into an awkward silence.

Cat glanced at her watch.

'Is that the time? Almost six. I'd like to watch the news, if that's alright?'

'There's no television here dear. Or telephones. I'm too old for that hokum. There's the wireless I use for listening to the races. Would that play the news?'

What Cat hoped might be wireless internet turned out to be an antique radio on a sideboard beside the coal range in the kitchen. She fiddled with the dials until she found a local station.

'... *false alarm. The security system at the storage facility in Nairobi was activated by an electrical fault, not by a break-in as was feared yesterday. The Kenyan President has given an assurance the sealed vials of Alo seeds were never under any form of security threat.*'

'There's no way they can guarantee that,' said Cat, throwing her hands in the air.

'I don't think he can hear you dear.'

'... *arrested in Wellington on Wednesday, has been transferred to a maximum-security cell at Trentham Army Base. We cross now to our reporter outside the base, Kahu Bennett.*

'Police are refusing to confirm the move, citing the new anti-terrorism laws, but Grassroots has posted that the heavily guarded convoy that entered the army base just on three hours ago was carrying Liddell, who has been transferred from Wellington Hospital. Sources at the hospital told the blog the Englishman was caught using a computer, hence the beefing up of security. A spokesperson for Victoria University confirmed earlier today Liddell was the person responsible for crashing the New Zealand Police information system minutes before he was taken into custody. More details are emerging of Liddell's background. Interpol now believes he used the pseudonym Turtle Dove, once ranked in the top ten on the International Cybercriminal Agency's most dangerous hacker list. Concern about the cyber threat from Liddell is almost certainly the reason Vestco closed down its website without warning on Monday. The corporation continues to deny this, claiming the site upgrade had been planned for months. They have admitted, however, that Liddell has tried to hack into their system twice in the last eighteen months. On both occasions the attempts were detected by Vestco's former IT specialist Henry Beck, the man Liddell is accused of murdering in Los Angeles a week ago today.'

Cat was considering whether the bad news about Matthew being moved to maximum security outweighed the good news that he'd got to a computer when a crash shook the house, causing Aunty Fay to spill the tea she was pouring.

'Never mind dear,' she said, putting the teapot down and reaching for the rifle.

* * * *

PETERSEN HAD chosen the firm carefully. The man sitting across the desk hadn't got to be Los Angeles manager of Barry and Eastmond, one of the world's most exclusive real estate firms, by delving into the private concerns of its clientele of A-list celebrities, Fortune 500 businessmen and Gulf State royalty.

Discretion and confidentiality were absolute.

After reading the documentation thoroughly and asking questions about the reef fringing the island in Cambodia's Koh Rong Archipelago, Petersen signed on the dotted line and confirmed the balance of the purchase price would be transferred in three days when he took possession.

* * * *

AUNTY FAY scuttled off with the speed of someone a third her age. As the crashing under the house subsided, Cat peeked into the hall and saw the fearless bow-legged warrior, rifle propped against the shoulder of her denim jacket, push open the vault door with her slippered foot.

The roar from her mouth was like a ship's foghorn. Cat crept down the hall to look over the old woman's shoulder. Jay was cloaked in white dust, like a child who just emptied the entire contents of a talcum container on his head. The sorry-for-himself look only made the foghorn louder.

Through the snorts and cackles, Jay was saying the door from the shaft came away from its hinges, taking half an overhead beam with it, which explained the dust shower.

He stepped towards the hall, but Aunty Fay, still pointing the gun, stopped him cold.

'You're not going down my hall in that state. Strip off in there and

269

I'll get the vacuum. Catherine, find some clean clothes for Jay from that wardrobe in the top room.'

A few minutes later Cat was briefing Jay on the news about Matthew being moved because he'd been caught using a computer.

'He might have got a message out.'

'Maybe he solved his part of the clue, but how in heck will we know?'

'Let's cross that bridge when we get to it. Got enough stuff on our plate here.'

In the excitement, Cat had forgotten about the CD.

'Did you see your other aunty?'

'Yep. Weird thing is, she got the disk and posted it to a bloke in Governor's Bay. Says she got the address from some random American who knew Matthew.'

'Sounds suspicious to me.'

'Couldn't agree more. Mind you, if our geek got to a computer, maybe he did get a message out.'

'How in heck could this person in Governor's Bay know about Aunty Joan and the package? Matthew and I didn't know about Joan.'

'And that's not all. Not only did he know about Joan, he knew she volunteered one day a week at the Save the Children store, and he knew the name of my mother's cat.'

'Which is?'

'John Fitzgerald.'

'After JFK? Is that where your name - '

Jay nodded.

'OK. Let's break this down. What's this American guy's name?'

'There's no name. Just this address.'

Cat took the piece of paper and started pacing the room. None of this made sense, but it was all they had to go on.

'Where is Governor's Bay exactly?'

'Near Christchurch.'

'We've got to go to Christchurch anyway Jay to see Professor Kane at Lincoln University. She wrote a thesis on Johann Miescher's work. The woman could hold the key to my part of the clue.'

Jay's face didn't share her enthusiasm.

'Every road's blocked Cat. There's a total ban on flying this side of the Alps, unless you're the Airforce or police. The navy's patrolling the coastline, not that the sea's an option in the time we've got. Paddocks round here are crawling with soldiers and cops and every man and his dog after the reward. Saw it all as I came back in. Only made it into the cave by the skin of me teeth. They've sealed off this town Cat. And even if we did make it to Christchurch, Lincoln's where they'll be expecting us to head. The closer we get to the university, and the closer to release time, they'll be throwing the kitchen sink at Lincoln.'

This was not what Cat wanted to hear. Jay was supposed to be the optimistic one, the rock. Pushing her on when all seemed lost. They couldn't give in now.

'There's gotta be something we can do.'

Aunty Fay was fussing over the kettle, saying everyone would feel better after a cuppa.

'There is one way,' Jay said quietly. 'Not sure we've got time though. There's this river, the Whitcombe. Comes down from a pass over the Alps. Gets ya into the headwaters of the Rakaia Valley on the other side.'

Cat thought of the view through Aunty Fay's curtains. She was reminded of the scene in *Lord of the Rings* where they tried to cross the Misty Mountains. She thought of Matthew in a prison cell somewhere in Wellington when he should have been visiting the studio that made the movie. Filmed in the very Southern Alps Jay was talking about. Frodo and the fellowship failed and had to go through the Mines of Moria. There were so many parallels. But the mountains Jay was talking about crossing were real. She looked at him helping himself from one of Aunty Fay's biscuit tins. Far from seeing some wizard with magical powers, he looked suddenly small, vulnerable.

'Do you know the way?'

'Been over a few times, years ago. Always from the other direction. And that was back in the days when the Conservation Department maintained the track. Even if we made it over the pass, you've still got to cross the Rakaia. This time of year, you get snowmelt from the

271

glaciers up there. Couple of big ones – Lyell and the Ramsay – feed the Rakaia. Then there's the nor-westers. Reason you have rainforests over here is that the prevailing wind hoons in from the west, scoops up bucket loads of water from the sea. She hits the coast and comes up against a brick wall of mountains. There's only one way to go. Up. As she rises she dumps rain like there's no tomorrow. Fair pisses down. Doesn't take a rocket scientist to work out where all that water goes. There's this valley off the Whitcombe called the Cropp. Gets more than fifty feet of rain a year. That's four times the height of this ceiling Cat, and she's high as ceilings go. Your big rivers like the Rakaia can rise from twenty-five thousand gallons a second to four-hundred thousand inside an hour. Doing the Whitcombe's one thing. Crossing the Rakaia could be a whole different ballgame. We're talkin absa-bloody-lutely last resort.'

49. Not the killing type

JAY SIDLED toward the section of tunnel that partially collapsed on his return from the Wildfoods Festival. Part of the ceiling beam lay diagonally across the opening, but after clearing rocks away it was still possible to crawl through the gap. Once safely through, he stood and adjusted the flashlight.

The map was a copy of an original updated by protesters who repaired, extended and used the tunnels to evade the police during the 1970s. Most of the holes in the ground were slabbed whim-shafts up to one hundred twenty feet deep, joined in places by horizontal drives known as adits. Many passageways collapsed in the first half of the twentieth century, but by adding a handful of short connector chutes in strategic locations, Jay's father and his mates opened up several miles.

A shower of dust fell as a large vehicle passed on the road overhead, vibrating the tunnel. Since deciding to tackle Whitcombe Pass, time had become their enemy. While Cat was packing some of the gear they'd need back at Fay's, Jay was off to church. Among other places. All going well, he'd return to pick her up, then they'd use the tunnels to get out of town.

Quarter of an hour and Jay was climbing through a trapdoor in the base of the wooden pulpit of the Church of the Nativity. Standing on a pew, he looked through stained glass to the street outside. Almost dark. Other than the pubs, which notoriously never closed on the Coast, Ross would normally be calming down by this hour. Tonight, the town was humming because of the invasion for Wildfoods.

Jay slipped outside and into the shadows between a jade emporium and the barbers. An alley led to a fence at the back of the Imperial Hotel car park. He scaled the fence, landing beside an electrician's van as the back door of the pub opened and a man swaggered out of the public bar. Hair tussed up like some reef coral. Crotch of his jeans round his knees. Swaying unsteadily in a way you couldn't pretend if you were sober. Jay slunk behind the rear of the van as the man walked towards him, trying to read a text message on his cell phone. He stopped, teetered, put the cell phone on the bonnet, unzipped his fly and started doing the business against the wheel. Seemed to go on forever. Six or seven jugs worth at least. Then he turned and swayed back to the bar.

The cell phone was still on the bonnet. Jay put it in the pocket of his backpack and ran across the car park, climbed through a number-eight wire fence and jogged along the side of a large corrugated iron building. Two more fences and he was in the rear yard of the Mainland outdoor equipment shop. He studied the alarm system. Seemed straightforward. Probably connected by phone to the police station or a security firm. He took a small canister from the pack, sprayed foam into the mechanism, then got the pliers ready on the phone line. As the alarm popped and the foam stopped the bell ringing, Jay snipped the line.

Your typical outdoor gear shop. Walls and display stands lined with sleeping bags. Hiking packs. Clothing. Mountaineering equipment. Camping kit. You name it. A copy of that morning's *Press* was on the counter. Jay turned to the weather page. A warm conveyor belt of air ahead of a cold front in the Tasman Sea was heading for the Southern Alps. Likely to bring torrential rain to the Coast. The question was *when?*

Choosing a green medium-sized pack, he moved quickly round the store, grabbing packets of dried food, a cooker, gas, boots for Cat, polyprops, Gore-Tex rain jackets, an ice axe, two sets of crampons, ropes, gloves and a few other essentials. He was about to leave when the door rattled. Jay ducked behind a display of maps. A cop was standing on the sidewalk with a hand over his brow, peering through the glass doors into the store. Would he notice the pack sitting in the middle of the floor?

Fortunately, not. He tried the door again, then continued his patrol along the street.

Staring at the maps while waiting for his breathing to return to normal, Jay had an idea. He took a map showing the Three Passes route and dropped another map onto the floor.

* * * *

'SOMETHING wrong dear?'

Aunty Fay didn't miss much. The packing was going fine until Cat saw the calendar. February 16. She'd missed Pop's birthday. First time ever. She imagined him sitting in his favorite chair beside the phone, looking at his favorite photo of the two of them, a tear rolling down his cheek. The same one running down hers.

'What is it dear?'

'It was Pop's birthday yesterday.'

'There there dear. I'm sure he'll understand.'

'I've never missed before. Not once.'

'Why don't you give him a call dear? I'm sure he won't mind if you're a day late. In the circumstances.'

A day late. Of course. The States were a day behind. She looked at her watch. Nine-forty. The time difference made it twenty minutes to midnight February 15 in California.

'It's no use. I can't call him.'

'Why ever not dear?'

'For one, you haven't got a phone. And two, they trace the calls. They'll know within minutes where I am, and the police will descend on this place like there's no tomorrow.'

'I think the police already know about Ross dear. They've had the town surrounded since yesterday afternoon. Not to mention those queer folk over at Joan's. You could call your father from the public phone booth in town.'

Cat closed her eyes and ran her fingers through what was left of her hair.

'Family's everything dear. If you were my daughter, I'd want to hear you were alright and what have you.'

'But we can't leave the house. They'll recognize me straight away.'

'Nonsense dear. Put this cardigan and hat of Joan's on. All they'll see are the same two harmless old relics they see on the footpaths of Ross every day of the year.'

'It's dark outside Fay. Grannies don't use public phone booths this late at night.'

'You'd be surprised dear. Don't tell Jay, but we've got a telephone account with the bookmakers in Australia. They give better odds. And they're two hours behind us over there. Joan and I often go down later than this to ring through our quaddies. Then we listen to the races on the wireless.'

'Jay'll kill me if he finds out.'

'Don't be ridiculous dear. Jay's not the killing type.'

* * * *

'HOW'S IT feel to be lined up in crosshairs Bradley?'

The voice on the other end of the phone was almost certainly bluffing, but Kaufman wasn't about to take a chance. Not after the last call from Duggan, just after the smartass sabotaged Deakes' rifle. He started walking, glancing round the garbage dump as he talked. They were hemmed in by hills covered in thick bush. Loads of places Duggan could be hidden with a weapon trained on him. With the dump lit up with spotlights, Kaufman would be an easy target. Play it cool. Keep him on the line.

'Your Aunty Joan's a lovely lady. Makes a mean possum pie. Sure she'd love you to stop by for one.'

'I did Bradley. At the festival. Right under your nose.'

'Course ya did. You and Elvis just waltzed up to her stall, bought ya pies, parked yourselves down on one of those picnic tables, chewing the fat while all those cops just sat back and watched. You're full of horseshit Duggan.'

Kaufman moved further away from the grumbling of the digger, pressing the cell phone to his ear for a clue. The call-waiting signal beeped. He ignored it.

'How was the bacon, mushroom, hash browns and eggs for breakfast Bradley?'

'Fine cook your aunty. Be a shame if anything happened to her.'

Duggan laughed. Cocky sonofabitch. With the faint sound of an echo. Like he was in a small room or enclosed space. Kaufman scanned the perimeter. Could be in one of the sheds in the compound next door. Or up that conveyor belt at the shingle works. Both had been searched and cleared.

'Joan's more than capable of handling a dropkick like you Bradley.'

Definite echo. Could be in a car or truck cab. But none had been allowed within a mile of the dump. The closest members of the public were the fifty or so reporters and rubber-neckers behind the barrier at the entrance. No one could go unnoticed holding a rifle in the middle of that lot.

He focused on the media circus. None were using a cell phone. Time to call the bluff. Kaufman put his left hand on his head.

'Tell me what I'm doing right now Duggan?'

'You're at the Hokitika dump, up to ya neck in rubbish.'

Common knowledge.

'What about my hand? What am I doing with it?'

'You've been jerking off ever since you arrived.'

Hansen entered Kaufman's line of sight. He pretended to be scratching his head, then put his hand down.

'I can do better than your hand Bradley. The crosshairs are between your eyeballs. Is that a zit or a sandfly bite at the top of your nose?'

Kaufman swallowed, hung up and walked briskly towards Hansen, grateful suddenly for the presence of the New Zealand detective.

* * * *

'WHICH HOSPITAL have they taken him to?'

'Saint Johns in Santa Monica. Don't bother calling Catherine. He's far too weak to talk.'

Her mother had answered the phone at Pop's. A surprise in itself. But the news her father had been rushed to hospital after a heart attack rocked Cat.

'For God's sake Catherine, give yourself up. Your ridiculous idealism almost killed him once. Now you're doing it all over again. Where are you calling from anyway?'

The voice was the same superior tone – almost the same words – as the day Pop was attacked in the alley.

'Are you there, child?'

Cat was facing the window of the booth, but couldn't focus through the blur of cracked glass and Mom and tears and snow and rain and shadows and Pop on his back unconscious. People were shouting and laughing, and music was playing and ...

'Where are you Catherine? Don't you dare hang up on me!'

What sort of coin do I need for to make a call please?'

A tourist, German or Dutch by the accent, was talking to Fay.

'Catherine! tell me where you are or I'll - '

'Gotta go Mom.'

* * * *

'THANK YOU for your co-operation Mrs Tayler. I believe we got enough.' The technician sitting at a screen in the van of the LA County Public Works Department Sewer Maintenance unit began triangulating the data to locate the spot where the call was made.

'You've done the right thing, Mrs Tayler. Your daughter will thank you for it one day.'

'What about her father?'

The technician looked through the tinted window of the van across to the white wooden house with ivy-covered carport. A light was on in a front room. Guy was probably reading in bed.

'He'll never know.'

50. Serious backup

'IS EVERYTHING OK, Mr Kaufman? You look kind of...bleached.'

'Never better.'

He was unnerved by the call from Duggan. And annoyed Hansen noticed something amiss. 'Anything shown up here yet?'

'Closest they've come to finding a computer disk is a McDonalds frisbee.'

Kaufman nodded towards a mob of civilians to the side of the media pack, recognizing some from the brawl at the Wildfoods Festival.

'Who the hell are they?'

'Few locals. They've volunteered to help. Plenty of folk round here have no time for greenies. I've told them thanks, but no thanks. They're more likely to get in the way. See anything at the Wildfoods?'

'Plenty. Drunks. People barfing. Wizard of Oz. Juggling clowns. No terrorists.'

'Hope none of the clowns was your man Duggan. Pretty good juggler according to those kids on the bus.'

Kaufman was saved from further embarrassment by his cell phone.

'Seems you're a popular man, Mr Kaufman.'

He ignored her and took the call from his deputy.

'Good news and good news Brad. You're about to get serious backup. Don't ask me how, but Petersen's arranged for a Special

Forces Pave Hawk and crew to be flown out to New Zealand on a US Air Force Galaxy.'

'When?'

'Arriving Saturday night your time. Landing in Christchurch. Turns out there's a US Airforce unit near the city. Supplies America's Antarctic program. They're offloading a bunch of scientific widgets to make way for the chopper.'

'Jesus. I thought Petersen agreed that was a bad idea.'

'He's getting worried Brad. Coming under serious pressure from above.'

Kaufman moved away so Hansen couldn't overhear.

'This could complicate things. Tell Petersen it'll only work if I can be in charge of the Hawk.'

'Will do. Think you're dreaming though. Those military guys are very protective of their whirlybirds.'

'You said you had two bits of good news. Tell me you've got a fix on that little prick.'

'Which one?'

'Cut the crap.'

'We've got fixes on both of them. Catherine Tayler tried to call her father from a pay phone outside the Goldfields Hotel in Moorhouse Street. It was intercepted, just like you asked. Duggan used a cell phone a few yards away. Far as we can tell he was standing in the middle of the street. Got balls, I'll give him that.'

'How long ago?'

'Less than five minutes.'

Kaufman whispered: 'Do the cops here know yet?'

'She's just taking the call about Tayler. Must be monitoring the phone booths, but their IT system's a bit slow. They won't know about Duggan.'

Kaufman could see Hansen talking on her phone.

'Wanna hear what she's saying? Just push your hash key.'

He caught the end of the conversation, with Hansen ordering squads to converge on the pay phone to begin a search to turn the town upside down.

51. The Chinaman

CAT CROUCHED as low as she could on the seat, hunched over the handlebars and followed the taillight of Fay's mobility scooter down the sidewalk and up the path to the house.

The old woman opened the front door – which was never locked – and Cat's heart skipped a beat as she heard the voice of Professor Keith Stedholme, her mentor from Berkeley. The radio was replaying a *Grassroots* interview from England.

'*... exhaustive analysis of the test data previously suppressed by the manufacturer and found no alterations in the protein, vitamin or mineral content of the coated seeds. As a scientist I am bound therefore to declare the seed coating safe for human consumption.*'

'*So, what you're telling us, Professor, is that the world has nothing to fear from the release of Alo?*'

'*I'd go further than that old chap. Having also reviewed the results of the latest laboratory tests on anticipated yields, I agree with the revised estimate of an average five tons per hectare for maize, in all probability even more for wheat and rice. With those sorts of yields, I believe Vestco is not exaggerating in its claim that Alo could make starvation history.*'

Cat stared at the radio, refusing to believe her ears. But it *was* Keith. The voice was unmistakable. And he would trust *Grassroots*. This, surely, was the end.

She'd screwed up everything. Pop. Melville. Her parents' marriage.

Her career. Matthew rotting in a cell. All for an insane pigheaded campaign to stop what everyone – even Keith Stedholme for heck's sake – thought was going to save the lives of millions.

Her cheeks and jaw quivered as she tried to keep it together.

A helicopter trembled over the house.

She let go, unable to stop her body shuddering in a deluge of tears and coughs and Pop glaring at her from a coffin.

'Tea, dear? I find things always seem better with a cuppa.'

Cat wiped her nose and... smiled. You had to, really. The planet was on the verge of a quantum change, the wolves were sniffing at the door, Pop near death in a hospital on the other side of the world, and here was this little old woman in pink slippers solving everything with the tip of a rainbow tea cozy.

'That'd be lovely thanks Fay.'

* * * *

PROFESSOR STEDHOLME looked up from the desk and made eye contact with his granddaughter.

He smiled, hoping it would make her feel better. But the terror clung to her face, the gag over her mouth and the barrel of the gun inches from her head.

* * * *

KAUFMAN WATCHED as Hansen ordered squads of police to fan out in house-to-house searches. The sidewalk and half the street outside the Goldfields Hotel were cordoned off with the now familiar yellow tape shouting POLICE LINE – DO NOT CROSS.

Beyond the barrier reporters and locals and tourists were packed nine or ten deep, the spectator ranks swelled by scores of out-of-towners lured to the West Coast by a rousing call-to-arms on the *JayStalker* blog. Detectives were trying to interview hotel patrons to see if anyone saw Tayler use the phone booth. Drunken men in red and white striped rugby jerseys who had been turfed out of the hotel were slinging abuse, souping up the tension.

Kaufman considered the phone booth with its peeling paint, broken window and graffiti. Had Duggan called from there as well? Could explain the echo. But hadn't his deputy said the middle of the street? He stepped off the sidewalk and moved towards the police barrier, ignoring the selfie frenzy, jeers, whistles and advice – even a marriage proposal. Standing on the white center line, he turned his back on the mob and looked back at the booth. An alley ran up the side of the building between the hotel and a museum. Light from windows in the bar illuminated part of a mural on the wall. There was a bearded prospector with a pick over his shoulder, a wooden tower and a horse standing on a small circular track. The near side of the mural was distorted by bricks that had slipped out of place, perhaps in an earthquake. There'd been a big one in Christchurch a few years back, and he wondered if the damage had extended this far?

As he looked around, Kaufman noticed several other buildings with similar damage. Every one had subsided only on the corners facing the street. Both sides of the road. He looked back at the mural. The horse was harnessed to a beam attached to a pole in the center of the circle. It must have had to walk round and round all day working a windlass to raise buckets of pay dirt from beneath the surface.

Kaufman smiled. What had Duggan said? *Under your nose.* Too smart for his own good. He returned to the sidewalk, tapping Nazim on the shoulder.

'They're using the old mining shafts.'

* * * *

JAY WAS approaching the collapsed beam near Fay's house when he thought he heard voices. He killed the headlamp, masking the passage in a pit of black.

The sound seemed far away, but he knew from experience noise played tricks underground. One could get muzzled, another amplified, for no rhyme or reason. He was reasonably sure these came from a lower level, so he risked the lamp. A stream of footprints – his and

Cat's — scarred the floor, Hansel and Greteling the way to Fay's place.

Bugger. He hurried back along the passage. The voices came and went as Jay navigated the labyrinth, silently tracking one level above until they stopped at a point midway between the Ross United Shaft and the branch leading to the Koninoor. He couldn't make out individual words, but the jabber was clear enough to distinguish one of the accents. American. From the buzz of the voices, they were on to something. Tracks, Jay assumed.

He gently scuffed the ground with his shoe and saw why the volume had suddenly increased. He was standing on a wooden beam that must span a winze, or secondary shaft, that would have been used for ventilation or to allow the miners access between levels. The old workings were riddled with these false floors. He looked up and saw the giveaway signs — the roof was higher here and the sides blotched with mineral dregs. Trouble was that decades of dirt and gravel made the false floors impossible to tell apart from the rock. You never knew how many were rotting time bombs waiting to give way, though this one seemed solid enough.

Kaufman and co were moving off. Jay's idea was only half formed, and a long shot after all these years, but it was now or never.

'This way,' he shouted. 'We can get out through the church.' He jumped on the beam. The voices stopped. Game on.

Jay darted off. For his plan to have half a chance he'd have to lead them down the Cassius shaft, which meant dropping onto their level in the main tunnel under Simpson Street. Kaufman would be armed for sure, so the more distance between them the better.

Jay was banking on his memories of the mine giving him an edge. Light and sound were no longer issues. The more noise the better, so he grabbed a tin cup from a cavity in the wall and banged it against beams and the rock as he went.

He arrived at the main tunnel so far ahead of his pursuers he had to toss the cup into a rusted wheelbarrow to keep them on task. From now on the glow from his headlamp should do the trick. He ripped along the passageway, grateful for the kinks and debris snubbing out the line of fire.

The Cassius was one of the deepest shafts under Ross and nigh on vertical, which could be a problem. No place to hide. Jay had a quick look at the map to refresh his memory. The cross section showed the Halcrow North tunnel – where he needed to position Kaufman – veering off horizontally two levels below. He started down the ladder, concentrating on keeping three limbs attached to the wooden rungs while the fourth was moving. He passed the first level – the Pilbrow tunnel – without drama or inkling of his chasers. He pointed the lamp down the shaft, relieved to see the ladder still intact and the beam of light not quite reaching the entrance to the Halcrow. He descended quickly and, as lights began flickering above, jumped through the framed opening.

The tunnel was just as he remembered. The first twenty feet or so was dry, up to the remains of the blacksmith's forge and bellows. Beyond that the floor disappeared under about six inches of water. The pipe running along the wall to the forge looked solid enough. He marched to the water, leaving a loud set of prints, then climbed onto the hearth and monkey-barred back along the pipe, stopping just before the shaft. Hoping like hell the voices were still outside lamplight range, he judged the distance to the ladder, switched off his lamp, and leapt across the darkness.

His grip held, but his feet, which he expected to land on a lower rung, hit something soft. A clot of rotten wood was blocking the shaft like a bird's nest in a chimney. The edge of the light beam would reach him within seconds. He trod down on the clot. It moved. He pushed some more, using his knees to force open a gap wide enough to scramble through. The ladder was slippery, iffy as, and four rungs below the clot she ceased to exist, leaving Jay's legs dangling over a chasm of unknown depth. At some time, water must have risen up the shaft, carrying the clot with it and rotting the ladder. Once the water receded, the clot was left wedged and the wooden ladder disintegrated.

The light from above was dimming, and the sound of feet splashing in shallow water confirmed his pursuers had taken the bait. Jay scarpered up the ladder, feeling his way in the gloom until a change in air pressure told him he'd reached the level above. He switched on his lamp, swung into the Pilbrow tunnel and starting running. He knew without looking at the map Kaufman would be finding the going tougher in the tunnel below, which had a lower roof and a longish tight channel which should slow them down enough for him to reach the reservoir ahead of them.

Jay had discovered the large mirror-clear pool one school holiday. Dammed by the miners for storing water, according to a withered former curator at the Ross Museum. It filled a natural hollow in the tunnel and was rimmed on one side by a narrow ledge. Halfway round was a wheel arrangement used to open and close the 'plug' over the outlet hole. Some water was always seeping through, which explained the ankle-deep puddles in the Halcrow below, but it was constantly being replaced from a drip in the ceiling, hence the transparency of the water.

Jay stopped at a winze fifty yards this side of the reservoir and pressed his ear to one of the wooden beams spanning the hole. No sound came from the tunnel below. There was a tiny gap between two hunks of timber. He picked up a pebble and pushed it through. It plopped into a puddle on the floor below, echoing nicely. From the muffled shout that followed, Jay reckoned Kaufman and his cohort would be under the plug in about three minutes.

He reached the reservoir and scurried round the ledge. The water level had dropped a shade, but there would still be at least a hundred thousand gallons. Enough to flood the narrow stretch of tunnel below. The wheel was stiff, but she was going to turn.

Sixty seconds.

Two distinct sounds messed with his head.

The rhythmic *drip-drip drip-drip* from the ceiling.

And the ominous thrumming of water pouring through invisible veins in the rock.

Jay had always considered human life as sacrosanct. He never agreed with the death penalty, even for the most low-life serial murderers. People had to accept there were bad apples who should be locked away for life. No human had the right to take another human life. So much of the grief he'd witnessed – civil wars, terrorism, child slavery – came down to the lack of value put on a single human life.

Ten seconds.

Jay gripped the wheel.

The American had killed two cops, and was going to kill again. There was a better than even chance his next victim would be Cat.

The cocky bastard had crossed the line.

Eye for an eye.

Self-defense.

He steadied one leg against the rock wall to take the strain.

* * * *

EVE WOULD think this place was heaven. She was the only kid Kaufman knew who had no fear of spiders, the dark or confined spaces.

And she'd be short enough to splash through this tunnel without bending her head. His neck was aching from the constant stooping, so he was relieved to reach a bulb where the roof rose enough for him to stand upright.

He had a hunch Duggan was close. He flicked off the safety and sloshed knee deep towards the center of the chamber to wait for Nazim.

'You hear that?' said the Israeli, wading to catch up.

'What?'

'We got company. Listen.'

Through an annoying drip from the ceiling, Kaufman picked up distant echoes, then voices, then shouts. They seemed to be coming from several directions.

* * * *

JAY RELEASED his grip on the wheel. The voices were everywhere. As if the whole of Ross was invading the mine.

Killing Kaufman he could live with, but not cops or civilians, however misguided they were.

Lights were glimmering off the walls of the tunnel back towards the Cassius Shaft. His footprints would be like runway flares.

There was still no sound or light in the other direction, so he shimmied round the rest of the ledge and high-tailed it, trying to visualize the layout ahead.

The tunnel ended at the Koninoor, which he reached sixty seconds or so before Kaufman, judging by the movement of light entering the shaft from below. He had a similar lead on the pack in the tunnel behind him, so there was no time to consult the map.

He scrambled up the ladder towards the main passageway under Simpson Street, calculating the chances of it being empty.

Zero.

A shimmering glow was already rumbling from that direction. All three main horizontal tunnels were no-go zones.

Which left only one option. The Chinaman.

Jay had always stayed clear of the infamously unstable adit that bore off at forty-five degrees from the Koninoor just below the main passageway. It was marked on the map with two crosses. One for the Chinese mine laborer crushed in a ceiling collapse whose body was never recovered. The other for the presence of black damp – the oxygen-depleting plague of the underground.

Beggars can't be choosers.

Jay swung across to the narrow entrance of the adit, just as a bullet from below thudded into the frame and the ladder was splintered from above by a falling pickaxe. Must be the local vigilantes' weapon of choice. She'd been a while since Jay felt this scared.

He was counting on a leg-up from the adrenaline coursing through his blood. The sides of the adit were butted every now and then by timber of dubious condition. Two shots hissed past his head and ricocheted off the uneven walls as he crawled over a pile of rubble. Kaufman obviously didn't know – or care – about the danger of shockwaves in a mine.

Jay grabbed a length of timber and rammed it into the ceiling above the pile. The end of the plank was so rotten it disintegrated without dislodging any of the rocks. He spun it round and tried with the other end, bringing down a decent amount and choking the adit with dust. Should slow them for a while.

The passage leveled to a more manageable incline and Jay was able to crouch and jog over debris and fallen beams, unintentionally knocking loose another section of roof as he passed. He used the breathing space for a quick look at the map. The far end of the Chinaman came out on the main tunnel under Simpson. All might not be lost, if the chase was concentrated behind him.

The adit steepened again, and Jay had to move rocks to squeeze through in places. His hunters had reached the second blockage. The air was getting thinner and his heart rate rising. Round a corner the passage fell to horizontal, the roof rose, but his path was bunged almost to the ceiling by a tangle of wood and boulders. Water trickled from the middle of the dam and ran off through a fist-sized gap at the base of the wall. The remains of a boot appeared to be levitating in front of the pile. As he approached, Jay saw it was attached to a tibia and fibula, or whatever they call leg bones in Mandarin.

'Sorry mate,' he muttered, as he tackled the blockage.

Removing half a dozen rocks and hunks of wood turned the trickle into a stream. The more he hacked away at the mush of rotten wood, the more gungy water was released, but the exertion was taxing him. He jammed a beam into a gap between two rocks, and used a third for leverage. Nothing budged. Coughing and gagged cries from behind drove him to one last effort.

The lower rock gave way and Jay just managed to leap aside before the central section of the mass collapsed and a torrent of scunge poured through to quickly fill the chamber to chest height. The movement of air produced a pocket of oxygen. Jay took a heavy-duty gulp and dived through the gap. The mush was freezing, dark as night, but thinned out below the surface scum. He swam in a frenzy, surfacing only when his hand struck a rock wall indicating he'd rounded a bend in the adit.

The lamp was still shining, just. And he could tell from the spluttering of words that his pursuers were turning back. Scuppered by black damp and a Chinaman. You wouldn't read about it.

52. Some hick town gumshoe

CAT HELPED Jay get the sodden backpack through the opening into the vault. He quickly closed the hatch, and they dragged the chest over the top to conceal it.

He was soaked, shivering, and plastered head to toe in grit from another collapse he said he'd deliberately triggered to seal off the tunnel running under the house.

'But that's our escape route.'

'*Was*. The mine's crawling with blokes you don't want to meddle with.'

'What now?'

'Guess we'll have to take our chances above ground.'

'I'll put the kettle on,' Aunty Fay said as she leant the rifle against a night store heater in the hall.

'There's no time Aunty. How'd you get on with the rest of the gear, Cat?'

She told him about the Keith Stedholme interview on *Grassroots*, but couldn't bring herself to admit the phone call to Pop. It would have to wait for the right moment.

'It's all laid out in the front room.'

Jay started sorting the gear into two packs. A helicopter made a jarring pass over the house, trailed like salt in the wound by a loudspeaker. Cat tugged the edge of the curtain. Soldiers were filing into a house at the end of the street.

'Oh my heck Jay, they're searching houses.'

He stopped packing and sagged back into an easy chair as Fay walked in with a tray of tea and muffins.

'We might as well, Aunty. We're done for. We'll never get out of this town now. She's sealed up tighter than a fish's arsehole, if you'll excuse the French.'

'What do you want to leave for, Jay? Surely you'll stay a few more days. You haven't seen Joan yet.'

'We've got to get to the east coast by Monday.'

'Why didn't you say, dear? Come with me.'

* * * *

KAUFMAN WAS conscious of the television cameras beyond the barrier. The mob had gone quiet, stunned by Hansen's hysterical outburst and 'demand' to know why he hadn't told her Duggan was using the shafts.

He tried to brush her aside by saying she was too busy organizing the house searches. She wasn't buying it.

'I've had an absolute gutful of your behavior, Mister Kaufman. You've been obstructive, manipulating. Highly unprofessional. You bloody Yanks come in here like you're Hollywood action heroes with God-given rights to take over, push your weight around. Expect every Tom, Dick and Harry to cave in, do what you say. And you wonder why America is so loathed around the world? Anyone who disagrees with you's automatically a terrorist. Try looking in the mirror, Mister.'

Kaufman wasn't going to stand there and take that, no matter who was watching.

'You're out of line lady. Way out of your depth. You and your Keystone cops wouldn't know the meaning of the word *professional*. If I'd been in charge from the beginning these terrorists would've been caught before they left Auckland. Instead, what do they do? Who do they put in charge? Some hick town gumshoe with no experience in terrorism, no idea how to run an operation, no hope of catching chickenshit. Do us all a favor lady and go back to your namby-pamby detective work. Leave the terrorists to the experts.'

He turned his back on her and walked away, noting there were far more cheers than jeers from the audience.

53. Deadly serious

SENIOR SERGEANT Jeff Kay would gladly forgo the overtime for a night in his own bed. On duty since ten in the morning, and this was his fifth twelve-hour shift in a row, not including the time spent traveling the country following the manhunt.

Five minutes and he could knock off from his current task in charge of the roadblock at the intersection of Harihari Highway and Donoghues Road west of Ross. His equally exhausted team was searching another car full of tourists or locals heading back to farms and roadside cottages in the south. Many were drunk, but there was a fair smattering of parents with kids eager to see the goings-on in town.

Every adult passenger was lined up against a spotlit wall and checked off against photographs of the two terrorists. Hats had to be removed, and facial hair checked for wigs and fake beards. While that was happening, constables were ferreting under seats, bonnets, chassis, any place someone could hide. Most of the farmland between the ring of roadblocks had been as good as turned over to the growing gangs of vigilantes. There simply wasn't the manpower to sort them out.

The beat-up Ford was waved through. The senior sergeant, who came from an inner-city suburb in Auckland, watched as an old truck rolled up for its turn, accompanied by a strong whiff of sewage.

'Give me strength. What we got here?'

'It's the night tanker sir,' replied a local constable on the team.

'Goes round all the farms pumping the shit and sediment from their septic tanks.'

The driver was ordered out and walked towards him. An old woman. Obviously not Catherine Tayler, but she was asked to wait while the vehicle was searched.

'Found something sir.' A constable jumped down from the cab and handed him a shotgun.

'Do you normally carry this with you when you do your, ah, rounds?'

'Course not. But with those terrorizers and what have you in these parts, and you fellas not exactly giving me a lot of confidence you can catch…'

'We can't let you take things into your own hands, mam. I assure you we've got everything covered. No-one's leaving Ross that shouldn't be. I'm afraid I'll have to confiscate the firearm.'

Senior Sergeant Kay realized how stupid this must sound, given the rumors about the weapons carried by gangs of vigilantes. But what he couldn't see wasn't worth the grief.

'Cab's clear sir,' announced the constable. 'So's the engine and spaces under the rig.'

'What about the tank?'

'You're joking.'

'I'm deadly serious, constable.'

The senior sergeant turned to the old woman. 'We need to check inside the tank mam. How do we do that?'

'There's a hatch at the top. Be my guest. Hope that young fella hasn't got a queasy stomach.'

The constable took a flashlight and climbed reluctantly up the ladder on the outside of the tank. He turned a lever on the hatch and pulled it half open.

'Awwwh,' he gurgled, turning his head away in disgust.

The rest of the team thought it was a great joke. The senior tried to keep his voice serious.

'Open it constable. You need to check inside.'

The young man took several deep breaths of fresh air, and, taunted by his colleagues, threw the hatch open, peered inside and threw up. Even the senior sergeant couldn't resist joining in the laughter. It was welcome relief at the end of a long day.

'OK son. Close it and you can come down.'

He turned to the old woman, who was chuckling with the other officers. Under normal circumstances, certainly in Auckland, he'd charge the woman for having the firearm. These were anything but normal circumstances and cars were queuing up behind the truck. Horns blasted impatiently.

'Ok mam, you can move through.'

'When can I get my gun back?'

She had a nerve, but Senior Sergeant Kay was past caring.

'Pop down to the station on Monday with your firearm license and I'm sure the local officers will be able to help you.'

* * * *

HANSEN WAS still seething about Kaufman's tongue-lashing.

Officers in blue overalls with yellow bags over their feet were inspecting prints near the entrance to a side room behind the altar. A dog team had found another entry point to the underground mines near Jack's Stream. It didn't take a forensic scientist to see how Duggan and Tayler had breached the cordon.

House-to-house searchers had gone through three-quarters of the town and found zip, and police manning the roadblocks reported nothing other than lengthening queues and abuse.

What was it Kaufman said?

Stick to namby-pamby detective work.

Have it your way, hotshot.

She did a rough calculation of what time it would be in Washington, then took the black notebook from her pocket and found the number. She tried to dial on her mobile, but the battery was flat.

She borrowed a phone from a police photographer and went outside to find a quiet spot in the cemetery.

'New Zealand Embassy. How can I help you?'

'Caroline Phillips in the trade section please?'

'Putting you through.'

'Phillips.'

'Gidday stranger, long time no see.'

'Chris Hansen, is that you?'

'Fraid so. Got a minute?'

'For you, always. You in town?'

'I'm in *a* town. It's a tad smaller than Washington, Caroline. Place called Ross. Near Hokitika.'

'Don't know it.'

'Look I'm a bit pushed for time. Wondered if you could help me with some information.'

'Ok… Let me call you back in a minute on my private line.'

Hansen knew her friend's *trade attaché* title was a front for her real job in DC. When the call came, Caroline briefed her on the background to the request for the Special Forces chopper and team of mercenaries. How the New Zealand Government had willingly accepted an unorthodox chain of command, with Kaufman calling the shots.

'The President put pressure on our PM to enact an executive order granting Kaufman and his colleagues immunity from prosecution for any crime they might have to commit in pursuit of these terrorists. Between you and me Chris, the PM was so keen to suck up to the President he didn't put up a fight. It's scary stuff. They had to wake up the Governor-General in the middle of the night to sign the order. All very hush hush. You can't say anything about this. I'd lose my job.'

'Of course. Another favor though Caroline, if you can manage it. Some things about Kaufman don't add up. Reckon you could dig around a bit on the quiet?'

'I'll see what I can do. Hear you've made Inspector since I last saw you. Congrats.'

'Keep the cork in the champagne. The way this investigation's going I'm more likely to be back on the beat drinking flat beer.'

Hansen noted Caroline's private number, and returned to the church.

54. She's special, this one

THE TRUCK petered to a halt and the engine was cut. Jay pointed for
Cat to move to the back of the tank. A few moments later he heard
the dull thud of gumboots on the metal ladder outside.

Fumbling with the fingers of his gloves, he reached up to turn off
the flashlight, chucking the stainless-steel dungeon into darkness. The
screech of the bolt being unscrewed surrounded them like fingernails
on a blackboard until the hatch was lifted open and faint moonlight
spilled, accompanied by Aunty Fay giggling.

Jay switched the flashlight back on and gave the thumbs up to Cat.
Her mask was partially clouded but the relief in her eyes plain as day.
She was wearing a full-body hooded wetsuit, silicone mask and
breathing through a regulator attached to a four-gallon tank on the
floor. Jay reached up to unhook the fish tray of shit suspended beneath
the hatch that fooled the young constable at the roadblock.

A knotted rope dropped through the opening. He pulled himself
up, then helped Cat out with the packs. Jay jumped the last five feet to
the ground and took off the mask. He was overwhelmed by nausea,
throwing up over the tire of the truck. He indicated for Cat to keep
her mask on.

They were in a picnic area beside the Hokitika River. Jay led her to
the water's edge, then downstream to a point where the bank
ballooned into a basin with a decent current. He led her in, gesturing

for her to sink down and wash off the remnants of shit. He did the same to the plastic bags covering the packs. Back at the truck they changed into hiking gear and shouldered the packs.

Aunty Fay gave Cat a hug and some words of advice Jay couldn't hear.

Then the old girl led Jay aside and they embraced.

'Look after her Jay. She's special, this one.'

'I know. Reminds me so much of Aroha.'

Fay looked bluntly up into his eyes.

'Women like Cat and Aroha don't come along every day, boy. Promise me you won't be a typical New Zealand male and wait till it's too late to let Cat know how you feel about her.'

'I'll try Aunty.'

'You do more than try, Jay Duggan. It's what Aroha would want.'

He gazed over at Cat. She was gripping the trunk of a young rimu and leaning to stretch her calf.

'The hell you got against that tree?'

'I'm warming up my muscles.'

'They'll be heatin up soon enough.'

The reflected moon sparkled in midstream as the river flowed silently towards the deep crystal pools of the Hokitika Gorge – the West Coast's *second-best-kept* secret. Jay would have loved to show them off to Cat, but their route lay upstream. They waved to Aunty Fay and headed up the track. The weather was holding. Jay wondered for how long.

* * * *

'YOU'RE OUT of your mind, after everything we've done to build her up.'

Vestco's communications manager was clearly livid with Petersen's decision to leak the truth about Joy McCarthy, who had become a pin-up girl for the entire genetic modification industry following her highly publicized transformation from green fanatic to biotech convert.

The world's media had lapped up the amazing tale of McCarthy's

298

pilgrimage from founding member of the organics movement to champion of genetic modification.

'This is not negotiable Shelley. And I want this dossier to go to *Grassroots*. Now.'

She snatched the file showing how McCarthy's green credentials had been fabricated, and blustered out of the room.

The exchange had come to a head during a crisis meeting on how to get a White House hopeful and personal friend of Jozef Pyjas out of the headlines and off the front page of Google searches. *Huffington Post* had broken the story about her receiving millions of dollars in contributions from the biotech industry, including Vestco. The exposé had snowballed into one of the hottest news items on the net, and was starting to be picked up by the mainstream media. It needed to be gazumped.

Shelley's head appeared in the doorway.

'And why on earth do you want to leak it to *Grassroots*? If we must do this, I could get it straight into the prime news cycle.'

'Trust me on this. I have my reasons.'

* * * *

VEHICLES ENTERING Ross weren't being searched, so Aunty Fay passed through the roadblock and continued towards town, parking the truck beside a phone booth on the outskirts.

She took the piece of paper from inside her bra and dialed the Christchurch number Jay had scrawled across the top. After several rings, a male voice answered. Fay read the short message, hung up, and drove home.

55. Simply orchestral

AFTER WINCHING themselves across the river in a cage suspended on a wire cable, Cat and Jay stuck to the true left bank as the track wound through forest peppered with tree ferns the size of giant's umbrellas.

Cat wasn't convinced by Jay's claim that the most dangerous creature in New Zealand, 'give or take the odd greedy politician or businessman', was the sandfly. There were hardly any at their first rest stop.

'Wait till dawn. Little buggers go berserk. Female ones anyway. The males don't bother you.'

Cat pounced on the light-hearted moment to confess about the birthday phone call to Pop that must have led the police to the shafts and almost given away their location.

Jay said nothing for a while. Just stared at a plump black robin picking at crumbs near his boot. The response, when it came, was unexpected.

'Really sorry about your dad, Cat. Hope he's alright. Your call wasn't the one that gave away the shafts. That was my fault. I phoned Kaufman from down there on the way back from the outdoor shop. I was showing off, plain and simple. Trying to put the bastard in his place. Stupid thing to do.'

He threw a piece of water cracker to the bird. 'Just as well your mother was there to call the ambulance eh? Thought you said they didn't get on.'

'That's the weird thing. She loathes Pop. Has had nothing to do with him, or me, for years.'

'It was his birthday.'

'You don't know my mom. She's as sentimental as a block of ice. Being his birthday would be all the more reason for her to keep away.'

'And you would have thought if he was that sick she would have gone with him in the ambulance, instead of waiting round at his house.'

'Hadn't thought of that.'

'Sounds a bit sus, just quietly.'

'Sus?'

'Suspicious. Like a jack up. They're sure to have your dad's phone tapped. And would have known it was his birthday. Simple to divert the calls and have your mother primed and ready on the off chance you'd ring.'

'Wouldn't put it past Mom.'

'Which also means there might be nothing wrong with your father. Could be just trying to make you feel so guilty you'll give yourself up.'

'That was the other weird thing. Mom was far more interested in where I was than how Pop was.'

'Hold on ta that thought,' Jay said, standing. 'We better get a move on.'

Although Cat knew he was trying to put a positive spin on it, she did feel better as they headed off.

With every turn the river grew. By dawn they'd reached the swing bridge across Collier Gorge and, with no sign of pursuit, Cat began to relax. Words could never do justice to the wild beauty of the place. The exquisite birdsong. The primal power of water gushing through the gorge. It was simply orchestral.

Every now and then the rainforest deigned to allow glimpses of the jagged peaks of the Alps, beckoning like the spires of mystical cathedrals.

The trail was becoming more undulated as it rose and fell to skirt bluffs and rockslides. The sandflies were the least of Cat's worries.

She'd started seeing hour glasses in the shapes of tree trunks, rocks and shadows. Her calves throbbed. Big strides up rocks were killing her until she stopped trying to match Jay's steps and gave up trying not to puff. Suppressing natural airflow was using too much energy. Small, machine-like strides were more efficient.

She even gave up complaining when Jay's arm materialized to help her up the steeper sections.

He took the lead, pushing the pace along a flat stretch parallel to the river, before suddenly turning off the trail and taking off his pack.

'Something wrong?'

'There's a hut just ahead. I'll get you to wait here while I check it out.'

'Why don't we just go round it?'

'Never know what you might miss.'

He returned a few minutes later, smiling like a kid who'd just seen his first Christmas stocking.

'She's all clear, and there's someone I want you to meet.'

Smoke was rambling from the chimney of the hut set at the back of an open plateau overlooking a bend in the river.

A chair made of driftwood was positioned for the million-dollar view.

Cat noticed a thin red wire going from the window up into a coat hanger high in a tree.

Their boots clomped on the wooden verandah as they ducked under a line of possum pelts draped across the entranceway.

Bouquet would be a generous way to describe the potpourri coming through the open door, though the mixture of wood smoke, cooking meat, sweat and marijuana was pleasant enough, bordering on homely.

The sole occupant of Frew's Hut, introduced by Jay as The Plucker, was a wiry rooster with glazed eyes and hair so thick it had to be the origin of the word *mop*.

His greeting, which sounded to Cat something like gidyhwyrite, was translated by Jay as *Gidday, how are you, are you all right?*

'Spect yous'll be up for a brew,' The Plucker said, eyeing Cat up and down as if she was the first woman he'd seen in years.

'Cheers mate,' said Jay. 'Mind if I try the tranny?'

'No worries.'

Jay sat on the bunk and fiddled with dials on a small transistor radio hooked up to what Cat realized was the other end of the red wire. Must be some sort of aerial. The strong black billy tea was good. So was the first item on the news bulletin. The manhunt was still centered on Ross. Special machinery had arrived from Greymouth to help excavate more rubbish at the dump, and a team of professional speleologists was being flown in from Nelson to help the police search the maze of underground tunnels beneath the town.

The second item made Cat drop her cup.

Professor Keith Stedholme, the renowned British biochemist, has been killed in a motor accident, along with his granddaughter and a Grassroots journalist. The trio were returning to the professor's home near Cambridge University when his Range Rover failed to take a bend and careered off a bank and into a swollen river.'

Cat's head slumped into her palms. Jay sat beside her.

'Wouldn't rule out suicide you know, after what he said about Alo.'

'Not with his granddaughter in the car Jay. And a journalist.'

'Sounds bloody dubious to me.'

'For heck's sake, when's this going to stop?'

Her voice was quivering.

'I know it's tough,' said Jay, putting an arm round her shoulder. 'But the only chance we've got of stopping all this crap is to get to Governor's Bay, and find out what's in that virtual box before the release.'

'Even if we sort out my part of the riddle, we're no closer to solving it without Matthew's.'

'Been thinking about that. The answers to the first two clues were movie titles, right? *Los Olvidados* and *Never Cry Wolf*. Remember what Matthew said about patterns in the answers? Chances are the last one will also be a movie.'

'So, you're saying if we have half the clue it might be possible to search on Google for the rest, based on movie titles?'

'You're onto it. And we know we're looking for thirteen letters.'

They were grasping at straws. Even if they found the CD they still had to work out a way to recreate the website without Matthew.

'We can do this Cat. You can do it. I need you to take a few deep breaths, get a grip, while I have a wee chat to The Plucker here. Then it's time to hit the breeze.'

He stood and turned, putting his hands lightly on her shoulders and looking into her eyes.

'You with me?'

It was a moment of intimacy and reassurance she desperately craved. She sniffed, wiped her face with her sleeve and nodded.

The conversation between the two men might as well have been in Japanese for all Cat could understand.

Something about *buying the tranny*, the Plucker saying he'd *settle for a shag*, Jay shaking his head, something about *a saddle*.

Then caps were being swapped, hands shaken and The Plucker was reaching under a bunk for a coil of red wire while Jay disconnected the radio.

Back on the track heading east, Cat resolved to fill her mind with anything but thoughts of Pop and Keith Stedholme.

'Why's he called The Plucker?'

'That's just what I call him. Came across him the first time we did the Whitcombe. He was telling us how he gets the skins off the possums. Grabs em in the right place and plucks em off in one pop.'

'Who's *us*?'

'Me and Andrew. Old hiking mate.'

'What's The Plucker's real name?'

'Wouldn't have a clue. Blokes like him prefer it that way.'

'Why's that?'

'Less people know what he's doin up here the better. Never asked him. My guess is he's on the dole and half a dozen other benefits he's not entitled to. Think there's a wife and kids in Australia he's supposed to be paying maintenance to. Long as he can earn a few extra bucks under the table from his skins and get stoned every night, reckon old Plucker's happy as a pig in mud.'

They continued on for a few more hours, and by early afternoon were approaching Price's Flat.

Cat was relieved when Jay suggested a break.

'We'll have a feed here and rest for a few hours.'

'Shouldn't we go as far as we can in the light?'

'We've gotta cross a stretch of open ground round Price's Hut which I'd rather do in darkness. You've done bloody well so far Cat, but that was the easy bit. She gets tougher from here on, and we need to save our energy for the pass. Been lucky with the weather, but she could turn to custard tomorrow. We need to get as far up the valley as we can tonight. Should be a good walkin' moon.'

After a meal of tuna and crackers, Jay went down to the river to wash up and check the surroundings. Cat arranged bunches of fern leaves into a mattress. She toyed with the thought of making the bed wide enough for two, before chiding herself for even considering sex at a time like this.

She was so exhausted when she finished the second bed, not even the attention of a swarm of sandflies could keep her awake.

* * * *

THE MATTRESS was so new, pieces of plastic wrapping still stuck to the brand patch near Matthew's feet. The room was smothered in antiseptic spiked with the syrupy metallic smell of welding from the new steel door and window bars.

The rest of the hastily converted cell was more what you'd expect from an ABC army building. Concrete walls. Clapped-out wooden floor. Single light bulb noosing from a very high ceiling, eighteen-foot or so, tarnished with mildew. Screw holes at regular intervals on the walls suggested it was a storeroom until very recently.

Matthew had hardly slept since arriving almost thirty hours ago. The little shuteye he managed was filled with images of exploding eyeballs and chunks of red rashers of human skin spitting in a frying pan. He forced himself to stay awake, which helped. For a while.

Never had he felt so alone. A mute guard came once to swap the bucket and three times a day others came with meals he didn't touch because he knew they were drugged or poisoned. Each silent visit lasted less than sixty seconds. For the other fourteen hundred and thirty-six minutes of the day he seemed to have the building to himself.

He tried to shut out thoughts of metal skullcaps and moist sponges and two-thousand-volt currents by concentrating on the only constant sound reaching him. A loose bit of roofing iron banging in the wind. Measuring the gap between bangs was a distraction until, with the record at forty-six seconds, he caught himself imagining the doctor counting down until the body was cool enough to see if his heart was still beating. He'd yelled until his lungs smoked. Nobody gave a toss.

If he hadn't kicked the bucket, literally, he'd have gone mad for sure. The lame play on words rebooted the old gray matter. What a tosser he'd been. Too full of himself to realize the Millbrook job was a set-up. From start to bleedin finish. What cash-strapped voluntary outfit pays over-the-top dosh to a geezer from the other side of the world, when all they really want is someone to hack into another outfit's system? You do it, three times, and out come the envelopes too fat with greenbacks to fit in your wallet. *Nudge nudge, wink wink.* You're so pleased with your high and mighty self you don't stop to wonder why the hacks are spotted straight away and sorted quicker than a lizard drinking. Even Henry Beck isn't that good. Wasn't. Must've got the word from Deaver, the two-faced con artist. Who, surprise surprise, is thick as thieves with his old mate Bradley trust'im-with-ya-bleedin-life Kaufman. And here you are Matthew me old son. Last clue sorted and without a computer. Might as well be on Mars.

A car horn pierced the concrete wall. Matthew looked up at the barred window and for the first time noticed a scratch on the beige paint on the outside of the glass. The bottom of the window was at least ten feet from the floor, which is why he'd ignored it till now. He stood, pulled the mattress off the bed, careful to keep it out of the pool of niffy liquid from the overturned bucket. He dragged the metal bed frame across the room and tipped it up against the wall. On his second attempt he managed to reach the top and grab hold of the metal bars over the window. The scratch was only an eighth of an inch deep by about half an inch wide, but by closing one eye and squinting he could make out the group of journalists hunched outside the gates. There were only half as many as when he arrived.

He yelled and banged on the reinforced glass with his fist. They showed no sign of hearing him. In frustration he tried to shake the bars but only succeeded in knocking over the bed frame. It crashed to the floor, leaving him dangling.

* * * *

A FEW minutes after ten in the evening, a massive Lockheed C-5 Galaxy touched down at Christchurch Airport, home of the United States Antarctic Program since the early 1960s and a staging point for American scientists heading to the Ice.

Packed at the front of the thirty thousand cubic foot cargo compartment, alongside pallets of polar clothing, snow shelters, food, medical supplies, core sample drills and other scientific gear, was an HH-60 Pave Hawk. The chopper's crew slept for most of the flight from the States and anticipated having the bird unpacked and cleared for takeoff to the West Coast by midnight local time.

* * * *

THE WOMAN behind the Air New Zealand check-in counter at Los Angeles Airport recognized the gold pendant even though the man was still three places from the front of the queue.

She had no doubt it was the Shoshone arrowhead design featured in photographs beside every check-in counter at every airport in California. She picked up her phone and told her supervisor. As the passenger reached the front of the queue, two men in black business suits appeared at his side. The shorter of the two held up an identity card.

'Homeland Security, Mr Tayler. Afraid we can't allow you to leave the United States at this time, sir.'

56. Cloak and dagger

'AH, MISTER Kaufman, how nice of you to grace us with your presence.'

Kaufman ignored Hansen's sarcasm as he entered the outdoor equipment store. Nothing had been found in the house-to-house search, and there were no reports of anything useful from the roadblocks.

Kaufman, though, felt reinvigorated. The Pave Hawk with its Special Forces crew arrived in Hokitika in the early hours of the morning and he'd just returned from a short reconnaissance flight. The chopper's forward-looking infrared was little use in the town, but would do the job nicely if the terrorists tried to break out. As would the externally mounted .50 caliber machine guns.

The police had received a call from the manager of the store, who discovered the break-in. Hansen was strutting round with him as he pointed out what was missing.

'Gotta be our boy right?' Kaufman asked.

She ignored the question and glanced at her notepad.

'So far it looks like they've taken a backpack, one pair of hiking boots, raincoats, cooking gear, packets of dehydrated food, torch, Swiss Army knife.'

'Here's something else, Inspector.' The store manager was pointing to a display of mountaineering gear.

'There's a pair of crampons missing. Hang on... make that two pair. And an ice axe.'

'Where would you use that sort of gear round here?'

'Lots of places Inspector.'

The manager led them to a map on the wall and pointed to a sweep of mountains. 'There are dozens of popular climbs right through this area, extending deep into the Alps. Then there's your more serious peaks in these ranges – the Birdwood, the Rolleston, Ragged. But they'd need a lot of high alpine experience to go near any of those.'

'We don't know much about Tayler, but Duggan's climbed Mount Cook.'

'And several peaks in the Himalayas.'

'Impressive,' said the manager. 'None of these are out of his reach.'

Hansen scratched her head.

'But why? What are they going to achieve by climbing a mountain?'

Kaufman was looking beyond the band of mountains to the plains stretching to the east coast on the other side.

He had a worrying thought.

'To get to the other side. What's the name of the place they're having the New Zealand end of the Alo release?'

'Lincoln University.'

'Show me.'

Hansen pointed to a red dot just south of the built-up area of Christchurch.

'There's your answer, Inspector.'

Kaufman stepped in for a closer look at the map. 'Must be trails through the mountains to the other side, right?'

'Several,' the manager replied, 'depending on how adventurous you want to be. We've got more detailed maps over here.'

They walked to a display stand holding a dozen different topographical maps. One lay on the floor.

'Any way of telling if any are missing?'

Kaufman went back to study the map on the wall while the manager cross-checked the stocks in the stand with records on his computer. It didn't take him long to discover a map for a route known as the Three

Passes was unaccounted for. They spread one of the maps on the counter and the manager marked the route with a yellow highlighter.

'Those passes don't look very high,' said Hansen. 'Why would they need crampons this time of year?'

'Whitehorn Pass. She's got permanent snow. Most guidebooks recommend crampons, though not everyone takes them. Hardy types have been known to run The Three Passes in light all-terrain shoes.'

'And where would this route normally come out?'

'Here. Where the Waimakariri River meets the main road, south of Arthur's Pass Village. Called Klondyke Corner. Big transition point in the Coast to Coast endurance race.'

That name was familiar to Kaufman.

'Duggan's done that race, hasn't he?'

'Several times,' said Hansen.

'And once they reach the road, they're less than three hours' drive from Lincoln,' added the manager.

'You could be onto something here Mr Kaufman.'

He nodded acknowledgement, then turned to the manager.

'How long would it take someone to get through these Three Passes?'

'Depends how much hurry they're in. There's several huts and spectacular scenery. Most people take three or four days.'

'And if they're not doing it for the scenery?'

'I've heard of multi-sporters running it in a day.'

Kaufman had heard enough.

'Right. I'll follow the route in the Hawk. I suggest you seal off the other side Inspector. Move most of your personnel over to this Klondyke Corner. And send in armed squads from the eastern end.'

He grabbed the map and was out the door before she could answer.

* * * *

HANSEN WAS on the phone to the police station in Arthur's Pass, asking for local advice on the best way to deploy searchers along the alpine track.

Teams from Christchurch could be in place at Klondyke Corner inside three hours. Some would go in on foot from the eastern end. Others would be ferried by chopper to drop points along the route, using several backcountry huts as bases. Reinforcements would be bused to Klondyke from Christchurch and the nearby Army camp at Burnham.

On this side of the Alps, groups were being driven to the start of the track near Lake Kaniere. Hansen put her deputy in charge of the logistical nightmare of moving the bulk of the manpower over to the east coast, focusing on Lincoln as the likely target.

The store manager was tapping away at the computer, no doubt filing a claim with insurance. Hansen interrupted him.

'You said an ultra-fit multi-sporter could run The Three Passes in a day. What about a person of only moderate fitness, a woman, with no experience of multisport or the New Zealand bush?'

'She'd be doing well to do it in three days. Browning Pass has some relatively steep sections. Gets a fair bit of ice. There's also some pretty serious river crossings through there.'

'And you wouldn't carry a big pack and ice axes and crampons and all that food if you were running it in a day?'

'Hell no. Your multi-sporters travel incredibly light. Shirt, shorts, shoes, water bladder, light raincoat. Few muesli bars. Bloody mad if you ask me.'

Hansen considered this.

It was possible Duggan and Tayler had split up, but unlikely given what Liddell said about Tayler holding the key to unlocking this virtual deposit box. And she'd need Duggan as a guide. What if they were not heading to the east coast at all? What if they were merely running away? Where would *she* go if she were Duggan? She'd go bush. To a place she was familiar with. Duggan may well have committed some or all of these crimes he was being accused of, though clearly there was another side to the man. Hansen didn't know many environmentalists. The ones she had come across tended to be anally responsible when it came to things like the bush, the mountains. Responsible hikers filled in backcountry hut intention books.

She phoned the base in Auckland and asked for checks to be made of all Department of Conservation hut books back in the days Duggan was hiking in the area.

The Three Passes was still the most likely scenario. But if they were going to be stuck in the bush for up to three days they posed no threat to the Alo release.

Why then was Kaufman so desperate to find them?

More than twenty-four hours had passed since she spoke to her friend in Washington.

She grabbed her cell phone, started punching keys, then stopped and stared at the screen.

How did Kaufman find out so quickly about the break-in at the outdoor store?

Surely he wouldn't stoop to tapping my phone?

'Mind if I use your landline?' she asked the manager.

'Not at all.'

The news from her contact in Washington was half expected.

Kaufman was your all-American hero. Served with distinction in a string of operations with US Special Forces in Panama, Kuwait, Somalia, the Balkans, Liberia, Congo, Kenya. Most with ridiculous Hollywood names like Operation Just Cause and Just Endeavor. He returned to the States to work in counterterrorism, including a stint on secondment to LAPD homicide.

'I'm barking up the wrong tree with my suspicions?'

'It would seem so. Officially.'

'And unofficially?'

'My husband's cousin works for the records section at the Department of Justice. It seems while Kaufman was at the LAPD there was some controversy about false fingerprinting. Allegedly. There was an internal inquiry, but nothing was proven.'

Hansen thought of the murder of the technology geek at Vestco that started this whole saga.

Liddell's prints were found on the gun.

'Interesting thanks Caroline. One more favor. Any chance of asking this contact in Justice to check the file on the murder of that information technology guy at Vestco? Name was Buck, Beck, something like that. I'd be interested to know where Kaufman was at time of death.'

'Can't promise anything, but I'll have a go.'

She hung up.

Fingerprints. Duggan's were found on the gun that shot Constable Shaw at Auckland Airport. After his neck was broken. Inquiries into the flight logs revealed no evidence of tampering. What if Liddell was right and it could be done without a trace? She used the store phone to make another call.

Neill O'Reilly was a former colleague who was always pointing out how his investigative skills were worth more money outside the force than in. A personality conflict with a fellow officer – he was caught in bed with the guy's wife – tipped the balance into premature retirement and the seedy world of private investigation.

'That favor you owe me, Neill. I need to call it in. And the job needs to stay on the quiet.'

'Shoot.'

'I'm going to email you a list of passengers on a flight from Los Angeles to Auckland a week or so ago. I'm also emailing a mug shot of a man. I need you to track down as many of the passengers as you can and ask them if they remember seeing the man on the flight. As I said, this needs to stay very discreet.'

'It's not like you to play the cloak and dagger routine.'

'You'll understand why when you see the identity of the person I'm interested in.'

57. Legs of jelly

CAT STUMBLED, misjudging the height of a tree root yet again. Her shoulders and head and lungs were hollering for relief, and the rest of her body was a punch bag of misery.

They'd been hiking all night, often through bush too thick to shed moonlight. Each time she thought the track couldn't possibly get steeper or more overgrown it laughed at her. She lost count of the times they had to brawl through undergrowth to get past whopping trunks felled by storms or scramble over the top of slips the size of high rises. They could have been going north, south, east or to the moon if it wasn't for the ever-present bellow of the river, its volume a gauge of how high they were up the side of the valley. Several times Cat was convinced they were lost. Jay always found the triangular orange trail markers. It was like he had a sixth sense.

Concentrating step by step was accelerating the fatigue, but a necessary distraction from thoughts of Pop, which circled to torment her each time they rested. Short breaks on the hour, every hour, like a boot camp. Jay climbing the nearest tree with the wire aerial to try to get reception. Once he got static from Mars. Then even the little green men abandoned them.

Downhill on legs of jelly was only marginally easier than up. This time the track dropped all the way to the river. Cat could see a footbridge, suspended above the torrent in the mist and spray and moonlight like a Japanese postcard.

'The track to the pass stays on this side,' Jay shouted over the fizzing of the river. 'There's a hut on the other side. About ten minutes' walk. I wanna try something. We'll leave our gear here.'

She had a thousand questions but no energy to ask. Probably didn't want to hear the answers anyway. They hid their packs under a tree fern and Jay, flashlight and transistor in one hand, led the way over the bridge. A sign on the door said the hut was closed because of an unstable slip on the ridge above. Too bad, Cat thought as she collapsed onto a bunk.

Jay disconnected the solar powered radio receiver and hooked up the transistor, jamming its aerial into the receiver's socket. He tweaked the tuning dial until he found a news station. The first item was about a donation from Vestco towards restoration of a world heritage site in Asia damaged in an earthquake. Cat started drifting off to sleep, but was jolted awake by none other than Paul Deaver, chief executive of the Millbrook Foundation.

'... last two days I have personally been given unrestricted access to Vestco's scientific data, and can vouch that our foundation's concerns about the veracity of their research is unfounded. As much as I hate admitting it, we were wrong. Based on the evidence, we are now convinced Alo is set to become the best thing since sliced bread, hula hoops, Alexander Graham Bell and the Wright Brothers all rolled into one.'

'Deaver would never say that,' said Jay. 'Gotta be some trick.'

'Yes he would,' said Cat, the penny finally dropping. 'In fact, he's said it before. Remember back in his office. The day we left. He wouldn't look at me when he said it. Deaver's part of the whole conspiracy - '

'... at a joint press conference in New York. The three-way joint hosting arrangement will ensure maximum coverage of the global release across television and online media platforms. The announcement took many media watchers by surprise, given Grassroots Intelligence's track record as a critic of big business and Vestco in particular. The blog's editor-in-chief Joe Shaw said the decision to co-host the release was influenced by the Millbrook Foundation's unequivocal backing for Alo, and the earlier endorsement of the seed coating by the eminent English scientist *and long-time genetic modification critic Professor Keith Stedholme.'*

Cat gulped. 'Oh my heck. They're everywhere - '

'... bulk of the estimated four hundred troops and police to Arthur's Pass, suggesting the terrorists are heading to the east coast. Police sources now believe Lincoln — the site of the New Zealand release of Alo in two days — is the likely target.'

'Must have discovered the break-in at the shop,' said Jay. 'Which hopefully means they've taken the bait about The Three Passes route.'

He looked back at Cat. 'How ya feelin?'

'Fetchin angry.'

'You're allowed to actually swear in moments like this, Cat.'

'I was.'

'Right. Bottle it up for now then. She's almost dawn. Let's get cracking.'

* * * *

WITH ITS sophisticated radar, the Pave Hawk could comfortably follow the terrain contours at speeds up to one hundred forty knots, its forward-looking sensors transforming the pre-dawn gloom into a ghostly glow of infrared light.

Kaufman looked across at the kid controlling the port machine gun, his face lit by the gleam of the night vision goggles attached to his helmet. Wouldn't need them much longer. The first traces of sunlight were hitting the top of the ridgeline far above. So far they'd spotted four people, seven deer and two wild boars. Closer inspection revealed the humans as middle-aged hikers sleeping in a hut.

As the Hawk emerged from a gorge into a widening river valley, the FLIR detectors picked out the glowing hotspots of two figures up ahead. The gunner armed the weapon.

Kaufman squinted through binoculars. He could make out two people running along a trail on a flat beside the river. They were heading for the cover of the forest at the top end of the valley, which they would reach in about ten seconds.

'Take em out,' he yelled.

'We're not sure it's them,' the gunner replied calmly.

'Take out that rock then, ahead of them.'

The gunner adjusted his sight, flipped the trigger guard and squeezed. An angry growl erupted as the cannon churned out several rounds. The two people were flung to the ground in a hail of exploding rock and foliage and dirt. As the Hawk moved in to land, a large tree with half its trunk blown away toppled to the ground less than five yards from the targets. Both remained head down, motionless.

Kaufman was first out of the chopper, his excitement growing as he recognized the shapes of a male and female. He aimed his pistol at the back of the male's head.

'OK asshole. Up slowly. Hands on your head.'

A groan but no movement. He prodded the man with his boot. When this got no response he used his foot to turn him over. It was not Duggan.

'This one's definitely not Tayler.' Deakes was helping the woman to her feet.

A sandfly buzzed in front of Kaufman's face, as he felt a second bit his neck.

Followed by a drop of rain on his forehead.

58. Like there's no tomorrow

'THAT WAS thunder, right?'

It was more statement than question, so Jay chose not to give a direct answer. He'd heard the sound of canon fire in the hills behind them to the northeast.

'I'd say the front's reached the coast by now. The air will have sucked up so much moisture on the way she'll be close to a hundred percent humidity. Once she hits these mountains she'll only have to rise a couple of hundred yards or so to cool enough to form cloud.'

'That'd be a good thing for us, wouldn't it?'

'If it was just cloud. Problem is that air's not going to stop rising till she reaches the main divide. As she goes up, the water vapor condenses. Before you know it old Hughie'll start pissing like there's no tomorrow.'

'Hughie?'

'Weather god of hikers. Round here the old fella can send it down in truckloads. We better shake a leg.'

They'd made good time since Wilkinson Hut, but Jay could tell Cat was exhausted. The chin tapping was back. She needed rest before they pushed on for the pass.

'There's a place not far away where we can stop and have a sleep.'

The track hugged a bank cloaked in kidney ferns and umbrella moss, taking them on an arc away from the river to avoid a slip carved out of the hillside in a previous downpour. At the top stood a matching pair of rimu trunks with grey bark furrowed like fingerprints. The stream trickling between the trunks always made Jay picture Shrek having a leak.

'Time for a little detour,' he said, heading up the middle of the stream. A few feet before a waterfall he climbed onto the bank and brushed through a grove of tree ferns with skirts of dead fronds hanging like bundles of kindling sticks. Before them was a vertical face of lichen-covered rock framing a mountain totara. Beside the trunk of thin papery bark was the stem of a climbing rata vine, dangling over the cliff. Jay wanted Cat to go up first. To discover it for herself. Like he did several years ago. He helped her start the climb, then waited for about a minute before scrambling up to join her.

She was standing there, mouth still open. It was, as they say, a sight for sore eyes. The Coast's *best-kept* secret. They were on the edge of a moss-carpeted plateau about the size of a tennis court enclosed by a near perfect semicircle of green miro trees with hundreds of bright red berries glowing like Christmas lights. Half a dozen wood pigeons, metallic blue and green and purple against plump white breasts, were tucking into the fruit. The stream dribbled over rocks into a shallow basin near the center of the amphitheater, before splitting into two beds and choosing the lower channel. From the seemingly dry channel to the right rose a single flute of steam. Sulphur swamped the taint of decomposing leaves.

'Tell me that's what I think it is.'

'Too right,' said Jay, walking towards a cave-like overhang formed by a buttress spreading from the base of a gnarled pukatea tree growing on a ledge above the flowing channel. He took off his pack and leaned it against one of two breathing roots sticking out of the stream like tombstones.

'We'll stop here a while. If you wanna take a dip I wouldn't muck about. Old Hughie can convert this creek into a roarer which'd be like turning on a bloody great cold tap full bore.'

They stripped to their underwear and slid into the hot water. Cat closed her eyes and purred, stretching those creamy shoulders back and giving Jay a front row eyeful of cleavage.

'If this spot was in the States I swear there'd be a hotel, airstrip, bunch of souvenir stores, the works,' said Cat, eyes still shut. 'How many people know about it?'

'Bugger all I suspect. Me and Andrew found it by chance years ago. Told no one. Been back half a dozen times and never seen any sign anyone else has been here.'

Thunder boomed. Jay counted the seconds till the lightning. Four miles. He looked at Cat and knew this was the moment Aunty Fay was referring to. Don't be a typical New Zealand male and wait till it's too late. *Easier said than done.*

'Met this arty bloke near here once. Glass caster he was, from Nelson. Anyway, he'd studied all this cloud-to-ground lightning data from the Met Service and worked out the most likely place for lightning to strike was on a ridge over that way called the Gelena. He sets up these great long rods connected to PVC tubes packed with various stuff you need to make glass. Soda ash. Lime. Silica from memory. He reckoned lightning would strike one of these rods then arc through the minerals to create natural glass. Had some fancy name I can't remember.'

'Fulgurite?'

'Yeah. Something like that. Never heard how the bloke got on. Bit of a dreamer if you ask me.'

'Interesting idea though. They do occur naturally. Fulgur is Latin for thunderbolt. The glass is also known as petrified lightning.'

Rain started falling.

Jay got out of the pool and started collecting clumps of moss to make a mattress in the cave.

He laid a raincoat on the moss, then a fleece blanket.

Out in the open the rain was getting heavier.

He looked behind him.

Cat was rising like a goddess from the pool, trickles of water dripping from her chin and each breast. The darkness of her nipples clearly visible through her wet bra. He turned back towards the cave, hoping she hadn't noticed his hard on.

'Tell me Mr Duggan, what did your possum plucker friend mean when he said he'd settle for a shag?'

Jay was struggling to think of an answer when the tips of two swollen nipples brushed against his back.

* * * *

HORIZONTAL RAIN was pummeling the window of the police station in Hokitika as Hansen waited for a car to take her to the airport. Her flight to Christchurch had been delayed by the late arrival of an inbound plane held up by the deteriorating weather. The phone rang and a desk officer picked it up.

'It's a Sergeant Pulepule from Christchurch, Inspector. Says he's got some info from the hut books.'

'Put him on speaker.'

The accent was Samoan Kiwi.

Duggan's name appears in virtually every hut book in the region. Except ones on The Three Passes route.'

Kaufman walked in. Hansen ignored him.

'What other huts sergeant? Are there any he's stayed in more than others?'

'Half a dozen. The Neave. Prices. Frews. Wilkinson. Lauper. Reischek.'

Hansen laid a map on the table. She asked him to repeat the names, and circled each with a red marker.

Joined together, the route became obvious.

It followed the Whitcombe River over the Whitcombe Pass and down the Lauper River to the head of the Rakaia Valley.

'Thank you sergeant.'

'One other thing Inspector. Every time he stayed in those huts he was with the same person. Guy by the name of Andrew Budd.'

'Where have I heard that name?'

'He's one of those extreme multi-sporters. The *Stuff* website ran a story on him breaking the record for the Coast to Coast course, but not during the event because he refused to pay the entry fee. Almost certain he lives here in Christchurch.'

'Track him down and interrogate him,' Kaufman yelled, heading for the door.

Hansen resented the intrusion.

'Where the hell are you going?'

'The Whitcombe Valley. My boys and I'll start searching it from this end. I suggest you get your Keystone Cops to start working from the other.'

The desk officer cleared his throat.

'That might not be such a sensible idea sir. The weather's packing up big time. Visibility's diminishing. I know that valley. If this wind intensifies, as forecast, flying's going to become extremely marginal. We've already had reports of torrential rain down the coast to the south. Slips blocking roads in the Haast.'

'He's right Mister Kaufman,' Hansen pitched in. 'You and your *boys* aren't used to the conditions we have in these mountains. Duggan and Tayler won't be getting up to much mischief up there. They'll have to sit out the storm. We're best to seal off each end and work in from the ground.'

'The Hawk can fly through anything lady.'

He left. Rain bat-bat-bat-bat-bat-bat-bat-batted the window until Sergeant Pulepule's voice interrupted from the speaker.

What do you want us to do about Duggan's hiking friend, Inspector?

Hansen sighed.

'Get him in.'

* * * *

CAT WAS home in her upstairs bedroom, rain falling on the iron roof, the smell of coffee drifting up from the kitchen. Had to be the weekend, which meant no school. Sleep in. She gathered the sheet tighter round her shoulders and rolled over.

Her back hit something hard and she opened her eyes. Her favorite dolphin poster had become a wall of jagged rock. She rolled to the other side, hitting the tree root again. Jay was squatting over a portable gas cooker, stirring bacon with a fork while coffee dripped through a little stainless-steel contraption on top of a cup. A curtain of rain flowed from the overhang behind him.

Memories of the lovemaking came back. She smiled. Something else was different. Like an inner warmth that went far deeper than the sex. A bond had been consummated. How had Jay described the Maori nose touching? An exchange of the breath of life. Cat raised the splayed fingers of her right hand, but stopped short of her chin. She had no desire, no need, to tap.

'How long did I sleep?'

'Hours. Must have needed it.'

'Any girl would have, after - '

'About that. It was, you know - '

'Beautiful Jay.'

'Yeah,' he smiled. 'It was pretty choice.'

He stood and cleared his throat. 'Ah... truth is... ah ... I think the world of you Cat.'

She walked towards him, reaching up to put her arms round his shoulders and kissing him. 'The feeling's mutual Mr Duggan. And aren't you full of surprises? Expressing your feelings like that. Eco-warrior meets sensitive new age guy.'

'Cut it out,' he said, grinning mischievously. 'Aunty Fay put me up to it. Made me promise to say it. The thought of her hunting me down with that sixteen gauge and pink slippers would put the fear of God into any bloke.'

As they kissed, a gust of wind drove a shower of rain into their faces like an alarm clock. Cat looked at her watch. 5.50pm.

'There's only nineteen, no, eighteen hours to the release.'

'Good news is this rain and cloud mean we won't have to wait till dark to push on for the pass. She'll be pea soup up there. Soon as we've had a feed, we better scarper.'

59. Raw. Wild. Unpredictable.

AS THE ROLLS ROYCE Silver Spur left the carpark beneath Zurich's most discreet bank and turned into Freigutstrasse, the backseat passenger switched on the television. The lifestyle report held no interest, so Petersen lowered the volume, opened his briefcase and looked over the speech his chairman would be giving at the G7 summit in a few hours.

Zurich was a city to be admired rather than liked. It got on with the business of wealth accumulation in a backroom sort of way. The stately yet subdued buildings and small-town Swiss charm attracted far less attention than the Monacos or Lombard or Wall Streets.

Petersen felt a tingle of excitement as the familiar countdown sequence to the news bulletin came on, with the voiceover tantalizing viewers with a world exclusive – the results of the most comprehensive poll in history.

Twenty thousand people in sixty countries were asked if they supported the release of Alo. A resounding eighty-seven percent said yes – up from forty-seven a week before the fire in Tolminsky's lab. Regional breakdowns showed the highest backing – between ninety-four and ninety-eight percent – in five countries. No mention that the five were homes to a well-known actor, golfer, television anchorman, football player and singer. The lowest level of support – seventy-two percent in New Zealand – was still described as overwhelming. The television producer had earned his bonus.

Petersen poured a celebratory drink from the decanter cabinet, toasted himself in the reflection of the window and settled back in the soft leather for the ride to Kloten Airport.

* * * *

CAT TREMBLED as another blast of icy water got under the collar of her coat and leeched down her back. Her thighs were red, and knees ghost white from the exertion and cold. She'd give anything for a pair of miniature windshield wipers.

You could brace yourself against rain driving in at a constant angle like a high-pressure shower. There was no predicting the direction of this spray as the river jerked and corkscrewed in its stampede for lower ground.

This was nature at an entirely different end of the spectrum from the comforts of a biology lab. Raw. Wild. Unpredictable. And it would be terrifying if not for the presence of the man walking a few paces ahead of her. Jay was in his element. At one with the land, in sync with its moods. There was no one on the planet Cat would rather be with right now.

It was mind-boggling how much the river had grown in ten minutes.

'I thought rivers were supposed to get smaller the closer you get to their source,' she shouted.

Jay turned.

'The pass is a narrow saddle between a couple of decent-sized mountains.'

His face was only inches away and she could barely hear him.

'She's like a massive funnel with two outlets. This is the biggest of them. We basically follow the river from here to the top, so she's gonna get a bit wetter yet. And steeper. You up for it? Here, let me carry your pack.'

'I'm fine,' she lied.

60. Smoke rising

IT WAS a while since Kaufman had run into a downpour like this. The windshield wipers were next to useless as the Hawk followed the river upstream, the pilot doing his best to keep the bird in the narrowing band of visibility between the mist and raging water.

Up ahead the valley widened a little, and on a plateau above the right bank they could see a hut. Smoke rising.

Before the skids touched the grass Kaufman was out the door and running towards the hut. He paused on the porch until Deakes and Nazim were in position. Guns drawn.

He turned the door handle and tromped inside.

The sour, burning rope stench of pot slogged his nose as he panned the gun round the room, stopping at a bottom bunk in the corner.

A head rose slowly and turned towards him, eyes struggling to focus.

No makeup artist could make Duggan's face look like that.

'Who the hell are you?'

The pothead's legs swung off the bed and he woozed to his feet, scratching his head.

'Name's Joe Bloggs. The fuck are you?'

Kaufman looked around the hut. Woodstove. Piles of firewood. Battered billies and fry pans. Candles. Packets of food on a shelf. Animal pelts pegged to a wire beside shirts, underwear and socks.

'No-one else here Brad,' said Nazim, kneeling to look under the last bunk.

Clothing and camping gear hung from a line of nails along the back wall. Coats, an old canvas backpack, towels, a scarf. And a cap. Blue with a brown brim. Remnants of an egg stain. Same cap the clown was wearing at the Wildfoods Festival.

Kaufman grabbed the scrawny pothead by the shoulders and rammed his back into the wall. He slumped to the floor, groaning.

'Where'd you get that cap asshole?'

'What cap?'

Kaufman moved towards him, preparing to kick. The threat was enough.

'OK OK. Didn't steal it. I swapped it OK?'

'When?'

'Yesterday. Last night. I can't fuckin remember.'

Kaufman's boot smashed into his shoulder. He screamed and keeled over, cradling his arm.

'How long ago were they here?'

'This morning,' he gasped. 'Round breakfast. Ten, maybe twelve hours ago.'

'And where were they going?'

'Over the saddle. Frew's Saddle.'

'You lying little shit,' Kaufman said, pointing his gun between the deadbeat's eyes, now fully focused.

In one movement Kaufman tweaked his aim and squeezed the trigger. The bullet smashed into the wall an inch above the deadbeat's head. Before he knew what was happening Kaufman jerked him up by the throat and pinned his whimpering frame to the wall, the gun pressed to his forehead.

'Where were they *really* going? Bullshit me again and I promise this time I won't miss.'

'Frew's Saddle. Swear to God. Said he was going over the saddle and down the Mathias Valley.'

'Show me. Over there.'

The pothead limped over to a map on the back of the door, and pointed to a route, which would take Duggan and Tayler out to the Rakaia River east of the Whitcombe Valley.

'How far along there would they get in twelve hours?'

'Depends. The guy looked in good shape. Way he talked, he knew the area real good. But the lady, she looked pretty knackered. Be surprised if she made it to the saddle. Specially in this weather.'

Kaufman raised his gun, then decided it would be a waste of a bullet.

The rain was even heavier as they headed back to the Hawk.

The pilot shook his head as Kaufman pointed up the steep side valley towards Frew's Saddle.

'In this rain and with the downdrafts and turbulence likely up there, we've got a marginal situation sir.'

When the rotor head started going on about a heavy buildup of water degrading the lift and increasing drag, Kaufman had heard enough.

'Just get us up there, captain. Now.'

∗ ∗ ∗ ∗

ONCE CLEAR of the Alps the roaring nor-wester catapulted the twin-engine flying pencil carrying Hansen and seventeen other passengers towards Christchurch Airport.

She was relieved to see the back of the intimidating clouds and rodeo turbulence.

Ahead was clear blue sky and the calm patchwork of the Canterbury Plains, divided here and there by rivers of braided mud.

With large sections of the mountain region declared too marginal for helicopters, Hansen's commercial flight was likely to be the last to leave the West Coast for hours.

Possibly days.

Most of the manpower would have to cross the Alps by road. She'd arranged to rendezvous with advance teams at Glenfalloch Station, the last farm at the end of the road up the Rakaia River.

First she had a matter to take care of at Christchurch Airport.

Sergeant Pulepule was waiting on the tarmac.

'Is he here?'

'Fraid not Inspector. He left home several hours ago. Got his wife in the interview room though.'

Mrs Budd was a female version of the stereotypical multi-sporter. Clean cut. Fresh faced. Not an ounce of flab. Dressed in a seamless triathlon suit made of over-priced anti-sweat anti-bacterial fabric. Fear in her eyes pegged her for a serial rule follower. The interview was a pushover.

Husband Andrew left before dawn for the Rangitata River, after receiving a phone call in the middle of the night from a woman called Fay. He'd taken mountaineering gear for a crossing into the top of the Rakaia near the valley leading to Whitcombe Pass. Hansen thanked her for being so cooperative and let her go, as an Airforce helicopter landed outside.

'I'm not familiar with this part of the country Sergeant. If Budd somehow hooked up with Duggan and Tayler, and they exited the same way he went in, would they get to Lincoln any faster?'

'No way. The Rangitata comes out much further south than the Rakaia. And you heard the wife. You need special climbing gear to cross between those valleys. Catherine Tayler's no mountaineer.'

There was a knock on the door and an Airforce officer in green overalls entered with news an advance party of SAS soldiers had been dropped at the Lauper bivouac on the west bank of the Rakaia.

'They were heading up towards Whitcombe Pass. Weather's still terrible up there, Inspector, even on the east side of the divide near the top of the Rakaia. River's running unbelievably high. We'll fly you in as far as we can.'

61. Robots in sand berets

THE AMBUSSON tapestry on the wall was priceless in more ways than the eight men gathered round the table beneath it would ever know. The focal point of the sixteenth century masterpiece was a hunter thrusting a sword full hilt into the back of a majestic beast.

No shortage of irony there, thought Petersen, looking on from the aides' table as the leaders of the so-called G7 nations chatted over breakfast at the ostentatious Chateau de Rambouillet southwest of Paris.

Might as well be called the G8 again, thanks to the presence among the presidents, prime ministers and chancellor of the man of the moment – Jozef Pyjas. Too big to fail. The Vestco chairman's speech hit all the right buttons about ending the world food crisis. They nodded in chorus as he told them of the latest independent estimate that within twelve months their nations would collectively be many billions of dollars better off through increased taxes from agricultural sectors, reductions in farm subsidies, foreign aid payments, social security payments and a reduction in crime. Pyjas was lapping it up like one of the truly powerful, which to all intents and purposes he was.

What Pyjas didn't know was that four of the leaders nodding their heads also stood personally to gain millions of dollars from the success of Alo, thanks to bribery so cunningly creative, Petersen wondered if he was blushing.

He thought of the words on the digital recorder sitting in a safe deposit box in LA: *Whatever it takes. I don't want to know. Just get us to the release.*

White dials on the cast-bronze clock showed it was 9am in Paris. Fifteen hours to go.

* * * *

WHITCOMBE PASS can be a dicey place on a fine day. Rocks like banged up teeth spike skywards to mountains towering on both sides, as if reminding them of a promise not to unleash their tons of snow and ice and rock onto whoever is foolish enough to cross the exposed saddle below. Avalanches are as common as toast, especially during the spring thaw. Or, thought Jay, on days like this when Hughie was working himself into a lather.

The rain was lashing in sheets as he led Cat to the sheltered side of a rock the size of a bus, thinking how impressive the avalanche must have been to bring that mother down.

'Wait here a tick Cat. Gonna do a wee reccie up ahead.'

'Reccie?'

'Yeah. Y'know. Reconnaissance. Have a gander ta make sure she's sweet.'

He took the binoculars and headed up the lower slope. Patches of cloud and mist were coming and going in the howling wind like Brown's cows, letting you see a half a mile for a few seconds then closing up shop. The pass ahead seemed empty, so he scampered higher to get a view of the beginning of the narrow Lauper Valley falling away on the other side. Spray from the cascading torrent conspired with the rain to obscure the midriff of the valley. Jay was just about to give up when he detected movement on the true right of the river.

Five, six figures in green, brown and black camouflage uniforms. Full kits. Rifles. Fancy mouthpieces. Advancing like robots in sand berets. SAS. Fifteen minutes, Jay estimated. Bugger. The pass was out. He slid down the shingle scree towards Cat, pondering their options.

'Fraid we've got company,' he said, throwing the pack over his shoulders and lifting her little daypack as she stood.

'Where? Who?'

'Soldiers. Up from the other side.'

'Then what's the plan?' The question was asked with just enough enthusiasm to convince Jay the second of his options was a goer. The first was to hide and hope the soldiers would miss them, although the bottom of the pass would almost certainly be watched. Option two had always been in the back of his mind.

'We'll have to go round the back. Over the Ramsay.'

'Over? Tell me you don't mean a mountain?'

'Not exactly. She's a glacier.'

Before Cat could protest, Jay was headed back the way they'd come, veering to follow the line of a ridge ascending towards an outcrop jutting like a groyne from the hillside. Confident the howling wind would drown out any sound they made, he led her skywards until the pass was lost in the murk below. He stopped and asked for her pack.

'I'm OK.'

'We're gonna dump stuff here. Take just what we need for the glacier.'

It went against all Jay's instincts to jettison the sleeping bags, cooking gear, food, spare clothes. Speed was now the priority. Time the invisible assassin. He repacked essentials like the ice axe, crampons, rope, then stood in front of her, adjusting the bootlace holding her glasses on her head.

'You've been this way before, right?'

'Once. When the pass was blocked by an avalanche.'

'How long will it take?'

He couldn't lie. 'She's gonna be a tough grind Cat. Specially in these conditions. We're gonna have to dig deep. It'll take a while. And we'll be cutting it fine.'

'We've no choice right?'

'Correct.'

'Let's do it. Point me to the first marker.'

'There are no markers.'

AT THE HEAD of the Rakaia Valley stand matching four-thousand-foot pyramids of rock so dense they withstood the movement of glacial ice that gouged the valley long before human memory. They're not much to look at from the floor of the valley, which is why they are shown on maps as knobs rather than mountains.

But the view from the top of the southern sentinel, named Mein's Knob after a Scottish chap who immigrated to New Zealand in the 1850s, is well worth the climb. Glaciers point down from the west and north, and the skyline through two hundred seventy degrees is etched with barbarous pinnacles of rock and ice and snow.

Even in this deteriorating weather, there was enough moonlight for the man lying on his stomach near the bluff at the northern end of Mein's Knob to see across the valley to the point where the Lauper River ended its short journey down from Whitcombe Pass. He had arrived at his vantage point to see a helicopter land with difficulty near the Lauper and disgorge its cargo of troops, who immediately headed up towards the pass. Now, as he watched through a miniature telescope, a second group of soldiers who had been contemplating crossing the Rakaia were heading back towards Reischek Hut.

The man looked at his watch. By his calculations, the first group of soldiers would be approaching the pass in the next ten minutes. He moved the scope to the left, following the course of the Rakaia where the river was joined by the flow pouring from the lake in front of the Ramsay Glacier. He made his decision. Checking the rope was securely anchored, he wrestled the heavy pack over his shoulders, tightened the straps, pulled on his gloves and ghosted over the edge.

* * * *

HAD TO BE close to five because breakfast was arriving. Matthew tried to get the guard to talk but the bloke just slid the tray through the trapdoor, took last night's dinner tray and hopped it.

The commander had convinced Matthew the meals were safe by eating yesterday's lunch in front of him. They talked briefly about the weather, football. Anything to do with Cat and Jay was off-limits.

When Matthew said he'd be willing to hold a press conference to let the world know how well he was being treated, the commander upped and left.

Matthew listened to the guard's boots disappearing and waited for the door at the end of the hall to slam before reaching for the food. Bacon. It was like the bastards knew. He left the tray on the floor and stared back at the ceiling. Light rain was falling on the iron roof. Seven hours to the release of Alo. His stomach rumbled so loud he almost missed the mouse. He shooed it away and it ran under the bed.

'Hang on a mo.' He'd got into the habit of talking to himself. 'How the bleedin hell did you get in here?'

There was no gap between the steel door and its frame. The trapdoor for the food could only be opened from the outside. The mouse could have come in with the food, but that was unlikely. The guards were mute, not sadistic. Matthew looked under the bed. The little guy was against the wall, nibbling a piece of egg. When it finished, the mouse ran along the floor to the corner and, without missing a step, scuttled up the gap between the conduit piping and the wall. It crouched for a moment six inches from the ceiling, then wriggled through the hole carrying the wires through the wall.

Matthew stood and walked to the corner. There was a little puddle of water on the floor. He looked at the ceiling above the hole. No sign of any leak from the roof. Water must have been blown through the hole by wind. Which meant the hole went through to the outside. Maybe there was a way to get a message out.

62. Like a caged animal

THE SECRET SERVICE agent in charge of pre-visit setup stood in the middle of Central Park's Great Lawn and visualized what the arena would look like in a few hours.

President and First Lady on the stage. Two hundred Secret Service agents. Four thousand police officers. Teams of elite National Guard green berets in reserve. Helicopters in the air. Police launches on the reservoir. Three mega television screens. *Nourish, Sustain, Cherish* banners almost outnumbering trees. And two hundred thousand carefully selected and vetted citizens. Every last one questioned, body-scanned and searched as they arrived at the perimeter.

Never before had such attention been paid to ensuring a supportive audience. If anyone wanted to exercise their First Amendment rights they were welcome to do so in the designated free speech zone set up at Thomas Jefferson Park in East Harlem.

* * * *

S N A F U. Situation Normal All Fucked Up. Kaufman could think of no better way to describe it, despite assurances from the pilot the compass could be recalibrated easily enough by an engineer.

Problem was the Hawk's engineer was back in Hokitika and the chopper was grounded where it crash-landed within a stone's throw of

Frew's Saddle. Brought down not by rain. Not by heavy buildup of water. Not even by enemy fire. By fucking lightning.

They'd been closing in on the saddle, flying just above the tree line when the flash struck, temporarily blinding the pilot. As he struggled to read his instruments, the Hawk was hit by what Kaufman had since learnt was a squall line, produced by a downdraft from the electrical storm hitting the ground and spreading out horizontally. This one slammed them from the rear at close to fifty knots. Given the sudden loss of transitional lift, the pilot did well to get the bird down with only minor damage to the nose.

The lightning strike had, however, damaged the Hawk's sensitive electronic equipment, knocking out the magnetic compass and putting the radio out of action. Kaufman was in no position to complain about the absence of the engineer. He'd made the call to leave him back in Hokitika and bring Nazim in his place. Kaufman looked at his watch.

'Call her again. Tell her the weather's clearing up here.'

It wasn't, but Kaufman was convinced Hansen was deliberately blocking the engineer making the flight. Nazim took the crew's satellite phone and trudged up to the top of the ridge to make the call. Within minutes he was back with the news a New Zealand Airforce Iroquois had taken off with the engineer ten minutes earlier but had to turn back. They'd try again in an hour. If the weather improved.

Kaufman felt like a caged animal. He didn't have an hour. He knew from earlier calls the search for Duggan and Tayler had shifted to a hut at the top of the Rakaia River, on the other side of the Whitcombe Pass. Still no signal on his cell phone. He grabbed the sat phone and jumped out of the cockpit. Tightening the hood of his jacket, he headed uphill. Visibility was less than fifty yards.

Just over the rise the mist cleared momentarily, and he saw the bivouac. It was little more than two hunks of iron and a door. At least it kept him dry. Desperate for any scrap of good news, he phoned Eve. His heart sank when the call was answered by Dr Hamilton, the oncology consultant. Eve was unconscious and being taken to hospital.

'Paramedics have just arrived with the ambulance Mr Kaufman. She's in good hands sir.'

It was like being stabbed in the guts. He buried his face in his hands and cried for the second time in his life.

'You there, Mr Kaufman? Don't give up on her now. Not with the treatment all lined up. Eve's the toughest kid I've come across. She'll fight this all the way. Never surrender. Gotta go with her now sir. To the hospital.'

Kaufman took the photo from his pocket and stared at it, using light from the phone's screen. He stroked her hair. Touched her nose. Ran his finger over the smiling lips.

'I'm not ready to say goodbye Princess.'

He studied the sat phone and worked out how to get online. A search gave him the number of a private helicopter company in Hokitika advertising deer hunting flights and kayak transporting in the Whitcombe Valley. He dialed, praying it was a home number. After the fourth ring a gravelly voice answered. 'Have you any bloody idea what time it is?'

'Sorry sir. It's an emergency.'

'My oath it's an emergency. Think I'm having a feckin art attack.'

Kaufman tried to explain his predicament. The man was having none of it.

'You out of your bloody mind? No one's gonna fly in this storm. You're just gonna have to sit tight cobber and wait for - '

'I'll pay you ten thousand dollars.'

That shut him up.

'That's right. Ten thousand American dollars to pick me up and take me over the pass to this Rieschek Hut. You know it?'

'I do.'

'Lives are at stake here, man.'

'Still say you're bloody nuts wanting to fly in this weather.'

'Twenty thousand.'

'Sweet Mary and Joseph. I was on the grog till two o'clock. Booze'll still be in me system. Could lose me license if the cops find out.'

'I am the cops. Twenty-five grand. Final offer.'

'Got yourself a deal Mister. Frew's Saddle eh? Give us half an hour.'

Forty-five minutes later Kaufman, who had been joined at the bivouac by Deakes, squinted through the rain as the Bell Jetranger landed on its third attempt. Hopefully it was because of the wind rather than the state of the pilot. Seeing an airsick bag taped to the front of the guy's helmet wasn't a good sign.

* * * *

'A DOCTOR Hamilton on the line sir.'

Petersen took the call, spinning round in his chair so the conversation wouldn't be overheard.

'Kaufman took the bait. Hook, line and sinker.'

'Course he did. He thinks you really are an oncology specialist. How's the girl?'

'Eve's fine. Sleeping peacefully in her bed next door.'

Petersen hung up and picked up the four-page draft. The journalists at the *New York Times* and *Grassroots* had been thorough. They had documents, emails, taped phone conversations, photographs and signed affidavits to back up their claim Petersen was the man behind voter registration irregularities in three gubernatorial elections, two of which tipped the balance in favor of the incumbent. There were a few inaccuracies, but the impact would be sensational if the newspaper and blog went to print with it tomorrow. Two Governors would have no option to resign, and one would be sharing a long-term cell with Petersen.

He folded the draft in half, then in half again, and kept folding until he was satisfied. He leant back, took aim and sent the dart flying through the air towards the trash bin in the corner of his office.

63. It ends here

THE BOY had never seen words printed on paper, let alone *TIME* magazine. He had no idea the hill he was climbing was the same one used on the front page of the latest issue announcing Jozef Pyjas as Person of the Year, and overlooked the release site for Alo in southern Somalia.

Abdikarim was only nine but already the man of his family.

His father died last month.

His mother and three sisters would die tonight if the white tents of the relief camp he'd been told about weren't over this hill.

He struggled up, using his last reserves of energy to whisper a prayer.

'Magaca Eebe, Eebaha Raxmaana, dhaafe Naxariista…'

The sight from the top terrified him.

Suns on sticks taller than myrrh trees shone bright light onto an area covered in huts and giant sleeping snakes and more people than Abdikarim knew existed.

Huge women with white skin and painted faces danced across a rectangular board and suddenly turned into a man with rings over his eyes and a red cloth tied round his neck.

On the far edge of the light, he saw the white tents with blue markings and thought of his mother and sisters.

He headed down the hill towards the light, heart pounding, his mouth so dry he could hardly swallow, his stomach beyond pain.

'Piss off.'

Abdikarim froze. The words spoken by the white man meant nothing. But the tone was clear. So was the shooting stick pointed at his head. He'd seen one of those. The day death found his father.

* * * *

JAY HAD been in surreal places before. Cave diving in the bowels of the Taurus Mountains in Turkey. The bat tent perched up the side of Shipton Spire in the Pakistani Karakorum. That cuddle party in LA last year was up there as well, just quietly. But this took the cake.

Crossing the Ramsay Glacier in the middle of the night with Hughie giving it the full orchestra. Pelting rain hitting you from left, right and center as it bounced off the ice or sprayed from torrents rushing in manic search of sinkholes darker than the night. Every sound, from the scraping of crampons on ice to the deep groaning and creaking of the glacier's internal machinery, was replayed in echoes off and around shapes defined by the crossing beams of two half-arse headlamps. You wouldn't read about it.

Progress had been snail's pace till Cat got the hang of the crampons. Then came the fall. Scared the hell out of her. Jay was probing with his ice axe for hidden crevasses, but misjudged the depth of a snow bridge. Down he went, both feet. Saved by the pick of the axe catching on just enough white stuff. He was jammed up to the waist, legs dangling in a weird emptiness colder than a freezer. Couldn't believe the temperature could be so different in the space of a few feet. Cat actually laughed, and everything would have been sweet till she heard the tinkling of ice falling into the hole beneath him like glass breaking against the side of a steel recycling bin. On and on and on and on. She had no idea the crevasse – and therefore the glacier – was so deep. A wake-up call for Jay as well.

From then on they'd been roped together. Was the only way he could get her to move forward. They were three-quarters of the way down. He knew this because they'd reached the place known to local mountaineers as the Great White. They were standing on a ledge twelve feet down the side of a wide crevasse, staring up at swords of ice rimming the lip like a row of shark's teeth. Getting down to the ledge had been a bit of a drama, costing one of the axes, half a dozen karabiners, all but one of the ice screws and, most importantly, the rope. All washed away in the Niagara cascade on the wall behind them.

Jay could think of only one way to get out of the crevasse. Walking up the wall by kicking the two spikes poking from the front of each crampon into the ice and using the remaining axe to cut handholds. He rated his chances of getting up at fifty-fifty. Without a rope, Cat would have to go up the same way. An impossibility in her state of near exhaustion.

Cat's scream pierced the inky dinge as a silhouette came hurtling over the wall towards them, the shock all but knocking her off the ledge.

'Coffee anyone?'

The look on her face was worth the entry fee.

'Bout bloody time,' said Jay, stepping forward to shake the hand of their visitor.

'Dr Catherine Tayler, I'd like you to meet me old mate Andrew Budd.'

'Honored madam,' he said with an exaggerated bow.

For once the woman was speechless.

Using Andrew's rope, they helped her up the wall and into the shelter of a glacier table, a sheet of rock balanced on a column of ice. Then it was Jay's turn to be surprised as Andrew whipped out a flask. Bugger me days, he wasn't joking about the hot coffee.

Cat perked up in no time, and a glance at her watch had her on her feet so fast she banged her head on the rock. An hour later they'd left the glacier and were skirting the scree at the side of the terminal lake, dodging boulders loosened by the rain that showed no signs of letting up. They could see barely twenty feet, but could tell they were approaching the end of the lake by the bellowing ahead. And this was just a secondary stream compared with what must be coming out of the Lyell, the larger of the two glaciers feeding the mighty Rakaia River.

LESS THAN a mile downstream, Kaufman peered through rain lashing the Bell Jetranger's windshield as they descended towards Reischek Hut. He'd been on a rough trip in the Galgodon Highlands of Somalia, but nothing like the wild ride over Whitcombe Pass in this storm.

They'd taken a roundabout route to keep as high as possible on the downwind side of valleys, the pilot explaining in his hayseed way how he was giving a wide berth to the strong drafts lurking lower down. At one point when thick cloud forced them downwards, the chopper struck violent turbulence and dropped three hundred feet in seconds. Moments later an updraft yanked them back up like a yo-yo. Captain Hayseed handled the cyclic like a pro to counter the extreme variations in pitch.

Drunk or not, the guy was wasted in this place.

On the ground, groups of soldiers were fighting the wind to erect tents in the little shelter offered by a stand of straggly trees beside the hut, using the headlights of two Pinzgauer trucks to illuminate the gloom.

Half a dozen stunned faces greeted Kaufman as he entered the hut, a low-tech wooden three-bunk affair with a billy of water bubbling on a camp stove. He recognized Hansen's second-in-command studying a map laid out on a stainless-steel bench.

'Where's your boss?'

'On her way. They've been held up at a side stream a couple of miles away. Army engineers are building a temporary bridge to get the vehicles across. With help from a mob of deerstalkers who arrived before her in four-wheel drives. Apparently the fact we're here was posted on Facebook a while ago. She's an hour or so away.'

'Then what are you lot doing sitting on your hands? You think these terrorists are gonna just walk in here and give themselves up?'

Hansen's deputy bristled at the criticism.

'We managed to get one team across the river before it became impassable. They're checking the pass. We've got a unit moving up the far side of the river from the east, though I'm told there's no way past these bluffs about a mile downstream.'

'What about this side of the river?'

'Got a couple of men here.' He stabbed his finger at a point between the cliffs and river. 'But frankly, there's no way anyone's crossing to this side in these conditions.'

The pounding on the tin roof intensified, like an exclamation mark. Kaufman looked at the map, noticing a dog bone symbol at the gorge at the base of Mein's Knob.

'Isn't that a bridge?'

'*Was* a bridge. Got washed out in a similar storm a few months ago.'

'Cobblers.'

It was the gravelly voice of Kaufman's pilot, lying on one of the bunks.

'I beg your pardon?'

'Most of that bridge got washed away copper. One cable was still intact after the storm. Bloke with a karabiner who knew what he was doing could get across. Seen them do it.'

'We're pretty sure Duggan's climbing colleague is heading this way Mr Kaufman. And Duggan himself has climbed - '

'I'm familiar with his background, thank you.' Kaufman grabbed two headlamps and started for the door. He declined the offer of soldiers to accompany him, saying it was probably a long shot, and they should wait for Inspector Hansen. Calling for Deakes, they set off along the track towards the gorge.

'They are not leaving this valley. It ends here.'

64. The least of your worries

IT WAS the easiest five hundred quid Jamie Benpatrick ever made. Ticket touts were not being allowed near any of the entrances to the stadium, but the ban didn't extend to Wembley Railway Station down the road.

Warnings about delays because of over-the-top security meant half the ninety thousand punters expected at the ground for the London Alo release were already inside, with close to five hours still to the whistle. It took Jamie less than ten minutes to hock off all his tickets, at three times the price he paid for them.

* * * *

CAT REMEMBERED the Los Angeles quake of ninety-four like it was this morning. It wasn't the six-point-six jolt that woke her. It was the microscope crashing down from the bookshelf beside her bed. The shaking and rattling went on forever, killing scores of people and injuring thousands, but the vibrations were nothing like this.

The math was simple. A river flowing at its normal summer velocity of around six miles per hour could shift a boulder the size of a basketball. Double the velocity and you increase the moving power sixty-four-fold. A river in flood, like the one she was staring at, flowing at say twenty miles per hour, could shunt a rock weighing two hundred fifty tons. Throw into the cauldron the hundreds of thousands of gallons being forced through the narrow gap every second, and the ground could be forgiven for shuddering.

Right now, Cat was more worried about the fingers on her left hand. There'd been no feeling in the tips for more than an hour. They'd reached the terminal moraine of the Ramsay Glacier where the flow issuing from the Lyell Glacier gouged its way beneath bluffs at the end of Mein's Knob. A single wire cable, all that remained of a footbridge, sagged to within three feet of the surface of the onslaught. Cat's heart sank at the thought of having to cross the wire.

'Careful round this bit,' Jay shouted as he helped her down a narrow channel between two rocks ending in a sloping shelf no more than twelve inches above the river. She clung with two hands to the slippery rock as she edged towards the hazy beam of Andrew's headlamp. The rock face ended abruptly at the mouth of a shallow cave.

'Well, we knocked that bastard off,' said Jay, an instant before a tree trunk the size of a power pole slammed into the rock just below the cave, splintering like a matchstick.

He walked over to where Andrew was unzipping a large pack. They pulled out what appeared to be a folded black air mattress, poles, yellow objects like stretched table tennis bats and a pump of some sort.

'You wanna set her up while I check the flow?'

'Sure mate.'

Andrew unfolded the black mattress, attached a cord to a valve and started pumping with his foot. Cat couldn't believe her eyes.

'It's a raft!'

'Well yeah. They call em crocs. As in crocodiles. Not that you're likely to run into any on this river. And they'd be the least of your worries, just quietly. Here, screw these together.'

He tossed over the poles and table tennis bats which she now realized were oars. 'You did say you were in a hurry, didn't ya?'

Cat was trying to think of some witty reply when Jay reappeared.

'Headlamps approaching from the other side.'

'How far away?'

'Three minutes from the wire.'

65. Ignorance is bliss

THROUGH THE scratch in the painted glass Matthew watched a cab pull up outside the gates to the camp. Only two journalists left. One of them opened the door to the cab and was about to get inside when he turned to the other, offering her a ride.

She walked towards the car, stopped, exchanged a few words and looked at her watch. Then she turned and it seemed to Matthew she was looking straight at him. He shouted and waved with his free arm. There was no sign of recognition. She looked at the sky, thirty percent black with the coming of rain, then back at her watch. She said something to the person in the cab, closed the door and it drove off, leaving her alone on the sidewalk. Matthew had to find a way to get a message through that hole.

* * * *

'GOOD LUCK mate. You're going to need it.'

Jay shook Andrew's hand, then watched as his friend attached a karabiner and tape to the wire, clipped the other end to his belt and started winching himself across the madness.

The faint lights of headlamps appeared round a bend on the other side, less than two minutes away. Jay lifted the raft down to the shelf.

He'd ridden big water before. Never anything like this.

Or in such a state of exhaustion.

And never with such a rookie as Cat.

Hydraulics and down currents completely unpredictable. Strainers from hell. The river would be nigh on impossible to read. Sort of water even the hair boaters would look at and say *maybe tomorrow*.

He turned to Cat. There was absolute terror in her face but, surprise surprise, no chin tapping.

He put a hand on each of her shoulders, shouting to be heard.

'Ready?'

'Heck yes. You've done this sort of thing before right?'

'Plenty of times. Heaps of fun.'

'No life preservers right?'

He kissed her forehead.

'Tell me what to do.'

'Jump in the stern and hold on to the line. Never let it go. I'll do the rest.'

'Which end's the stern?'

Ignorance is bliss, Jay thought as Cat stepped into the back chamber. She was going to get tossed like a pinball in the stern, but they needed his weight up front to keep momentum through the recirculating holes and to counter the water they were bound to take on, most of which would end up in the back. Reaching across to grab the hand line, he took a couple of deep breaths, psyching himself up. Holes and waves were going to be the best markers. Keep the bow pointed square to them, not the current. High side like crazy. Take the munter hydraulics up the guts. He looked for the right moment to launch. It was never coming. He slipped the raft over the edge.

Pain shot through his right arm as it was nearly wrenched from its socket.

* * * *

LI BO had dreamt of creating the ultimate display since he was a boy growing up in the city of Liu Yang in Hunan Province. As a descendant of Li Tian, the monk credited with the invention of firecrackers, Bo lived in the shadow of a legend. His heritage brought him great honor, but always as a descendent of Li Tian.

Surrounded by batteries of shells and port fire tubes, mortar racks and troughs, Bo looked up from the discharge site over the sea of faces waiting patiently in Tiananmen Square. The world record for a waterfall display was 10,255 feet at the Ariake Seas Festival in Japan in 2003. *Niagara Falls* they called that one. Bo's *Great Wall*, to be ignited the instant Alo was released, would smash more than the height record. The turreting detail in the cascades would blow minds.

From this day on, Tiananmen Square would be remembered throughout the world not for a lone protester facing down a tank, but for the spectacular display that took pyrotechnics to a new level. And Li Bo would step from the shadow of a monk.

* * * *

KAUFMAN SCOOTED up the path of mud and looked over the chasm, his headlamp spotlighting the single strand of cable above the foam.

Detecting movement above to his left, he moved his head, and the arc of light crossed the end of a moving rope.

He edged across the ledge with his back to the rock wall, reached up and behind for a finger hold, then swung up to grab the end of the rope.

Peering up, he made out the shape of a person frantically trying to climb higher.

He fired a shot and got a scream. A second shot dropped a hunk of rock so close to Kaufman's head he felt it pass before it landed beside his feet. The figure above was hanging unsteadily using only one arm.

'Come down or the next shot will be the last thing you don't hear.'

After a moment's hesitation, the figure slowly but expertly slid down under the power of one arm. Kaufman aimed his headlamp above the figure but could see no one else. He stepped aside and drew his gun as the figure reached the ledge, facing him in a balaclava.

'Take it off. Slowly.'

It wasn't Duggan. Must be his climber friend.

'Where are they?'

'I don't know what - '

Kaufman grabbed the prick by the scruff of the neck and shoved him back till he was standing inches from the edge, gun aimed at his forehead.

'On the river.' he blurted out.

'Bullshit.' Kaufman shoved him closer to the edge.

'Fair dinkum. Riding a croc. It's a - '

'I know what a croc is you moron.'

Deakes appeared, holding a pump and mumbling in Afrikaans. Kaufman lowered the gun.

'It seems I owe you an apology, Mr Budd.'

He relaxed his hand around the man's neck, adjusted his grip and was just about to jerk upwards when the guy shot his arms into the air and dived backwards.

Kaufman looked at his watch. Three hours thirty minutes left.

They covered the distance back to the Reischek Hut in under fifteen, guided over the last few hundred yards by floodlights and revving engines indicating Hansen had arrived. Through the window of the hut, he saw her talking to her offsider. The pilot was beside the chopper, peeing on the grass while steadying himself against a rope anchoring the rotors to pegs in the ground. Kaufman made a beeline for him.

'We're off.'

'No bloody way. Wind's too strong. I've done what you asked.'

The wind had picked up, but the rain seemed to be easing, and visibility improving. They could see the near side of the river across the drenched rocks of an upper bed.

'I'll double your fee.'

'No money's worth that risk.'

Kaufman pointed the gun at his head. The pilot looked round for support. The nearest soldier was out of earshot.

66. The only scream

CAT'S RIGHT arm spasmed from the grip on the rope but she clung on, knowing her life depended on it. With no feeling in her frozen left hand, she transferred as much of the burden as she dared, despite the agony as the raft was jerked and tossed by monster waves and flung towards rocks, often rearing up at the last minute from nowhere.

It was a miracle they were still afloat.

The first part of the nightmare might as well have been in darkness for all Cat could see through the rain and froth and spray.

Total disorientation.

Like dropping into the black hole of the Dragon's Den at Emerald Pointe and never coming out.

The only plus was that if Cat couldn't see anything, it was unlikely the raft could be seen from the banks. It didn't stop her throwing up till there was nothing left.

Thankfully there were stretches of relative calm as they charged down channels where the water rippled rather than surged, as if the bucking bronco suddenly figured out how to gallop.

Cat marveled at the way Jay read the river, changing the angle of the raft to guide them round obstacles. One moment he'd push with one oar while pulling the other and they'd pivot. Then he'd dip the right oar deep into the water, leaving the other just below the surface to bring the backside round.

The rain eased and the blanket of mist began unclogging as they got further from the main divide.

Cat could now see they were traveling down one of several braids in the middle of a vast glacial valley.

Up ahead the three main braids joined as the valley narrowed.

'Brace yourself Cat. Gonna get rough as these currents fold into each other. Eddy lines left, right and center. The gorge isn't that long, but she'll be a hairy old ride with this much water. Whole new meaning to the word bottleneck.'

The raft tilted violently to the left as they struck the first junction. Cat was sure they were going to flip, then a massive surge from the channel barging in from the left thumped them back into line.

Jay looked back with a nervous smile. Suddenly his eyes darted over her shoulder and his mouth dropped. Cat swung round. A helicopter was following them into the gorge, ten feet above the water and closing rapidly.

The raft lurched as they hurtled round a bend, then gathered speed as they charged into the vee of two converging waves. Jay plunged deep with one oar, sending the raft into a spin and giving Cat another glimpse of the helicopter. Someone was stepping out onto the skid, causing the aircraft to tilt for a moment.

They swept round another corner and Cat saw the bridges. The river split in two around an island. The wooden top of each bridge was clear of the flood, but metal supporting beams jabbed diagonally into the water. Jay appeared to hesitate, raising both oars, before driving towards the smaller chute. The current was taking them directly towards one of the struts.

An instant before impact waterspouts detonated around them and sparks ricocheted off the metal. Cat opened her mouth, but the only scream came from Jay.

* * * *

ISHWAR SINGH was too frightened to move. An American woman with hair too white for her age, breasts too visible and a scent too strong to be natural was painting his face with filthy paste.

Until today he had never seen an elephant.

Over the young make-up artist's shoulder were at least twenty, decorated tusk to tail with flowers and jewelry.

Each beast had four feet. That added to more than eighty giant pestles trampling the field he and his wife had so carefully prepared for planting.

They'd have to do it all over again.

67. The mother of all holes

KAUFMAN LOST sight of them as the pilot powered the chopper into a rapid climb. They'd seen the raft spring up, but weren't sure if their prey had been hit. He held his breath, crimping the muscles of his stomach for the moment the chopper would dive for the next attack.

The pilot kept climbing.

'What the hell are you doing?'

'I could ask you the same question,' replied the pilot, looking straight ahead, knuckles taut white against the controls as he carried them higher and higher above the river.

Kaufman was floored.

Hayseed filled the vacuum.

'Correct me if I'm wrong mister, but I thought the object of this exercise was to catch these blokes. Not shoot them in the back like deer on the run.'

'Jesus F Christ man. Have you any idea - '

'You might get away with that in America mate. In this country we call it murder. I ain't gonna be no accessory to murder.'

The rapid climb was making Kaufman nauseated. He raised his gun and pointed it at the pilot's head. The man turned towards him and laughed.

'What ya gonna do about it, Sunshine? Shoot me?'

JAY WAS in the Amazon, tumbling through froth. Lungs bursting as he tried to swim to the bank where he'd see Aroha's elbow wrapped round a branch.

He was in a violent hydraulic with no idea of the direction of the surface. He saw the bubbles and followed them. His head broke the surface for an instant, granting half a mouthful of air before he was dragged under into the backwash of the mother of all holes. He tried to swim sideways but was trapped. Rolling arse over kite. What did that hair boater on the Zambezi say about holes? Use the down current to push you under and out. Swim into the fall. Curl up like a ball. Hang on like there's no tomorrow.

It worked. Sort of. He came up on the boil line and had to freestyle madly to avoid being sucked back into the tumble dryer. This time he managed two mouthfuls of air and a glazed view of his surroundings. The bank was moving too fast for a bearing. His line was taking him headfirst towards a gigantic pillow formed by the current rising over a rock. Instinctively he spun onto his back and twisted his feet to point downstream like shock absorbers. He braced for the impact, but was swept up and over the boulder and thrown forward.

He was in midair when he saw her. Not Aroha. Cat. Twenty, thirty feet ahead. Clinging to what was left of the raft. He dug deep, snatching breaths in the troughs and twisting his head to avoid the froth. As the gap closed he noticed Cat was still gripping the hand line, attached to the only chamber inflated.

'Hold on,' was all he could think to shout.

Her head turned and her mouth opened to reply but got a mouthful of water. He plunged the last few feet, grabbing her leg and pulling alongside.

'Bout time,' she coughed.

Jay fought back tears. Of relief. Adrenalin. Exhaustion. Joy.

Below the bridge the valley opened as the river fanned into braids. The current gradually eased. Half a mile downstream they managed to haul themselves ashore, where they lay face down on the boulders, panting. Jay flexed each part of his body in turn. Stiff. Sore as hell. But alive. It was only then he remembered the attack at the bridge. He helped her over the rocks into the cover of scrub above the bank. No sign of the helicopter. Cat's hair was slicked over her face, the Dame Edna glasses still tied to her head with a bootlace. The arm of her raincoat was ripped and flapping. He saw the hands of her watch and looked up at the sky, pretending to estimate the time. The rain had stopped. To the east the sky was vivid blue. He held her shoulders and kissed her forehead.

'Must be close to ten. Better shake a leg.'

She looked at the watch.

'For heck's sake Jay. Less than two hours to go.'

Cows looked up at them as they ran across a field towards a shelterbelt of macrocarpa trees.

On the other side was a driveway and at the far end half a dozen people were grouped near the back of an ambulance. Heads bowed. A female ambulance officer closed the back doors, walked up the side and opened the driver's door.

'This way,' whispered Jay, leading Cat behind a hedge.

The ambulance came slowly round the corner and stopped as it reached the road. Jay sprinted across the front, jerked open the door and dragged the startled driver out before she realized what was happening. He twisted her arm behind her back and covered her mouth.

'Cat. Find something to tie her up with.'

Jay heard her open the back doors, then stifle a scream.

'There's an old woman in here. I think she ... is ... dead.'

'Just our luck.' Jay eased his grip on the ambulance officer's mouth.

'What's the story with the old girl?'

'She passed away last night. Taking her to the morgue at Darfield Hospital.'

Cat appeared holding rolls of bandages.

Jay wrapped one around the driver's head, covering her mouth and eyes, keeping her nose and ears free. The woman trembled in front of him.

'Don't panic. We're not going to hurt you. Just need to borrow your wheels for a tick. Dr Tayler here is going to lead you behind those bushes and help you take off your uniform. We'll have to tie you up and leave you here. Won't be for long. We'll let someone know where to find you.'

'What about the old lady in the back, Jay?'

'Don't think she'll mind making one more wee trip.'

They left the officer tied to a post behind a shed. Jay found a spare cap and green St Johns Ambulance jacket and leggings in a small closet in the cab.

Cat, dressed in the driver's uniform, climbed into the passenger's seat. A tear was rolling slow motion down her cheek.

'Worrying about your dad again, aren't you.'

She nodded, avoiding his eyes.

'Make you a deal Doctor. I'll worry about your old man. You worry about what the hell we're going to do when we get to Lincoln University.'

She leaned over and gave him a peck on the cheek. 'Deal.'

Half a mile down the road, Jay switched on the siren and planted the accelerator to the floor.

68. Quite an entrance

DAVE LOWE figured this was how Walter Cronkite must have felt as the lunar module maneuvered towards the landing site in July of sixty-nine.

There had been much bigger television audiences since the moon landing, but nothing came close to the impact that single pioneering event had on the human memory. Today Dave Lowe – with a little help from the *Grassroots Intelligence* blog – would change that.

The timer at the corner of the console said one hour forty-five minutes to release. Lowe, sitting in the executive producer's chair, wouldn't want to be anywhere else.

* * * *

THE HEAD of the bed was taking too long. Slotted screws holding one side to the base came out using the end of a spoon filed down against the steel door. The head was held with bleedin Philips screws. The fork was Matthew's best option, but the prong had to be in exactly the right position before applying pressure or he'd strip the thread.

Rain pounding the roof made it hard to concentrate. Finally, the last screw yielded. He dragged the base to the corner and propped it in position. Lifting the detached side panel in one arm, he tried to climb but the base tipped over straight away.

He adjusted the angle of the base to the wall and wedged the side tighter against the conduit covering. It was unsteady as hell but somehow he made it to the top of the base and grabbed hold of a bar over the window. Using one of the wire bedsprings looped round his wrist, he attached the side panel to the bar then jumped back to the floor.

So far so good, though he knew that was the easy bit. Biting onto the plastic serviette tube containing the message, he picked up the bed head and started climbing. Halfway up, the base shifted under the extra weight and over he went. Pain bolted through his ankle, and as he looked up, the side panel swung once, twice, then crashed to the floor beside him.

He lay gasping, dreading the echo of boots in the corridor. The only sound was the rain on the roof. Although Matthew realized this was a hero moment, he wasn't thinking Robert the Bruce and spiders. He was thinking bacon.

This time he used two springs to hold the side panel to the bars and two more to attach it to the base. He slid the head behind the side panel, attached it to the base, then untied the side and eased it higher up the wall. The top was clearly going to be unsteady. And would she still be out there?

He peered through the scratch. There was no one at the gate. A flicker of blue and white caught his attention. There she was, standing under the verandah of the adjacent building, shaking a *Newstalk ZB* umbrella. The army camp commander must have taken pity and invited her out of the downpour. From there she would not only see the tube drop. She'd be in a position to reach it.

His heart started racing as he grabbed the tube from the sill, put it in his mouth, and started climbing. Reaching over to wedge his right foot and right hand into the gap between the corner and the conduit cover, he was able to inch towards the hole. The higher he got, the further the side panel tilted away, forcing his legs wider apart.

Two inches to go.

He steadied for a final push. Salt from sweat dripping off his brow stung his eyes. The pain in his groin was almost unbearable. It surged up his spine as he craned his head and twisted his wrist to take the tube from his mouth. The ladder creaked but held. With supreme effort he pushed upwards, jabbing the end of the tube into the hole. The ladder creaked again, the side panel shifted too far, and Matthew knew he was a goner.

He keeled backwards. The last thing he saw before hitting the floor was the end of the tube. Still stuck in the hole.

* * * *

KAUFMAN WAS grappling to hold himself together as the pilot flew over farmland. Nothing had worked. Hard cop. Soft cop. More money. The little creep was holding them hostage. Kaufman had never felt so powerless.

'What are you going to do? Keep flying around till we run out of gas?'

Hayseed ignored him. The chopper continued to circle above the tablecloth of fields laid out beneath them. Beyond the Canterbury Plains to the west the tops of the Southern Alps were lost in black cloud. In the other direction, across the sprawling city of Christchurch to the beaches of the east coast, the sky was postcard blue.

They were passing over a horseracing track and stabling area when the fuel low-level light started flashing. As if he'd been waiting for the signal, the pilot changed direction and headed towards the city.

Kaufman looked at his watch. Eighty minutes.

They lost altitude as the chopper crossed the edge of a large tree-lined park a mile or so from the sprinkling of high rises marking the city center. Dropping to within fifty feet of the grass, they flew over a rugby field, scattering players and narrowly missing the goalposts.

Just when Kaufman was sure they were going to land beside a small lake, the pilot accelerated over the stone buildings of a school, crossing a sleepy stream low enough to see the spooked face of a canoeist.

They shot up the middle of a street, almost collecting a tram. Directly ahead was the multi-storied glass wall of the Christchurch Art Center.

Surely not, thought Kaufman, with a vision of the 9/11 planes ploughing into the World Trade Center. He looked across at the pilot, expecting to see a madman. Hayseed calmly turned his head, winked, then banked the chopper so hard Kaufman's shoulder smashed against the door.

They charged up a street, narrowly missing the tops of cars, and over a river before Kaufman realized what the pilot was up to.

Cunning bastard was going to land in the one place he thought he'd be safe. The Police Station. The engine spluttered as they closed on the wall around the compound.

Beyond was a line of police cars and motorcycles surrounding a black limousine flying the Stars and Stripes. Horns blasted and people scattered as the chopper gimped, losing altitude too quickly.

The port skid clipped the top of the wall, sending them catapulting onto the roof of a police van parked inside. It probably saved their lives, cushioning the impact. The pilot and Deakes were knocked out, both wedged against the crushed starboard side. Blood seeped from a cut on the bridge of Kaufman's nose. Nothing serious. He was able to open the door and jump out to greet the police officers running towards the fallen bird. He recognized the tall figure of the American Ambassador.

'Quite an entrance Kaufman. We're on our way to Lincoln for the local release of this seed of yours. Care to join us?'

* * * *

THE SIREN did the trick as the ambulance was waved through a police roadblock at Darfield, so Jay was feeling confident as they entered Rolleston, five miles from the release site. Cars pulled over to let them cross the main highway and follow the signs to the Lincoln Road.

Trouble was waiting beside the golf course on the edge of the university town. The road was barred by dozens of people in bush shirts, fluoro vests, motorcycle helmets, folded arms and no intention of moving aside for an ambulance. Cat slipped through to the back just before the vehicle was surrounded.

A guy with an enormous beer gut who on any other day was probably pulling pints at the local public bar ambled up to the driver's side. Jay saw uncertainty in several faces of the butchers and bakers and candlestick makers behind him. Going on the offensive was his only chance. He slipped the cap lower over his face, wound down the window and bellowed over the whine of the siren.

'Have you bastards got no respect for the dead? I'm already late for the post-mortem thanks to another mob of you bloody idiots in Darfield. Either get out of the way or you can drive this bloody thing to the morgue yourselves.'

Jay had no idea if there was a morgue at Lincoln, let alone a hospital. The pawns in the background started crumbling, but not their self-styled king. He blew cigarette smoke into Jay's face and reached through the window to yank the keys from the ignition.

'Turn that siren off lad.'

Without the keys, resistance was hopeless. Jay flicked the switch and put his face in his hands as Captain Beergut peacocked down the side of the ambulance towards the back door.

* * * *

CAT'S HEART was beating so fast she was afraid it would show through the sheet. The back door swung open and cigarette smoke skulked in.

'Murray. Get over here lad and check out these stretchers.'

'No bloody way I'm going near stiffs. Do it yourself.'

'Bloody hell. You just can't get decent staff round here can ya?'

The tired line got a few laughs.

'Out of the way. I'll do it.'

The voice was butch female and drew a barrage of whistles and hoots and no doubt embarrassment for Murray.

Cat heard boots step up onto the metal floor of the ambulance and move towards the other stretcher. A sheet was pulled back.

'This old-timer's dead all right.'

'What about the other one?'

'I can see from the hand that he or she's kicked the bucket as well. Fingertips have gone blue.'

The boots clomped back down the steps. Cat held her breath until the doors were closed, and remained motionless until they were on the move.

69. A part in history

LINCOLN UNIVERSITY began life as an agricultural school in 1878 and promoted itself to the world as a center of excellence in land research.

It was particularly proud of the contributions made by a long line of eminent scientists beginning with Marmaduke Luxley in the 1920s and ending with the internationally acclaimed geneticist, Professor Valmai Kane, current head of the Center for Advanced Biotechnology. These factors, plus the proximity to the city of Christchurch, made Lincoln an obvious site for the New Zealand release of Alo.

The actual release site was an experimental field about two miles to the east of the main campus. *Nourish, Sustain, Cherish* banners fluttered in the breeze at the top of three grandstands filling with dignitaries watching the global build-up on a giant screen on loan from the city's rugby stadium. The hundreds of guests were outnumbered by police and soldiers scrutinizing every person, structure, blade of grass. Two helicopters patrolled overhead. Sharpshooters were positioned at every vantage point, and barricades were in place on every road, track, bridge, tunnel and farm gate within hundreds of yards.

Hansen stood at the epicenter – a square of green artificial turf fringed with gold tassels on the edge of a small rectangle of prepared earth into which the first seed would be planted. A siren could be heard from the direction of the university. Just an ambulance. Her eyes followed a line from the fake green turf up steps to a raised walkway of red carpet, bounded by fancy gold rope. At the far end, guarded by six soldiers holding rifles Hansen knew were not loaded, was a specially constructed capsule the size of the red telephone booths once common on street corners throughout New Zealand. The phallic glass-sided capsule supposedly symbolized growth and purity and all that nonsense. It looked like an oversized vase from Briscoes. Inside was a sealed vial containing a single seed.

Identical vases were in position at release locations around the world. Some in fields like this where the seeds would grow. Others in stadiums or large public areas with elaborate boxes of soil for ceremonial plantings. In sixty minutes, Professor Kane would enter the vase, remove the sealed vial and walk down the carpet with the Prime Minister to the plant zone.

In the VIP section of the grandstand, the Prime Minister and his wife were being shown to their seats beside the American Ambassador. Hansen felt proud and excited. Although a professional here to do a job, she was playing a part in history.

'She's not here Inspector.'

It was her offsider.

'Who's not here?'

'Professor Kane. Guest of honor. Supposed to be here ten minutes ago. We've called her office. Just goes to voice mail.'

'What about other people in her department?'

'Same thing. No one home. Think they're all here.'

Hansen looked across towards the buildings of the university.

'How far is it to her office?'

'It's in the Center for Advanced Biotechnology. Far corner of the campus. Five minutes by car. Want me to go check?'

Hansen thought of the siren. Perhaps something had happened to the professor. She also realized she'd been so carried away with the moment she'd stopped thinking about the terrorists. And Kaufman.

'Take over here. I'll go.'

* * * *

IT WASN'T until rain hit his face that Matthew discovered he had no feeling below his neck. He tried to lift his hand to shield his eyes. Nothing happened.

He was being carried on a stretcher across an open space between two buildings. As they approached a set of glass doors, the stretcher-bearers slowed.

Matthew tilted his head to stop the rain driving into his eyes. She was less than ten feet away, clutching a blue and white *Newztalk ZB* umbrella.

'Harvest,' he shouted. 'Harvest bleedin harvest.'

* * * *

PROFESSOR KANE wouldn't have been out of place as the matron of a private girls' school. No-nonsense green eyes behind sensible glasses. Hair with a tint of gray parted conservatively to one side. Silver brooch necklace over the plainest blue blouse.

The office matched the woman, Jay thought, as he listened to Cat doing her best to extract the information she needed.

The handwriting on the whiteboard was precise.

Black ring binders neatly labeled.

Certificates and family photographs framed in matching wood and arranged just so between a filing cabinet and glass fronted bookshelf.

Jay had one eye on the professor and one on the half-open door to the lower level of the biotron backing onto the office.

White benches and basins and microscopes. Shelves of sample jars. Racks of forty-five-degree wooden pegs holding upturned beakers. Yellow lines painted on the floor around a sophisticated looking machine, like warning lines on a railway platform.

As Cat quizzed the professor about Miescher and his descendants, Jay glanced at the spines in the glass bookshelf.

He did a double take when he saw a book titled *In Mendel's Footnotes*.

'What was Mendel's first name?'

'Gregor,' replied Cat, resenting the intrusion.

'No, it wasn't,' said the professor. 'Mendel took the name Gregor

365

when he entered a friary in his early twenties. His given name at birth was Johann.'

Jay bolted towards the cabinet.

'It's locked,' the professor protested.

Jay reached for a paperweight.

'Please, that's not necessary.'

Professor Kane took a set of half a dozen keys on a Peugeot ring from her drawer.

'Use these. It's the small copper one.'

Jay opened the case, handed the book to Cat, and slipped the keyring into his pocket.

Cat leafed through the first few pages, mumbling something about a home, a house.

'Random,' she said triumphantly. 'The home of Johann Mendel's footnotes is a house. Random House. The publisher of the book.'

Raised voices torpedoed the smile from her face.

* * * *

CAT WATCHED in shock as Jay leapt over the desk, clamped his hand over Professor Kane's mouth and dragged her through the door to the biotron.

The door swung shut, leaving the reflection of an ambulance officer staring back from the glass. The clock over the door said forty minutes to go. She knew what she had to do.

She ran out the other door into the corridor.

It was empty.

She started sprinting towards the clipped orders of soldiers in the reception area, getting just beyond the entrance to a stairwell when the doors were thrown open and four black rifles barged into the hall.

'Help,' she shouted, running towards them, trying her best to use a New Zealand accent. 'It's the professor. She's had a heart attack.'

The lead soldier hesitated.

'Where is she?'

'Up those stairs. First office on the left. Got to get the defibrillator.'

She pushed past them and through the doors into the carpeted reception area. The ambulance was still outside.

Telling herself to calm down, she walked up to the main door and reached for the handle.

She heard the click of the safety catch being released an instant before the numbing metal of the gun barrel poked into the back of her neck.

70. Like a neon sign

'OUTSTANDING JOB, Petersen,' said Pyjas, as they watched the flashing lights of the lead SUV in the motorcade approach the sector for VIP vehicles outside the Central Park Precinct House.

'Thank you sir.'

They got the signal from the Secret Service liaison to move to the curb ready to greet the President when he stepped from the limousine. Petersen slipped into the background, out of camera shot. The leader of the free world and the chairman of a seed corporation – equals in the eyes of the flag-waving do-gooders massed behind the barriers – shook hands and began the short walk through to the stage.

'You coming or what?'

It was the President's Chief of Staff.

Petersen wavered.

Plan A was to leave now to be at the intersection of Park Avenue and East Ninety-Sixth for the rendezvous with his kidnappers at precisely 6pm, the moment Alo was released and the focus of the planet and every law enforcement agent within miles would be on the image of a half-naked peasant farmer in India.

By the time the burnt remains of the kidnap vehicle, complete with teeth to confirm the victim's identification, were discovered two days later at a quarry in Pennsylvania, Petersen would be recovering from cosmetic surgery on the island of Song Saa. His island.

Plan B was identical except for the timing of the kidnapping, which would take place at precisely 6.30pm, the moment the lead singer walked on stage to begin the post-release benefit concert.

The head said Plan A. Always did. The heart said Plan B. This is your creation, your greatest work. *Carpe diem quam minime credula postero.* Petersen always preferred the full sentence from Horace's poem. *Seize the day, trusting as little as possible in the future.*

He pressed two buttons on his cell phone to send the pre-set coded text message, and followed the victorious entourage towards the Great Lawn.

* * * *

THE ROADBLOCK at the junction of Lincoln Tai Tapu Road and State Highway 75 was one of several around the perimeter of the university. Police officers backed up by soldiers were stopping and searching every vehicle approaching the release site.

They paid no attention to the blue Peugeot heading *away* from the campus on the other side of the road, or to the driver with the Paisley headscarf, sensible sunglasses and hint of red lipstick.

Jay accelerated slowly away from the intersection, waiting till he was well out of sight before stepping on the gas. The three-liter V6 engine responded, and headed for the peninsula.

He pushed the button on the steering column to turn on the radio. They were broadcasting live from Lincoln, interspersed with segments from international sites counting down to the release. The Royal Family was arriving at Wembley. The President of the European Council was approaching the Arc de Triomphe. The President of the United States was waving to crowds at Central ...

'Can I break in there please... we've just been told by the police that one of the ecoterrorists has been captured. We understand it is the American scientist Dr Catherine Tayler. Just been apprehended on the grounds of Lincoln University that is less than a mile or so from where we are at the New Zealand release site. That's all the police are saying at the moment. No word on the whereabouts of the third terrorist, Jay Duggan. But to repeat, Dr Tayler is in custody. That will be an

enormous relief, with just under thirty minutes to go. Back to you.'

Jay hoped the reporter was right. That Cat was captured by the New Zealand police and not the psycho Kaufman. As soon as he realized she hadn't followed him into the biotron he had to make an instant decision. Suspecting Cat sacrificed herself to give him time, he'd led the professor up a flight of stairs to the upper level where he gagged her and tied her up. A door opened onto a fire escape. There was only one Peugeot in the car park.

He changed down to fourth as he approached the turnoff to Gebbies Pass. The radio was concluding an interview with the New Zealand prime minister.

'Thank you sir. Now, just to repeat the breaking news. The American terrorist Dr Tayler has been arrested at Lincoln University. There has also been a development with the English terrorist Matthew Liddell in custody at Trentham military base, where we cross now live to our reporter Kahu Bennett.'

'Yes, it seems Liddell has been injured in some sort of accident. In the last few minutes, he has been transferred to the base hospital. There has been a flurry of activity, with two helicopters hovering overhead, armored vehicles blocking entrances and soldiers moving to the perimeter of the base facing out, as if they expect an attempt to break him out. They're clearly taking no chances.'

'Are the army saying anything about how Liddell might have been injured?'

'No. They're refusing to comment.'

'Any idea how serious his injuries are?'

'They don't appear to be life threatening. I saw him being carried in a stretcher. He was conscious, although we may be talking head injury because he yelled out something strange as he was whisked through the door to the hospital. Harvest. Said it more than once.'

The word hit Jay like a neon sign. *Harvest.* Harvest Random? Random Harvest? Thirteen letters. Didn't sound like much of a title for a movie, but you never know.

He glanced in the rear vision mirror. Still wearing Professor Kane's headscarf. He pulled it off and eyeballed the mirror. As a teenager doing small acts of sabotage against logging companies he used to psyche himself up by imagining he was saving the world. This could be for real.

71. Not of this world

PETERSEN TOOK in the floodlit forest of humanity decked in coats and scarves and hats of every color to ward off the raw winter air.

Close-ups of their spellbound faces filled the *Grassrroots* feed monitor beside him, peppered with shots of the President and First Lady being introduced to other big kahunas in the pavilion behind the stage.

With the cameras focused elsewhere, Petersen slipped to the front of the stage to sip the aura. You could taste the expectation. A voice called his name from the crowd, and he looked down to see a woman from his college days. He waved at her. Hundreds of nearby arms suddenly shot into the air to wave back. Annoyed at the attention, he turned away, only to see himself on the giant screen at the side of the lawn. *Pope flaming Petersen.*

* * * *

THE GOVERNOR'S BAY hill road was empty as Jay pulled up outside the colonial style wooden cottage with a large satellite dish out of place on the corrugated iron roof. All the neighbors must be indoors glued to televisions. He pushed the doorbell, no idea what he was going to say.

'Cutting it a bit fine aren't we?'

The voice was Canadian and came from below. A head with John Lennon spectacles, single earring and silver ponytail poked out and Jay could see there was an overgrown path down to a black door. Presumably a basement.

'Have you got the code for the final clue?'

'Think so.' Jay ran down the path, more relieved than concerned the stranger knew so much. He stepped through the door into another hemisphere. A private museum of monitors, keyboards, scanners, printers. The innards of dead computers. A curved television that had to be close to 80 inches. Maple leaf flag. Single bed. Small kitchen. The whole nine yards for self-contained survival. Plus a webcam thingy in the ceiling.

'I've recreated most of the old website from the disk, but held off loading the final sequence because when I hit this key, our location to within a couple of inches will light up on security monitors in a dozen jurisdictions.'

The ponytail was sitting in front of a fancy terminal, talking as he tapped away at the keyboard.

Living proof blokes could multi-task.

'When I got the disk, I'll tell you straight up, didn't want anything to do with it. Left it there in its envelope a good five hours before curiosity got to me. Then when I loaded the thing and saw what was on it, I nearly returned it to sender.'

He continued typing. Jay wandered over to have a closer look at a set of framed newspaper articles on the wall. From *The Times*, *Washington Post*, *USA Today*. All speculating about the identity of a notorious hacker.

'Are you this SwordPhish bloke?'

'Was. I suspect this escapade will blow that cover.'

'So, you know our mate, Matthew Liddell?'

'No. I've heard of Turtledove and his work. His email the other day was the first contact we've had. Must have sent it from Wellington Hospital before he was moved to the army camp.'

He talked as he typed, explaining how Matthew mentioned the CD sent to Ross, and how he'd worked out the connection to Joan by hacking into Jay's mother's hard drive.

'How did you even know about my mother, let alone where she lives?'

'Her blog of course. It's been taken over by the dark side, but the original source code's still there, with the keys to her drive. Frankly I'm surprised whoever's hunting you didn't work it out. Joan was on your mother's Christmas card mailing label list. I got the name of your mother's cat from a spreadsheet showing payments to a vet. A search linking Joan's name with Ross came up with a list of volunteers at Save the Children.'

'Strewth mate. There's still loads of dots here not joining up for me.'

'The CD didn't make a lot of sense at first, till I found Maipi Kenana.'

'How the hell do you know about him?'

'Simple. The file was created on his computer.'

'I thought Maipi and Whatu were in jail. How did you get hold of him?'

The SwordPhish smiled, still typing. The bloke was not of this world.

'When I said *found* him, I mean I *hacked* him.'

'But Maipi's computer was blown up. I was there. She was toast.'

The SwordPhish shook his head as if talking to an imbecile. Jay was clearly out of his depth. No more questions.

'A computer is nothing more than a client my friend. Information is stored on servers. I hacked into Maipi's file, mail and web servers, to see what Matthew got up to at Waikaremoana. The password, the entry portal, the denial-of-service attack on the Vestco site. Your friend also moved a rogue active server page onto his personal site while he was there. Took me a while, but I was eventually able to access the root of his system. That's like the dude's soul.'

All this time the bloke's fingers never left the keyboard.

'To cut a long story short, I was able to make sense of the file on the CD. I know about the virtual safe deposit box, the clues, the entry location. All we need is the final password.'

'Pretty sure its Harvest Random or Random Harvest.'

A Google search revealed *Random Harvest* was a movie about a veteran of the Great War.

'Have a seat my friend. This final set-up will take a wee while.'

Jay flopped into a recliner and stared at the muted television. Images from release sites flashed across the screen. The digital clock counting down in the corner, beside the *Grassroots* logo, showed twenty minutes fifteen seconds.

FROM BENEATH the temporary grandstand, Kaufman looked through the legs of VIPs at the same images on the big screen at Lincoln. He'd just heard Hansen had caught Tayler. Duggan had slipped away, but the police were a hundred and ten percent sure he wasn't within the three-mile secure radius of the release site.

He turned and saw the smiling face of Captain Falconer, the SAS commander. As he ambled towards him, his cell phone went off. It was his deputy back in the States.

'You're not gonna believe this. Our old website's being recreated.'

'This better be a joke.'

'Wish it was. The data needed to recreate it is being downloaded from a house in a place called Governor's Bay. Very close to where you are at Lincoln.'

'Can't the download be jammed?'

'No chance. Not without throwing out the entire global release. The stuff being downloaded is linked to critical release data on the new Vestco site which as of two hours ago became fully integrated with the television network system and *Grassroots*... wherever that exists in cyberspace.'

Kaufman got the Governor's Bay coordinates. Pretending to still be talking on the cell phone, he walked past Captain Falconer to the cockpit door of one of the Air Force choppers. He climbed in, shut the door and had his gun in the face of the pilot before he could protest.

72. The Women's Weekly

THE FRONT door of the house in the fashionable Auckland suburb of Remuera was opened by an elderly woman with eyebrows matching the blue rinse in her hair.

'Sorry to disturb you Mrs Lancaster. My name's Neill O'Reilly. I'm a private detective.'

'Is this about that peeping tom who's been bothering Mrs Stokes?'

'No Mrs Lancaster. I'm working another case. The one involving the three young environmentalists trying to stop the Alo release.'

'I was on the same plane as those scallywags from Los Angeles you know. You're not going to arrest me are you?'

'Of course not.'

'You better come in then.'

O'Reilly followed the woman along a wood-paneled hall to the sitting room. It was like a furnace. Must have the heat pump turned to maximum.

'Can I get you a cup of tea Mr O'Reilly?'

'Not for me thanks.'

He took out the photograph and handed it to her.

'Do you recognize this man, Mrs Lancaster?'

'I'll just get my glasses. Sure I can't get you some tea? Coffee perhaps?'

'Quite sure thank you. I'm a bit pushed for time.'

She returned wearing a surprisingly modern set of rimless frames.

O'Reilly showed her the photo again.

'Yes of course. That's the Jewish gentleman with the American seed corporation. One wonders how those young terrorists got away, with that clever man on the plane.'

'I beg your pardon?'

'He was sitting across the aisle from me. Looked quite different of course. A very clever gentleman. Had a bushy beard and those half-rimmed glasses. And the skullcap. That's how I knew he was Jewish. What's his name again?'

'Kaufman. Bradley Kaufman. How can you be sure it was him?'

'The *Women's Weekly*.'

'I don't follow.'

She walked over to a magazine rack, and came back thumbing through the latest issue of the women's rag.

'Here we are. I realized it was Mr Kaufman when I saw this photograph of him with his daughter.'

The double-page spread was about the all-American hero and the sacrifices he'd made for his country.

There were photos of him in army fatigues in war zones, receiving a medal from the President outside the Pentagon, and one taken at a theme park. Kaufman and his daughter were smiling at the camera from each side of a someone dressed in a chipmunk suit.

'I wasn't sure it was him until I saw that caption. There. His daughter's name is Eve. Same as my middle name. I distinctly remember the Jewish gentleman on the plane talking on the telephone to his daughter. Extraordinary what you can do on planes these days. It was soon after we took off from Los Angeles. He called her Eve. I suppose one shouldn't have been eavesdropping, but it was such a lovely conversation. Have you a daughter, Mr O'Reilly?'

* * * *

MURMURS ROLLED through the grandstand as the Pave Hawk cruised behind the giant screen at Lincoln.

Hansen had to smile.

After its hapless trip to Frew's Saddle where this symbol of American military and technical might was brought to its knees by the New Zealand weather, here it was repaired and making a grand Hollywood-style entrance sixteen minutes before the release as if to claim credit for getting us this far.

A constable walked up, holding a cell phone.

'It's for you Inspector. She says it's urgent.'

It was Caroline Phillips in Washington.

'You sitting down, Chris?'

'You kidding? I'm at ground zero here with this mega clock ticking. What you got?'

'Not only was your friend Kaufman at the Vestco building at the time Henry Beck was murdered, digital records from the security system show Kaufman's swipe card was used to unlock Beck's office at 5.58am. He locked it again two minutes later.

'What was the estimated time of death?'

Between six and seven. But the air-conditioning was switched down twenty seconds before Kaufman left the office. He was back at 6.43 and seconds later the air-conditioning was cranked back up to seventy degrees. The murder wasn't reported for several hours.'

'Interesting. But it doesn't prove much. Someone else could have swiped his card.'

'There's more. I've had my friends at the FBI take another look at that amateur video footage of Liddell running through Pershing Square. They've used this experimental enhanced resolution software to zoom in on other people in the square at the time. Guess who they found?'

'Our friend Mr Kaufman.'

'Correct.'

'Still doesn't do it for me Caroline.'

'But wait, there's more.'

She sounded like one of those infomercials. Call in the next ten minutes and get two for the price of one.

'A colleague at our embassy in Berlin ran a check on that cancer clinic in Frankfurt you mentioned. It doesn't exist. There is a Dr Berlangen in Frankfurt. He's a doctor of linguistics, not medicine.'

Her own phone rang. She looked at the screen. Neill O'Reilly, the private investigator in Auckland.

'Thanks Caroline. Owe you big time.'

She took the call from O'Reilly, and within seconds was sprinting towards the police tent.

* * * *

SAND WAS falling into Cat's eyes. She tried to raise her arms. They wouldn't move. The sand was up to her neck. She lowered her face, but got a mouthful of grit. She closed her eyes tight and concentrated on her body. Shoulders. Stomach. Knees. Feet. She was treading barefoot through an alley. It was pitch dark. There was music behind the wall. Or was it water? Yes. She could hear a river, but not see it for the mist.

A voice was calling her name. Jay? Pop? She turned. He was standing in the shadow. Kaufman. Holding something. A gun? No. A guitar pick. She looked back at the face. Professor Tolminsky.

Her head started flopping from side to side. She opened her eyes. Someone was standing over her. The face seemed familiar. Brown skin. Brown eyes. Flat nose. Big lips. Fishhook pendant dangling from the neck. Was it Sir Jack? Whatu? Skip? No. Those were woman's eyes. It was the cop. What was her name? Hansen? Yes. Inspector Hansen. Right in her face.

Cat blinked. Then blinked again. She was sitting in a large green tent, hands cuffed to the back of the chair. The droning rumble of hundreds of voices drifted through the walls, interspersed with the *thu-thu-thu* of a helicopter. The ground trembled from the base of the sound system.

'Where is Jay?' Hansen was shaking Cat's shoulders.

Cat smiled. Jay must have got away.

'What time is it?'

'Eleven forty-seven. Thirteen minutes to go. Doctor Tayler, I need to know where Jay has gone.'

'You must think I'm stupid.'

'Far from it, Catherine. We know about Kaufman, the American. That he was in Henry Beck's office in LA when he was murdered. I've just found out he came to New Zealand on the same flight as you, which puts him at Auckland Airport when Constable Shaw was killed. And he was first on the scene in Napier when Constable Wilson was killed. I've crossed all the *t*'s Catherine. I need your help to dot the last *i*. We need to know where Jay is. And what all this has to do with Alo.'

'This is all about Alo. Henry Beck must have found out about it, so they killed him. He managed to get a message to Matthew with a code sequence for a virtual safe deposit - '

'I know about the virtual box Catherine. Matthew told me.'

'The box must contain evidence of what's wrong with Alo. Why it's got to be stopped. Why this psycho Kaufman's trying to kill us. We may have worked out how to open it. Jay's on his way there now.'

'Where is he?'

Cat hesitated. A police officer stuck his head through the flap door of the tent.

'Kaufman's been and gone Inspector. Took an Air Force chopper to the east. Pilot's not responding.'

'Damn. Is the American helicopter still here?'

'Yes mam.'

Hansen looked at her watch. 'There might still be time Catherine. To save Jay at least.'

73. Show time

SWEAT FORMED on the SwordPhish's forehead, sliding down his nose to form a single droplet which he ignored as he tapped furiously at the keyboard.

'Right my friend. It's show time!'

Jay watched over his shoulder as he typed *randomharvest* into the login box. The filename *meggido.mov* appeared above a black video box in the center of the screen. The SwordPhish hit the play arrow, then moved to another terminal. Jay took his seat.

The clip opened with a view of a laboratory similar to parts of the biotron at Lincoln, but with cages of rats instead of glass tanks with plants. A voice began. Polish accent. Speaking slowly. Deliberately. And with a lisp Jay hardly recognized as belonging to the Professor Tolminsky he'd heard on television several times.

'I tort I create da perfect seed coating. Den I discover anomaly in data vitch, if substantiate, raise doubt about safety for human consumption of crop produce by da Alo. I alert Vice President Petersen, along with revise timetable for retest.'

Tolminsky coughed before continuing, his voice getting weaker.

'I was force, by tret to my family, halt test for toxicity and make false report to Food Standard Agency.'

Jay noticed almost all the rats were motionless as Tolminsky methodically outlined how he continued with the toxicity testing in secret, injecting the seeds with an accelerator gene to speed up the growth of the crops and using himself as a guinea pig for human trials.

'Though I base my trial on consumption of long-grain basmati rice, becos of genetic makeup of da Alo I have no doubt toxicity issue will replicate in any plant produce using da coating.'

The image jerked and the cages went out of focus. Tolminsky was rotating the camera to face himself. As Jay stared at the screen, the door to the basement exploded open.

74. You are us

KAUFMAN completed the roll, coming to his feet in a fluid movement with his gun aimed at the head of Duggan.

'I believe you're familiar with the drill. Stand up, nice and slowly, hands in the air where I can see them. And move away from the computer. You too Ponytail.'

'This has got to be some sort of record,' said the nerd, rising and putting his hands on his head.

Kaufman smiled. 'You ain't seen nothing yet.'

The television showing the build-up to the release was muted, but he could see the clock counting down. Less than five minutes.

'Have you seen Tolminsky's clip you moron? Have you any idea what's going on?'

Kaufman was thinking of Eve. The chemo. The vomiting. Fevers. The bleeding. The plane they would be on to Germany. A creep like Duggan would never understand.

'You know you'll never get away with this.'

Kaufman kept the gun pointed at the New Zealander's head.

'We've done pretty well so far don't you think? The fire in Tolminsky's lab. I kept one of the gorilla suits as a souvenir. Henry Beck when he tried to get in the way. The cop at the airport. The constable in Napier. That madcap professor in England. Your obese receptionist. All taken care of. Cleanly. Clinically. That's the difference between you and me Duggan. The professional and the amateur.'

'Why us? Why drag us into this?'

'You are us Duggan. We're on the same team. Your precious Millbrook Foundation was set up by Chas Petersen as a front. A manageable front. Paul Deaver was a puppet chief executive. You were all part of the plan, headhunted for your unique contributions. You Duggan were the Trojan horse, supplying us with intel on other eco-terrorists. Liddell was used to test the security of the Vestco information systems. Recommended for the role by Henry Beck, believe it or not. Tayler was considered the most dangerous anti-genetic modification fanatic of them all, so she was ring-fenced and kept under the watchful eye of Deaver. It was his idea to spike her drink with flunitrazepam to induce the blackouts. And the doctor, the one who prescribed the rest that led to your vacation, was an actress.'

'Unbelievable.'

'That's not the half of it. Petersen's true genius is manipulation. Some might call it bribery. It's such a callous word, and doesn't begin to describe the man's mastery. As they say, everyone has their price, and Petersen has a sixth sense when it comes to determining that price. The Food Safety Agency. Regulatory bodies from Washington to Brussels. Governments. Prime Ministers and Presidents. Judges. Journalists. Media executives.

'And the biggest coup of all... Grassroots Intelligence. The blog was created, funded and controlled all along by Petersen. He had his hand firmly on the faucet, turning the leaks on and off at will.

'Oh, and I forgot to mention your climbing buddy. Andy was it? Squealed like a stuck pig just before I helped him join you in the river.'

Duggan's shoulders slumped.

The digits on the television clock changed to amber as the countdown entered the last sixty seconds.

'I'd make you watch it. But as you Kiwis say, I've got things to do, places to go.'

He shifted the aim from Duggan's head to his heart.'

'See you round.'

75. Nooooooooooooo

A SINGLE gunshot in an enclosed space sounds more like a pop than the blasts typical of Hollywood movies. Jay knew that hearing the sound meant he wasn't dead.

He opened his eyes to see shock register on Kaufman's face and a crimson patch appear on his shirt just below the heart. The American collapsed to the floor. Standing behind him was Inspector Hansen, holding a pistol.

Through the ringing in his ears Jay heard his name shouted, as Cat blurred past the detective and flung her arms around him.

He was aware of the SwordPhish rushing to a computer and starting to tap on the keyboard, but Jay's eyes were drawn over Cat's shoulder to the television. Hansen grabbed the remote and hit the sound.

Twenty, nineteen...

They'd failed.

Cat turned to the screen.

'Noooooooooooooo...'

76. Frenzy of anticipation

ISHWAR SINGH knelt in the only untrammeled patch of soil on his plot and looked up in awe at the Prime Minister of India, who was standing on the green carpet holding the seed vial above his head like a sports trophy. Ishwar's faded head scarf had been replaced by a new turban with *Nourish, Sustain, Cherish* in bright red, the same color as the little light on the lock arrangement flashing in time to the digital clock on the larger-than-elephant screen. Voices chanted from all around.

'Terah, bara, gyaarah...'

As the countdown reached ten the light on the vial changed color and gained in intensity, sending the crowd to a new volume.

'Nau, aat, saat...'

Images on the screen flashed rapidly from Somalia to Tiananmen Square, Red Square, Wembley Stadium and Estadio do Maracana in Rio de Janeiro as billions of people were whipped into a frenzy of anticipation.

'Seis, cinco, cuatro...'

The screen filled with the chanting faces of the President of the United States and the Chairman of Vestco, shouting and thrusting their fists in time to the crowd in Central Park.

77. The raised palm

STANDING BEHIND the President and Chairman, Petersen was swept up in the emotion of the countdown. Even though, as architect of this extravaganza, he knew exactly what was about to happen.

At the count of zero, locks on seed vials all over the world would click open, releasing the ceremonial seeds for planting. At precisely that moment twenty million dollars would be electronically transferred from the Los Angeles branch of the Bank of America to an untraceable account in Zurich.

Three, two...

Petersen looked at the screen, at Ishwar Singh, the illiterate Indian set to become the Neil Armstrong of the twenty-first century.

One, zero...

Fireworks boomed from barges on the reservoir as two hundred thousand voices erupted.

But the image on the screens, instead of showing a green light as the vial opened, was frozen on the raised palm of the Indian farmer.

78. Some sort of record

THE TELEVISION flickered.

The image of the raised palm disappeared, and Cat was looking at the interior of Tolminsky's old lab in Pasadena.

What were rats doing in a plant biochemistry lab?

As Tolminsky talked about the anomaly in the data, how he was forced to abandon retesting and falsify reports, Cat looked at the dateline at the bottom of the clip.

It was the day before fire destroyed the lab and killed Tolminsky.

The professor's voice became emotional, his breath short as he explained how he'd used himself as a guinea pig in a human trial.

The cages went out of focus and Cat raised her bandaged hand to her mouth as Tolminsky turned the camera on himself.

An enormous tumor covered the left side of his face, completely smothering one eye and ear in a weeping mass of red and black.

His nose had ballooned to cover his upper lip.

Cat gagged as the grotesque image dissolved into static, replaced by the voice of Kaufman and a view of the room she was standing in, filmed from above.

'You ain't seen nothing yet...'

Cat watched in amazement as the American, gun pointed at Jay, confessed to everything.

In front of the biggest television and online audience in history.

It ended with the gunshot and Kaufman falling to the floor.

As the producers at the television network regained control of their broadcast and started showing images of shocked faces in Central Park, Cat turned to Jay.

'Could someone please tell me what in heck I've just seen?'

'Cyber justice.' The Canadian accent came from a man in the corner of the room Cat hadn't noticed until now.

'When I was recreating the Vestco site I came across links to the system behind Grassroots Intelligence, which gave me access to the television network center controlling the release. You know how long us hackers have been trying to crack their mainframe? For eons. The steps they had to take to hook up with the blog lowered their defenses for, like, the first time in history.

'I'd just finished keying in Tolminsky's clip when Rambo here turned up to spoil the party. Fool didn't realize that when I said this must be some sort of *record*, it was an audio cue for the camera up there to begin filming.'

* * * *

THE ARREST on stage of Chas Petersen, the publicity-shy Vestco vice-president, was broadcast live to billions, as was his hysterical finger-pointing rant about taped evidence implicating a mortified Jozef Pyjas. Hundreds of police had to form parallel human walls to shield the pair from incensed spectators as they were led away in handcuffs towards the Central Park Precinct House.

The SwordPhish's timely hack into the television network's computer controlling the global release prevented seals on all the seed vials unlocking. Countless tons of seeds coated with Alo were destroyed over the following days, as relief at the near miss turned to a worldwide clamor for answers, compensation and justice.

Commissions of inquiry, hearings, white papers, investigations and probes in dozens of languages were launched into the roles of the biotech industry, judiciaries, law enforcement agencies, Xecintel, the media, government officials and politicians – including several presidents and prime ministers. Within hours of the announcement by the United Nations Secretary-General that a Crisis Conference on Food Production was being organized for Los Angeles, the same presidents and prime ministers were outbidding each other to promise the most comprehensive overhauls of food safety regulations, agriculture standards, media ownership – and the largest increases in humanitarian aid.

Bradley Kaufman survived in an induced coma on life support for three days. He died without knowing about the confession of the actor playing the part of his daughter's oncology consultant, and the subsequent examinations by actual specialists at the Center for Cancer and Blood Diseases in Los Angeles.

They found Eve Kaufman's medical records had been altered. Instead of neuroblastoma, she had ganglioneuroma, a benign tumor that could be removed by surgery.

She should never have had chemotherapy.

Her chances of recovering were high.

Epilogue

JAY CHOSE a rimu seed from the tray and carried it in the palm of his hand to the middle of the clearing.

The bandage was off Cat's hand. Surgeons managed to save all but one of her frostbitten fingers. Matthew was in a wheelchair. His leg was in a cast, and he had a pin in his hip, but was expected to walk again. Dozens of planks had been laid end on end so he could be wheeled to the clearing by Detective Inspector Hansen, who made sure no media were allowed within sight of what Jay insisted was a private ceremony.

He knelt on the soil, took the greenstone pendant from his neck, kissed it, and placed it in the hole. He took the black seed between his thumb and forefinger and held it up as if raising a glass.

'To keeping it natural.'

Nods all around. Words were unnecessary.

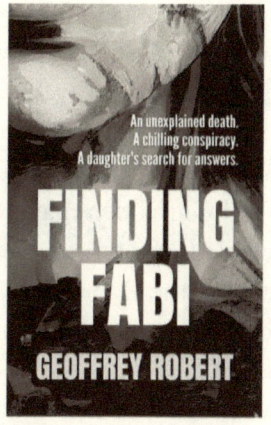

THE GHOST SHIPMENT

When a young American tourist dies in a surfing accident in Bali while high on cocaine, his billionaire father hires the Aristotle investigative journalism team (including **Jay Duggan**) to track down the drug kingpin ultimately responsible for his son's death.

Ped Garland, a maverick with a troubled past who is campaigning to become the Republican presidential candidate, captivates voters with his candid and unorthodox approach to politics, and bold plan to end the nation's drug nightmare.

With Garland's bid gaining momentum, the journalists' investigation leads them from the exotic resorts and nightclubs of Bali to the lawless backstreets of Colombia, seemingly tranquil neighborhoods of New Zealand and rarefied halls of Washington's elite as they battle powerful adversaries determined to protect their secrets.

For more details:

www.geoffreyrobert.com

ALL IT WILL TAKE

In a land where the earth remembers every injustice and the wind still whispers the names of forgotten heroes, two rabbits are born on opposite sides of a deepening divide.

An epic tale of injustice, rebellion, and the fight for freedom

All It Will Take

GEOFFREY ROBERT

Nell, the son of a black warren leader, longs for open fields and a life without fear. Levi, heir to a white supremacist governor, clings to a vanishing past.

When Nell meets Ollie, an orphan doe with nothing to lose and everything to believe in, their protest becomes a movement, their defiance a revolution.

As loyalties are tested and long-buried truths come to the surface, can these rabbits find a path to unity, or will the cycle of hatred keep turning?

Inspired by the legacy of Nelson Mandela and literary traditions like *Watership Down*, *All It Will Take* is a timely allegory of resistance and reckoning – a tale for an age when history threatens to repeat, and silence is no longer an option.

For more details:
www.geoffreyrobert.com